From reader reviews on Amazon

- Twilingmarche is a fun read with appealing characters and lush descriptions of its Edwardian England upper crust setting.

- Wheels within wheels mystery. Rags to riches, orphan to heiress, surface glitz to real power, loneliness to deep love. Everything is different from what you expect, the happy ending is teetering on a knife edge.

- The author did an excellent job of incorporating many themes using a multitude of both major and minor characters.

- Vera Mont's 'Twillingmarche' is a lushly written historical mystery set in Edwardian England

- This intricately woven plot is filled with major and minor characters who all have a common thread; they're deceiving someone …Mary, a young servant girl, is suddenly plucked from thankless drudgery and whisked away to a sprawling country estate.

- I thought this was a very well thought out mystery.

- This was a charming book about life upstairs and downstairs in an English country home. Focused on an heiress named Felicity, there is much drama and conniving and I enjoyed every minute of it.

Twillingmarche

a novel

by

Vera Mont

Published by Montland Books in 2015

Second Printing

ISBN-13: 9780994909411

Cover Photo by: © Rad100 | Dreamstime.com

Contents

1

Mary tiptoed down the stairs, carefully avoiding the fourth step with its loud squeak. The parlour door stood slightly ajar; the male voices issuing from within were quite subdued but, knowing the Master and his friends, would of a certainty become rowdy after a while. If they should waken the baby, she would have to spend another hour rocking him to sleep and by then it would be little Missie's bedtime. Mary might never get to her own supper. She must somehow, without being noticed, close that door.

"If indeed she is the one we seek," an unknown voice was saying, "there would of course be a reward...."

And the Master: "Well, I dunno.... We've got fond of her, you see, and she's good with the kiddies."

"I understood you to say that she was - how did you put it? A daft little thing."

"Not so's it'd matter," the Master qualified. "Slow she is, for t'shop, but not so's she can't do housework."

The stranger said: "Now, Mr. Barlow, there is no need to worry. I have not yet determined whether she is the right girl. It is only a slim possibility."

"Who else would it be? All them things you said, all true."

"Well, if so, my client will be pleased to compensate you and your good wife for any inconvenience occasioned by the loss of Mary's services."

Why, they were talking about herself, she realised. Somebody was looking for her! After all this time, could it be?

The other man asked in a tone rather of command than request: "If I might see the girl?"

When the Master rang, she had almost reached the kitchen. She straightened her shift, smoothed down her hair, stopped a moment to peek into the cloudy hall mirror, took a deep breath and scratched timidly at the parlour door.

"Come in, come in, Mary," said the Master in the hearty accent he usually reserved for his richest customers and the tax assessor. "This gentleman wants a word with you."

"In private, if you please," added the other.

Mr. Barlow heaved himself out of the chair slowly, not wanting to go, but he went. Mary shut the door behind him.

"Come here, child," said the stranger. "Let's have a look at you." He was older than the Master: his pink, indoor face had wrinkles and his hair was grizzled, even to the lush and curly side-whiskers. Old, but not unhandsome in his way, and by his clothes, truly a gentleman. He wore trousers and coat of rich charcoal worsted, like to the dearest in the Master's shop, and a black striped waistcoat and his wing collar - the whitest and stiffest that she had ever seen - was adorned with a cravat of dove grey silk. The silver stick-pin which held it in place matched the studs in his starched shirt-cuffs. She wondered if he always dressed so swell or was he perhaps stopping on the way to some grand ball? "Don't be afraid," he said. "Sit down - no, here, across from me."

Mary had no option but to take the Master's chair. She could not prevent herself giving an apprehensive look about lest she be caught committing this monstrous infraction, then perched upon the very edge of it, barely touching the seat.

"Well, well, well," the stranger leaned back comfortably in the chair usually occupied by the Mistress. "You *do* have the look!"

Mary's hand wanted to fly to her hair but dared not. She had always, ever so secretly, thought herself pretty, with her thick, dark red hair, green eyes and wide brow. Surely the village boys had more than glanced in her direction - often, truth be told; nor did she mind, so far as that went.... But what did he mean by 'The Look'?

"Yes, sir," she mumbled.

"Yes, sir!" rejoined he. "Yes, indeed. Now then," he lowered his voice with a sidewise glance at the door,

2

"Mary, is it? Mary, your employer tells me that you are seventeen years of age, is that correct?"

"Yes, sir."

"Hm. Might you not be closer to eighteen?"

Mary could not say for a certainty, short of laborious calculation, but assented with a small inclination of her head.

"He further tells me that you came here three years ago, without references, and could not say whence you had come?"

"Yes, sir. That is, the Twinsdale vicar brought me. I'd no references on account of I'd not been in service...."

The gentleman seemed displeased; Mary did not continue. He did. "And you have little recollection of your life before that time." He said this so firmly that Mary once again felt obliged to agree.

"The right look, the right age, the right circumstances.... Should you indeed be the girl we - that is, the girl my clients - lost at about that time, things could turn out very well for you." He thought a moment, staring down at his expertly polished buttoned shoes. "If not, well, you can always come back here."

"Come back from where, please, sir?" Mary ventured.

"Why, from Twillingmarche," said the man.

Mary had heard stories of Twillingmarche - a very grand and wonderful place; like an enchanted castle. Was this gentleman suggesting that she go to live in a castle? Yes, he was, for now he said: "I propose, with the Barlows' approval, to take you there myself this very evening."

"Sir? Are there babies? Am I to be a nursery maid?"

There had been a fleeting smile about the gentleman's lips earlier, when he had first beheld her; now he chuckled aloud, a sound like thunder moving in from the sea. "No, my dear girl," he said. "There are no babies - as yet. One may hope." With another far-away laugh, he added: "No, you are not to be a maid of any kind. Rather a dear companion.... That is, if the lady finds you satisfactory."

3

"I shall do my very best, sir."

"I'm sure you will, I'm sure you will. I take that to mean you are agreeable to my proposal."

"Oh, yes, sir!" Mary breathed. To be a lady's companion was more than she had ever hoped. And there were no babies - at least, not as yet.

"Very well, then. My name, by the bye, is Elijah Forkes. Solicitor to the Sommelroux family. I have a carriage waiting outside. If you could pack your belongings with reasonable despatch...." He smiled at Mary's look of blank puzzlement. "Quickly. Meantime, I'll just have a word with your employers."

Master and Mistress were both near; one might almost suppose they had been hovering in the narrow hallway. For once the baby was silent and the little girl out of sight. She had to make her farewells brief. Then she had only to bundle her second shift, underthings, nightdress, Sunday pinafore and shawl. By the time Mr. Forkes had finished his transaction with the Barlows, Mary was ready, waiting at the door she would never again run to answer. Sitting alone inside the carriage hitched to two fine brown horses, she looked once more at the front stoop she would never again have to scrub. If only the Lady would like her! Oh, she must! She *must*. The carriage pulled away, Mr. Forkes in his finery looking somewhat outlandish upon the driving seat. Mary thought this is how Cinderella must have felt, in the fairy tale she had so often read to Missie - rather, to herself chiefly, for the child never would sit quiet.

The hour was very late when they arrived; Mary saw almost nothing of the castle: an immense, angular deeper blackness beyond the silhouettes of trees. Nor had she time or presence of mind properly to take it all in: she had been up since dawn and scarcely managed to keep her eyes open. Mr. Forkes steadied her elbow as she stumbled out of the carriage. It had stopped, not at the building, but outside tall iron gates. A dark form detached itself from the shadow of a flanking tree; the hooded lantern it carried was not bright enough to reveal a face. It said in a soft murmur: "So, you have brought the girl."

Mr. Forkes replied: "I believe she will do very well." He gave a gentle nudge to Mary's shoulder, handed over her bundle. "This is Roberts; she will take care of you."

With that, he was up on his conveyance and driving away, leaving behind a quite bewildered young maid.

"Come along," said her new companion. "Be very quiet when we reach the house; you don't want to start by waking everyone."

Some people, nonetheless, were already awake: as she trudged toward the bulk of the house, Mary noticed one window on the first storey, then another, lit behind their curtains. They entered by the central doors, one massive wing of which had been open a crack. Roberts swung it silently to behind them. All was in midnight darkness. Cautioning silence with a firm grip on her arm, from which Mary was too much awed to flinch, Roberts led her up a flight of stairs, along a corridor and finally through a more ordinarily proportioned door. There was light inside, if only a dim light, issuing from a pair of wall-sconces shaded with pink glass in the shape of lilies. Everything else in the room was equally pretty: a carved canopy bed, its rose-coloured curtains pulled aside, made up with fluffy white pillows and lace-edged sheets; night-stand and dressing table covers, even the window drapes were pink. Why, she thought, this must be the Lady's own chamber! If only she had had a moment to comb her hair and tidy her clothing.

Roberts said: "Wait here," and exited by yet another doorway.

Only a moment passed, however, before Mary heard the approach of not one, but several people. She stood quite, quite still on a lush cabbage rose, in the center of the patterned carpet, far too delicate to be trampled by her rough work boots. The Lady entered first. It must be, for she was opulently dressed in a silk dressing-gown of brightest red with blue and yellow birds upon it all over. She was large and fair, not unlike the Mistress, but far handsomer. Behind her was Roberts, without her cloak, seen clearly at last. She looked severe in grey and white, dark brown hair pulled back in an old-fashioned tight bun.

Close upon her heels came a young man with very much the look of the Lady upon him - only his face was stern in contrast to her warm smile. Mary wondered fleetingly about the propriety of a man entering the Lady's bedchamber but supposed it permitted with others present - and especially as they two must be related.

"Well, well," said the Lady, inspecting Mary up and down, from tousled locks to dusty boot-caps. "Elijah is to be congratulated. She is lovely, is she not, Roland?"

The young man muttered: "Yes, Mater, lovely. Lovely. Can I go to bed now?"

His mother sighed. "All right, Darling. We'll talk in the morning." The young man withdrew. "Mary?" the Lady turned to her. "Mary. I am not overly fond of the name."

"I am most sorry, Mistress."

The Lady smiled, waved a plump white hand dismissively. "Don't let it worry you, my dear, it can be helped. Now, you must be tired after your journey?"

Mary, afraid to admit this, afraid not to, looked down at the gorgeous figured carpet.

"Never mind, never mind," said the Lady kindly. We'll get to know one another tomorrow. Night-night." She left by the way she had come.

"Well," said the woman Roberts. As everyone she had met today seemed to say everything twice, Mary waited for a second 'well'. None came. "We must get you ready for bed. Have you anything decent to wear?"

"I have a clean nightshift in my bundle," said Mary. "Where am I to sleep, please, Ma'am?"

"Why, here, of course; this is your room, for now. And I am not ma'am; I am Roberts."

"Yes, Roberts."

"Not 'yaze Raabets' - yes Roberts. Say it properly."

"Yess R-o-berrts," Mary dutifully repeated.

Roberts sighed. "We certainly have our work cut out.... Never mind; it'll do. Remember, you must always call a lady's maid by her surname, parlour maids and footmen by their Christian names. The housekeeper is Mrs. Golightly; the cook, Mrs. MacRory; the butler is Makepeace. You will meet them all eventually."

Mary tried hard to take in all of this; at the end was certain of only one thing. "Yess, R-o-berrts."

"Good," said the lady's maid. "Now, take off those horrid rags, and wash your face - here." The door lately used by the Lady opened into a smaller room which housed enough wardrobes and chests of drawers for all the clothes owned by the Barlow family and several of their neighbours as well. There were three other doors: the one through which Roberts conducted her led to a bathing-room. It contained a rack of fat towels, one padded footstool and a huge claw-footed zinc tub. Mary just managed to stifle a giggle at the idea of a bathtub having a whole room to itself. "You can take a proper bath tomorrow," Roberts said. "I'll see about finding you some food."

"Yess, thank you, R-o-berrts," she said to the retreating back. The outer door closed.

Only at that moment did the girl realize that she had altogether missed her supper, that hunger was her most pressing need - but one. There was nothing for it but to investigate. No chamber pot under the bed, none in the nightstand, nor in any corner of the wardrobes. She must either dare one of the two remaining doors in the dressing-room, or make her way outside, in total darkness, in a foreign place...

Roberts entered softly with a tray covered in white cloth. Imagine, someone else bringing Mary a tray! Then, really, *anything* was possible. She dared to ask.

Roberts, for the very first time that evening, smiled. It changed her face entirely; she looked, if only for the most fleeting of moments, more gentle than alarming. "Come."

Next to the room inhabited by the formidable tub, she opened a door Mary had feared to try. Wall-sconces sprang to life when Roberts touched a round thing on the wall which looked like a small - Mary, blushing, abandoned the unseemly thought, but fixed into her mind how one made light in this amazing place. Revealed was the tiniest room of all. Aside from the washstand, its sole occupant was not a chamber pot, but an elegant throne with dark oaken lid hinged to an oaken seat. The girl restrained herself from clapping in delight, but was too late to stifle a gasp. "Oh, yes," said Roberts, "we are quite modern here. When you're through, pull this." Over all, affixed to the high ceiling was a wooden box. The long copper chain hanging down from it ended in a handle of polished oak. "And don't forget to wash your hands afterward."

"Water?" Mary asked timidly.

"You are an ignorant little thing. Here." Roberts twisted one of three brass fish over the washstand and from the mouth of the largest one, water spouted. *Hot* water! The left-hand fish gave cold. It was quite magical. "The late Lord Farwell had plumbing put in - at great expense, I might add."

"Plumming," the girl repeated. "Water comes out of fish..."

"Dolphins. These are meant to be dolphins, not fish."

"How does plum-ming do it?"

"You needn't concern yourself with how it works - just use it. And look smart - it's very late."

Having taken care of her ablutions, having watched the water disappear down a sink-hole - no need to carry buckets to dump outside! - having given her hands and face a pleasurable rub on the soft pink towel, Mary slipped into her nightshift and reentered the bedroom.

She padded over to the little table on which Roberts had set her food: the whitest of bread and lean cold ham sliced very thin, soft yellow butter, jam in a small silver pot that had its own dainty spoon; warm milk in a fine china cup with forget-me-nots painted on – and even inside!

"Not like that!" reproved Roberts. "A lady does not fall upon her food like a starved animal. You must take a slice of bread, put it on your plate and break it into quarters: thus."

Under constant instruction, and with more than one reaffirmation of Roberts' opinion on the size of the task ahead, Mary finished her meal in thrice the time it would have taken, left to her own devices. While she could not altogether see the sense in dawdling so, if this was what a lady did, this is what she would do from now on.

When the last drop of milk was gone, Roberts said: "Now, you must sleep." She doused the lights, whispered good night and softly went away. Mary had no more than a minute to wonder at her good fortune before she fell deeply asleep.

She had an idea that the baby was crying; a feeling that she ought by now to have gone to him.... The baby must have his nappy changed and be taken to the Mistress for his feeding.... Yet, it was still quite dark and her bed was softer, warmer than she had ever known.... Now she could hear nothing; thinking she must have dreamed it, Mary turned over and had almost fallen asleep again when the curtains about the bed parted.

"Good morning," Roberts said.

Curtains? Even so, the room was in semi-darkness.

"Roberts," she mumbled. There was some hazy recollection in her mind of this woman who now, tugging on the quilt, said: "Best go to the closet, girl, and then have your bath." The little room, called a water closet, was familiar enough for Mary to know what to do. But where was the baby? And the Mistress, scolding her tardiness, and Missie, whining for her breakfast?

"Where?" she asked vaguely.

Roberts had no time for questions. She let water into the tub, saying: "I'll put some of this in." 'This' was pink bath crystals in a glass-stoppered jar, such as the Mistress would use only on very special occasions. "Come along, get undressed. Shy? All right, I'll leave you. Be sure to get yourself thoroughly clean. Here," Roberts handed her soap and a long-handled back brush. "We'll have to do something about those hands. And your hair! Wash your hair properly."

Mary, alone once again and beginning to realize that she was not, after all, dreaming, did as instructed. The water was deliciously warm; the tub, large and deep. She nearly dozed off. Something is wrong with me, she thought. Am I sickening? Oh, it must not be, not now, when she so desperately wanted to make a good impression. She roused herself sufficiently to wash. The bath smelt heavenly. Would she be allowed to do this often?

Soft voices drifted in from an adjoining room; she could only make out phrases here and there: "How long...?" That was the Mistress - no, the Lady - Mary did not yet know her name. And Roberts: "Hard to say... ignorant..." "...someplace else... no choice..." "...obedient, so far..." If they were discussing herself, Mary thought, and if being obedient ensured treatment like this, she would always remain so.

There were no babies. She was almost certain someone had told her this. No babies to diaper. And, it dawned upon her fuzzy mind as a brilliant revelation, that meant no diapers to *wash*. Even if nothing more wonderful happened, if her childhood fantasies were not all to come true, this alone was happiness enough. Mary sank blissfully back in the silky water.

Afterwards, Roberts brought food again - porridge with cream, a soft-cooked egg under a quilted cosy, toasted bread, marmalade, steaming tea; lovely, lovely food! Roberts gave her loose underthings of soft white cotton and a white woollen robe to put on. "For now," she said. "I must see to a proper wardrobe in time."

Mary's bundle, her coarse grey shift and bleached apron, were nowhere to be seen. Nor could she locate her lace-up boots. Instead, Roberts brought rose-embroidered pink slippers for her feet. It was not very cold in the room, perhaps because the heavy drapes at the window were closed. Yet neither was it dark, for in their glass shades, wall-lamps burned all the time. Roberts brought an array of things for her hands: emery boards and orange stick, pumice and buffing chamois. Roberts filed Mary's fingernails round and even, polished them fine, like a lady's, rubbed the roughened skin with scented oil and gave her cotton gloves to wear. All the while, Roberts talked in her genteel accent, telling Mary what everything was called and correcting her pronunciation patiently, like a - not quite a mother; rather, a stern but caring aunt. Mary tried especially hard to earn one of Roberts' rare transfiguring smiles. She was growing quite fond of Roberts.

"And now, my girl, it is time for a hot drink and rest." Not more than three hours could have passed since her waking, and she had done no work of any kind, yet Mary felt she might do with a short nap. She must truly be sickening for something. "Mr. Forkes tells us you can read." Mary nodded. She vaguely recalled the kindly, jolly old man and was gratified to be reminded of his name. "Here is a book for you to study."

It was called "Miss Fairfield's College for Young Ladies Compleat Book of Etiquette" and written by Miss Fairfield herself. There was such a very great deal to learn! But Mary had scarcely finished her delicious rich cocoa - made with scalded milk instead of water - when she dozed off.

By the time she awoke, evening had come. Roberts brushed her hair and helped her put on a dress of sprigged polished cotton. It was a trifle snug but the lady's maid said: "I can let out the arm-holes. The rest will be all right, once we get you into stays. Come along, now, don't keep the lady waiting."

At last, she was to be shown her new duties, Mary thought. But no: she was to have supper in the Lady's red, gold and white parlour. A small round table was set with dazzling china and glassware. Roberts conducted her to one of a pair of red plush chairs.

The lady said: "Tonight, it's only the two of us. Perhaps tomorrow, or one day soon, we'll invite Roland to join us. You'd like that, hm?"

"Yess, M'lady," said Mary.

"No, no, my dear! You must call me Esmee. Come now, say it like a good girl."

"Esmee?"

"That's better. We shall be great friends, you and I - shan't we?"

"Yes, Esmee."

"Very good. But," the lady added thoughtfully, "I really do not care for the name Mary. I wish to call you by some other name. What do you think of Felicity?"

"Oh, m'lady..." She recovered herself and tried to speak slowly and distinctly, as Roberts had taught her. "Esmee, I think that is a beautiful name."

The lady smiled. She had a charming smile full of small pearly teeth. "Very well, then. Henceforth, I shall call you Felicity."

Mary-Felicity was now expected to sit down and eat sliced chicken in raisin sauce, flanked by roasted potatoes and glazed carrots. With meals like this three times a day, she would soon be as plump and round as the lady herself, though probably she would never, never in her whole life, attain such amplitude of bosom. She suspected that it was impolite even to think of bosoms in company, although revealing a fair portion of them evidently was not. She would consult Miss Fairfield on the subject, later when she was less busy trying to remember how to make food last a long time. Once, she had believed herself well-versed in etiquette; had endured mockery and accusations of 'putting on airs'. Only now, watching the lady choose with confident ease from the bewildering array of cutlery and crystal, did she fully appreciate the Barlows' crudity. She was well rid of them. Mary had always secretly thought that she herself was made of finer stuff: now, she was certain. She vowed inwardly to become worthy of her new companions. On the whole, she must have acquitted herself satisfactorily, for, when it came time to take her leave, the lady, setting down her empty wineglass, smiled.

"Do keep working on your table manners, my dear," she said. "Speak as little as possible, except to Roberts or myself, in private. I do hope you will stay with us."

"Oh, M'Lady," Mary sighed, "so do I!"

"You like it here, do you, Felicity?"

"Yes, I do, Esmee, truly."

"Well then, be a good girl, and perhaps things will turn out to make us both quite happy."

In these surroundings, with these kind women to guide her, Mary thought, good behavioiur should not prove difficult.

2

The night was cool for summertime; morning, uncomfortably so. When Mary woke at dawn from force of habit, she discovered that she could not start a fire, for no kindling had been laid in the grate. Where might she find some? There were other servants - Roberts had mentioned servants - if she could only seek them out, surely someone would tell her. Gliding in her soft slippers to the door, however, she found it locked! How strange.... Out the window, she saw only a deserted garden: terraced flowerbeds, lawns silvered with dew, along the curving drive, trees ghostly in the mist. An old man in a ragged straw hat hove into view, carrying a pitchfork. He and his long blue shadow stopped beside one of the beds of red and yellow flowers. Moments later, a young man in knee-breeches pushed a wheelbarrow 'round the flank of the building.

He set down his burden, spoke an inaudible word or two with the other, turned. It was not the lady's son. He was dark-haired, taller than Roland, more supple of body and slender of limb. As he stretched, graceful as a cat, his shoulders strained against the thin stuff of his shirt and the rising sun tinted his features as delicately as the finest artist might enhance a daguerreotype. Mary watched him in fascination. The young man, perhaps sensing eyes upon him as cats are said to, looked up. The wide-eyed startlement on his face was so quickly replaced by stern, hard lines that Mary stood frozen with apprehension at the sight of it. Had she done wrong, spying upon him? As soon as she felt able to move, she drew the draperies closed and slipped back into bed, pulling up the covers and squeezing her eyes shut, as small children feign sleep in order to escape punishment.

Ah, but in the darkness thus created she continued to see the young man's face. Sharply defined and clean, it

13

was like a head carved from marble. She could think of but one face beautiful enough to compare. The image arose from a long, long distant past, almost from another life. An angel... yes... atop some grand monument... in a churchyard.... On a gravestone, she realised now, examining the memory, and shivered. But where? The Twinsdale Protestant cemetery, with which she was sadly familiar, contained nothing so magnificent. And, too, that angel had been white and stiff, expressionless, while this one was ever so much alive; ruddy of cheek, full of health and the vigour of youth.

"Good morning, Felicity," Roberts broke into her daydream.

She proceeded with their usual routine, giving no sign of any wrong having been done. Mary dared hope that all might yet be well. She soon forgot the morning's fright in the busyness of breakfast, lessons in speech, grooming and deportment, an after-luncheon (*not* dinner) nap, a new blouse of white lawn.... Her day was, in fact, so very full that she even forgot to ask about firewood until bedtime.

"It's not as cold as all that," Roberts told her. Then she relented. "If this chill persists, the central heating will be turned on soon. The radiator," she explained, indicating a tall narrow box under the window. It was pierced all over the side in flower and leaf designs; Mary had already peeked through these at an odd metal contraption shaped like a concertina.

"That gives heat?"

"Yes, and -"

"But, *how*?"

"A young lady does not interrupt. The heat comes from a furnace below stairs. Never mind how - have I not already told you, Felicity? A young lady need not understand matters mechanical. If you really are cold, I suppose we can bring over a little wood from the Lady's chamber."

"Yes, but why can't I.... Oh, you'll only tell me that a young lady doesn't. Well then, why can't a maid bring wood in here?"

14

Roberts sighed deeply. "Oh, you *are* a slow one! Because, little goose, nobody is to know of your presence here. It is a secret - for now. Someday, *if* you learn your lessons well and do as the Lady and I tell you to, you shall have the run of the house. Then you shan't have to make up the bed or tidy the bath. You might even have a maid of your own. But if you disappoint us.... Now, drink your cocoa and get into bed; you'll be quite warm enough."

Mary obeyed and very soon drifted into sleep. Her dreams were filled, not with a crackling fire, nor yet the central heating which she had hitherto believed only a fable, but with the sharp-lit figure of the angelic young man. Who had seen her and not told anyone; with whom, therefore, she now shared a secret. And the secret - oh, how delicious! - was Felicity!

Thus passed more days; Mary lost track of them. Her hands no longer bore the marks of rough work - indeed, she had only a vague recollection of life with the Barlows. All of her memories were growing indistinct, as if this magical place were somehow outside of time; as if the past were a mere backdrop, insignificant.... The present hour itself assumed a dream-like quality. And yet, there was a rightness to it, too - she did feel so at home in this fairy tale. Food was brought to her; she had neither to serve nor to wash up. Fine clothes - plain daytime skirts, tea gowns, robes, even unmentionables - were skilfully adjusted by Roberts to fit her. Felicity wondered where they came from; all had evidently been made for someone narrower of hip and chest, since every garment needed letting out. She now knew better than to ask too many questions. In any case, she was not required to wash or iron; Roberts took care of everything.

Much as she enjoyed this life of leisure, Mary worried secretly that the rich food might spoil her figure. She did not wish to hurt Roberts' feelings by leaving more than a morsel or two of each meal on her plate (as a young lady ought). She could, however, spare the butter-knife and gravy-boat without causing offence. When Roberts left the room, it was a simple matter surreptitiously to pour her twice-daily cocoa down the was-basin drain and drink water instead. This, in the absence of work or vigorous exercise, was a small enough measure of prevention, yet she began to feel somewhat less heavy. She was no longer drowsy all day long - whatever had ailed her before must have passed off. But early mornings and afternoon nap times hung heavy upon her!

Miss Fairfield had palled; a slim volume on the history of Twillingmarche fascinated her for a while. What an immense building it was! Three sections, all connected, yet discrete and quite different, one from another. The original monastery was built in the eleventh century (the author himself had not known more precisely). From 1538 to 1610, the Palladian wing (Lovely word! She longed to see the structure it described; the drawings in the book, fine though they were, surely could not do justice to its scale!) had been added by the first and third earls (Raymond, she knew, but had to look up Roderick). Yet another section, at the end of the last century, was the achievement of Roland, tenth Lord Farwell. Roberts said that it was not a castle and must always be referred to as Twillingmarche or simply, 'the house'.

When she ventured to complain of boredom, Roberts brought in more books - novels, they were called, like fairy tales for grownups - all about modern young women, their lovers and their various tribulations. On the contents of these books, Mary was questioned at intervals until she knew each story almost as well as if she had herself been its heroine. Esmee was pleased when she recited passages by rote, without drama or emphasis, like her multiplication tables. Roberts was pleased when she reproduced the diction correctly. This was not so difficult, for she had a good ear; her crude country accent disappeared rapidly.

Oh, but how she yearned to go out of doors! Already, her skin was fading into pallor. Roberts said that was good - that a young lady must be careful to shield her face from the sun; that redheads were especially prone to unsightly freckles. It was true that in summer Mary always sported a sprinkling of light brown spots across her nose and cheeks, what she had never before realised was that people of breeding consider these repellent.

When she was left alone, Mary would pull the drapes apart - only a little crack, very cautiously: being a secret was really rather tiresome – and watch the garden. She spent hours sitting at her window, hoping for a glimpse of that handsome, dark-haired young man. Twice, her persistence was rewarded, but never again did he look up at her. In the afternoons, she often saw the fair Roland astride a tall brown horse, trotting down the drive. It would be exciting, she thought, sometime to go horseback riding, though she found the great muscular beasts more than a little daunting. She knew not why this should be so; there had been massive drays aplenty, and some few hacks, in Wayne Fell and none had ever threatened her with bodily harm. Yet, from a small child, she had always kept well clear of horses.

Other people passed across her field of vision but rarely; the only one she saw most days was the old gardener. She wished she could go down and talk with him, ask him the names of the red and yellow flowers by which he appeared to set such great store. Sometimes he would be accompanied by one or two helpers in overalls and homespun shirts. They looked rough country lads: certainly their manners would leave something to be desired.... But they were Mary's age! When she saw them laughing together and cavorting, as boys will, she felt more than ever alone. Grateful as she was to Roberts and Esmee, how welcome would be the company of servants - or any youthful company at all.

Esmee, on her frequent visits to Mary's room.... No, to Felicity's. This, above all, must she fix in her mind: always to answer to her new name. She must learn, even in her private reveries, to think of herself as Felicity. On her visits, and on the more exceptional occasions when the girl came to tea in the lovely (not parlour - sitting room) beyond her own bed-chamber, Esmee was unfailingly patient and kind. However, when Felicity assayed a question of which she disapproved, her smooth pastel features assumed a certain hardness and her silken voice, a certain edge. "All in good time," she would reply. Or wonder aloud what a girl could do on her own, without references....

It wasn't that Felicity wished to leave Twillingmarche - far from it! The more she learned of the estate, its history and past inhabitants, the more she hoped it would become her home. Only that she would dearly love to see it whole, inside and out. Only that she was restive to do something - anything - besides eat, read, recite, walk about the room with books on her head and pretend to take unnecessary naps.

Ah but today, today something different would happen. Roland was to join the ladies at supper in Esmee's rooms. Roberts dressed her with more than the usual care. For the first time, she had to wear stays. She had believed that corsets were made for women like Mistress Barlow, who carried an overabundance of flesh. Horrid it was, until she grew accustomed to being laced in tight. "That's nothing," Roberts said, as close as ever she came to outright laughter. "When you attend formal occasions, they shall have to be much tighter."

Was she, therefore, to attend formal occasions? With very grand people, in ballrooms full of candles and an orchestra? Was she to wear a gorgeous ball-gown, like the heroine of a novel, and dance with elegant, witty gentlemen? Oh, *when*? But, too, if that were so, she better had learn her lessons especially well, so as not to bring shame upon her patroness and mentor.

Roland was tardy. Esmee carried on a conversation that consisted, as usual, largely of having Felicity relate what she had learned of Twillingmarche and manners. All the while, she chafed visibly. A lady must never show impatience, Felicity had been taught, yet Lady Farwell kept glancing at the door. At last, after the most perfunctory rap, it opened. Roland gave his mother a light peck on the cheek; she returned the kiss warmly, lingeringly, as if they had not seen one another for ages. It was not so: Felicity herself had seen them earlier in the day, walking arm-in-arm about the terraces. He offered no excuses; Esmee asked for none.

She said: "Darling, this is our sweet Felicity. Has she not grown even lovelier since you last met? Felicity; Roland Wilkins."

Wilkins. Not Sommelroux? Of course, Roberts had once explained the relationships: Esmee was Lord Farwell's second wife. She, too, had been married before. Wilkins must have been her first husband. Felicity had privately to respect the young man for sticking by his father's name, be it ever so humble. Roland smiled wanly, made a very slight bow, and sat. He was wide-shouldered and deep-chested like his mother and his pink cheeks were set off by a fine fluff of yellow hair that would not long remain flat on his head, however assiduously he brushed and wet it down. A little fringe of similar hair adorned the soft curve of his upper lip. He had sturdy legs encased in tight fawn trousers; an exquisite brocade waistcoat with shell buttons was exposed by the parting of his royal blue coat. His eyes were a much lighter shade of blue. He was attractive in a tender, boyish way.... Ah, but how pale, how insignificant he would appear next to Mary's dark angel of the dawn!

Roberts served from covered chafing dishes on a side table. Felicity was too much occupied with what each utensil was for, to wonder more than passingly how the food and three elaborate sets of china and silver could have been brought to Esmee's rooms without any servant knowing it. Was the third setting meant for Roberts, and she had given up her place? No wonder, then, that she remained so slim. Roland's conversation was minimal, as was Felicity's perforce: she had been trained to keep attentive silence, except when asked a question, then to answer as briefly as courtesy allowed. Too, she understood that Roland was not much taken with her. This caused her no special chagrin, except that Esmee obviously wished otherwise.

"It is too bad that you two children were together such a little while, before," she remarked. "You were fond of each other then. I'm sure you will be so again."

The five courses appropriate for an informal supper seemed to last forever. Felicity's mind had begun to cloud even before the fish, perhaps because she was unaccustomed to wine with her meals; by the sweet, it was all she could do to remember that a young lady must not take cheese while in company. Beans were never served at Twillingmarche.... Then, why not ban cheese from the table, too? Because, Roberts had answered with more amusement than irritation, the gentlemen enjoy it with their port. It popped unbidden into Felicity's mind to challenge the injustice of this arrangement: why should gentlemen be immune to gas? She was sufficiently awake to stifle the highly improper question before it passed her lips.

Over brandy, Esmee announced: "She'll do. She will have to do, won't you, Felicity? It might go very hard with you, otherwise."

Mary was startled out of her somnolence. There had been veiled threats before, yes - never anything so bald and harsh. She bowed her head. "Yes, Esmee."

"One had hoped," the lady adjusted her tone to the gentler one she generally used, "to give you more time, but that has now been made impossible. Listen very, very carefully. Are you paying attention? You are Felicity Sommelroux. Don't stare like a ninny. And close your mouth. You *are* Felicity Sommelroux. Three years ago, shortly after your father, Lord Farwell's, death, you had a terrible accident. You recall nothing of it. You were missing for some time, and when found, you were quite addled in your brain. Therefore, we sent you to a clinic of excellent repute, in Switzerland." Esmee interrupted her strange narrative, turned to Roberts. "She knew this yesterday,"

Indeed, one of the novels Mary had been given to memorize was all about a girl who, having suffered a head injury, was sent to such a clinic, where she met and fell in love with a consumptive young German count. He had died in the end. Very sad.

"There," Esmee resumed, "you regained your health but, alas, not your full memory."

The girl in the novel had despaired of ever knowing her own history, had finally become resigned to life without a true identity - until, told of her lover's passing, she fainted dead away. When revived by her devoted nurse, the girl -

20

who was much like Felicity, but had a different name - remembered everything. "But she did! She - I mean, we - I - had fallen from a runaway horse."

Esmee exchanged glances with Roberts and then Roland. "No," she said slowly, distinctly, "you're confused. It was your grandfather who fell from a horse. You fell over a cliff, into the ocean. You were rescued by some fishermen farther down the coast, and since you could not tell them who you were, they brought you to the nuns at Eastmills House. That is why it took us so long to find you."

"Nuns," the girl repeated. Yes, her mind, unreliable as it was at the moment, did contain scenes from a convent. Was this her own memory? There was a girl who decided to become a nun because her father would not allow her to marry the low-born fellow she loved. But it had also happened to Mary; there now came into her nostrils a scent of candles and incense, and into her inner eye, a glimpse of stained glass window. "Eastmills House... Only she - I - did not take the veil, after all...."

"All right," Esmee said briskly. "We haven't much time. Mr. Forkes will rehearse you more on the way."

"Way," repeated Felicity. She was growing quite drowsy, but she did recall kindly old Mr. Forkes, who had taken her for a ride in a carriage - oh, a long time ago. "Elijah Forkes - with whiskers - I like him.... "

"About ten minutes," Roberts told someone else.

"Is she packed?"

"Of course. All is ready."

"Then take her away. Felicity," Esmee added severely, "be a good girl."

As the door was swinging shut behind herself and Roberts, whose supporting arm she would have preferred not to need, words drifted past: "...couldn't be helped..." "...known he'd come so soon..." "...will never work..." "...hope..." That last word echoed reassuringly. Hope.

Vaguely familiar was Mary's stumbling progress through darkened halls and into pitch-black night. She and Roberts were both wearing cloaks now, with hoods to hide their faces, and Roberts was encumbered not only by a lantern, as on the previous occasion, but by a hefty portmanteau as well. Had Mary been feeling less weary, she would have offered to carry it. Had she not been so nearly asleep on her feet, this all might seem exciting: it was the first time in weeks that she had felt fresh air upon her face - this, perhaps, kept her from falling down. This, and Roberts' frequent admonitions to be quiet, to watch her step, to be careful.

At last they reached the gates. Here was the carriage; even in the darkness its shape was somehow comforting. And here was Mr. Forkes, recognised primarily by his scent - a warm and spicy smell - into which she gratefully collapsed. She overheard some whispered conversation between the other two, made little enough of the words and cared less: she was inside the carriage now and permitted, finally to rest.

3

"Well, well, well," said Mr. Forkes cheerfully. "Sleeping Beauty awakens."

Mary was almost certain that nobody had kissed her, although there was the image in her mind of a dark young man with features clear and sharp, as if carved from stone. That must have been Prince Charming. "Where..?"

"Don't fret, my dear. Everything is all right."

"It is?" She felt motion, as of a carriage, and would have looked out the window, had it not been close curtained. Only a little twilight allowed her to discern the gentleman's long-nosed profile. Ought he not to be on the driving seat, instead of inside with her? He had been with her the night before, in some stationary place; he had been tolerant and generous; had given her a soothing drink from his silver hip-flask, between sleep and more sleep.

"Where's Roberts?"

The old man chuckled. "Just where she ought to be - at home, minding her mistress."

"And where are we?" Felicity was coming fully awake now; aware that the journey, her second one in this man's company, had lasted some considerable time.

"We are going to Twillingmarche," he said.

"But I was at..."

"No," said he, very sternly. "You were not. You have not been at Twillingmarche these past three years."

"Yes, sir," she answered meekly.

"Good, good. Now, who are you?"

"Mary... No... Felicity Sommelroux."

"Excellent. And where have you been?"

"I have been at the convent."

"Yes. And then?"

"And then..." It was hard to remember. "Somewhere. At a sanatorium?"

"Switzerland. It was called?"

In a book. The girl who fell in love at the...
"Alpenweiss." She began to realize the importance of the
correct answers. "There was a boy named Reinhard and
he died.... It was very sad."

"Yes, my dear," Mr. Forkes agreed, "it must have
been. But that is all behind you now. You are much better.
I came to fetch you from the sanatorium. We travelled on a
train and on a boat. Do you recall?"

Felicity searched her memory for trains and boats,
found both in a not very gay setting: Madeleine was sent to
finishing school in Paris, because her stepmother was
jealous, because her father loved Madeleine best of all. "If
Esmee is my stepmother, will she not send me away
again?"

"You must not think of Esmee as a stepmother.
She has cared for you from a tiny child, as if you had been
her own. Nor would she ever send you away, so long as
you continue such a good girl as you have been."

"Esmee was very kind to me," said Felicity. "I was
happy with her."

"Good, good," said Mr. Forkes. "And she has
missed you sorely. She will be gratified to see that you
have grown into such a lovely young lady. As will Master
Roland, naturally."

"But," Felicity began to protest, "it was just yester..."

"No!" She flinched at the violence in his voice; he
saw her flinch and put a reassuring hand upon her
shoulder. "No, my dear," he repeated more softly. "You
have not laid eyes on one another in the last three years.
Do remember that."

"Three years," she said.

"That's better. Lady Esmee wrote you many letters,
which you still keep, and sometimes read over. They will
be in your trunk."

"Yes," Felicity agreed, although she had never, to
her certain knowledge, owned a trunk. "Many letters."

"Now, we are almost there. Tell me your story from
the beginning."

"My name," she recited obediently, "is Felicity
Sommelroux. The Earl of Farwell was my father. His

Christian name was Randolph. He died. My poor mother died, too, when I was little. Esmee is my stepmother, who is very kind and wrote letters. Then I fell over a cliff and got am-nee-si-ah. And then there was a convent - Eastsomething. Eastmills? Yes. When I was found, Esmee sent me to a clinic in Switzerland, which is on the Continent. The clinic was called Alpenweiss. Doctor Weiss helped me to begin remembering again..."

"Yes. And now, to our great joy, the good doctor believes that your recovery might best be completed in familiar surroundings."

"You came and fetched me in a boat."

Mr. Forkes nodded approvingly. He drew aside the drapes to reveal sunlit vistas of field and wood. "Soon you will be safely home again."

That means, she thought in secret amazement, that I am the daughter of an earl! Also that I shall finally see the house (not castle). I shall wear fine dresses and attend grand balls and dance with handsome young gentlemen, just as Mother said that I should.

"Home again." She gave Mr. Forkes her most radiant smile.

Twillingmarche, The House, was even grander than she had expected. As the carriage entered the wrought iron gates and made its stately way along the gravelled drive, she was able to see it all of a piece, in daylight. There was the southernmost end, largely hidden by trees, which must have been the abbey: a square, nondescript low building beyond crumbling grey walls, and a blocky tower. There was the central section; three storeys, all in dazzling white stone, its tall, narrow windows separated by flattened columns, which could only be the Palladian wing. And here, as the carriage came to a halt, was what must surely be the most recent addition: a red brick structure with gables on the topmost floor. The front (facade, she recalled) was decorated with horizontal bands of intricate brickwork and iron railings outside every window. Far up, on the edge of the roof, stood a row of stone pots, each on its own little pedestal. In the centre, directly over the main entrance, stood a female figure of heroic proportions, carved from pink granite.

Mr. Forkes alit, immediately extending a supportive arm to Felicity. He signalled at the man on the driving seat (buckboard? No.... Where did that silly word come from? Never mind; a young lady needn't concern herself with technicalities.) who did something to the top of the conveyance, releasing a great wooden box. Felicity accompanied Mr. Forkes up the wide stairs between terraced flowerbeds, giving only one apprehensive look behind.

She had scarcely time to note low relief carvings of the Farwell coat of arms upon either wing of the massive doors (on shield sable, a cock displayed gule, bearing aloft twain chalice d'or) before they were flung wide. The man who stood there was tall, spare, hawk-featured and dark-haired - familiar. Either she had seen him before, or he reminded her of someone else, she was not certain which.

"Makepeace," said Mr. Forkes, "here is our young mistress, home at last. I trust her room has been prepared? Good, good. Later on, Lady Farwell will no doubt wish to present the household. Oh, and Makepeace, get a footman to help with the luggage."

She smiled at the butler: "I think I should know you."

"No, Lady Felicity," said Mr. Forkes ever so gently. "Makepeace was not with the family at the time of your accident. You will find, I'm afraid, very few faces from the past."

The girl began to frame a suitable reply, when there appeared from some unguessed depth of The House, none other than her dark young man of the morning. He was neither stretching nor lively; he was as stiff and formal as the angel on a monument. "Edward," Makepeace told him, "take the young lady's trunk up to her room."

Edward! A footman? Well, why not? Mary had been a maid in some other, very distant life.... He did look handsome in green and gold livery. But he gave her only the briefest of glances, though she was now dressed quite becomingly in a brown velvet travelling suit trimmed with

26

cream lace. And she was not a secret anymore.... Perhaps he did not recognize her. Or perhaps he was keeping the secret of her first visit here, of which no-one must ever know. If only people would tell her what was expected! If only people would say whom she ought to remember and whom not!

All Edward did was hasten past with a respectful dip of the head and hurry outside to assist the coachman. Meanwhile, Mr. Forkes was explaining to Makepeace (Butler and lady's maid are called by their surnames, maids and footmen by their given names; the housekeeper and cook are Mrs.) that he had fetched her home on the train (She knew this, and the boat, though Mr. Forkes did not mention the boat.) and that, being yet rather frail after so long and tiring a journey, (although Felicity did not feel in the least frail or tired) she would require a few hours' rest.

Before the solicitor was able to finish his instructions, however, Esmee appeared at the top of the staircase. She was gorgeous in a gown of deep pink, the colour of her cheeks. She flew down the steps to envelope the girl in loving arms, push her away and gaze upon her fondly, only to embrace her yet again, the whole time saying, over and over: "I'm so happy to see you!" This was not the manner in which Esmee had been used to dealing with her and Felicity hoped that it would not become habitual: so much hugging made her uneasy. "Come along my dear," Esmee released all but her hand. "We have prepared your old room, naturally. We shall have Kate run you a bath, and then you'll take a nice nap."

Only, her room was not the same at all. The one to which Roberts, after a restrained curtsey, which greeting Felicity could not help feeling was a little cold, however appropriate to their new roles, was larger and far more lavishly appointed than her previous one. Like Esmee's own chamber, it had a sitting room attached, and a separate bath. The pale green drapes had been caught back in loops of thick gold tasseled braid; no lamps were lit. Outside, she saw not lawns, trees and circular drive, but the back of the old abbey directly across and part of the

Palladian wing along the right-hand side of a courtyard. In it were outbuildings, the purpose of which she could not guess, and beyond, a kitchen-garden within tall brick walls. She sighed happily: there would be more activity on this side of the house. Even now, three muscular men in shirt-sleeves were straining to push barrels up a ramp onto a wagon harnessed to a pair of massive black horses. There would always be something interesting to watch when she woke early or did not wish to take her afternoon sleep. Everything she beheld was delightful.

"May I," she asked Roberts, "have some cocoa?"

In the ensuing days, two significant new dimensions were added to Felicity's daily routine. She took breakfast and occasionally luncheon on a tray in her own chamber, but now shared tea each afternoon with Esmee and Roland in the blue drawing room on the main floor. Supper, a meal for which one changed, even if one had done nothing to soil one's daytime clothing, was always served by Makepeace in the great, oak-paneled dining room. Here, she felt insignificant and dwarfed at one end of an oak table large enough to seat twenty people, with only three places laid. Mr. Forkes, after but one night, had returned to London. Felicity soon grew accustomed to the new arrangement and hardly ever needed correction in the use of fish forks and fruit knives. Between meals, Roberts still came, as before, to instruct her in the finer points of deportment.

The more important change was that her door, when she ventured to try it, opened readily! She was free to go anywhere in the house. Not that she had much need: firewood, clean towels, freshly ironed linens and clothing were brought by Kate, a girl of her own age, or the younger maid, Evelyn. Felicity continued, nonetheless, to make up her bed every morning, to clean her bathtub and washbasin after use, to rinse out her stockings and delicate new underthings. Roberts would not have approved, but doing these trivial chores gave Mary a tiny measure of independence, despite Felicity's total helplessness. Well, Roberts need not be troubled by the knowledge; certainly, the maids had no objection.

Her outdoor activity was confined to sedentary walks about the garden, usually in the company of Esmee, each lady carrying a silk parasol, and Roland in his straw boater, whenever that young man could be persuaded to come along. This enlargement of horizons, however appreciated, nevertheless inspired a hunger for more. She longed to explore farther afield – the farmlands and pastures, the woods, the road beyond those wrought iron gates; village, town, riverbank... She told herself: only be patient, and someday, all those things will be yours.

A week after Felicity's reintroduction to Twillingmarche, Mr. Forkes joined the family at supper once again.

"He has arrived," said the solicitor to Esmee - over Felicity's head, for he sat on her right. "He has taken rooms at the Garfield Hotel in Dover Street. We may expect a visit, I'm afraid, within the next few days."

Esmee sighed. "It *is* awfully soon..." and turning to the girl, explained: "We are speaking of your cousin once removed, Roderick Sommelroux, from America. He is the son of your late father's uncle Raymond, younger brother of the tenth earl."

"I didn't know," Felicity began, but was interrupted.

"No, of course you didn't. Raymond was believed to have died in the colonies some time ago - without issue. Nevertheless, Roderick exists and he is coming here."

"Yes, Esmee?"

"We must all be very hospitable, no matter how uncouth the man turns out to be."

"Yes, Esmee."

"Roderick supposes that he has a claim to the Farwell legacy, by virtue of his gender. As if *that* was a virtue!" Esmee stifled an unladylike snort, only to don an even more unladylike, not to say unbecoming, expression, very like a snarl. "But we shall have the better of him when you and Roland are married."

Felicity forgot to say yes in the shock of this dramatic revelation. She did not find in her heart any passion for the fair Roland - who had, in any case, been keeping himself out of her way. "Married? I am to marry Roland?"

"Oh, yes. It is crucial that you produce a son, for none of us may legally succeed to the title. Isn't it fortunate that you two always got on so well, even as children? And now that innocent attachment has suddenly - as soon as you set eyes on one another - blossomed into love!" Esmee sighed deeply and fluttered her long, unnaturally dark eyelashes. "So romantic!"

4

It was unusual in that largely silent house for voices to be raised in argument. Yet, contention was evident, even through the thick door; moreover, alarmingly, contention between Esmee and Roland, those most affectionate of mothers and sons!

"I don't care!" Roland was saying. "Even if he is real - *if*, I say, because he could be a pretender. Have you thought of *that*, Mater?"

"Of course I have," retorted Esmee. "D'you take me for a fool? Elijah has inquiries in hand, over there."

"Then what's the rush? Why have I got to be engaged?"

"Come here, darling." The woman's tone grew softer, so that Felicity was forced to put her ear close up against the wood. "She will turn eighteen soon, and then -"

Roland interrupted: "She can't inherit 'til she's twenty-one. There's bags of time."

"Yes, I *do* know that." Esmee's voice regained the edge of impatience. "But we have yet to bring her out; we must give her some kind of debut..."

"I don't see why."

"Because she is meant to be a countess. At the very least, she has to be presented at court. She's fragile, poor thing, and won't be expected to attend a full season.... Even so, we can't risk her meeting someone - perhaps someone more eligible. Besides," the voice was silken now, caressing, "you will enjoy being in town again, won't you, my sweet?"

"Yes, I suppose," the son grudgingly allowed. "It's beastly dull here."

"Look on the bright side," his mother said. "Once you're safely married, you shall be in charge. More cash will be forthcoming too: you'll be able to live in Town. Marriage needn't be so hard to bear. Certainly, it never interfered with your stepfather's - shall we say private? - life. I know."

Roland muttered something unintelligible. It sounded as if the argument were winding down; Felicity hurried away, not to be found lurking when the young man exited. Evidently, Roland was no more eager to marry her than she, him. At least she was to have a debutante season. She knew from novels what that meant: London, balls, new dresses, parties, the opera... being presented to the King.... How glorious it all would be! And we shall see, Felicity said to herself, who is too fragile to enjoy every moment.

Cousin Roderick's arrival threw the household into a tizzy. He came not by train or carriage, like a civilised man, but drove his own motorcar. Those of the staff who could find any pretext to be occupied in the front part of the house were at the windows, peering out; those who could not, gathered about the kitchen door, waiting for the vehicle to be taken round to the coach-house. This was not to happen for some little while, however, for the stable-master refused to have it near his charges and in any case, no footman knew how to operate the thing. There it stood - black, square, very much at odds with its setting - in the circular drive. And he came, not alone, nor yet with a wife, but accompanied by his solicitor, an American named Mr. Goldsmith. Fortunately, Mr. Forkes was on hand to engage the unexpected guest in legal conversation.

The family found the encounter more awkward. What was one to say to a complete stranger from across the Atlantic Ocean, who suddenly turned up in the guise of a relative? For Felicity, the problem was solved: she had been taught to speak as little as possible in any situation. She was duly introduced, looked over, complimented, then excused until luncheon. Roland, never the most loquacious of young men, responded in monosyllables, ungraciously. Therefore, the entertainment of Cousin Roderick fell upon the plump white shoulders of Lady Farwell. That burden might turn out, Felicity reflected as she withdrew, less heavy than one might have expected, for Roderick seemed disposed to carry on a conversation all by himself. He commented on everything, touched everything; he picked up and replaced ornaments, gazed upon the portraits in the hall and laughed aloud in the solemn faces of his putative ancestors.

"That one," he said, pointing with his index finger and whole extended arm, as Felicity had been admonished *never* to do, at the sixth Earl, a Roland, "is the spittin' image of my poor old dad. What a puss! And that wig! Underneath there, he must be hiding the same flaming red hair we're all cursed with, right?" He gave a wink to Felicity who was already half-way up the stairs. His own characteristic feature was somewhat thin on top but still curled luxuriantly about the ears. Unlike the gentlemen of Felicity's recent acquaintance, he did not sport any facial hair; his cheeks were red and round as September apples, and as smooth. Indeed, but for his costly suit - Felicity could recognize good stuff, however garishly plaid - he seemed no gentleman at all.

The tour proceeded without her. Felicity did not wish to remain in her rooms, watching people come and go beneath her window. In any case, soon there was no servant left in the courtyard except for one young boy who took his time over the cleaning of a boot. Therefore, being no longer confined or a secret, she slipped down the service stairs, into the back regions of the house. Voices issued from what must surely be the kitchen. She knew Kate and Evelyn moderately well now, had met Mrs. Golightly and Mrs. MacRory. She had exchanged good-mornings, though little more, with Makepeace. Might she enter and join them? Would she be made unwelcome?

While she stood there hesitating, the kitchen door swung open. Uncomfortable at the thought of being found thus, undecided of destination, she drew back into the shadowed entrance of the butler's pantry. Edward emerged, carrying a tray covered with a white cloth, such as the one on which Felicity was accustomed to receiving her own breakfast. To whom would he be taking a meal at this time of day? He hurried past, unaware of her, continued on through the baize doors at the end of the hall.

Amazed and curious, Felicity fell in behind. She had never seen this part of the house. Here was a corridor, lit by small square panes along its left-hand side. She did stop briefly to look out. The cobweb-covered window gave onto the courtyard; this must be the eastern wall of the Palladian section. She had been told that no-one lived here; the wing had fallen into disuse since the erection of the modern building. Nor did Edward stop or turn anywhere along its considerable length. A lucky thing for his pursuer: there were but two side-passages in which she might have concealed herself.

Another door; this one of dark mahogany, whose hinges did not creak as the footman pulled it open. The girl waited a moment before following suit. She found herself in yet a different structure. The walls and vaulted ceiling were of bare stone, rough to the touch. The temperature dropped several degrees; Felicity shivered in her light summer frock. The left-hand wall of this corridor was a series of bricked-up archways, barely visible in the meager light from narrow slits of window left in each, except the one which held a sturdy wooden gate, closed and barred. Along the right, three smaller recessed doorways deep in shadow seemed vaguely menacing. They exuded a stale odour reminiscent of doused charcoal braziers and ale-houses.

Suddenly, she came to a dead end. Stone stairs, too ponderous to be called a flight, angled upward to what must be the ancient abbey's belfry. A niche in the wall, large enough for a grown man to stand in, where perhaps a statue of Saint Barnabas had once stood, contained twin wrought-iron sconces but no candles. Such illumination as there was came from the passage behind her. On the far side of that wall section, a closed door of massive oak planks, blackened with centuries of smoke from rush torches. Edward had disappeared from sight. Straining, she could discern a whisper of movement somewhere above; a very soft echo of steps. She placed one, then another wary foot in the hollows worn by the sandals of long-forgotten bell-ringers.

The faint sounds halted. So did Felicity. A knock, a pause. She felt by a disturbance of air, the opening and closing of a door. Edward would be returning by the same route, perhaps immediately. She could not explain her presence here and might not have sufficient time to run back the way she had come. Hiding anywhere along the route was hopeless: even in this murk, her pale green dress would glow like a beacon. How humiliating to be caught thus, spying upon a servant! She retreated to the niche, which wasn't deep enough to conceal her, then felt her way around the curve of the tower. She heard Edward say: "Naturally, I shall keep you informed," and his quick, light steps descending the stair. She pressed herself as flat as possible against coarse wood, two rivets of the ornate iron hinge jutting into her back. The door yielded - slowly, heavily - but silently.

The cool dimness of the large space was relieved by a pair of stained-glass windows, high in the far wall. The pervading smell was not of abandonment, but of sanctity: oiled wood, parchment, the lingering sweetness of incense and bees-wax. Of course! In this chapel generations of Sommelroux, their household staff and tenant farmers had worshipped. For all she knew, Esmee and Roland still came here sometimes, though there was no resident cleric to officiate. She stood perfectly motionless, breathless, while Edward passed.

And now? She had a choice to make. There ought to be another exit from the chapel to the outside; she could look for that. The gate she had passed along the corridor had to be an exit the courtyard. Would she be able to replace the bar from outside? It might be worth investigating. Or she could wait a while and return the way she had come. Or again - daring thought! - she could go up the stairs and find out who lived in this isolated tower. Not Mr. Finch, the steward; he had a cottage on the riverbank. All the servants' quarters were supposed to be on the top floor of the newest wing. Perhaps it was a servant indisposed and quarantined, lest the others come down with an illness. If that were so, visiting him or her might be unsafe. But it would also be a gracious gesture, such as might be expected from the daughter of the house.

In the end, curiosity proved stronger than caution. Almost before she was aware of having decided, she stood on the landing.

"Back already?" a woman's voice answered her knock.

"It isn't Edward," said the girl, taking a shy step into the room. "It's Felicity Sommelroux."

"Is it? Is it really?" The occupant was seated in the very centre of the chamber. She wore a wine-red velvet cloak so large and full that her lean face seemed tiny as a doll's among its swathing folds. Her hands, white and delicate, fluttered like doves, folding and refolding the napkin on her tray. This lay on a small table before her throne-like chair. To her right, pushed aside, was a tapestry frame. Felicity had never seen one before but knew what it was by the unfinished work stretched upon it: a picture in yarn, as depicted in her favourite book. Once upon a time, priceless tapestries graced many of the walls at Twillingmarche. She had not supposed that anyone still made such wonderful, old-fashioned things in the twentieth century. "Come closer, let me look at you."

Sunlight entered the chamber by two tall casement windows, fitted with sheets of clear modern glass. All the furnishings - a great profusion of chairs, tables, footstools, cabinets filled with curios - were dark, heavy, ornate. So full was the room that Felicity could hardly imagine anyone moving about without knocking things over and barking their shins. "I wondered," she hesitantly offered, "whether you might be ill."

The woman gave a small laugh, like sheets of old parchment rubbed together. "No, my dear, not ill. It's quite safe to approach."

Felicity edged closer. "May I ask who you are?"

"You may ask," said the other. "And so might I, of you."

"I have just -"

"Ah, to be sure, you said Felicity Sommelroux. Indeed!" Emitting another dry cackle, the old woman peered up into her face, intently as a bird, with startling green eyes. "And you do have the look."

"I was given to understand so, Ma'm...." Sudden recognition escaped her unintentionally: "But, so have you!"

"Oh yes, I suppose I must, being of the tribe. Yes, yes." She nodded so hard that Felicity was for a moment alarmed by the fancy that her thin neck could not long sustain such vigour. "Has no-one mentioned me?"

"No, Ma'm."

The other sighed, shook her head. The hair exposed by her movement was almost as bright a red as Felicity's own. "Unkind of them. And sloppy. That's to be expected, I suppose.... Still, you must have been told not to go about calling anyone Ma'm."

The girl nodded, confused. "Yes.... Only, what may I call you, please?"

"You must call me Auntie." Taking Felicity's hand in one of her narrow, pale ones and holding it firmly, the old woman nodded some more. "Oh yes. Yes indeed. I am Letitia Sommelroux. Do you not remember at all? Your dear old Aunt Lettie? For shame, child!"

Felicity began to feel just a little bit frightened. There was a mental echo about this peculiar overstuffed room, though she was quite certain she had never been here before. Had someone, sometime in the past, told her of it, or of its occupant?

She stammered out, "Aunt Lettie?"

"That's right, that's right, Aunt Lettie." She finally released the girl. "Sit you down, child, and talk to me."

Not daring to do otherwise, Felicity pulled up one of the antimacassared chairs and seated herself gingerly. "I can only stay a little while; Esmee expects me for luncheon."

In the short time, however, she did learn that Aunt Letitia had herself chosen this remote apartment and that she did not desire contact with the outside world, which she considered vulgar, disorganised, inadequately managed.

"Like entering a convent?"

Letitia nodded. "Yes, yes, something like that. Mine is a sad story. I may tell you sometime. If you don't mind visiting a crazy old woman."

"I should love to! I mean... you're not...." The girl dissolved in embarrassed confusion.

Lettie merely cackled. "You never know, do you?"

Felicity, by now somewhat accustomed to the teasing, regained her composure, "I don't care. I shall come to visit whenever I can."

"Good girl. And don't chatter, will you? I'm moderately sure they wouldn't approve."

Felicity knew whom she meant by 'they'; had already guessed that Esmee and Roberts would not look kindly upon independent exploration, nor of her making the acquaintance of a relative about whose very existence they had chosen, so far, to keep her ignorant. "I won't say anything. I used to be a secret myself."

"Doesn't surprise me," Aunt Lettie said. "This house is filthy with secrets. What do you think of the new cousin?"

The girl reflected, wanting to formulate an intelligent reply, yet having little knowledge upon which to base it. "He seems very brisk, energetic. Perhaps a little crude?"

Letitia nodded in her own energetic way. It no longer alarmed Felicity: the woman was not, after all, so old and delicate as she had first appeared. "I imagined he would be. But is he genuine? That is the question. That is the most urgent of questions."

"I don't know. He does have The Look: bright red hair and green eyes.... He does resemble some of the portraits.... Yet, I believe Esmee has doubts. Mr. Forkes - our solicitor, d'you know of him?" She waited for the nod. "It seems Mr. Forkes is making inquiries."

"Excellent. Well then, we must wait and see, mustn't we?"

"Is that what Edward is to keep you informed about?"

This had been a mistake, she saw as soon as the words left her unguarded mouth. Aunt Lettie's features lost their readiness to break into laughter. "Have you been a naughty girl, listening at doors?"

"No! Not at all," she protested. "I only happened to be at the foot of the stairs..."

"Well, all right," the older woman relented, luckily foregoing an exploration of how the girl had 'happened' there. "I shall forgive you this one time."

Felicity was relieved. Soon thereafter, she made her apologies and departure. She did not quite know how to feel about this encounter: excited by the discovery of a secret, but apprehensive too, lest she betray it and be punished. What form the punishment might take, she dared not contemplate. She might even be sent away - never to live again at Twillingmarche! That possibility did not bear thinking of: Twillingmarche, she felt - obscurely, perhaps unreasonably, but nevertheless strongly, in the depth of her very being - was where she belonged.

5

This is *some* place!" Cousin Roderick said for the fifth or sixth time, attacking his roast pheasant in a manner unlike any Felicity had been taught. "Talk about old! So, how come you've been letting it fall apart?"

The question, which could as easily be construed as an accusation, was aimed at Roland, who looked vaguely about for help. His mother supplied it: "Twillingmarche is hardly 'falling apart', as you so quaintly put it. The older wings are not currently in use, naturally. We've not needed a great deal of living space," she glanced at Roland and Felicity, "for only three of us."

"Besides, we spend winters at the London house," added Roland. "We should be going there soon."

Cousin Roderick nodded; to Felicity's relief, he swallowed before resuming speech. "Fine. But I'll want to do something about those other wings. Guess I'd better have a peek 'round the property, too, soon's I can."

Esmee, quickly changing her expression of displeasure into one of bland graciousness, said: "Roland will be happy to show you around this afternoon, won't you, Darling?"

Roland, not so adaptable, mumbled: "All right."

Mr. Forkes put in: "Perhaps it would be helpful if Mr. Finch were to accompany the gentlemen?"

"That'll be the foreman, eh? Or whatever you call him."

"We call him Mr. Finch," replied the solicitor mildly. "He is, in fact, the Steward of Lands."

"He can come," Roderick allowed, helping himself to more meat. The action caused the hovering Makepeace a barely visible dismay; at the earliest unobtrusive moment, he moved the serving dish out of the visitor's reach, proffering one of buttered peas in its stead. This was waved impatiently aside by Cousin Roderick, whose attention had, in any case, wandered. "And the little girl. She can come too." Quicker than Makepeace, he now refilled his wineglass - with claret, which even Felicity knew to be inappropriate with fowl.

She looked up in alarm, first at him, then at Esmee, Roland and Mr. Forkes in turn. It was Esmee who came to her rescue. "I'm afraid our dear Felicity does not ride since her accident."

"Ride?" repeated the American. "You mean, like horses? I figured we'd go in the car."

"That," Mr. Forkes explained patiently, as if to a backward child, "might prove impractical, given the condition of the roads. Or, more accurately, the lack thereof. A farm cart, possibly -"

"All right, fine," the other cut him off, "we'll ride. It's been a while, though." He half turned in Roland's direction, "so find me a horse that doesn't jump around too much. I'll take the cute little cousin for a spin some other time, eh?"

Felicity, mindful of her manners, however unenthusiastic she might be at the prospect of spinning anywhere with this man, said: "That would be very nice."

Luncheon somehow drew to a close. There was more conversation, into which she inserted the occasional 'really' or 'how interesting' wherever she detected an expectant pause. This did not prevent her observing how Cousin Roderick's eyes tended to stray from his plate - or, for that matter, from the face of whomever he was currently addressing, to the front of Esmee's extremely fetching tea-gown. The other man of law, Mr. Goldsmith, spoke almost as little as Felicity - and, like the girl, missed nothing. She had the feeling that he did not entirely approve of his employer's ocular fixation. As the gentlemen repaired to their rooms to change into riding costumes and Makepeace went off in search of Mr. Finch, Esmee tarried a moment.

"What do you think of your cousin, hm?"

The girl hardly knew what to answer, but her face must have given her away.

"I don't like him either," Esmee smiled. "Especially the way he looks at you.... Never mind. He might turn out not to be a cousin, after all."

"I hope so," Felicity sighed with such depth of feeling that her stepmother meted out one of her tinkling laughs.

"Even if he is, we've got you, haven't we? He may end up with the title but without the property or income. If he is proved a mere pretender, he shall end up with nothing. Go on being a good girl, and don't worry."

Left alone, Felicity sat at loose ends. Should she go to her room and re-read those letters in her trunk? She knew their contents well. Esmee had written about the changing seasons, about the affairs of Twillingmarche, including such events as the passing of the old butler, Fennimore, and the hiring of Makepeace. ("So devoted to your dear Father!" the letter said. "So aged and bent he seemed in the last months, one might almost believe that the Earl's death broke his poor old heart." Knowing Esmee today, it was odd that she would, only two and a half years ago, have been so compassionate toward a mere servant. But then, perhaps she had felt a warmth for the faithful retainer that she never could for a new butler, however competent. Perhaps the memory of Randolph had made her sentimental.) There were long descriptions of social occasions: the theatre, balls and suppers, which the Felicity of those days would not have been old enough to attend, but the like of which the grown-up young lady of today soon would see for herself. There was an account of Roland's eighteenth birthday, so vivid that the reader could almost imagine being present in the company. The coming of Mrs. Golightly was mentioned, and the conditions of travel back and forth between Twillingsford and London, and the latest fashions in evening wear. So immediate and detailed were these communications, one truly would not guess that they had been written only a fortnight ago.... Perhaps they had not. Suppose Esmee had been writing to her all along, keeping a sort of journal against a hoped-for day when Felicity should be restored to her?

Sweet as the thought was, she knew those letters practically by heart, as if she had been reading and re-reading them during a long sojourn within the confines of the Alpenweiss clinic. Certainly, this was a memory preferable to one of life with the Barlows; their crude manners, loud voices, their nasty, demanding children - and no-one in the whole world to think of poor Cinderella Mary with affection.

Perhaps, in all that time, Esmee had Mr. Forkes looking for her, as her own dear mother would, had she lived.

These idle thoughts - but then, she had no duties neglecting; if Roberts wanted her for a lesson, she would come and fetch her - were passing through Felicity's head, as she sat on alone in the dining room. "...a complete vulgarian," she heard. That was Makepeace, and the voice which answered him belonged to Kate. "How long will he stay?"

"Forever, he seems to thi- - I beg your pardon, Miss! One had expected the room to be unoccupied. Shall we come back to clear?"

"No, no," she said. "It's perfectly all right. And you're right about Cousin Roderick, too; he does seem to think he'll be staying forever, the ghastly man!"

"Yes, Miss," Makepeace inclined his head to hide the ghost of a smile. He might actually be rather handsome, Felicity thought, if only he would really smile sometimes. Kate, who had stopped in the doorway, made no attempt to hide her own wide grin.

Felicity asked impulsively: "Can I help? With clearing the table? I've nothing to do."

The butler's features hardened into severe perpendicular lines. "No, indeed, Miss. That would be most unseemly."

"Thanks, anyway," Kate piped up, for which she received an even harder look.

"I'll go then."

But where? Suddenly, Felicity began to feel a little bit lost - even a little bit superfluous. The library was cool and silent. There were novels she might read, more challenging than those she had been given: novels by Charles Dickens, Alexandre Dumas, Thomas Hardy, R. L. Stevenson, and quite recent ones, too, by the fabulously popular Mr. Kipling; even the very latest from Mr. Galsworthy.... Not now; she was too restless. There was a group of slim volumes bound in white kid, lovely to the touch. She opened one whose gold lettering proclaimed it to contain the love poems of Lord Byron. On the flyleaf, in an exuberant hand, was written: "To Felicity on her twelfth birthday, with all my love, Papa." And so were they all, the entire matched set of poetry books, from 'A Child's Garden of Verses', on her second birthday, to 'The Sonnets of Shakespeare', gifts from Lord Farwell to his daughter. He must have had them bound especially. How sweet - and how achingly sad! She would not linger in this haunted, forlorn place.

She longed for the comfort of a warm kitchen - friendly faces, laughter, gossip, the smell of baking bread.... Mrs. Golightly had made it clear that the young lady should not concern herself with household affairs. The housekeeper approved of her, apparently, even less than did Makepeace. Esmee would be having her after-luncheon rest; Roberts must be busy at her sewing - another skill Felicity had once begun to learn, which was not now supposed to continue, except, of course, for the fancy needlepoint appropriate to young ladies, for which she had no patience. How did other girls of good breeding manage to occupy their time? Perhaps one day Aunt Lettie could be persuaded to teach her how to weave a tapestry? But not today. She sighed. Today, the best occupation she could find was a leisurely, lonely walk in the gardens - remembering to wear a broad-brimmed hat lest the early autumn sun bring out unsightly freckles. Old MacRory, thus far the most friendly toward her of all the servants but Kate, might cut some flowers for her to practice arranging.

Indeed, he did better: he showed her how to use the secateurs - special clippers that severed the stems cleanly, without crushing. He let her cut her own flowers. It was there, in the lower terraces, MacRory following along with a laden basket of greens and late roses, that Felicity became aware of a disturbance. Male voices, shouting orders and advice, trying to outdo one another; a footman (the younger one, George) was seen galloping down the drive, incongruously mounted on one of Roland's fine horses. Felicity and the gardener hastened back to the house. The disturbance had, by this time, moved through the entry hall and was proceeding up the curved staircase. Edward and one of the grooms carried Cousin Roderick between them, amid conflicting directions from Roland, both solicitors and Mr. Finch, the steward. The burden himself added no little volume to the commotion. Esmee, in one of her gorgeous Chinese robes (the bright blue one with golden dragons, which matched, respectively, her eyes and - at the moment, loosely tumbling - hair) had rushed to the top of the stairs, seemingly just this moment roused from her post-prandial sleep.

Mr. Forkes, nearest the front entrance, noticed and came over to inform Felicity. "Mr. Sommelroux has had a fall,"

"From a runaway horse?" she asked hopefully.

"No, my dear, only from a rock, which he had misguidedly climbed in order to take in a particularly fine vista. Or so I am told, not having been present. It is possible that he has broken his ankle," the man added with a grim face, but Felicity did not miss the fleeting look of satisfaction which preceded this statement. "We have, of course, sent for Doctor Gillivray, post-haste. It would be best for you - if I might suggest? - to be occupied elsewhere, while he attends the patient. There may be sounds not altogether suited to the ears of a young lady."

Felicity, upon reflection, construed this to mean that Cousin Roderick might scream and carry on and become excessively vulgar in his speech under duress. There was, however, another possible interpretation. She asked: "Do I know Doctor Gillivray?"

Mr. Forkes smiled thinly, nodded once. "Yes. At least, you *have* known him, although, fortunately, not very closely. Blessed with the famed Sommelroux constitution, you suffered very few childhood ailments; thus the good doctor, who has attended the family for many, many years, was rarely called upon on your behalf. He did visit often during your dear father's final days. I don't suppose," he gazed steadily into the girl's wide green eyes, "that you recall much of that."

"I don't remember anything about Papa's illness or death."

"Good, good." Mr. Forkes nodded approval, then elaborated: "It is perhaps better to be without such painful memories."

The noisy procession, meanwhile, reached the apartment, once Lord Farwell's, which Cousin Roderick had commandeered for himself. Edward and the groom departed by the back stairs; Mr. Goldsmith and Esmee remained by the sick-bed; Makepeace was even now returning to his station to await George and the doctor.

"Ought I to go up?" Felicity asked.

"Briefly, I think," said the solicitor, "to show one's concern and sympathy."

This she did, then hurried down the hallway to her own room at the far end of the house. From the window, she watched knots of servants form, dissolve and reconfigure; evidently, the news of Cousin Roderick's misadventure was transmitted by what Mr. Kipling would call the Jungle Telegraph. There was Edward, hurrying across the courtyard and out of sight, in all likelihood, to inform Aunt Lettie. There must be access to the tower, other than by way of the Palladian wing and the abbey. Next time, she would herself seek entrance by this route: her presence in the courtyard might be more easily explained (Inspecting the kitchen garden? Looking for MacRory? Going to the stables in a valiant effort to overcome her fear of horses?) than would be the case if she were seen wandering about uninhabited sections of the house.

The doctor arrived; spent some considerable time with the injured man. Indeed, there was a certain amount of profanity issuing from that quarter. Felicity busied herself at the William and Mary secretary cabinet in her sitting room, trying not to listen, while her ears, of their own accord, remained alert to every sound. It was truly a fine piece of furniture, she lectured to her unheeding self. It had intricately inlaid doors and drawer fronts. Esmee's letters were safely housed in four pigeon-holes; the remaining four waited, in forlorn hope, for new correspondence. There were little drawers with keyholes, carved ornamental panels... One of these, under her absently caressing touch, sprang open to reveal a secret compartment. She ceased to register Cousin Roderick's complaints. Inside were papers rolled up in a neat bundle. She began to pull them out.

Just then, Roberts came in without knocking, to announce that Dr. Gillivray was asking to see her. Felicity shoved the papers back hurriedly and slammed shut the compartment. She would have to speak sharply to Roberts about this cavalier attitude toward her privacy. Not this minute, though, for the maid had urgency as her excuse: in a moment, Dr. Gillivray bustled in.

He was old. Not lightly-grizzled like Mr. Forkes; not creased of mouth and thinning of hair like Makepeace, but truly ancient. What hair he had, a fringe from ear to ear to ear again, was snowy white, as was the drooping moustache. His stature had obviously never been great; now he was stooped and shrunken to Felicity's own unimpressive height. His little beach-pebble grey eyes, behind round wire spectacles, peered out of a criss-crossed maze of wrinkles.

"My dear child!" he effused, seizing her hand in both his own liver-spotted talons. "My dear, dear child. It is so good to see you again. Recovered, I hope? And all grown up! My, my, yes, all grown up. The image of your dear father, too. You won't remember me, I don't suppose?"

"Not well, I am afraid," said Felicity, at pains not to show her revulsion at the physical contact - after all, this poor little man seemed genuinely attached to her, in his way. "Things are coming back to me, but slowly."

"Yes, yes, it must be very trying," the old man said, "not to remember.... Can't imagine.... Why, I clearly recall the night I brought you into the world. A true Sommelroux...." He gazed through the living girl, into a long-dead past. "That shock of bright red hair, voice like a foghorn... a fine, lusty infant.... Pity your poor dear mother had not the same hardihood.... None of the wives seemed to...."

Felicity would have liked to enquire further about the frail, aristocratic mother and newborn brother she had lost at the age of three years. But Roberts was in the doorway, making shooing motions over the doctor's head. "I do not like to think of that," she said.

"No, no, of course not... callous of me." He dropped her hand, at long last, but continued to peer into her eyes. "All is well with you, otherwise? In the pink of health, and so forth?"

"Yes," Felicity replied. "I am perfectly well, thank you. Dr. Weiss believes my memory will come back."

"They treated you well? In that foreign hospital?"

"Oh yes, they took very good care of me."

"Good, good," he said. "Well, must get on. Wonderful to see you again, my dear... wonderful."

"It was good to see you, too, Doctor Gillivray."

Crablike, he scuttled out, giving a few more nods and smiles over his bent shoulder. Roberts closed the door after him.

"That went tolerably well," she said. "I'm quite pleased with you, Felicity."

The girl nodded assent, wondering privately how much pleasing Roberts mattered any longer. Roberts, after all, was only Esmee's personal maid. Perhaps, before her London season began, Felicity ought to think about having her own lady's maid. Kate or Evelyn? She must find out which of them was more adept at ironing and hairdressing. On the whole, she would prefer Kate for her sunny disposition and willingness to talk....

"Felicity?"

"Yes, Roberts."

"Are you paying attention?"

"Yes. You were saying?"

"Your cousin,"

"Roderick the Vulgarian. Yes?"

"Don't be flippant, my girl. And don't you get too cocky either - that vulgar man may yet end up in possession of Twillingmarche, and we could all be left out in the cold. Your own claim is hardly unassailable, don't forget."

"I'm sorry, Roberts," said Felicity. She truly was: she must not let her mind wander so, and be caught off guard again. "I *am* paying attention."

"That's better. It's more important than ever that you do. Mister Roderick has broken his ankle. This means that he cannot travel - cannot return to London - for some time. And now he has sent for his family."

"His family?"

48

"Yes," Roberts said, with an air of profound resignation. "A wife and three daughters. The eldest is about your age; the twins are nine years old."

"Oh dear," sighed Felicity, who had no desire to be among children, at least until such time as she should have her own. And then, of course, there would be a nurse to help take care of their most troublesome needs.

"Oh dear, indeed," Roberts echoed. "You shall have to assume some of the duties of hostess, a task for which I'm not at all sure you are prepared. Being American, they won't notice your speech, and if they do, we can blame it on Switzerland.... They are expected in two days' time. I will show you over the house before then. We must have MacRory - a great friend of yours, I believe? - take you over the grounds and stables. This afternoon, as soon as possible. There is one other thing you need to know about.... Sit down, Felicity."

The girl perched on the edge of her bed, wondering what surprise lay in store now, what new information she must assimilate within a mere two days.

"You recall," the other resumed, having paused only long enough to convince herself that her audience was hanging on every word, "the Sommelroux family tree? The tenth earl, your grandfather, who passed away when you were still quite small, had four children: three daughters by his first wife, and a son, Lord Randolph, by his second."

"Hortense Partridge, 1858," the girl recited cheerfully. "My father was born the following year. But the book doesn't mention three older sisters."

"That is why, if only you'd keep quiet, I am trying to tell you. Penelope, the eldest, married against her father's wishes - married a colonial adventurer. That doesn't matter, for they were both killed in the early stages of the war. They had no children. Dorothea was another disgrace: she decided to pursue a career - on the stage!" Felicity drew a startled breath; she never would have imagined a member of that family doing anything so daring, so romantic. Why then, Dorothea must surely have been, if not a Suffragette, at the very least an Emancipated Woman, thought the girl admiringly. She held her peace, however, as Roberts continued the narrative. "Needless to say, she was disowned. Her name has not been spoken in this house from that day - nor will it be again. Do you understand?"

Felicity nodded. "I am not to talk about Dorothea." At least, she amended secretly, in front of you or Esmee. Or Mr. Forkes, or Cousin Roderick or Roland. Aunt Lettie, on the other hand, must know the whole story; she had been here, while Roberts had not. Felicity would ask her someday, leading up to it carefully, in case Aunt Lettie shared her father's prejudice. But she was curious now. "What happened to her?"

Roberts leaned closer, lowered her voice yet more. "She lives in London. She has retired from the stage, fortunately, but is still active in Society. Surrounded by a disreputable crowd of Bohemians... and even some who ought to know better. I tell you this in strictest confidence, only because it might chance that you meet her. In that most improbable event, you must pretend that you have never heard of her. You must have nothing - take this to heart, Felicity - nothing whatever to do with her. As I said," Roberts lightened a fraction, "it is unlikely in the extreme: Lady Esmee intends to see that your season is an altogether proper one. You may put Dorothea out of your mind."

Felicity knew what was coming next, yet, like a child being told a favourite tale, was all suspense. "And the third daughter?"

"The youngest is Lady Letitia. She never married. She lives at Twillingmarche still."

"At Twillingmarche? Here?"

"In the old abbey tower, yes. Now pay attention. Letitia being your aunt, it is necessary that you meet her. Esmee will introduce you tomorrow. Now, don't be alarmed. Letitia is not quite like other people. She, well -"

"Is she *mad*?" asked Felicity, her eyes round as saucers. "Is she locked up in the tower? In a secret room with no windows?"

Roberts shook her head gravely. "I see it was a mistake to let you read so many novels. No, she is not locked up. She chose to live there and she has been made quite comfortable. Lady Letitia is... um... withdrawn. It's perfectly safe to visit her, so long as you are quiet and polite and do not stay overlong."

"Why is Letitia so withdrawn? Did she suffer a tragic loss, long ago?"

"Felicity, you really must curb that fanciful imagination! Oh, very well, I'll tell you." For all her protests, though, the girl could see that she was eager to relate a story. Roberts had not gone in search of those novels especially for Felicity's education; she'd read them, every one, and many others like them. Moreover, the girl now understood that the pretty, feminine pink room in which she had been hidden on that earlier stay, was Roberts' own. The lady's maid, beneath her severe grey and white facade, had a romantic streak even wider than Felicity's. "When she was just a girl of your age, Letitia formed a – an attachment - to a quite unacceptable young man. Lord Farwell, naturally, refused to countenance the misalliance."

"Why didn't she go to a convent, then, like Eastmills?"

"Well," Roberts answered rather testily, "for one thing, the Sommelroux are not Catholics. Nor even devout Anglicans, except to the extent required by good form. You will attend services, by the way, from this Sunday, at the church in the village." Why not in the grey stone abbey chapel? Felicity wondered. Because, she answered inwardly, the family had stopped using that a generation or more ago. She must not voice her disappointment: she wasn't meant to know about the chapel. Possibly, some day, when Felicity and Roland had large - separate, she hoped – families, she would reopen the chapel.... Roberts was going on: "Letitia, as an act of defiance, moved into the tower. Her father, thinking that her pique would soon pass, allowed it, but took the precaution of having her declared mentally incompetent. He intended to revoke the decree as soon as she should agree to marry according to his wishes. She never did. I suppose it was of no great consequence to the earl, since he already had an heir. So, Letitia has remained in her self-imposed exile. She has chosen isolation over marriage, over the pleasures of Society."

"Then, she must be mad, after all...?"

"Stop saying that! It is not a polite word. Try, rather, to think of Lady Letitia as living in a world of her own."

Felicity thought. It appealed to her, the notion of inventing a whole personal world. She also thought that it paled in comparison with having Twillingmarche for one's own. Anyone who made that choice must be at least *a little* mad, whatever Roberts said, however in possession of her wits Aunt Lettie had appeared. Perhaps, like some patients at Alpenweiss, she had her good days, which this happened to be... Which meant that tomorrow would almost certainly be a bad one. On her visit in the company of Esmee, then, Felicity resolved to be very quiet and ever so polite. She said as much to Roberts.

"That's right. You won't be expected to remain but a few minutes. One more thing: if she wants to show you her tapestry, or talk about the House of Sommelroux, you must indulge her. She makes up her own version, so do not correct her."

"Yes, Roberts."

6

It *was* a bad day - for everyone. Felicity woke early - a habit she had all but broken - feeling vaguely apprehensive. Evelyn, not a very communicative girl at the best of times, brought her tea with the barest of courtesies: this morning, there was no pleasant, idle chatter. When the time came to choose a lady's maid, she would certainly opt for Kate. Everyone at breakfast was tense and taciturn. Mr. Forkes and Mr. Goldsmith had evidently run out of property laws to compare. Roland was more of a sourpuss than usual; Esmee was out of sorts, perhaps because of having risen hours before her accustomed time. Cousin Roderick, though confined to bed, made his presence felt throughout the house. Every few minutes, he was ringing or shouting for coffee, a hot water bottle, the fire to be stirred, his leg rearranged, his pillows fluffed: he kept Kate and George on the run all day long. His family - could they be any less awful? – were expected on the morrow.

Shortly after breakfast, Esmee conducted Felicity to the tower. She took a different route from Edward's of the day before, but the girl had been shown the Palladian section by Roberts, comparing each room to its diagram, so this was now familiar terrain. Through the ballroom, stripped these many years of furnishing and ornament, their footsteps echoed; through the magnificent, abandoned dining room; past salons and games room, across the main hall with its gilded twin staircases. The whole way, Esmee kept quizzing her on the house and its history.

"Twenty-eight bedrooms, on the two upper floors, all named after Royalty. It's a good thing Queen Victoria had so many children, isn't it? When Palladian wing was built, its bedrooms were called only by their colour. When Grandfather built the new wing, after his brother Raymond left for the colonies, he moved in there, with his new wife, and so there was a new blue bedroom as well as an old one, a new pink room, and so forth and it got confusing. Anyway, the main floor and first storey were open all the time, but *these* bedroom were only used when they had balls and weekend shooting parties with dozens of guests and... and even the King stayed once, when he was Prince of Wales. Grandfather renamed the bedrooms in his honour."

"That's right," said Esmee, "you learned well."

"Only, why don't people come anymore?"

Esmee frowned. "It was Lord Farwell who liked to entertain. After his death.... Well, Randolph preferred London. It's not important. Tell me about the family. Lord Farwell had three daughters," she prompted.

Felicity picked up the narrative. "Penelope married an adventurer and died -"

"Where? When?"

"In South Africa, in 1889. The Boers killed her, I think. And we don't talk about Dorothea, who went on the stage, and Letitia is not mad, exactly."

"And Lord Farwell was?"

"Terribly displeased with his daughters."

"No, Goose. The last one - Randolph."

"My father was the youngest child and the only male. The first Lady Farwell died in childbirth." She paused, seeing an odd look on her stepmother's face. "Didn't she?"

"Near enough, I suppose," Esmee said. "Never mind. It was a long time ago. Continue."

"So then, the earl married Hortense, sister of his friend, Sir Henry Partridge. She was eighteen and my grandfather was - let me see - thirty-six? Sir Henry must be very ancient. Shall I meet him, d'you think?"

"I doubt it," said Esmee, with a hardness in her voice that signaled close of subject. "And Lord Randolph died?"

"Three years ago, but I don't remember anything about it."

Esmee sighed. "It'll do."

Felicity thought, but decided not to mention aloud, that nobody was ever likely to ask her questions of such an obvious nature, least of all Cousin Roderick, who seemed utterly unconcerned with other people, dead or alive. Still, his wife might be a quite different sort of person; women often feel entitled to pry. Perhaps that was what made Esmee so nervous - for, nervous she definitely was. Of course, this might equally well be caused by the impending interview with her withdrawn sister-in-law.

"I've sent Makepeace to prepare Letitia for our visit. One must. You see, she dislikes surprises. She becomes flustered and put about, poor thing...."

Felicity ventured: "Did she know Felicity... er... me very well? Were we close?"

They had come through under the staircase into the service corridor; Esmee approached the door to the old abbey. "No, but she may remember... It's so hard to tell! As a little girl, you were afraid of her. Nor was she keen on you."

"Oh, good. There won't be much reminiscing about the old days. I shouldn't ask her what happened to the little dog, Fluffy - things like that?"

Esmee stopped as suddenly as if she had walked into a stone wall. "Fluffy?" she demanded in a voice abnormally sharp and high. "Where did you hear that name?"

"I - I don't know," Felicity stammered. "It - it sort of popped into my head. Roberts must have told me and I'd forgotten, until just now. Esmee, don't look like that - please? I didn't mean to forget. It's only... there's so much...!"

Esmee sighed, relaxed her body by a visible effort of will. "That must be it," she said. "Don't be frightened. It's all right. Actually, there *was* a little dog."

"Where is Fluffy now?"

"It died years ago."

She followed Esmee up the stone steps, past the curiously empty niches. She reflected that this might be a bad time to enquire whether they had once contained statues, and if so, what had become of them. Before the arched door of dark wood, Esmee stopped for a moment, drew a steadying breath, knocked and entered.

Aunt Letitia was ensconced, as before, in her throne-like chair; was wrapped, as before, in her voluminous velvet cloak. Her breakfast tray and table must have been removed: her chair now faced the tapestry, upon which she had evidently been busy. She slowly wound a strand of purple yarn around a wooden shuttle, placed it carefully among its vari-coloured fellows on the ledge of the loom, slowly turned. "Who is it?" she asked in a querulous old woman's voice.

"It's Esmee, Letitia. Didn't Makepeace tell you to expect us?"

"Yes, yes, he said something. Esmee, is it? And the other one? Who is she?"

"This," Esmee took a step closer, pushing the girl before her, "is Felicity. Do you remember your little niece? She has come back to us."

"She has?" The old woman peered round the tapestry frame, "Where has she been? Speak up, girl! Where've you been?"

Felicity took another step forward, and one, more or less sideways, to give her aunt a better view. "I have been in Switzerland," she said very distinctly, "at a clinic named Alpenweiss. I had an accident, but now I'm quite recovered, except for the amnesia."

The woman inside the heavy cloak nodded many times while she pondered this. "Sick, were you?"

"Not sick, Aunt Letitia. I had a fall, and was grievously injured, and lost my memory."

The other stared at her intently, straining as far as the folds of her garment allowed. "Not mad, are you?"

"No, Ma'm. I mean, Aunt Lettie."

"Well and good. We certainly don't need any more of *that* in the family. I'm quite mad myself, did they tell you?" She leaned back with a self-satisfied smirk.

"No, Aunt... I mean, I don't think...." Her limping response was cut short by a volley of cackles.

"And how," the birdlike head swivelled around, "is our dear – what's your name again? Esmee, is it?"

That lady, having stood still and white and silent all this time, now roused herself. "Very well, thank you."

"Is that all?" Letitia demanded. "Nothing more? Not married yet? Or at least expecting?"

"No, Letitia, nothing like that."

"You should, you know," the other woman admonished, "and soon. Before you're too old to have children. It would be a shame to waste your chances."

"Don't you remember, Letitia? I have a grown son. Roland. You have met him. "

"Roland? Roland.... No, can't say I recall any Rolands - except my dear late Papa, but nobody ever used his Christian name. His friends called him Rory - can't imagine why, but they did. Well, then, if you've already got one of your own, what d'you want *this* child for?"

"Oh, Letitia, do try to remember! Felicity is my step-daughter. Your brother Randolph's child, from his first marriage."

"Oh, all right! Have it your own way. All these begats are too muddling for me. I'm tired."

Felicity did not mind the dismissal. She would ask about the tapestry some other day - one of Aunt Lettie's good days. She said farewell politely, as did Esmee; Letitia only wiggled her thin white fingers at them.

"Well," Esmee sighed, once the heavy door had closed, "I suppose it could have gone worse. She really can be shocking!"

"Why don't you send her to the clinic in Switzerland?" asked Felicity. "Dr. Weiss might cure her."

"Wouldn't I like to!" Esmee replied. "She won't budge from this tower. Besides, you have no idea how much that place costs."

Felicity nodded agreeably. Anyway, the question had been prompted by nothing more than idle curiosity: she did not wish any such action to be taken. In fact, she rather liked the idea of a slightly mad - had she not used the word herself? - relative in a tower. She also liked Aunt Lettie, though she could hardly say so: it had required all her self-control to refrain from laughing. There was an unladylike and shameful satisfaction in seeing Esmee so discomfited. "I'm sorry. It was a silly question."

Her courtesy visit to Cousin Roderick before luncheon occasioned no such mirth. He was restless and mean - at least to George, when the footman brought up his tray. To Felicity, he made an effort at friendliness, even going so far as to take her hand and hold it for quite a long time. His own hands were large, pale of skin, with freckles and light red hairs on the backs down to the knuckles. Felicity kept looking at them, hoping the man would notice and release her. She should have known better; Roderick was not a noticing sort of man.

"And what has Pretty Little Cousin been doing," he asked playfully, "while I've been stuck to this d--d bed?"

"I had my bath," Felicity recited, "and then breakfast, and then I went with Esmee to see my poor aunt."

The man nodded thoughtfully. "I guess I'll have to see the poor old aunt, too, once I can get around again. Funny place, this. Full of weird people."

"Weird?"

"Strange," he explained. "Kind of spooky. All those rooms, empty, and the three of you, holed up in just one bit.... I guess you wouldn't see how odd it is, living here."

"It is my home," Felicity said primly.

"They tell me, though, you haven't been here for quite a while." He was gazing up into her face with a speculative look in his eyes which reminded her of Aunt Lettie. The question he had not quite asked must be important.

"That's true," she said gravely. "And I missed Twillingmarche, the whole time. Esmee - my dear stepmother - wrote many letters, full of news. They helped me feel less lonely, but it's so much nicer to be here."

Cousin Roderick wasn't paying attention; his thoughts had already moved along. "That, what's his name, Sparrow or something.... Is he honest?"

"Mr. Finch? Well, of course," the girl replied indignantly. "My father would never have kept on a steward who *wasn't*."

58

"Your father," he pointed out tactlessly, "has been dead and buried for three years. A lot can happen in three years."

"Nothing happened," she said firmly. "Everything is just as it was. Except that Fennimore, the old butler, died. His heart broke after my Papa; he was terribly devoted."

"Sure," said the cousin from America, at long last releasing her hand. Felicity retreated out of reach. "And maybe Finch is, too. Or maybe not."

"Of course he is. *All* of our servants are loyal." If she had no way of knowing this to be true, she was not about to confide in Cousin Roderick.

"I'll want Goldsmith to go through the books," he said, not precisely to Felicity. Then his gaze refocused on her face. "So, Pretty Cousin. Have you got a beau yet?"

"A bow?"

"You know - a boyfriend."

Felicity thought this a funny word, though rather a nice one. She surmised that it meant suitor. "I cannot be engaged to anyone until I turn eighteen."

"That isn't what I asked. And anyway, you'll be eighteen soon, won't you?"

"In just over two months." She hoped, secretly, that he and his as yet unknown family would be far away by then. "I am to become engaged to Roland."

He nodded, frowning. "The popinjay. Isn't that kind of, um, kind of like marrying your brother, or something?"

"Not at all! There is no blood connection - of any kind."

"And you're in love, are you?"

"Cousin Roderick! Perhaps you have different customs in the colonies, but even you must realize how impertinent that question is." She turned to leave, remembering her manners only at the last moment. "I hope you feel better soon. Good-bye."

His course laugh added fuel to the hostility which grew and grew in Felicity's heart, wholly overcoming her training as a young lady by the time she reached the bedroom door, which she slammed - and felt no remorse for slamming.

All afternoon, the three men of business were closeted in Mr. Finch's office. Esmee took to her rooms, as usual, but was too agitated to sleep. She had Roberts ask Felicity to keep her company and they spent an hour over embroidery. Felicity noted with satisfaction that the older woman's work progressed no more skilfully than her own. There was only sporadic conversation, even less sewing.

"I couldn't very well refuse, could I?" said Esmee.

"I suppose not," Felicity responded. Was Esmee still fretting over her altercation with Roderick? Having agreed, however reluctantly, to let the slick-haired Mr. Goldsmith look at the ledgers, it was useless now to regret her decision.

"He hasn't got any proven right," Esmee pursued.

"Hasn't he?"

"According to Mr. Forkes, no. Still, a refusal would look as if we had something to hide...."

Sensing that Esmee required, not more legal advice, which was, in any case, beyond her competence, but reassurance, Felicity said: "It doesn't matter, does it? I mean, everything is in perfect order."

"I expect so. And maybe he won't be quite so keen, when he finds out how little money there is."

Felicity was taken aback. "Are we not rich?"

Esmee laughed mirthlessly, almost harshly. "You wouldn't have any idea how much it costs to maintain this..." her gaze wandered to the gold-brocaded walls, red velvet draperies and beyond these, taking in the house, out-buildings, gardens, park and meadows. "...this white elephant! We can't sell it - and we can't keep it up - not without capital...."

The girl asked shyly: "The capitol? But we do have a place in London, you said."

"Goose." There was no malice in the word; Esmee was in the habit of calling her this whenever Felicity exhibited her vast ignorance. "I mean money. The real money's in trust until you marry, or turn twenty-one."

"Oh." She had never thought about money before. Beautiful furnishings, modern plumbing, fine food, many servants - Felicity had taken it for granted that there was money aplenty. "Only, what do we live on?"

"Income. This isn't your concern, but it might be as well for you to know something about it. Of course, Roland and I have an allowance that covers the essentials. The farms earn a little, and there is the interest from your legacy. Mr. Forkes handles all that part. But we have had to sell things."

"You mean, furniture and statues?"

"Yes, and paintings and chandeliers. You saw the old wing; there isn't much left."

Noting sadness and worry in Esmee's eyes, the girl was moved to ask: "It wasn't - not because of keeping me in the...?"

"Don't be silly!" snapped the other woman. "Anyway, it'll be all right, once you're married. If he...."

"If Cousin Roderick isn't really?"

"If we can prove he isn't. If he is, Elijah says the capital may be tied up in court for years."

"I see."

Felicity privately thought that the capital getting tied up in court need not matter so much. They could go on living on income - perhaps more modestly. Perhaps they should save money by giving up the house in London, which she had never seen, and to which she did not, therefore, long to go. Well, no; on second thoughts, should she decide against marrying Roland, she would not want him living here. And he, by all appearance, would be happier in London....

Those decisions could wait. She might never be allowed a title; Cousin Roderick might yet become the thirteenth earl. This gave her no pain. Of one thing, however, she was absolutely, unreservedly certain: she wanted to keep Twillingmarche.

7

George brought them in the carriage: Mrs. Sommelroux - "Rosalyn, please. I hope we can all be friends." - dark-haired, fashionably attired, perfectly smooth of figure and face under a marabu feathered hat, like a lady in a picture magazine.

A younger copy in perfect pink velvet suit and matching travel cloak, stiff with cream-coloured piping, applique and braid - Bettina, eldest daughter. "Oh, this is *heavenly!* Do you absolutely *adore* living here? How old are you? I was nineteen last birthday. It's just *too* wonderful, getting a brand new cousin almost my own age!"

"Second cousin," said Felicity, while thinking to herself, it's not removed nearly enough.

Two perfectly identical, small, red-haired, freckled girls in middy blouses, the image of their father. "Where does this hall go to?" and "When do we eat?" - Lucy and Lisa.

They must all troop upstairs to greet the patriarch; they must be shown to rooms prepared for them; they must be given luncheon and made welcome. Felicity caught Edward rolling his eyes at Makepeace, who gave a minute shrug. Kate, helping to relieve the visitors of outer garments and giving Edward a hand with their extensive baggage, never smiled once. Esmee tried, but the expression seemed to cause her pain.

Roland, having been ordered by his mother to put in an appearance, said as little as Felicity herself, though, throughout the meal, his eyes came to rest rather too often on Bettina. If not for the ruffles upon her blouse and gathered skirt, Felicity surmised she would have no figure at all: perhaps it was only her inexhaustible flow of twittering speech that held the boy's attention. The wife, naturally, had her meal on a tray in Cousin Roderick's room. But the children were much in evidence, nudging each other, giggling, spilling gravy on the white damask cloth, (It would be as well, during their stay, to find some table-covering better suited to the barbaric manners of American young...) asking incessant, often rude, questions. Fortunately, Mr. Goldsmith was present and took it upon himself to answer, ponderously, if inaccurately. Mr. Forkes, on Felicity's right hand, was largely silent.

With so many people in the house, Mrs. Golightly brought in two village girls, Maybelle and Jane. Though untrained in service, sixteen and fourteen years of age, they were at least extra pairs of hands. Even so, given the uproarious, demanding nature of these houseguests, the servants were hard pressed - especially after Cousin Roderick announced himself well enough to take short hobbles out of his room. Like his offspring, he was suddenly everywhere - always requiring a strong arm to help him down the stairs, to help him sit; he must have a hassock and pillow arranged just so - and stand up again two minutes later, to take the air upon the terraces. George, as junior footman, was assigned to his care. To judge by the hitherto unaccustomed frown upon his young face, he did not consider this duty altogether fair. Nor was it, Felicity agreed, but better than to have seen Edward so demeaned. In any case, everyone in the household found him- or herself taking on tasks equally unpleasant.

The entertainment of Rosalyn, whenever that woman left her husband's side, or he, more often, hers, fell naturally to Esmee. Felicity, by the same convention, must spend endless hours in the exhaustingly effervescent company of Bettina. Fortunately, in the afternoons Roland relieved her of the burden while he took the guest riding. Unchaperoned - and with no word of protest from Mrs. Sommelroux. Americans seemed to have little regard for the proprieties. There remained still the problem of the little girls. Their mother, although giving every sign of doting on them, nevertheless allowed them to wander at large; their older sister appeared to have no concern for their whereabouts or welfare, let alone the welfare of whatever they touched. A fine Chinese vase was the first casualty, that very afternoon; there soon followed an ormolu clock, which they had decided to study. Thereafter, delicate and valuable ornaments were tactfully removed to parts unknown. The house soon took on an austere look, which Felicity secretly found restful to the eye. The ears were quite a different matter; the children's progress could be followed at all times by the sound squealing and bickering, of furniture being knocked about. Only when they went out of doors was there peace. Outdoor activity, therefore, was strongly encouraged.

Thus it happened that upon the third day, Lucy came running breathless up to the house: "Help, somebody! It's Lisa!"

MacRory, weeding one of the terrace flowerbeds, caught her in mid-flight. "What happened to Lisa?"

"She's fallen into something. Let me go! I need Mommy!"

The old gardener held fast to her thin shoulder. "Fallen? Into what kind of something?"

By this time, Makepeace had appeared in the doorway; Felicity and Bettina, drawn from their post-luncheon stroll by the commotion, were in time to hear the child say: "A big hole. Back there!" Lucy waved her free arm in the direction of the stableyard.

"Oh, Gosh!" her older sister gasped. "Is she all right?"

Felicity considered this rather inane, even by Bettina's standards. Making no comment, she herself set off at a run, closely followed by MacRory and the released Lucy, with Bettina lagging far behind.

They found Lisa near the exercise paddock on the grass with the stablemaster, Cartwright, kneeling beside her. "She's had a fright, that's all. Nothing broken, eh, child?" Lisa only wailed the more; certainly her vocal cords had not been impaired. Cartwright explained: "She's fall in the old well, but Will here pulled er out. No harm done."

The youngest groom was hovering nearby, his sunburnt cheeks greyish with shock. "I dunno how it happened," he protested. "That well ain't used no more - no water in there, see, not to speak of...."

There must have been *some* water, Felicity observed, for the little girl was sopping wet up to the waist and more, her bloomers clinging in deflated folds to mud-encrusted legs. "Well then," she took charge, for want of anyone of greater authority, "we shall have to get her indoors, and dry. Lisa, can you stand?"

The child could, and once upon her feet was quite able to walk unassisted. Cartwright had been correct: she wasn't hurt at all. Nor any longer frightened; her crying soon gave way to complaints about her sodden condition.

Naturally, the incident did not end there. Later that afternoon, an inquest of sorts was held by Cousin Roderick. He had Will and the stablemaster called to the steward's office. Mr. Finch was nowhere to be found; Makepeace thought he might be out inspecting the farms. Present were Esmee, Mrs. Sommelroux, Mr. Goldsmith and of course, the twins. There were but two chairs in the office - the more commodious of these was ceded by mutual consent to the injured man; his wife, as if by right, occupied the second. All other spectators perched as and where they could find space to do so. Felicity need not have attended but was curious. Had Mr. Forkes not gone up to London that morning, the proceedings might have been conducted with a more court-like dignity.

"The little gals tell me," Roderick addressed Cartwright, who stood before him, battered hat in hand, "there's a well out there."

"There's two," the stablemaster corrected. "The one we use an' the old one, what's got hardly no water anymore."

"Why are the wells uncovered?"

"They're not. Leastways, the new one don't want covering, bein just a pipe, drilled like, so big around." The old man put his brown forefingers and thumbs together in a rough circle three inches wide. In order to perform this manoeuvre, he had disposed of his fedora in the most convenient place: upon his head, where it remained thereafter.

"Got a eel-ectric pump in -"

"I'm talking about the other one, you moron!" Roderick cut in, "the one my little gal fell in."

"Oh, aye?"

"Why isn't *that* well covered?"

"It were," said Cartwright.

"It were," Will spoke up. "We've took off the winch and chain, long time ago, but her covered, all right."

Roderick turned to his daughters: "Is that so?"

Lucy said: "Covered?" and Lisa shook her carrot head, no.

"Well!?"

The stablemaster calmly explained. "Aye. Carriage wheel what's got broke, right over top of er. Put on, way back, after the turkey cock wen in. Drowned hisself. Purty good ol cock, e were, too. But stoopid? You won't see nothin' on God's green earth stoopider an a gobbler."

"Tha's right," said Will. "Them stoopid birds."

Mrs. Sommelroux looked at her children, one at a time perforce, as they were nestled under either arm. "Try to remember, darlings, did you see a wheel of some kind?"

Lucy mumbled, "I dunno," and Lisa fixed an accusing stare on Will: "There wasn't any turkey."

"Never mind the damned turkey!" their father exclaimed. "I want to know how you came to fall in."

"We were playing, that's all," said Lisa. Lucy added: "There's nothing to *do* here!"

Esmee, who had been following the various exchanges only with her eyes, now remarked: "Such overactive children! They really ought to have a governess."

They really ought to be kept in a cage, thought Felicity darkly.

Mr. Goldsmith spoke for the first time. "The point here is. That well is not safe. It is not merely. A question of the children." The mother glared at him but he ignored her. "Anyone can fall. Into. An uncovered well."

"That's right," said Roderick. "I want it fixed at once."

66

"It were," Cartwright insisted. "Leastways, this mornin, at watering time. Anyhow, my boy pulled out the bairn."

"I guess that's something," Roderick allowed ungraciously.

"Had to," Will offered, "she were screechin an hollerin so. Spooked the Grand Duke of Twillingmarche, she did."

"The who?"

"The Duke. Him's our prize stud. Could'uv hurt hisself."

"A horse?" asked the bewildered mother.

Mr Goldsmith said: "There is still. The matter of liability. I believe we have. A case here."

Cousin Roderick gave an impatient snort. "Sue my own estate? Don't be an ass." Turning on the horsemen, he concluded: "All right, you can go. See to that well."

"Don't worry," Esmee comforted the other Mrs. Sommelroux, "Roland will make sure they do a proper job this time. And I shall have the housekeeper appoint a maid to look after the little ones. Of course, you see, we have never had such children about. Our Felicity," her gaze lingered affectionately upon her stepdaughter, "even as a small girl, never made mischief."

"Poor thing!" retorted Rosalyn. "She probably was never allowed out of sight."

"No," Felicity replied serenely, "Esmee took such care of me as she did of her own child."

George was summoned to assist Cousin Roderick back to his room, although his wife could as well have done so. Esmee, giving her a little pat on the shoulder, took leave of Felicity, who volunteered to tell Mrs. Golightly to make arrangements for the girls' supervision, then look for Roland. Both errands might better have been entrusted to Makepeace, who was in a position to mobilize more efficient forces - but she felt no urgency attached to them and wanted an excuse to get away. She was but a few paces behind the departing stablemen.

"Pesky things," remarked the senior Cartwright. Will agreed: "Into everything, they are." "And their pa - he's a real job of work." "Nasty," said Will. "I surely do hope they go back where they belong, and purty soon."

In the kitchen, where the recently scarce Mr. Finch was having tea with cook and housekeeper, all fell silent at Felicity's approach. She guessed by their expressions that they had also been discussing the Americans. Everyone here appeared to share her feelings toward these interlopers. What, she wondered, would happen to the household, were Cousin Roderick's claim to be successful? All the servants would leave.... But where would they go? What would become of them? And, with that man in charge of it, what would become of Twillingmarche? It was unbearable to contemplate.

"You've all heard, no doubt," she began. Three heads nodded assent. "This is a hardship, I know, Mrs. Golightly, but it seems those children are not safe to leave alone. Lady Farwell wondered if you could -"

There was a stifled giggle from Mrs. MacRory, a silent smirk under the Finch moustache, even a smile of sorts upon the severe countenance of the housekeeper.

"What did I say?"

"Lady Farwell wondered?" Mrs. Golightly mocked. "She doesn't wonder if a body could. She just comes out and demands what she wants. Can I find them a minder, you mean?"

Felicity, embarrassed but recovering, as she saw no malice in their amusement, said: "I suppose that is what she meant. I myself think most appropriate would be someone like Clarence." Nomination of the oldest, strongest and least tender-hearted of the three Cartwright boys for nursery maid inspired open merriment around the kitchen table - in which, this time, Felicity was a welcome participant.

Mrs. Golightly wiped her eye with a lace-edged handkerchief, sobered, sighed. "Maybelle's ma has four little ones, two of them boys. She'll manage all right."

Having passed on the message, Felicity wandered, as it were aimlessly, out the kitchen door and across the courtyard. She knew that Roland had gone riding with

Bettina; there was no chance of finding him for some little while. She had been denied an opportunity to visit Aunt Lettie these past three busy days. Checking both yard and upper-storey windows for curious eyes, she drifted alongside the Palladian wing, around a corner of the erstwhile bakehouse, now used as a storage shed. It was here that Cousin Roderick's automobile had been housed, Cartwright senior having adamantly refused to allow it anywhere near the horses. Now hidden from sight of the Victorian wing, she picked her way purposefully between piles of grey stone, once the outer arches of the cloister. About here, she had earlier calculated, must be a second entrance to the abbey. In the cool shade of tall stone walls, there it was - a little postern gate. Locked securely.

What a nuisance! Now, she must meander back the way she'd come.... No - she would find old MacRory instead. Past the north end of the greenhouse, past refuse from the stables, piled ready by the garden gate. Indeed, as she had hoped, the head gardener was supervising his apprentices, Janus and Albert, in the transport of manure to the cold frames. Its rich, warm scent filled the air. Felicity had been inside the garden but once before, and found it fascinating. Enclosed by brick walls twelve feet high, it was a world apart - a little paradise of peace, order and plenty. From here came all the fresh produce on the Sommelroux table, and much of the fruit. All the year round, MacRory explained, for the cold-frames under their cloches (warm frames, really, topped by glass pyramids), even now being prepared and seeded, would provide salad greens well into November and as early as April. Through the winter, the vast glass house along the western end would be heated, so that the growing of food need not cease. The old man appeared to enjoy sharing his special lore as much as the girl enjoyed learning it.

Yet, when she judged that she had kept the gardener from his work long enough, she was still haunted by a - more than desire; something close to need - for at least a short talk with Letitia. Through the kitchen and along the service corridors she went... and found the door to the older wing locked. So many locks! It occurred to her that these precautions might have been instituted in an effort to contain the two-headed menace. Who knew what harm to themselves and the house those girls might do?

Well, then, Felicity concluded, she would have to give up secrecy. "Is Edward busy?" she enquired of Makepeace.

The butler gazed about as if expecting to see the footman occupied in some work on the staircase; this was all his answer to her question. "May *I* be of assistance?"

"I wish to visit my aunt," she said.

The butler raised one eyebrow. "So soon, Miss?"

"Soon? It's been three days. The last time, I thought she seemed not quite herself."

Both Makepeace eyebrows rose high and remained up. In surprise? Disapproval? Felicity had made a mistake; the visit in the company of Esmee had been supposed to be her only one to the tower: how would she know Lettie's normal condition? "There is no need for concern, Miss. Lady Letitia is quite well. I personally delivered her most recent meal."

There was no alternative now but to brazen it out. "I still want to see her."

"Very good, Miss. I shall send to enquire."

There would be a longish wait. Makepeace must ring for Edward, who must then be despatched with her message and a hefty brass key, then return with Aunt Lettie's reply. Felicity, being committed already so far, insisted on going with the footman. "It might seem odd, my standing idle in the entry hall. I shall wait in the abbey. If she says she's not in - silly as that might sound - I shall come back with you." She did not miss the questioning look that Edward gave the butler, nor the other's infinitesimal nod of assent.

"You think it would look odd, waiting in Hall?" asked the young man as he relocked the first door. "And wouldn't it look odder still, what we are doing now?"

"Why? After all, should not one take an interest in one's only surviving relative?"

"Only relative?" He raised eyebrows not unlike those of Makepeace. Felicity thought he must have practised in a looking-glass: someday, he, too, would be a perfect butler.

"I do not consider myself related to - any others."

"That's as may be," said Edward, with a most becoming little smile, "but I wouldn't go shouting it all over the house."

"Nor do I. Only, well, I did rather want to avoid - them - for a little while."

His smile broadened to a spontaneous and youthful grin. It was the first time, but one, that she had seen him act naturally. Did this mean he had begun to trust her? "Can't say I mind terribly, myself. Lady Letitia has got it all her own way, hasn't she? Doesn't see anyone she doesn't like. Not that they've been clamouring to see her."

The answer, when it came, was affirmative. "She must have taken a fancy to you," her companion remarked. "Here's the key, then - there's no point in my hanging about. Don't forget to lock up, and return it."

Aunt Lettie was alone, working busily at her loom. "Felicity, is it?"

"I only wanted to.... Two things, really." The girl, without waiting to be asked, pulled a hassock near and seated herself. "One was to tell you what's happened - if you want to hear it?"

"In due course," the older woman said. "And the other?"

"I had hoped.... That is, I meant to ask about the tapestry. It seems to me so much more interesting than my silly needlepoint flowers! Does every young lady have to do needlepoint? Without exception?"

Aunt Lettie's laugh was not at all the witch-like cackle of last time. "Oh yes. Every young lady. The question is, do you?"

"Roberts - Esmee's own maid, d'you know her?" A wise nod. "Roberts has been teaching me. Oh, but it's so dull! And I thought, if I could learn to do tapestry instead?"

The aunt considered this. "Possibly. Come here."

Felicity joined her on the other side of the loom. The work in progress was an immense thing, some of it rolled up on a big wooden cylinder. The picture, as the artist revealed it, was wonderfully intricate - full of landscapes, people, buildings and animals. "It is the history of the Sommelroux, you see."

"Yes. Here's the abbey, all alone. There is the Farwell coat of arms. It was just issued then, wasn't it? And down here, the Palladian wing has been added, and this must be the new house, but it's not finished."

"Here is the eleventh earl - my late Papa - as a young man, supervising the building. Perhaps one day, I shall tell you the story."

"But I already know," said the girl. "Well, that is, Roberts gave me a book, and I did read it, though I can't pretend to recall every bit."

There was a thump. Felicity, startled, looked all around for the source. A fat rust-coloured tabby, which must just now have jumped down from the windowsill, stretched itself, then began to walk leisurely toward her. "It's a cat!"

"Clever girl. His name is Grimalkin."

"Isn't that the name of witches' cats?"

"It struck me as amusing, at the time. Well, never mind that. Sit down and tell me what you came to tell me."

Felicity described the arrival of Roderick's family, then recounted the most recent events. The older woman listened attentively, asked few questions, and made no comments. During the recitation, the cat Grimalkin circled her twice, sniffed at various reachable parts, rubbed his chin on her knee, and finally settled in a sunny spot half-way across the room. He groomed himself thoroughly, merely staring at her from time to time under his up-stretched nether leg. A vulgar creature, to be sure, but she found his native arrogance somehow endearing. "And now," said the girl in conclusion, "poor Maybelle has to look after them. Because - this is what Mrs. Golightly says - she has two younger brothers. I think it's terribly unfair on her, don't you? Having to take care of awful children at home, and then having to suffer more, just because she has."

"How do you know Maybelle's brothers are awful?"

"Because they're children. Oh, I suppose," she admitted, "there might be *some* nice children. Anyway, they can't be nearly as troublesome as Lucy and Lisa. Oh, dear! I just thought. Cousin Roderick said he wants to come see you. I hope he doesn't bring them all."

Aunt Lettie smiled. "I may be indisposed.... In any case, I am much too delicate to receive more than a brace of visitors in any one week."

"D'you mean," Felicity asked anxiously, "that I shouldn't have come again so soon? They told me - Makepeace did - but I wouldn't listen."

"Makepeace has my best interests at heart, bless him. But he can be overprotective," said Aunt Lettie. "No, I mean that there is a certain advantage in being slightly mad. One operates by different rules."

"Oh. Then I may come often?"

"Can't imagine why you should want to. The Felicity Sommelroux I knew never came here but once a month, when her Papa pulled her along by the hand."

"I thought that was because you didn't like me."

"I have said," replied Aunt Lettie in a careful voice accompanied by one of her sharpest green looks, "nothing about *you*, child. And now, perhaps you ought to be going back. Edward will be here soon with my tea."

"Mayn't I stay and have tea with you?"

"Not this time. A young lady must know where her duty lies."

Felicity heaved a great, resigned, not very grown-up sigh. She knew that Aunt Lettie was right; she would be expected and sought out, should she be tardy. But it was hard; she really would so much rather not go. For all her strangeness, it was Aunt Lettie with whom she felt most comfortable.

8

Felicity had learned to eat like a lady: that is, she now understood both how and why to make a small amount of food last a long time. Even so, her figure had noticeably suffered the consequences of too many fine meals and too little work. Roberts clucked over the fitting of every new frock and positively fretted over foundation garments. Strictly speaking, none of these things were new. At first, the dresses let out and altered by Roberts, then divested of superfluous bows and ruffles by the wearer herself, had been made for a Felicity of thriftier proportions and more girlish tastes; they were all in pastel shades and floral prints. The most recent offerings came from Esmee's wardrobe. This occasioned Felicity a certain dismay: the vivid blues and reds - not to speak of yellows! - favoured by Esmee were not best suited to her own complexion. In contrast, Bettina Sommelroux wore blouses, suits and frocks in the latest style, each one chosen for her with the greatest of care. Money or no money, the issue must be tackled very soon: she simply could not go to London in any of the costumes which had served but poorly in the country.

To her surprise, Esmee agreed so readily as if she had anticipated the problem. "Tomorrow," she decreed, "you and Roberts must go into town. Mr. Forkes is arriving on the three o'clock train; he can ride back with you. If you leave directly after breakfast, you will have ample time at the dressmaker's. There's only the one - Twillingsford is a rather backward place.... Never mind, we'll soon get you up to London and clothe you properly."

"I shall be most careful about spending money," Felicity promised.

"Leave that to Roberts," Esmee said.

Perhaps she ought to include in her immediate wardrobe an outfit for riding. Being quite certain that she wanted always to live at Twillingmarche, that skill had become a near necessity; it appeared to be one of the very few opportunities for exercise afforded a young lady. In winter, there would be balls and dancing, yes, but the need was far too urgent for that. And besides, if Bettina was able to do it, how difficult could riding be? This very day, this very hour, she would go to the stables and become acquainted with those formidable beasts.

The first person she encountered was Will, with the Grand Duke of Twillingmarche. The one she welcomed, for he was a pleasant-featured boy of fifteen years, with a hesitant manner; she supposed if anyone could be counted upon not to find her mission risible, it was Will Cartwright. The other caused her great trepidation. The stallion stood eighteen hands high, though Felicity had no knowledge of this; what she could see was that it rarely stood - rather, it pranced and reared and cavorted in a most unnerving manner. She was entertaining second thoughts on the whole enterprise when Will espied her.

He waved to her, grinning. "Wait there, Miss, while I puts the Duke into paddock. Him not fit comp'ny for young ladies."   He pulled the animal's head about and led it, sweet as a ewe-lamb, exactly where he pleased. Hardly a minute passed before he returned, alone but with the friendly smile still wide upon his face. "Now, then, Miss. Come to see bout the well, have you?"

"Not exactly," she said, "but as I am here, show me."

There was little enough to see. A low circular stone wall - over which an agile nine-year-old would have no difficulty clambering - topped by rough planks, upon which man-sized boulders had been piled. She inwardly dared Lucy and Lisa to budge one of these. "Well done," she told the groom. "Even Mr. Goldsmith would be hard-put to find fault with *this*."

"Old cover," the boy indicated a carriage wheel with two of its spokes broken, now leaning by the well, "keep out gobblers, not wee girls. Us never reckoned with girls."

"They took it off themselves, didn't they?"

Will nodded, his face darkening with disapproval. "Must'uv. Don' mind mischief - them bairns, what bairns do. But if me or my brothers ever **lied** like those two.... Well, Da would'uv ad more than words for us, he would. Still do, no matter us all bein out of short pants."

Felicity agreed with the perceived drift of these remarks; a spanking might go some way toward making Lucy and Lisa a more likable pair. However, this was not the primary objective of her visit. She confided as much to young Will.

"Ride, Miss? Why, sure enough, I know the very horse."

The stableyard and the building itself, were scrupulously clean, in excellent repair: there was no indication here of a shortage of funds. The weather being mild and dry, all the horses had been turned out to pasture. Will Cartwright led the way, past the exercise ring, past the Duke, now grazing peaceably in his private enclosure, to a whitewashed rail fence. In the near distance, she recognised the carriage horses: five all the same colour and a blond little one; they were heavier of body and thicker of neck than any of the others.

"They're pretty," she said in surprise, for the animals did not now present an intimidating aspect.

"Oh, aye. Best-matched team, here'bouts, them bays. Jessie's foal, him be a good un, too, someday."

Further off, singly or in pairs, fine-boned saddle horses, brown, white, and dappled grey, stood about idling in the sunshine. She counted eight grown and three young ones. "We have eighteen horses?"

"Not countin farm stock."

"But are they not expensive to keep?"

Will shrugged. "Dunno. That for Mr. Finch to figure out."

In the few minutes they had been standing there, some of the horses had already begun to saunter near. Her companion rummaged in the pockets of his bedraggled jacket, brought out a handful of sugar cubes, liberally coated with tobacco shreds and lint. The horses took notice and quickened their approach; in another moment, four dauntingly massive heads were thrust over the fence. Felicity backed away a step, but the boy did not laugh. "Them big," he said, "but gen'le. These here's my special pets, ain't you? Ginger, Blaze, Honey," he offered each of them a sugar cube, which they took from his open palm with an incongruous delicacy. He rubbed each forehead with his other hand, then gave their necks a slap. "Get on, now. Us wants Petunia." The fourth horse was a grey, less handsome than the others by virtue of its girth. "Her bone lazy," said Will affectionately, "a real soft ride. Here, Miss."

She was expected to proffer the furry sweet - to let the horse touch her hand with its flapping mouth and huge, mobile tongue. She must do it, or show herself a craven. No apparent harm had come to Will.... She thrust out her hand and tried to keep from flinching. The animal's lips were soft as eiderdown; they barely brushed her palm. She could - she did! - pat the velvety nose, scratch the stiff swirl of hair between the eyes, as she had seen Will do. "It's not afraid of me," she marvelled, meaning that she was now a little less afraid of it.

The groom said: "No, Miss. But, with respect, horses ain't its. Them he's an she's, same as ladies an gennulmen. Exceptin geldings... but I reckon, them still he's, anyhow."

Felicity did not understand the final statement, would have liked to ask for clarification. Only, from the darker hue flooding Will's brown cheeks, she supposed this to be a subject best avoided upon such tenuous acquaintance. She filed the question away for another time - one to put to MacRory, perhaps. "Petunia is a she?"

"Aye, Miss. Her an ol lady, dam to Ginger an Blaze an three more. Saddle 'er up for you?"

"Not now," Felicity replied, "I haven't dressed for riding today. But I'd like to give her another sweet, if it's all right."

That had gone very well indeed - had been far easier than she'd anticipated. Not tomorrow, but the following day, when she had bought a suitable costume, she would return. Walking back around the stableyard with her new friend, Felicity experienced a profound sense of the rightness of things. "Will, you are happy, aren't you?"

"Miss?"

"You really like horses..."

"Them's about all I knows, Miss," said the boy. "My Da, Cal an Terry an me, us horsemen born an bred."

"Have you always lived here?"

"Aye, Miss, I were raised with these here animals. Petunia an me, we're of an age."

"I don't remember you from before," said the girl sadly, "or the horses."

"That ain't no wonder," replied the groom. "Before - well, the Little Miss, she weren't much for ridin. Weren't much for much, beggin your pardon."

"Then you didn't know me very well?"

"No, Miss - none of us did, outside help. 'Cept for hitchin up the shay, an her sittin up there, next the Guv'nor. Real purty she were, like a princess in a storybook...."

His eyes were far away, as if seeing backward in time. Had he looked upon the Little Miss with impossible desire? Surely not; he could have been no more than twelve years old. With envy, then? Impulsively, she asked: "Do you ever wish you were -" She had been going to say, of my class, but it sounded to her internal ear dishonest, even offensive. " - someone else?"

"Beg pardon, Miss?"

"I mean," Felicity pursued, "do you *enjoy* your life? You don't dream about going to - I don't know - London, the colonies - seeking your fortune?"

He stared as if she had proposed something absurd. "This be my home, Miss. Got all I needs, right here."

Mr. Goldsmith was, for once, absent from luncheon, as were Roderick and Rosalyn. In the latter case, Felicity could surmise the reason. When she had gone up to change, she'd heard them quarrelling. She had stayed but a minute outside their door, listening to the harsh voices. Rosalyn's, accusing: "...promised, if I stay with you... Society..." and Roderick's, wheedling: "...a fine lady, and the girls...." She: "...see nobody, go nowhere.... These people don't like us!" "Just be patient," Roderick said. "Patient?! ...might be years! Years!" There was near-despair in her voice, "...buried in the country... Bettina marry? ... not safe here...." Felicity hurried away; the altercation continued.

Luncheon, therefore, was a less populous and yet livelier affair than usual. Roland overcame his taciturnity to the extent of entertaining the little girls - and they, because of this, were less obtrusive. Bettina disturbed her not at all; it was Esmee, mainly, at whom the girl directed her remarks about the tour of London the family had taken.

"The Parliament was really, really impressive," she prattled on. "Except, we couldn't get very near, because there were these women outside, and some of them were chained to the railing, and the police were trying to take them away, except they wouldn't move, and a huge crowd was standing around, making rude noises. I always used to think the English were, you know, polite and quiet-like. I never found out what happened in the end, because Mother wouldn't let us stay and watch.... Don't you think they're really, really brave, the suffragettes?"

"I imagine," said Esmee, "that they would have to be."

"Except, Daddy says, just arresting them doesn't do any good. He says, you English are too soft on troublemakers..." Bettina turned her eyes anxiously on Roland. "You don't think women should be publicly whipped, do you? For wanting to vote in the elections?"

That young man, obviously ill-at-ease with the subject, squirmed and blushed, but answered readily enough: "I think any man who raises his hand to a woman deserves to be whipped. Publicly."

Esmee stepped in. "This is hardly a suitable topic for table-talk. Especially with," she glanced at the girls, "children present."

"We don't mind," Lisa said. "We're going to be suffer-jest when we grow up."

Lucy explained: "Daddy wouldn't whip us. I don't think. Would he, Lisa?"

Her sister thought a second. "Guess not. He'll be too old by then, anyhow."

"And Mommy doesn't like it here, so we'll be home, where everybody knows us."

"Yes. We wouldn't get rested in Sacramento."

Conversation moved on into less controversial areas, and Felicity was free to pursue her own reflections.

All might yet be well. If Mrs. Sommelroux disliked the country so, she might persuade Roderick to take her home. Even if they remained in England, perhaps the other family would spend its time in the capitol, in Society. Bettina would no doubt find a husband there; Lisa and Lucy would be sent to school. Mr. Goldsmith, whose absence was such a relief, must surely go back, sooner or later, to his law practice. She herself, with Esmee, would spend the minimum necessary time at the London house, then come home again, and be as they had been before - at peace. And Roland? Must she marry him? If it were the price of Twillingmarche, yes. He was not, after all, such a bad sort; she might come to equitable terms with him.

He startled her out of her reverie. "Care for a stroll in the park?"

"Go ahead, my dears," Esmee said. "Bettina and I will find something to amuse us."

Maybelle was waiting outside the dining room to take charge of the children; there was no excuse for refusing.

They walked. Roland, though he had lost much of his animation, did attempt some amiable small-talk. Leaves were red and brown upon the oak trees, but had only just begun to fall; there was sufficient shade underneath that she did not need a parasol.

"Mater says I've been neglecting you," confessed Roland. "I apologise. Only...."

"I do understand," Felicity replied, "one has duties."

"Oh, good. Well.... It's a nice day."

"Yes."

"No sign of frost,"

"No."

"How are you enjoying... things?"

"Some things," she replied, "very much. I do love Twillingmarche, don't you?"

"I like it well enough," said her stepbrother, "I suppose. Not much doing. It's all right for a girl, but.... I mean to say, a man ought to have work to do. Something... important. Or, anyway, something that matters."

Felicity stopped in order to give him her full attention. Inarticulate though he might be, Roland was trying to express an idea close to his heart. "Don't you feel," she asked, "that running the estate is important?"

"That's just the thing," said he. "I *don't* run it - and never shall. Finch takes care of the land; Forkes takes care of the money - they wouldn't let me interfere, even if I really wanted to. Old Roderick, now.... He's not the nicest man in the world, heaven knows.... But he does run his own business. He didn't just sit on his assets, even though the properties his dad left could have kept him in comfort. He made the old livery stable into a garage. For repairing cars," he added. "Because he could see that's where the future was. He had to be sharp, to turn a profit, but he's never let competition stop him. You have got to admire that."

Felicity did not feel compelled to admire anything about Cousin Roderick, least of all his making money from broken automobiles. However, she did have an inkling of Roland's feelings. He was not cut out for managing an estate, yet he longed for control. An occupation of some kind ought to be found for him. "What would you like to do?"

Roland looked bemused. "I'm not trained to do anything. Mater never meant me to have an occupation - she wanted me to be a gentleman."

"Still, something must interest you. Many gentlemen are scholars or poets, some are explorers... even a few of the Sommelroux men were adventurers. Why, look at Roderick's father! He left home with hardly a penny, and he did all right."

"Yes," Roland said, "that's true. What I like - at least, I think I might like - motors."

"Well, there you are. You shall have motors. Perhaps you'll be a gentleman inventor."

This appeared to please Roland for a moment, before his features once again drew into lines of concern entirely unsuited to them. "Felicity? I mean, dash it all," he finally blurted, "d'you *want* to marry me?"

She stopped in her tracks. Were they meant to be honest with each other, or was this a rather awkward proposal? She said carefully: "I am prepared to do so."

"That's how I feel, too. I guess we have to,"

"I know," she said, liking him much better than she had.

"Only, see," Roland stumbled over his words, "your dad - I mean, you know, Lord Farwell? Well, he was married - twice..."

"Yes, I know."

"And that didn't stop him...er...." He reddened. It was a shocking sight; his pale skin turned the colour of a beet, from the collar all the way up into the roots of his hair. It seemed to her very unkind of Nature to make fair people blush so easily, when dark ones looked much more attractive, doing it. "...didn't stop him living his own life, if you know what I mean...." While she did not, completely, she nodded for him to go on. "And Mater told me.... But it's all different now! Bettina isn't..."

Felicity looked her intended squarely in his light blue eyes. "You've fallen in love!"

He nodded miserably.

"Oh dear!"

"Only, what are we going to do?"

She sighed. "I don't know. Perhaps nothing. Not yet. We can go on as before, at least for a while. Does Esmee know?"

"Of course not! She'd have a kitten-fit."

"You haven't declared yourself to Bettina?"

"No.... But it doesn't matter. She feels the same way - I know she does."

"To tell the truth, I'm not very enthusiastic about this marriage, either. Yet, Esmee is my guardian, until I come of age. We dare not upset her plans now - not with the threat of Cousin Roderick - and so much at stake...."

"Mater's plans!" sighed Roland. "I was never keen on this scheme. Truth is, I didn't think you could pull it off."

"Pull it off?"

"It's an expression Americans use. I mean, I never thought.... Even if you do look like the real Felicity, you're not a bit like her in any other way...."

"The real Felicity?" she asked icily. "I am Felicity Sommelroux. The only one there is. Understand?"

Mr. Goldsmith's failure to appear for tea was remarked only in passing. However, his absence from sherry before supper was to be wondered at; for him to miss three meals in a row was scarcely credible.

"Don't know what could be keeping him," said Roderick testily. "Sent him to check something in the village. How long could that take?"

"Oh, stop fretting," his wife said. "Sam knows what he's doing."

"Does he, though? Never been much of a driver."

"So it's just your old car you're worried about!"

"Not just," said Roderick, "but I don't want it wrecked. And it's dark. Peaceful - whatever your name is - roust somebody out to look for him."

Makepeace glanced at Esmee, who nodded. "I think it might be wise. Suppose poor Mr. Goldsmith is stranded? Send Edward and one of the grooms. He went into the village, you say, Roderick?"

"Amber-Whatsis. Only a couple of miles, ain't it? Don't see how he could have run out of gas, or got lost."

"Petrol," Roland said to Makepeace. "Have them take some petrol, just in case."

"Very good, sir."

When the butler had gone, Bettina turned to Roland. "You never told me you had a car! But that's wonderful! We can go for long drives!"

"No, no," he told her, "we haven't. We'll buy one, though, soon, won't we, Mater?"

Felicity noted the yearning light in his eye and decided, as soon as she should come into her inheritance, to give Roland an automobile. Perhaps as a consolation present for breaking off their engagement....

"Then, how come," Lucy piped up, "you have gasoline?"

"It's for the dynamo."

"What domino?" asked Lisa.

"Not domino," Roland corrected gently, "dynamo. It makes electricity for the lights. It's really an impressive machine - I'll show you kids tomorrow, if you like."

"Well," said Esmee, "let us go in. When Mr. Goldsmith is found, he may have something on a tray."

Mr. Goldsmith was not found. Edward returned late in the evening to report that Cousin Roderick's automobile had been discovered in the main street of Amber-upon-Twilling, undamaged and fueled, yet abandoned. Although he and Terence Cartwright had inquired all over the village, there was no sign of the lawyer. He had taken his mid-day meal at the Carter's Arms, and then, seemingly, disappeared. No-one whom they had asked could recall seeing or speaking to the man since early afternoon. Terry was scouring the countryside; Edward had come back only to mobilize a search party.

After the footman departed, Rosalyn said: "I'm sure he's all right. Sam has the wits to take care of himself."

"You'd know that better than me," remarked her husband darkly. "Too damn much better," he added under his breath. "Thick as thieves...."

"That's just like you," she retorted, "to think the worst of everyone."

"Yes, Daddy," Bettina joined in. "Sam's never done anything disloyal. You just can't trust anybody, can you?"

"I've got no reason to," her father answered, scowling.

They seemed then to become aware of Esmee, Roland and Felicity, who followed this family exchange, barely able to conceal their interest. Roderick fell silent and his heavy, brooding silence doomed any further attempt at conversation. Roland half-heartedly proposed a game of billiards, but Roderick could not stand for prolonged periods upon his injured leg, nor had he patience to watch the young people play. Esmee's suggestion of a game of cards was met with no enthusiasm. She soon declared herself ready for bed, and advised the others to retire.

"Makepeace can wake us if there is any word. I shall instruct him to do so."

There was no word that night. Felicity - and she supposed, everyone else - slept but little, expecting at all hours to be roused for yet another mishap of the American Sommelroux. She rose sluggish, out-of-sorts and puffy of eyelid. Since she could be of no possible help in locating Mr. Goldsmith, she saw no reason to put off her trip into town. It was just as well, however, that Edward was excused from duty after his long, strenuous night and would not be driving: she didn't want him seeing her in this state.

It was George who brought the carriage around and barely missed a collision with Roderick's automobile. Clattering up the drive in it was none other than Mr. Goldsmith. A most indignant and dishevelled Goldsmith. All the family, as well as any servants within earshot, flocked to the entrance-hall. Makepeace ushered in the tired, stubbled lawyer and quickly brought a chair, upon which that man - perhaps just a touch over-dramatically - collapsed. Bettina gushed with relief; Rosalyn fluttered and clucked like an old hen; Cousin Roderick made noise, some of it quite profane, demanding the very explanation that the lawyer was anxious to impart.

"Locked in! All night!" he exclaimed with a good deal more intensity than Felicity had ever suspected him capable of. "It was horrible! Spooky! And then. All the candles were gone. I couldn't find any more. I called. And called. Nobody answered! I'm not a superstitious man. But."

There was more, much more, in the same vein: questions from all directions, too fast and confused for orderly answers. Felicity waited only long enough to ascertain the bare facts of the story. Mr. Goldsmith had gone to Saint Hilda's. He had been alone, and somehow got locked in, until the verger opened for morning prayers. Why he had gone there and not informed anyone remained unclear. But now, Felicity thought, as the carriage took her and Roberts away, she would look forward to services tomorrow; the church had become imbued for her with an air of excitement, of mystery.

9

It was not her elegance that drew attention at church: Felicity had, contrary to her fond expectations, nothing new to wear. Roberts insisted that a young lady would rather die than enter an establishment which stocks ready-made clothing, of which Twillingsford boasted two, one for men and another for women and children. Ladies and gentlemen, Roberts said, have their apparel made to measure, whether they can afford it or not - and, in any case, they do not consider the problem of payment. Felicity had therefore spent an inordinate amount of time at the dressmaker's, being measured, handled and draped, having her body inspected, discussed and judged, rather as if it had been a side of beef. She must go back for fittings and adjustments; she would have the finished articles in two or three weeks. It all seemed a silly waste, but Roberts was in charge - for the moment.

Fortunately, at Saint Hilda's it was no matter what she wore. Every woman in the congregation, with the notable and much-noted exception of Felicity's companions, was at least ten years behind the London mode. She knew this because at Twillingmarche no periodical with tinted illustrations was ever thrown away or used to start a fire: she had spent many an idle hour in the study of fashion, past and present. No, it was her very existence that aroused curiosity. Evidently, the news of her return had spread to the village.

Cousin Roderick garnered his share of attention, being conveyed to a place in the aisle by George. Someone - Mrs. Golightly? - had remembered the bath-chair used during his final illness by Lord Farwell. It was, after a lengthy search, discovered in the attics and refurbished. The large, ungainly wicker contraption had spoked metal wheels and a raised foot-rest. With the beplastered appendage going before and a plaid blanket across his lap, Cousin Roderick looked, but for the high colour in his cheeks, every inch an invalid. He would have preferred to come alone, after the service, but his wife had convinced him otherwise. "After all," she had said, "if you're going to be the lord around here, you'd better let the locals have a gander."

This Sunday, the good folk of Amber-upon-Twilling were not cheated of a spectacle: the front pew was fully occupied by exotics. Esmee, in a brilliant chinoiserie floral of blues and reds; Rosalyn in more modest ivory silk, but with a frivolous dyed rabbit-fur trim and a broad-brimmed white hat too airy for the season and the place; Bettina in her tiresome pink flounces; Felicity in a moss green velvet suit, let out, though not quite sufficiently, at key points. The garment was uncomfortable, but not ostentatious. She had, however, been able to turn the matching green cloche hat into something remarkable by the judicious application of tulle and some roses she had fashioned from scraps of pink silk and green lace. Roland wore a modest russet tweed, set off by paisley waistcoat and foulard; Mr. Forkes had on his usual black and carried an exquisite walking stick with a silver handle in the shape of an eagle. Roderick's hideous tartan coat clashed and jangled with the blanket draped across his legs.

The Locals, in browns and greys and dowdy hats and gloves frayed at the cuff, provided background, chorus and audience.

Felicity's attention was riveted, from the first moment, upon the vicar of Saint Hilda's. The man looked eerily familiar. How, when, or where, she could not say, but she had seen him before. Did he also recognize her? Certainly, throughout the sermon and especially during the singing of hymns, in which he declined to participate, his gaze kept returning to her face. Perhaps he, too, had difficulty in recalling her? Or was it merely that, having known the young Felicity, he wondered at her changed aspect, after three years?

One half of the puzzle was solved directly after services, when the old man came to greet his most illustrious parishioners.

Esmee performed the introductions: "Reverend Gillivray - Roderick Sommelroux, the late Lord Farwell's cousin - from America. Mrs. Sommelroux; their daughters, Bettina, Lucy and Lisa. The children can be excused now, Maybelle. And, of course, our dear Felicity. She has come back to us, at long last. I daresay you will find her much changed."

The girl managed a polite enough greeting; for his part, the reverend Doctor Gillivray patted her hand lightly and let it go. He was younger than the medical one, not nearly so decrepit, nor so effusive. He said: "My brother tells me that you have quite recovered. Very pleased to hear it, my dear."

Rosalyn said nothing at all; Bettina spoke much and said little; the men offered a how-d'ye-do and moved on. Except for Cousin Roderick, who had been chafing visibly, waiting for the church to empty before tackling the real purpose of his visit. "I want to talk to you."

"Indeed?" the vicar answered mildly. "On a spiritual matter, or a worldly one?"

"About my man, Goldsmith. Get lost, George."

The footman gave a slight nod and withdrew - not out of hearing, quite, but to a courteous distance. The rest of the company, too, drifted away toward the carriages. It had been necessary to harness both for this occasion; even so, accommodation was somewhat tight. George would be required to help Cousin Roderick and to load the bath-chair upon the baggage-rack, but Edward had retired to the head of his team. While the other women climbed in, with a hand from the available gentlemen, and much shifting of skirts, Felicity thought to further her acquaintance with the bays.

"I know Jessie by the white stocking," she said to the footman. "What's the other one called?"

"This is Jewel, senior mare," said he, and with a stately bow: "Jewel, this is Lady Felicity, your new mistress."

She smiled at the impertinence, reached out to pat Jewel's golden head. "You don't have any sugar?"

"No, Miss. I'm afraid Will Cartwright spoils them."

She would have liked to pursue a conversation with Edward on any subject whatever, and she had the - possibly wishful - impression that he, too, was willing to promote their acquaintance. Only, at this moment, both were more curious about Roderick's interview of the vicar.

"Yes, he did come to see me," the latter was saying. "That would have been, oh, about four in the afternoon. He asked some foolish questions. Then he went away." The old man lifted up the hem of his surplice in preparation to move off, but Roderick followed with a determined push at his chair.

"That's not the way I hear it! What questions?"

Some of the answer was lost, for Dr. Gillivray was a soft-spoken man. Felicity could make out only that Mr. Goldsmith had wished to inspect some records and been refused.

Roderick's voice, on the other hand, carried perfectly. "Why not? What's the big secret, anyway?"

"No secret... a stranger, after all... not seemly..."

"So, he went away, did he? And where did all this happen?"

More by his gesture than his words, Dr. Gillivray appeared to be indicating the current premises; that is, the church itself. His next statement took in the cemetery; she guessed this to be the direction of Mr. Goldsmith's departure.

"Where were you?"

"...my tea..." The old man looked - longingly? - toward the house on the far side of a well-kept lawn. "...early... lock up,"

"And you didn't see him come back? You never heard him?"

"...appointments... my study... verger..."

"Where is this verger? I want to talk to him."

Dr. Gillivray spoke more, quietly, then beckoned to someone in the churchyard. Felicity had not noticed the little wizened man but he, apparently, had been aware of all that transpired, for he now joined the two by the church steps. He was, fully erect, of a height with Roderick, seated. He snatched off his cloth cap, revealing unkempt locks of yellowish white. "Ye wants me, Vicar? Guv'nor?"

"Were you here yesterday afternoon?" Cousin Roderick demanded, "about four o'clock?"

The bent old man nodded rapidly. "I cleans up the graves. Weeds, sompin awful."

"Is that what you were doing?" Roderick enunciated more loudly. "Friday afternoon. Did you see Mr. Goldsmith go back into the church?"

"With a hoe," the other elaborated, "an rake. Time I jes pulls em up with my hand."

"Did. You. *See*. **Goldsmith**?" Roderick shouted, so that the few people still standing about in gossiping knots turned toward him in unison.

"Not so bad now," explained the verger patiently. "Dyin off. Summertime, I can't hardly keep up."

"He's deaf as a post!"

"An then I sweeps, an I locks up of an evening, keep out them, whatyoucallem? Vegrans. Them gets in, anyhow. Found one, yestiddy it was. Slep inna church." He shook his scraggly head, more in sorrow than anger. "Inna church! Pore bastid,"

"I did try to tell you," Dr. Gillivray said.

"Oh, get him out of here!" cried Roderick in disgust.

The vicar patted the little gnome's shoulder, motioned him to depart. The verger, replacing his cap, added: "Him oughtn't to've burned up all the cannels, din leave a penny, ain't right..."

"Well," remarked Felicity to Edward, "that explains why nobody heard Mr. Goldsmith... "

"...but not," the footman finished, "what Mr. Goldsmith was doing in the church."

"Still, should he have burned all of the candles?"

"No, that was very wrong of him"

They smiled at each other, sharing another tiny secret. She gave Jewel and Jessie a last light scratch on their foreheads. Edward helped her into the carriage, then hurried over to give George a hand with Cousin Roderick's chair.

Sunday afternoon was meant to be a quiet time; most of the servants had the half-day off to visit relations in the village. After a cold buffet, the family had been accustomed to engage in sedentary amusements or to occupy themselves with spiritually uplifting literature. Felicity, declining an invitation to take the air with Bettina and Roland, proposed to do the latter, in her own room. That cabinet intrigued her: having shut the hidden compartment at Roberts' unexpected entrance, she had not yet found a way to open it again. She was determined to discover its trick, and read those papers.

It took almost an hour of persistent experimentation. You had to press down and outward on both carved tulips at the same time, with the same even pressure. But, finally having gained her prize, she judged it no prize. Here were nothing but poems, rendered in a round, childish hand, with much crossing-out and over-writing.

> Little birds to their nests hasten,
> And the river, to the sea,
> The wind whispers, 'Time's a-wastin',
> And I hurry home to thee.

What foolishness, thought Felicity. Again:

> If you could read
> The heart within this breast,
> A lonely heart, which only for you beats,
> And your sweet name eternally repeats,
> How could you fail to heed
> It's forlorn request?

Oh, dear, thought Felicity. Whoever wrote this must have been in love. Only, she hoped they had found some other way to win the object of their desire; these soppy verses would certainly not have done it. Now that she knew how to open the compartment, she could read more of them, any time she wanted to. If ever. Such an

92

ingenious device was quite wasted on the concealment of something so trivial.

It would be far more entertaining to slip off to the tower. She must tell Aunt Lettie about Mr. Goldsmith's mysterious adventure: she had come to feel it a duty to report all that happened at and around Twillingmarche.

There was no answer to her knock, once, twice. No answer when she called out. Aunt Lettie was either asleep or out of her room. Where could she have gone? It might be no easy matter to come back later, therefore the girl decided to explore every possible avenue. She had seen no other doors on the way up the stairs, but had never yet climbed any higher. She would try that.

On the landing above Aunt Lettie's room there was, indeed, another door, firmly shut. And yet one more at the very top, which was slightly ajar. Receiving no reply to her knock here, she gently pushed it open. Felicity found herself in a narrower stairwell, leading to what must once have been the bell-tower. Its arches had been glazed, turned into four tall windows. The north one looked out onto the roofs of the house, affording little interest. The other three offered wonderful views: of the park – a veritable sea of green foliage, spotted here and there with the yellows and reds of early fall - to the Amber road and beyond - eastward, past the hothouse and kitchen garden, farmland interspersed with outcrops of rock. The south window, bright with sunlight, gave on to a long vista of trees, meadows and, far away, a glimpse of the River Twilling in its deep rocky gorge. Close by were some quite picturesque ruins; closer still, beneath the tower, a miniature version of the walled garden. It looked sheltered and cosy - a place Felicity would dearly love, someday soon, to visit.

The small square chamber had a modern floor of unpolished planks, partly covered by a multicolored rag rug, such as she had seen in the servants' hall. Containing nothing but two commodious wicker chairs with a low table between, a bookshelf, tea caddy and a profusion of potted plants, it was the most pleasant room that she had ever seen. It was also unoccupied.

On the little table was a monthly, placed as she had been taught never to do: open, face-down. Its title was odd but promising: Journal of the Royal Society of Chemists. Whatever Chemists are, she thought, if they are in the Royal Society, they *must* be interesting. Disappointingly, there were no pictures, of Royalty or anybody else, only pages of closely-printed text, interspersed with incomprehensible line-drawings, mainly by people with German-sounding names: Hoffman, Buchner, Fischer... They might be Continental relatives of the old Queen. Not DeVries, though, surely.... She put the magazine down. A book pulled at random from the shelf was no better: the authors' names were Cannizzaro and Kekule. These could not possibly be real; they must have been made up - funny nommes-de-plume - but the book's contents were not at all amusing.

She would try once more the second door. As she came round the turn of the staircase, she caught a glimpse of someone making for Aunt Lettie's room. She could not tell who, or even whether it be man or woman; she had no more than an impression of a black and white figure moving rapidly. Felicity waited one full minute by pulse-count, then, as the person did not reappear, descended the last flight.

"Auntie," she called softly, "are you there?"

"Felicity, is it? Come in, my dear." The voice was strong and sure, with no trace of querulousness.

She carefully entered the chamber and looked about. There was Aunt Lettie, seated in her big chair, wrapped in her cloak, but no sign of anyone else. "Are you alone?"

"Of course I am alone. I am always alone."

"But," said the girl, "I saw someone. On the stairs, just now. I could have sworn they were coming here."

"Well, they're not here now," replied the older woman with a touch of impatience. "Kate left a little while ago with my luncheon tray. Maybe it was her you saw. You were not announced," she added with more than a hint of displeasure. "Did Makepeace give you the key?"

Felicity had not particularly wondered at finding the Palladian wing unlocked; if she thought anything at all, it was that luck was with her. She explained this, and also: "I didn't like to tell anyone. You see, it is becoming so difficult to get away unnoticed.... One hardly knows whom to trust.... Don't be angry, Aunt Lettie - please?"

The pale features within the dark red folds relaxed somewhat. "All right. As for whom to trust: Makepeace, Edward, Kate - Mrs. Golightly and MacRory, in an emergency. But you mustn't barge in - it upsets me."

"I am sorry," said Felicity. "Only, I did want so much to tell you. I went to church today."

"Hmph. Doesn't everyone?"

"Yes, and I met Doctor Gillivray. The other one, I mean, the vicar, not the physician."

"He's been neglecting me," said Aunt Lettie. "They both have. How is the old windbag?"

"I thought him charming. And the verger, he was so funny! Has anyone told you about Mr. Goldsmith? Cousin Roderick's solicitor, only *they* say lawyer. He was snooping around at Saint Hilda's because the vicar didn't show him some records, and they accidentally locked him in, and the verger is deaf, so there was nobody to hear him shouting, and he spent the night inside, and he was so frightened.... I don't see why he should be - I mean, a *church* would never be haunted, would it?" The older woman gave a minute nod after each statement, whether to indicate that she was following the narrative, or that she had heard all of it before, Felicity could not tell. "Roderick was yelling questions, and this funny little verger just kept explaining about weeds in the cemetery."

"Septimus Finch. Why, he must be a hundred years old."

"Finch? Like our manager?"

"Oh yes," Aunt Lettie said, "some kind of great uncle, I believe. Everyone hereabouts is related to everyone else. You will find Golightlys and Finches in every bush, MacRorys and Cartwrights and Markles... even some Makepeaces. It's a small, closed-off world."

Felicity was fascinated by her aunt's knowledge of village life and history. Amber-upon-Twilling had come into existence as a result of Twillingmarche itself. "When the first Sommelroux was entitled," Letitia explained, "by King Henry the Eighth, did you know? Good. Do you also know how it happened?" The girl shook her head, all attention. "Raymond Sommelroux had lent a great sum of money to the king, some time before. Rather than repay it from his own treasury, which was never adequately stocked, Henry gave him these lands in 1538, after the Dissolution. A good arrangement on both sides; it cost the king nothing and Raymond came up in the world. Of course, he'd seized all the Cistercians' gold plate and fine art for himself, and, sadly, half the cloisters were scavenged for building stone before Raymond took possession. "

"Was Raymond - before - was he a general?"

Letitia gave one of her witchly cackles. "Not quite. He was King Henry's castellan. A sort of glorified butler, one might say."

"But how did he get rich enough to lend so much money?"

"Ah, well," the other woman put a long white finger alongside her nose, "that *is* a question. Shrewd investments? A big win at horse-racing? The details, of course, are shrouded in the mist of time.... Raymond was in charge of victualling the palace; Henry entertained lavishly.... One *might* suspect, if one were of a nasty turn of mind, that the capital was skimmed off Henry's own cellars."

Felicity saw nothing untoward in this speculation, nor anything so terribly improper, were it true: King Henry robbed the Roman Church; his servants robbed King Henry. Those had been uncivilised times. Besides, Raymond and his heirs had done more for the district than the contemplative monks ever would have. "So, that's how the coat of arms came about. There it is, in the top corner of your tapestry: a red rooster, holding a pair of goblets in its claws."

"Still, the king had his little joke. The Earl of Farwell acquired his escutcheon and yet, placed in the very shadow of unruly Scotland, never got leave to build fortifications. Raymond must have had a few uneasy nights, don't you think?"

"Yes," Felicity retorted, "but the Sommelroux had the last laugh - the Scots never attacked. Edward told me that."

"He has always been keen on history, has our Edward."

They studied the yarn pictures for some time, Aunt Lettie pointing out the most remarkable events in the annals of Farwell. "The second earl, Roland, was perfectly useless. The next one bred sheep. It was the trade in wool that allowed him to finish building the new house... well, new at the time. The fifth earl, another Raymond, diversified farming, and improved his tenants' standard of living. His son increased the rents to finance some colonial adventure - but he, too, turned a profit in the end."

"And it was a Raymond who built the modern house."

"He began it, yes. The two sons finished the construction,"

"But only one moved in." The girl concluded. "Why did he go away?"

"Who?"

"Your uncle Raymond. You were very young then, but you must have known him. What was he like?"

Aunt Lettie nodded thoughtfully to herself. "He was the sort of uncle every child adores - young, irresponsible, amusing. As to why he left.... Well, I suppose, there was nothing to keep him. He and my dear Papa disagreed about - things."

"Raymond never got to live in the new house."

"I don't imagine he would have wished to."

Felicity took up the broken narrative, "Your brother Randolph had the conveniences added. He spent rather a lot of money on that, didn't he?"

"Rather a lot," Aunt Lettie agreed.

"Esmee says the farms aren't earning enough, and we have to be careful."

"Esmee, is it? Yes, she had better be careful."

"But, Auntie," Felicity asked, "who made the little room upstairs? Who lives there?"

Letitia started almost out of her draperies, her pale face taking on an unaccustomed flush. "The little room - where?"

"Why, why," the girl stammered, wondering what she had said to elicit this violent reaction, "at the, the," she pointed over their heads, "the very top. There is a sort of bell-tower room, with windows, and, and plants... Don't you know?"

"Oh, that little room," the older woman subsided in her chair. "It was mine, some time ago.... When I was young enough to climb so many stairs. No-one uses it now."

"Somebody still takes care of the plants."

Letitia, once more in possession of herself, smiled. "That will be Kate. Dear, sentimental girl - she can't bear to see anything die, not even houseplants."

And Kate escapes there when she's off duty, Felicity surmised. Kate has found herself a fine retreat for reading magazines and being alone. Or, Felicity emended, remembering the second chair, for meeting her young man? Only, one fervently hoped, that young man was someone other than Edward.

"Does Kate have a beau?"

"If she does, I doubt she would tell me."

"Would Edward tell you, if he had a sweetheart?"

Aunt Lettie gave a laugh - not the half-mad, frightening one she sometimes used, but a warm, amused sort of chuckle. "I imagine he might. Edward is a special friend of mine."

Well, that was a relief. Why should it be? Felicity was fonder of Kate than of any other female in the household, barring Aunt Lettie. Why should she begrudge her favourite maid the company of the most handsome footman? After all, admire Edward's face and figure as she might, she herself was pledged to Roland Wilkins. And yet.... She sighed. "It's hard, sometimes, being Felicity,"

"It's hard, sometimes, being anybody, my dear. And now, I think, you ought to return. Do remind Makepeace to keep that door locked."

10

The more Esmee talked about London, the less Felicity looked forward to it. She would certainly be barred from any chance of meeting her other aunt, the infamous Dorothea - the only reason she might not mind so very much being apart from Lettie. The London house had its own servants; none of the familiar people would be going, unless she insisted on taking Kate. Had she the power to insist? Certainly, it was worth a try. She would be kept busy with dressmakers, parties and polite afternoon visits with strangers, but, oh so lonely, if there was not one person with whom she could speak freely. The trans-Atlantic cousins would be there; though, with social activities to keep them occupied, they might be less insufferable.

There was a second matter which Felicity hardly dared to confess, yet, confess it she must: she was not at all confident that her dancing met the standard of Society balls. At village fetes she had been a partner much coveted by the lads; until quite recently, she had believed her skill in the art more than adequate. But now she suspected - nay, was quite sure - that a very different style was to be required, of which she knew nothing. To her mentor in all things lady-like she reluctantly confided her trepidation.

"Yes," said Roberts thoughtfully, "that is a problem. I don't suppose there was much dancing at the clinic. How should you have learned?"

"Perhaps I am too delicate for balls? Perhaps it is too soon for me to come out?"

"No, no - it cannot be put off," said the lady's maid. "You are almost eighteen. And you don't look at all delicate.... Well, we must teach you."

More tedious lessons! Roberts had the Victrola from the blue drawing room brought to Felicity's quarters, and there instructed her in the necessary steps, which were nothing at all like the lively turns and bouncing rhythms of the village green. Quite dull, really, but not difficult. In a matter of days, Roberts declared her ready to take the practice floor with a gentleman partner.

"But not in front of... of everyone!" she protested. "I should die of embarrassment."

Esmee, who had come in to see her progress, agreed. "We can use the ballroom in the old wing. I shall have Roland make himself available. It will help you to become accustomed to the right sort of environment.... The chandeliers are gone, I'm afraid - it'll have to be daytime. Tomorrow afternoon, then, while Roderick has his nap."

"What about the ... others?" Felicity enquired anxiously.

Esmee understood she meant the curious cousins. "I know! I shall take Rosalyn and Bettina into Twillingsford. Roberts will chaperon."

And so it was settled. Roberts hastily converted a gown of Esmee's which had fallen into disfavour. It was roomy, and of a phosphorescent green most unflattering to the girl's coppery hair and pale skin, but it would do, so long as nobody of consequence saw her. Roland was of no consequence, for he scarcely noticed her anyway. Nor was he altogether pleased to be commandeered for dancing in the obscurity of the old ballroom. "At least, couldn't Bettina come along?" he had pled, but his mother was adamant. "Perhaps next time, when Felicity is more - well, adept. The last thing I want is to be laughed-at by those Americans."

The little procession therefore consisted of Roland, Roberts and Felicity, with Makepeace in front, holding the key, and Edward bringing up the rear with the Victrola in his arms. This, for Felicity, was sufficient to undo all her precautions: being seen thus by him was a humiliation far greater than could be occasioned by any distant relations. Worse: she thought there was a fugitive smile playing about the footman's chiselled lips. But he said nothing and slipped tactfully away as soon as he had set up the music machine.

"I wonder why that door needs to be locked?" Roland asked. "Nobody ever comes here."

"The children might take it into their heads to do so," Roberts explained. "You remember all that fuss about one of them falling into the well? Think how many ways those two could find to injure themselves in this old building."

"I guess you're right," he allowed. "Only, I thought that maid Maybelle was supposed to keep them out of trouble."

"Yes - supposed," said Roberts with a frown, "but she can't manage very well. Twice already, she's lost track of them - just yesterday, they were brought back by the gamekeeper; they'd wandered all over the park." She sighed. "As soon as Mr. Sommelroux is well enough to travel, we shall all be in London. Then, perhaps, a proper governess can be found for them. It's high time those little barbarians had some discipline."

"I like them," Roland said, "the way they are."

"Ill-mannered and destructive?"

"Spirited. If you ask me, English girls have far too much discipline. They're boring." He had the grace to notice Felicity and to blush, adding: "Present company excepted, of course. Shall we dance?"

Soothed by the illusion of moving in his natural element, Roland's temper improved almost to the point of jollity. After the second waltz, he remarked: "Not too bad, for a girl who's spent three years in an asyl - er, I mean, a clinic. I'd teach you the Cakewalk, but Roberts wouldn't approve, would you, Luv?" He gave a broad wink to the lady's maid, who averted her head, but not before Felicity noticed her cheek colour slightly.

"Is that the latest dance-step?"

"Hardly," said Roland. "It's been around for years. Pretty tame, really, compared to some dancing we've seen, eh, Roberts?"

The lady's maid declined to answer and Felicity wished that Roland would stop teasing her and that Roberts could be less straight-laced. She was amused and a little irritated by both.

102

They stuck to the more sedate ballroom fare, and were doing tolerably well, when two carroty heads bobbed up at one window, then at another, laughing and grimacing. Before Roberts had a chance to go outside, Maybelle came and herded them away. Too late for Felicity's peace of mind; everyone would know within the hour. It was her desire to vacate the premises immediately, but Roberts was against this, and Roland said: "Oh, stop worrying. You do well enough. Anyway, who's to care?"

Who, indeed? Not two more turns had been completed, when Makepeace materialised in the grand doorway, a most lugubrious expression upon his normally vacant countenance, in an equally mournful voice to announce: "Mr. Sommelroux."

"Lord Sommelroux, you stuffed ape! Get it right, or you'll be looking for a job."

Makepeace withdrew without another word, disapproval writ large in every line of his back. The dancers had frozen in their tracks, while the cylinder wound down, untended. Roderick in his bath-chair occupied much of the entryway; in the background, George tried to make himself invisible. "Son of a Gun! The gals were telling the truth. What's going on?"

Roland being speechless, Felicity was first to collect her wits. "We are having a private ball. Would you care for a turn?"

The American laughed. "That's a point to you, Pretty Cousin. Guess I'll sit this one out - some of these days, mind, I'll take you up on the offer." He snapped his fingers at the footman, who pushed the chair forward. Roderick gazed about. "Nice. Didn't get much chance for a gander, before this pesky thing," he patted his plaster. "Very nice. Where's all the furniture got to?" Since the question was not addressed to anyone in particular, no-one volunteered to answer it. "Sold off, I'd guess. Rotten management, any way you look at it. Well, that's going to change. Get rid of all those horses, for a start. And most of the servants - they're uppity, anyhow, and lazy. Money getting wasted all over the place, and the house run down. This room, now... that ceiling's got to be twenty foot high....

Put in a few lights, nice carpet, some tables and chairs, this room is big enough for a hundred to eat in. You, Ronald, how many bedrooms in this here building?"

"Thirty or so," replied the young man, taken too much by surprise even to correct his own name. It was, Felicity happened to know, only twenty-eight, plus servants' quarters under the roof, but, for once, she kept her own counsel.

"And this floor? Let's have a peek around. George!"

Roderick was wheeled about, into the sumptuous central hall, through dining room, library and gun room, even the gentlemen's cloakroom and butler's pantry, talking all the time, while Roland, Roberts and Felicity trooped silently along. "Yes siree, Bob! This place sure could use a coat of paint. Something bright and lively, instead of all this dreary old panelling. No money, no money - but just look at it! Why, this'd make a luxury hotel to beat the Ritz.... Except, who wants to come to the back of beyond for holidays? I've got it! It could be kind of like that place where Pretty Cousin's been all this long time. Indisposed? Rich? Why go to Switzerland? Exclusive clinic, right here in Merrie Old.... How does that sound? Pretty good, eh? I'll need some capital to fix things up - lights and plumbing and so on.... The rooms are too big anyhow - a few extra walls, I could make twice as many. Hire a quack with the right connections, that'd be useful, and lots of pretty nurses..... By Gum, I *have* got an idea here! What d'you think?"

What they thought was etched on their faces as Felicity and the lady's maid glanced at each other: it was the most ghastly notion they had ever heard. Roberts made a strangling noise in her throat; otherwise, neither woman replied. Roland, however, looked thoughtfully up and down the hall in which the procession had halted.

"Yes-siree, Bob," Roderick continued without encouragement, "a heck of an idea! I'll get Goldsmith to scope out the details. Right away. Back to my room, George. As for you kids, go on with your party, or whatever it was."

But the mood had turned sour; the dancing was finished. Felicity pictured in her mind the wonderful building cut up into tiny bedrooms and stuffed full of strangers. It was a shame to leave it empty, yes - but to despoil it was surely not the answer. Get rid of the horses and servants, indeed!

"It really isn't such a bad idea," Roland said. "I bet he could make a go of it, too - he's shrewd enough. And it's not as if we ever used the place. Not even before the Governor's illness."

"Is that what you called Papa?" asked Felicity, desirous more of changing the subject than of discovering Roland's relationship with his late stepfather.

The boy looked abashed. "Tell you the truth, I never called him much of anything. We never did take to each other."

"That must have been very uncomfortable for you. Especially if Esmee was as fond of me as she says."

"Yes, well. Anyway, he seemed to think the sun rose and set on his little girl."

"Were you jealous? Did you resent me very much?"

Roland looked at her in surprise. "No. Why should I? Anyway, it wasn't all that long, me only coming here after..."

"What?"

"After Gran died. My real father's mother that was. She raised me, pretty much. I mean, don't get hold of the wrong end of the stick - Mater came as often as she could, even took me up to London, one time.... And she always sent money, which is more'n my dad ever did, even before he went off to India."

They had come through to the Victorian wing; Roberts hurried ahead to find Makepeace and lock up; they were alone.

"Do you mean," the girl turned to him, "your father's still alive?"

Roland shrugged. "Last I heard. What difference does it make? The bas... the man didn't even come back for Gran's funeral - his own mother! Well," he relented somewhat, "by the time he found out, I guess it would have been too late.... He wrote a letter, saying how it would be all right for me to join him out there, but he reckoned I'd be better off not, what with Mater's 'illustrious marriage'.... Illustrious was the word he used. Anyway, that's the last I ever heard from my dear old dad." There was such bitterness in Roland's voice, as if all this had happened yesterday.

"But that was years ago,"

"Six years - I was almost fourteen."

"Weren't you tempted by India?"

He shook his head. "If Dad had wanted me, he'd've come back for me. Mum did. In a four-horse carriage. You know, they never harness four, except for funerals and weddings, though I didn't know that, then. All I knew was the whole village turned out to see me off. That's the most important I've ever felt in my life. Mater thinks of that sort of thing."

Felicity, moved by his candour no less than by his pain, placed a comforting hand on Roland's arm. He smiled at her. They were, after all, becoming friends. If they must marry, she thought, an accommodation satisfactory to both parties might yet be possible.

Supper that evening was livelier - and more difficult to bear - than usual. Cousin Roderick began by what he evidently considered a comical description of the scene he had witnessed in the ballroom. Lucy and Lisa, encouraged by their father's rare mood of levity, added details, accompanied by fits of uncontrollable giggling. Felicity and Roland exchanged glances in which a strong desire to be swallowed by the earth could be read - and not only by themselves: Bettina, noticed it and stopped laughing. As nobody else said anything, the subject at last petered out and died. Only to be replaced by one of Roderick's hobby-horses, the rail workers' union.

"It's a disgrace, that's what it is. If they strike, they could paralyse the whole country! And *you* people," he looked at Esmee and Mr. Forkes accusingly, as if the two of them had been in personal charge of national transportation. "You'll most likely let 'em get away with it.

That's the trouble with this country - too soft. Me, I'd send in the Pinkertons, bust a few heads. That'd sort 'em out."

There was some light of intelligence in the eyes of the solicitor, but Esmee and Roland looked as bewildered as Felicity. She had never heard of a pinkerton, and certainly hoped never to meet one. Bettina and her mother appeared to find something of overwhelming interest in their soup; Mr. Goldsmith was lost in contemplation of a particularly blood-curdling still life (allowed these many years to darken with cigar smoke into the obscurity it so richly deserved). As the children had nothing to add, this subject, too, gave way.

Opposition to Roderick's great idea, which Felicity had been awaiting with some trepidation since the sherry, came from an unexpected quarter. When he began to propound it during the fish course, Esmee blanched, looked to Mr. Forkes for help and received it in the form of an uncharacteristic but reassuring wink; she therefore held her peace. Not so Rosalyn.

"That is the most hare-brained idea I've ever heard," she declared. "You drag me half way around the world, make me leave everything - just to be a - an - an innkeeper's wife...! How do you think the gentry will feel about us? Back home, trade is respected - but here...!"

Bettina wailed: "Daddy! You said we don't have to stay here! You *promised*! You said it's only for a little while -"

"Shut up! The both of you. I've had it up to here with your Goddamn squawking!"

Not only his womenfolk, at whom the outburst was directed, but everyone at table, froze into silence. Roland gaped at the man, his cheeks suffused with the disfiguring hue of rage, half-rose in his seat and was restrained by his mother's grip upon his arm. The two solicitors glanced at one another and then riveted their eyes to their respective plates. Lucy and Lisa swivelled alert heads in unison from face to adult face. Felicity was fascinated by the colour scheme: Roland was flaming red; Rosalyn had turned the exact shade of the tablecloth; Roderick's countenance had taken on a quite alarming tinge of purple. It was Esmee, her fair skin transparent as bone china, who stood up.

"Sir. You are a guest. Therefore, etiquette prevents me asking you to leave my table at once. However, my children and I are not accustomed to such manners - nor do we propose to become so. You will excuse us. Felicity, Roland,"

The two young people rose; with a dignity borrowed from Esmee, placed their napkins atop their plates, pushed their chairs silently under the table and sailed out of the room in the wake of their magnificent flag-ship. Neither had as yet found words, when the family was joined by Mr. Forkes, admiration shining bright in his eyes. He accompanied them to the blue drawing room, where, momentarily, the butler appeared.

"Shall I serve coffee and liquors now, M'lady?" Had Felicity not known better, she might have said Makepeace was positively smirking. Whether or not, he had deserted his post in the dining room – a breach of protocol unheard-of – to wait upon his mistress.

"Just the cognac, I think," Esmee said.

After the little girls had been removed by Maybelle (with considerable difficulty, as evidenced by the scuffling, whining and, yes, profanity, that could be heard upon the staircase) the Other Sommelroux remained in the dining room. Voices were raised, but little of their burden carried to the salon. Once, Bettina's dominated in a short burst: "Well, I'm going to bed!" and a door slammed. Soon, a more measured set of footsteps ascended - that would be Mr. Goldsmith, excused - or possibly escaping. The argument between husband and wife, growing ominously quiet, continued for some time. There being nothing to be learned of its content, the four (five, with Makepeace flitting in and out) repaired to the billiards room for a friendly tournament, dominated overwhelmingly by Esmee. And friendly it was: a little moral victory and two generous snifters apiece had both warmed and cheered the company. In the girl's estimation, Esmee and Roland had risen today. For their part, they appeared to look upon her without reservation, as a full member of the family. As to

Mr. Forkes, he had ever been a fixture taken for granted; now as always, he seemed prepared to fall in with the prevailing Sommelroux mood.

11

Eager as she was to impart the latest information to Aunt Lettie, Felicity could find no opportunity to slip away, until the medical Dr. Gillivray came to examine Cousin Roderick's leg. The invalid had kept to his room all morning; Rosalyn, having the night before demanded a room of her own, remained therein. Trays had been parading up and down the back stairs - even Mr. Goldsmith refrained from breakfasting with the family and had his morning meal by his master's bedside. Roland had invited Bettina for a ride - to distract her, or simply to remove her from the purview of feuding parents. Mr. Forkes, having eaten early and frugally, was closeted with Mr. Finch in the latter's office. Felicity felt it incumbent upon herself to keep Esmee company. Nor was it such an onerous task; the stepmother was more charming to her than at any time since those first weeks of their becoming great friends.

When the little old man had finished and come downstairs, shaking his wizened head, "...ought to exercise it, I told him. That chair, foolish... difficult patient..." Felicity had an idea.

"Esmee, do you think, while the doctor is here, he might visit Aunt Lettie? She seemed a little out of sorts, last time."

Dr. Gillivray pricked up his ears at this. "Lady Letitia? She isn't ill, I trust? Sommelroux are never ill, you know. Iron constitutions. Why, I recall..."

Esmee, setting his mind at rest upon the first point but ignoring further remarks, answered Felicity: "I suppose we ought not to neglect the old dear...." But she said it with a marked lack of vigour.

"I can take him."

"You wouldn't mind?"

"Not at all. I needn't go in - I shall wait at the foot of the stairs."

Kate was therefore despatched with the key; it had become something of a ritual. Through decades, the Palladian wing had been deserted but for periodic raids upon its saleable contents; in these past weeks, it was the scene of almost daily forays by members of the household. Though she made every effort to stay ahead of him, the little doctor nonetheless kept up a flow of talk directed at Felicity, on the subject, mainly, of the Sommelroux and their collective, legendary freedom from illness. How, then, she wondered, had the twelfth earl come to die at forty-four years of age - and the rightful thirteenth, in infancy?

"What did my father die of?" she asked impulsively.

As she ought to have anticipated, this was her companion's chance, previously denied, to seize her hand in both his skeletal ones and peer into her eyes - his own brimming with earnest sympathy. "My dear, dear child! You should not dwell on it. Not at all. Such an unhappy subject..."

"I really ought to know!"

"Well, yes, yes, put that way... perhaps... what with your poor memory gone and all..."

She stared right back with a sincerity to equal the doctor's. "I do so long to recover my last memories of Papa.... Please help."

"It was not a long illness, as these things go.... Oh, my dear, it would be kinder to say sudden, you know... but.... Well. Lord Farwell, contrary to the family history of robust good health, did contract an illness... a, well, a sort of wasting disease.... I must confess. I'd hoped it would never be necessary, but.... You see, Science is not as yet all that it ought to be.... There was really only so much I could do for the poor man. Only to ease his pain... give him some rest. He slept through the last days.... That is to say, most of them... "He continued to clutch her right hand; it was starting to ache. Felicity thought little was to be gained by pressing him further on this evidently distressing subject.

"And my grandfather?"

"There, now, there," the old man brightened, "I can offer some comfort. Well into his seventies, he was, and still active.... Maybe more active than he ought to've been, eh? Had one or two accidents already... I told him... eyesight, reflexes.... Wouldn't believe he wasn't up to it. In any case. I can truthfully say *his* passing was sudden and painless. A fall from the cliff. Yes, yes - dashed on the rocks. Died instantly. No question of it." Was there a certain relish in the doctor's quavering voice, or merely relief that at least one death was not attributable to his own lack of medical skill?

"What was he doing on the cliff?" enquired Felicity.

"Ah that, now that is question itself! Only Lord Farwell could tell us, I'm afraid. Out riding, they say.... He was a wild one! Why, I remember the time he and some cronies.... Well, never mind. Not for tender ears, eh? Oh yes, that last time. Well, it seems the earl was training some uncouth young stallion. Why he would choose the cliff path... beyond me, I'm afraid. But there it is - he did. Then, as I understand it, someone let out the dogs.... Quite a kennel he used to have - the old earl, that is. Master Randolph now, he was never a one for hunting - more the bookish sort. Fine tradition... pity..."

Before he wandered too far into the tangled wilderness of memory, Felicity recalled him to the topic at hand. "Out riding an uncouth horse. On the cliff path. Dogs. Yes?"

"Yes. Yes, well, it seems the dogs caught up with their master, thinking, no doubt, the chase was on, you know.... In any event, the horse was spooked, threw the earl, and ran off. That, in a nutshell.... Horse eventually got back to stables... Hue and cry set up. Body found next morning... and a terrible sight it was, too. Oh, my dear, how thoughtless of me! Quite unsuitable.... And with yourself having gone over the cli- um.... *Do* forgive a silly old man!"

"You have done nothing wrong, Doctor," the girl assured him. "It was I who asked an untoward question. Still, I am grateful for your frankness."

"Never kept dogs after that, Master Randolph didn't. Not a dog on the whole estate, ever since.... Still have them on the farms, of course... got to, I suppose, minding the sheep and so forth.... Why not sell off the horses, eh?"

"Perhaps because they were needed too. To get from place to place, and so forth. And my mother? Do you remember her?"

"Why, certainly I do. Lovely girl... delicate as a flower. So much like the others.... Never mind. Sad story."

"I should like to know more about her."

"Daresay you would, my dear. But only good things, eh?" The little doctor patted her hand absently and sighed. "I wasn't called on much, after that. You see, the old earl.... Well, I think he blamed me, rather. Wrong of him, though. Nothing and no-one could have saved that baby..."

At last, though only in order to excavate an immense white handkerchief from some internal pocket, and with it wipe his glistening pink forehead, he released her hand. Felicity passionately wished that people would not constantly take liberties with that appendage. Having stopped in deference to the weighty topic, she now seized the opportunity to resume their journey. And to lighten the atmosphere, after a little while she asked: "Has it been a long time since you last saw my aunt?"

"Not a *very* long time... some time.... I hardly know. Lady Letitia is never indisposed. Almost never... blessed with the Sommelroux constitution, if anyone is.... She's not overly fond of me, I'm afraid. Likes my brother George, though.... I believe it has something to do with the reverend George's gift of the gab. Never had it myself, at all."

"Are there many other Gillivrays hereabouts?"

"Many? Oh, my dear, dozens. Gillivrays galore!" He paused to chuckle, probably not for the first time, at this small joke. "Outside of female relations - because, you see, they marry and then they're no longer Gillivrays, strictly speaking - cousins, nephews.... The pious George himself - with his lady wife, of course - has produced seven. All hale and hearty to this day, thank the Good Lord. I myself have four children and - let me see now... Elizabeth married a Golightly... Richard, Henry, Albert -

and nine grandchildren. Why, why, there is one in this very house! Young George. Yes, a grandson of mine. And a fine, strapping lad!" The old man beamed as though this profusion of Gillivrays were to his personal credit - as indeed to some extent, it was. Certainly he was more in his element with birth than with death. He would, even now, launch upon a detailed account of young George's entry into the world, had they not - to Felicity's intense relief - arrived at the stone stairway.

Kate, who had been waiting at its foot, nodded for the doctor to go up. "I can show him out," she told Felicity. "You needn't bother."

"But I want to see her, afterwards."

Kate said: "To tell about the fight? It's all right, she knows." The maid smothered an unseemly laugh. "Wasn't it just the most? Like cats and dogs!"

"We couldn't make out a single word from the drawing room," Felicity admitted wistfully.

"We could, from the pantry, clear as a bell. She said if he'd wanted to build an hotel, there was plenty of room in San Francisco *and* without unions to bust. Then *he* said how he conducts his business is none of hers. And how she didn't mind the profits, and hadn't he given her everything? And then she said yes, even a black eye or two. Can you imagine? I can - he's that sort. So then she said she's only been putting up with him because he promised to make her a lady.... Much hope of that, if you ask me! He went on and on about how the place - he always means Twillingmarche when he says 'the place' - ought to earn its way 'cose it costs so much to keep up. And then a lot more of the same.... I could strangle that man!"

"You may have to queue up for the privilege," said her companion. "I think Lady Esmee has first rights. I'm none too keen on him myself."

"Nor's anybody else, come to that. You should'uv seen the face on Uncle Joe!"

"Who?"

114

"My uncle Joe Makepeace. Didn't you know? Of course - nobody tells you anything, do they - if they can help it?"

Felicity agreed, but with a conspiratorial smile added: "Sometimes they can't help it. Evelyn is your sister, I know that much. What's your last name?"

"MacRory. Not *that* MacRory - our dad is farrier, down in Amber. They're cousins."

"I'm not surprised, really. Aunt Lettie said once that everybody in the neighbourhood is related in some way to everyone else. Also, Dr. Gillivray has just been telling me about his family - that our own George is -" She broke off, for Kate was suddenly overcome by a fit of the giggles. "What?"

"Nothing," the other gasped. "Nothing...really! It's a secret. Promise not to tell?"

Felicity replied: "I am very good at keeping secrets."

"So you are. Well, he's not *our* own George – he's *mine*. We have an understanding, see? Only, Da's so old-fashioned, he thinks we ought to wait. I'm seventeen years old, for Goodness' sakes! And George is nineteen."

"But Kate, that's wonderful! He's very handsome." Not quite so handsome, she added to herself, as the senior footman.... Discovering that this pretty, vivacious maid had no possible romantic interest in Edward played some small part in her delight at the confidence. "And so sweet-tempered! Why, who else could be so patient with the beastly Roderick?"

"Yes, but he does suffer, poor lamb."

"Perhaps," Felicity said, more to cheer the other girl than from true conviction, "now that they can't agree, they'll go home. I know Rosalyn wants to. I don't know what Bettina wants - besides being introduced into Society. Perhaps she'll get her way, and they will soon go up to Town. Dr. Gillivray says he needn't be confined to that silly chair anymore."

Kate sighed. "Oh, how I wish they would go... anywhere! But he said no. Very crude, he was. Won't leave those stuck-up fossils - pardon, Felicity; it's what he said!

Won't leave Esmee and Roland and Mr. Forkes to - he said this, too, I swear! - to cook up something behind his back."

"What did Rosalyn answer?"

"She cried a bit, only I guess she was faking, 'cose, right after, she could talk well enough, and loud enough. Anyway, she said this is an awful place and it's not safe for the little ones.... Ask me, those girls are the biggest danger here. She said Bettina will never make a decent match, buried in the country. And he said something not very nice about she didn't seem to mind how Bettina carries on with.... Oh, I'm sorry!"

"It's all right. Roland and I have a different sort of understanding. Go on."

"Oh. And I thought.... Never mind. Anyway, he said, once he'd got hold of the capital, fixed this place up, got rich - he really thinks all that is bound to happen! - then the local gentry will be breaking down his door.... Something wrong?"

"No, not wrong," Felicity replied. "Only, you made me think, just now. Where is the local gentry? Has everyone gone down to London for the season? One would imagine that by now - if only out of curiosity - I would'uv received some invitations. For that matter, why does Esmee never entertain? Is it because of the Americans?"

Kate shook her head. "I don't think so. There wasn't any parties and that last summer, nor even before I started to work here, not for donkey's years."

"Since Lord Farwell died?"

"Yes," the maid allowed judiciously, "that'll be it. They say he was sick a long time, too. Listen. I think the doctor is ready to go. She'll be tired,"

"All right, I'll just pop in for a minute."

Actually, she was no longer aching to relay the news - which was no news to Letitia, and besides, both maid and butler seemed to know a great deal more about it than she did herself. Her mood had lost its buoyancy.

Aunt Lettie being out of sorts as well, the visit was prickly and brief. Felicity was blamed for bringing 'that addle-pated busybody' and her attempt at explanation, dismissed. Aunt Lettie said she had no time for such nonsense. In point of fact, the girl reflected, though she had the presence of mind to refrain from saying so aloud, what else had she but time on her hands? A tapestry as yet unfinished, after years and years of patient work, could hardly occupy all of anyone's waking hours. Meals and gossip, brought by one of three trusted servants, would not fill up much time. What did the woman do all day long? Sleep? Dangle a piece of yarn for her fat cat to play with? Stare out of the window and daydream, like the Lady of Shallot? Possibly her intervals of lucidity were few and far between, to be hoarded.... Somehow this explanation did not satisfy; during their acquaintance thus far, Letitia had not appeared insane, confused or even vague, except as and when she wished to do so. The withdrawn, utterly inactive life that she had chosen - well, it would certainly drive her niece into madness. This, to her immediate regret, she did say aloud. The interview was terminated on a note less harmonious than anything that had yet passed between them.

Felicity, wending her solitary way back to the new house, was filled with remorse, a feeling of abandonment - one might even call it melancholy - such as she had not experienced during her time at Twillingmarche. She did love 'the place'! Something in her deepest, most secret heart identified Twillingmarche as her home. Her fondness for Aunt Lettie was an integral part of that identification. They were kindred souls! To be rebuffed by one for whom she owned such an attachment was - painful, yes, but even more: disorienting, alarming.

Her mind said this was but a temporary setback: tomorrow, everything would be all right again. But her heart rebelled at the prospect of facing Esmee or Roland while she felt this way - not to speak of the unspeakable American contingent. She must have a little solitude.

The Palladian wing was deserted. She had been over the ground floor in minutest detail; Roberts had conducted her through a few and past many of the bedrooms, their sparse furnishings ghostly under dust-sheets.... She had never explored the top floor. That is what she would do now. Perhaps in those commodious attics where the bath chair recently demeaned by the Rodrickian posterior had been discovered, contained odder and more amusing things. The intimate possessions, portraits and garments of long-dead ancestors.... Who knew? - perhaps even a sheaf of love letters penned by a Raymond or Randolph of some bygone age, to his own Esmee or Hortense.

It was therefore to the top floor that she ascended. It was there, somewhat later, that she found herself prisoner.

12

The attic was every whit as interesting as she had hoped, and not nearly so dusty and cobwebby as she had feared. The space was divided into long, narrow rooms along a central corridor. Once, these had been servants' quarters: cramped, too hot in summer and too cold in winter; washing water had to be lugged four long flights up, and down again to discard.... She was glad nobody had to live here anymore. Used only for storage now, each cubicle nearly overflowed with shrouded furniture, orderly even in their crowding; with paintings, stacked against walls.... She would have liked to see, but feared to breach the crates lest she damage something of value. There were trunks full of clothing. One of these contained magnificent gowns of an age long past, some of which looked as if they would fit Felicity quite well with no more than a tuck here, a hem shortened there. And they were more attractive than the modern dresses she discovered in a wardrobe. There was gentlemen's clothing as well: waistcoats and trousers, neatly arranged on hangers and covered in cotton sacking. There was a tallboy full of cravats and shirts and... and more intimate masculine apparel. She quickly closed and turned away from this drawer. These garments must have belonged to someone quite recently - her father? How nicely they had been preserved, how lovingly stored away! Indeed, Lord Farwell and his lady wife must have been blessed with loyal, not to say sentimental, servants. By all accounts, he must have been a gentler, nicer man than Grandfather. There were swaddling-clothes and tiny shirtwaists - very probably from Felicity's own babyhood and the brief, pathetic infancy of her small brother.

And here, propped against a small table, draped in a sheet, was the most elaborate gilt-framed looking-glass that she had ever seen. It would make a fine addition to one's room. She would ask - whom? Mrs. Golightly; furnishings must fall within the housekeeper's jurisdiction -

to have it brought down. Unless it were as valuable as it was beautiful, and then Esmee would take it to sell.... No, she decided; better, after all, to leave this treasure buried - for now. She could enjoy it, meanwhile. No sooner thought than done; Felicity was stripping off her frock, an unbecoming cerise, handed down from Esmee.... Oh, how she longed for dresses of her own! From the trunk, gently folding aside the layers of tissue paper, she chose a delectable froth of sea-green and sky-blue. How well it suited her complexion! How flattering, if perhaps a trifle daring, the bodice; how prettily the green chiffon billowed out as she twirled before the glass! Quickly, she tried on another gown, and then one of the modern dresses from the wardrobe. This, and all its companions, were made for a figure more frugally endowed; nothing could be done to enlarge them. They might fit - not Kate, unhappily - but probably Evelyn, who was younger and slimmer. But perhaps there was more in the yet unexplored recesses of the attic.

How sad, she thought, that all these wonderful things should languish here, idle, unappreciated. And more than sad: profoundly wrong, that only three people should have, and yet be ignorant of, this vast house and its accoutrements. She felt sometimes that she, Esmee and Roland were little more than leaves, floating upon a pond, the depth of which they could not guess, nor influence the processes taking place beneath the murky water. If a chance wind should blow them away, it would make no difference to the pond; its submarine life would continue unchanged. Felicity, once she was old enough to take charge, would have things otherwise. Yet, Cousin Roderick's was not the solution: he meant to uproot all the native plants, eat all the fish.... She was quite pleased with her analogy - she would write it down. It was certainly more clever than those verses in the escritoire.... Had Felicity made up those dreadful rhymes? Well, as she could not have been more than thirteen or fourteen years old, she might be excused.

Oblivious of the passage of time, she went from room to little room, taking stock. She uncovered boxes full of china, silver and glassware; found cedar chests of bed-linen; came upon a carefully-crated chandelier of magnificent proportions; saw, but left for another time, bundles of books wrapped in brown paper and tied with rough jute. Light from the single small window had at first been adequate, and now was growing dim. Of course: this was an east-facing room; it must be afternoon. And she had intended to return for luncheon!

Felicity quickly donned the unfortunate cerise frock and replaced the drapery over what she fancifully thought of as "Mirror, mirror, on the wall". Well, someday soon, it would hang on *her* wall.... Then, with a last glance about to ascertain that all was as tidy as before her incursion, she hurried down the corridor to the attic door.

The handle turned - nothing further happened. She pulled, pushed and twisted, to no avail. On entering, she had noted with some surprise how easily, how silently the door opened: it was not stuck; the hinges were not rusted. The door was locked. Beyond any measure of a doubt, locked. There was no key, either inside or out; she could see the faint light of the landing through the keyhole.

Bewilderment was rapidly developing into fear. She had told no one of her destination; no one would come here, possibly for days - or even months. No one could hear if she called out. She did, all the same, with the anticipated lack of result. She must not panic; she must think. In this vast storage space, there must be tools. If all else failed, she would start an exhaustive search for some implement with which to force the lock. But first, investigate the windows. Yes, she could open them, only they were a dizzying way above the ground, with not even a ledge to speak of: climbing out was not feasible. However, MacRory, or someone, might hear her cries for help. Better to be embarrassed for a few minutes than to be stuck here for heaven knew how long. She could see not a soul in the gardens. The servants would be at their midday meal - except whoever was dispatched to search for her - in all the wrong places. The east side overlooked the kitchen-yard and stables, where was more likelihood of human activity. There, she would go next and try her luck.

But wait! Crossing the hallway, Felicity heard something. A step? She pressed her ear against the unyielding door and held her breath. Yes - soft-footed but unmistakably, somebody was coming up the stairs. "Kate!" she called out through the keyhole, "Kate, is that you? Bring a key! I'm trapped in here!"

"No," a masculine voice responded, "it isn't Kate. And please stop shouting, Miss." A sound of metal on metal, and as she stepped back from it, the door cautiously opened, to reveal Edward.

"Thank Goodness you've come! But how did you know?"

"It was, indeed, Kate who thought you might have wandered away and been lost in this wing. You not having returned from your visit to - to Lady Letitia, and with your well-known curiosity. Begging your pardon, Miss."

Felicity, fully aware of the need to make haste, was nevertheless reluctant to move, to end such a rare chance of proximity. If her feelings were inappropriate, even improper, well, so be it - she would repent some other time. Maybe. "Is Lady Esmee very upset?"

"Naturally, Miss. As who would not be, in the circumstance?"

She protested: "But I only missed luncheon! Everyone misses meals..." The series of expressions on the footman's face stopped her. Surprise, followed by enlightenment, followed by a fleeting smile, immediately replaced by the bland repose which servants cultivate, so that their employers should remain blissfully ignorant of a personality behind the mask.

"You are in error, Miss. The Lady is not distressed by your absence. In point of fact, I do not suppose anyone in the household, with the exception of Kate and myself, was cognizant of it. Nor is anyone partaking of a meal..."

Felicity interrupted. "Oh, do stop blathering! Did something else happen?"

The young man's eyebrows rose at this outburst - if not so eloquently as Makepeace's, even more elegantly. "You heard nothing, then? I suppose you would not; the mishap and consequent uproar occurred upon the terrace of the Victorian wing."

Felicity was almost beside herself with impatience. "What mishap? What uproar? Will you just tell me?!"

"I am attempting to recount the events, Miss," Edward said reprovingly. "Oh, all right, I was only teasing," he smiled, lapsing into a more natural speech. "You know those hideous great stone jugs on top of the facade? One of them toppled over and nearly landed on Mrs. Sommelroux. The other one, not our Esmee. They were taking the air - the Americans were - I think maybe, so they could fight without an audience. At any rate, himself was all purple in the face, the way he gets in one of his tantrums. He'd just stormed back inside; she was a step or two behind. The urn missed her by a hair - she says. Of course, she's probably exaggerating; nobody saw it happen. She was scared half out of her wits. She's having a lie-down now, with a cold compress and a brandy or three."

"But how...? When?"

"A little while ago. Half an hour? As to how...." Edward shrugged. "All the world and his dog's been up on the roof, trying to figure it out. He's hinted, and more than just hinted, that it may have been deliberate - meant to kill her. For my part, I can't imagine who'd want to do such a thing, or why.... If it'd been himself, now, that would make sense. And maybe that's what he's secretly thinking, too - why he's in such a tizzy. Be all that as it may, Mrs. Sommelroux is determined to depart at the earliest opportunity."

This resumption of his butler-in-training diction alerted Felicity to the fact that they were now approaching the new wing; presently, Edward held open the green baize door for her, standing aside with that blank face, that stiff posture she so disliked. Their little time alone was at an end - and they had wasted it on Rosalyn. How tiresome that woman was! But then, at least, the Americans would finally go.

The family, with the exception of the near-victim, was gathered in the drawing room. Cousin Roderick, still in his bath-chair, dominated by sheer excess of volume, blustering to no evident purpose, gesticulating with the hand in which he clutched a glass, slopping dark amber fluid on his wrist. Esmee, pale but composed, sat quiet in her usual place; Roland tried sporadically to interrupt the flow of invective with soothing, meaningless noises. Bettina sat apart, in a huddle with her young sisters, looking as young as they, and as frightened. Masters Goldsmith and Forkes stood tensely aligned with their respective employers, as if squaring off for a fist-fight. Felicity slipped into the room and made her unobtrusive way to stand behind Esmee's chair. That lady reached up and touched her hand lightly, in acknowledgment of her implicit support.

"I propose," Mr. Forkes began, but was drowned out by another spate of wild accusation from Roderick. He waited for a lull, then said again: "I propose to conduct an investigation."

"You propose," Roderick shouted. "*You* propose!? What we need here is a real investigation. Police. Where's the police? Why haven't they been called? That's what I want to know."

"In point of fact," replied Mr. Forkes, "they have. I myself instructed George to fetch the constable."

"Constable," echoed Roderick. "You mean some moron of a back-woods copper on a bicycle?"

"Oh, I hardly think Bernard Golightly ought to be characterised as a moron. Of course, one might send word to the Chief Con - chief of police - in Twillingsford, who would despatch a man, tomorrow or the next day.... But it was my understanding that Mrs. Sommelroux does not wish to remain at Twillingmarche. I would not presume to delay your departure."

Roderick snorted. "I just bet you don't. Well, think again, Fork. My wife may be leaving, and she can take the gals if she wants to, but I'm not going anywhere. You people haven't made a big fat secret of it - you all hate my guts. Well, that sure goes both ways. I've got a right, and I'm gonna see this thing through, even if it does take years in the courts. You can't scare me away, dropping pots off the roof. I want that police chief here - not tomorrow or the next day, but now."

Mr. Forkes heard him out with little visible sign of dismay. Then he said: "Very well. One of the grooms shall deliver a note this afternoon. As to whether the Chief Constable will consider the incident to merit his urgent personal attention - for that, I cannot vouch."

"Horseshit!" Felicity started at the expletive, as she also noticed Esmee and Bettina doing. The very room could almost be felt cringing; of a certainty, it was not accustomed to such language. "I'm going to bring him myself. Goldsmith!"

"Sir?"

"Get the car. George! Dammit, he's not here. Call the other one, Whatsisname."

Mr. Forkes put his head around the door to summon the footman. "Edward, Mr. Sommelroux is in need of assistance to reach his automobile. In the circumstances," he glanced around to Esmee, who nodded minutely, "we should extend him every courtesy. His manner notwithstanding," he added softly.

Mr. Goldsmith and Roderick having slipped away and been removed with great fuss, respectively, Mr. Forkes closed the door. Then, turning, he said: "Possibly Mr. Sommelroux was correct to some small degree. We must wait for the constable. It may be wise to seize the opportunity to take a bit of sustenance."

Esmee agreed; the others followed obediently, scarcely knowing why they did so. Felicity joined the exodus with alacrity; she had only this moment realised how ravenously hungry she was.

Though every one seethed with conjectures and questions on the same topic, none at table felt sufficiently at ease to share their concerns. With neither parent on hand, even the little girls were oddly silent, and Bettina looked so isolated and forlorn that Felicity was moved to pity for her. In any case, all jealousy had gone from her heart; the surreptitious glances passing between Roland and the American girl aroused not resentment but sympathy. She did not want Roland for herself, and Roland did not desire her. In the past hour, secret wish had crystallised into stout resolve: she would never marry Roland. Nor would she ever give up her inheritance. A way must be found for Felicity to have both Edward and undisputed possession of Twillingmarche.

After a short and subdued meal, the children were dismissed to the care of Maybelle. Bernard Golightly, who had meantime arrived and been cooling his heels in the servants' hall, was summoned and taken in hand by Mr. Forkes. It seemed appropriate that the solicitor should be in charge, with Esmee's and Roland's tacit approval.

"Well now, well now," the constable began, laboriously extracting from the inner mysteries of his uniform coat, a crumpled pad of paper and a blunt pencil. "George here tells me there was a haccident."

Mr. Forkes gave a bare outline of the mishap.

"I see, I see. Well, now, I'd best have a look at this here roof, where the whad'youcallem fell off of. Right?"

"Correct," said Mr. Forkes. "This way."

They all trooped up the stairs and along the top-floor hall, past the maids' rooms, through an undistinguished wooden door, and up a narrow flight at the back of the house, of which Felicity had previously known nothing. They emerged, one by one, on the rooftop. It was flat, its expanse broken by clusters of yellow brick chimneys and surrounded by a wrought iron railing, hip-high to Felicity, whose sections joined into square brick columns. Atop these were stone containers shaped like loving cups and adorned with bass-relief garlands of flower and fruit. Having seen them only from below, she had not realised how massive these urns were. Originally eight, now there were but seven. In the centre, dominating all, stood the heroic female figure which, with her arms raised and garments unaccountably swept back- and down-ward, exposing an abundance of shoulder and bosom, greeted visitors to the House, long before they came in sight of the main entrance. The statue, commissioned at the height of the Picturesque Period, was meant to portray Britannia, spirit of the empire. The household staff affectionately called it 'The Lady'. Only at this moment, at close quarters, did the pet name make itself clear to Felicity: there was an unmistakable resemblance between the marble figure and … Esmee! It was not so much a likeness of face, or any physical particular, but one of posture, of attitude, of... how could one put it delicately? Of a flamboyant, bold, defiant presentation of the Feminine.

While she had been reflecting upon this observation - one that, incidentally, she longed to share with someone (Edward, for preference; less improperly, Kate) - policeman, solicitor and the rest had gathered about the empty pediment nearest The Lady's feet. When able to insinuate herself into the semicircle, Felicity saw, as they all did, where two corner bricks were missing, and how the mortar had crumbled away from some of their remaining fellows. Constable Golightly touched the damaged place, rubbed mortar-dust between his thumb and two fingers, tut-tutted softly to himself and made an entry in his notebook. Mr. Forkes imitated all but the last action.

"But, but we had no idea," Esmee protested. "Why, it might have killed any one of us, at any time!"

Mr. Forkes said: "It shall be seen to. The masons shall be summoned, first thing tomorrow morning. In the meantime, I believe it would be wise to remove the rest of the urns."

"And that there statoo," Mr. Golightly said, gazing up at the figure with no little admiration in his eyes.

Reluctantly, Esmee concurred. Mr. Forkes promised to set matters in train immediately. The procession then returned by the way it had come, Felicity bringing up the rear. It seemed to her, pushing at a brick here, tugging at one there, that none of the other plinths were in poor repair; privately she felt that these precautions were unnecessary. She understood, however, why something must be done - and seen to be done. Also, she noted a shallow flight of stairs at the far end of the roof, connecting it with that of the half-storey taller Palladian wing. She would return at the earliest opportunity to explore this hitherto unsuspected dimension of the house. Sadly, that opportunity would not come until the workmen finished dismantling and securing the ornaments - perhaps not for some weeks.

Now, the constable wished to speak to Mrs. Sommelroux. "Alone, if you please. In her bedroom? Ah, well then, somebody'd best come along." Felicity, her curiosity unextinguished by the afternoon's adventure, would have volunteered, but even as she was making up her mind to come forward, Mr. Golightly asked Bettina - and there was justice in his choice.

The interview did not last very long; presently Makepeace, who had been hovering a tactful distance from the proceedings, escorted the policeman downstairs. They all followed him outside, where he prodded the remains of the eighth urn with his boot, cocked an eye at the top of the facade, wrote laboriously, and put away his notebook. "Well then, that's clear enough. A haccident. Pore lady got herself a scare, but no bones broken, eh? You'll see about repairs, Mr. Forkes?" The solicitor, Esmee and Roland chorused yes, indeed, they all would, nodding collectively, co-operatively. "Well then, that's me a-gone. M'lady, Miss, Miss, Sir and Sir...." He touched his helmet to each one in turn, thanked Edward, who had fetched his bicycle, and pedalled off toward the Amber road.

"Put that way," Mr. Forkes mused, placing a solicitous hand beneath Esmee's elbow, "the incident assumes less tragic proportions, does it not?"

His companion smiled, accepting the unneeded support. "Trust common people to have common sense."

Roland, emboldened, perhaps, by witnessing a physical contact, offered his own arm to Bettina, and was not rebuffed. "A little walk to take your mind off things?" Politely, he turned to include Felicity in his invitation, but his eyes beseeched her refusal, which she willingly granted. "I think I shall take a brief rest."

Having both stated and desired it, once in her room, she found rest impossible to attain. Her body was not tired and her mind, all a-twitter with the residue of excitement. There was no activity in the kitchen-yard; a wagon full of barrels had just rumbled away; everybody was gone out of sight. Even Gus the boot-boy had deserted his post; there was no entertainment to expect. She carefully recorded her pond-centred thoughts of the morning. On paper, she believed they still looked rather clever. Now, pen in hand, she caught herself writing:

See how day breaks open the night,
Hear the song of the meadowlark:
All things are wond'rous, fresh and bright,
As light defeats the dark.

See where my Love comes gladly to me,
Over the dew-drenched lawn,
He is beautiful, strong and free,
His smile is like the dawn.

"Twit," said Mary to Felicity.

But I believe he loves me, she retorted, or at least likes me very much. I really think so. It's terribly unfair that Roland, who - let's face it - isn't all that long on intellect, can be so sure of his silly Bettina, while I have to guess about Edward. Anyway, she thought, it's got to be better than the old poems. Though maybe 'dew-drenched' is a bit much, and 'free' may not be strictly accurate.... She would review it another time. She slipped the pages into their hiding place.

When, between tea and supper time, Roderick arrived in his automobile, bearing along a sheepish Mr. Goldsmith and a most uneager plain-clothes policeman from Twillingsford, work on the roof was already well advanced. Before dark, all the urns had been moved from their pediments onto the surface in the lee of the railing. The Lady, more difficult to shift without damage, was swathed in burlap and festooned with ropes. Behind her, a wooden platform was being erected; upon this, with padding to protect her fragile limbs, the statue would be laid - until such time as her plinth could be reinforced to the satisfaction of all concerned.

Roderick was not best pleased by these developments. The detective, an inspector named Markle - for the chief had not, after all, seen sufficient merit in the complaint to come himself - did approve. "The important thing," he said, "is to prevent any further incidents, is it not, sir?"

"Yes, yes," Roderick waved him aside. "But they could have waited! They've wrecked the evidence! You dolt, can't you see? They've done it on purpose - to cover up the crime!"

Inspector Markle visibly hardened with offence at the appellation, but maintained his stoical good manners. "I myself spoke to Constable Golightly..."

"And *that* little detour," interrupted Roderick, "gave them time for all this! It's a damn conspiracy is what it is!"

The officer continued unperturbed, "...who, having viewed the scene, is satisfied..."

"Satisfied! That yokel? He wouldn't know a crime if it jumped up and bit 'im in the arse!"

"...that the occurrence was accidental. He..."

"I've been telling you, somebody pushed that thing off of the roof!"

"...cautioned the householder and agents thereof, to take such measures as he deemed advisable to prevent any risk of a similar occurrence. How- "

"Attempted murder, I'm telling you! Just because they're some kind of big wheels around here, an idiot of a copper believes them!"

" -ever, to satisfy yourself, sir, and to clear up any possible misunderstanding, I should like to interrogate each member of the household."

"That's more like it!"

"I should like to begin, if I may, with the alleged victim."

As Rosalyn had, meanwhile, sufficiently recovered to take tea and was currently ensconced in the blue drawing room with her daughters, it was not necessary for the inspector to go upstairs. "Is there," he asked Esmee, "a room in which I may conveniently conduct some private interviews?"

For the district chief, the library might have been made available; given his relatively modest rank, Inspector Markle was offered the use of Mr. Finch's office. The farms

130

manager was not, of course, consulted in the matter. Esmee did find in herself the grace to order tea and sandwiches brought to the officer. "Feel free to send Makepeace for anyone with whom you wish to speak. Only, do, please, try to keep it brief - we've had a most exhausting day."

"You can say that again," Cousin Roderick, for the first time in living memory, agreed with Esmee. "Before you toddle off, Peacekeeper, get me the whiskey. And leave the bottle."

13

Inspector Markle did not finish his interrogations until close on eleven in the evening. Felicity's own conversation with him was the shortest and most insignificant. She was obliged to admit that she had been, throughout the excitement, trapped in a disused attic.

Instead of showing the least sign of amusement, he asked: "Have you any idea, Miss, how that came about?"

"I cannot say for certain," she replied with as much dignity as the fact allowed her. "I told no one of my intention to go there - did not myself know it, until the moment. It was an impulse, merely. I can only suppose that one of the servants, on some errand or other, noticed the open door and relocked it."

"Are the attics always kept locked in this house?"

"No," Felicity explained, "they never used to be. Only since the two children are here. They *will* get into mischief! We - well, that is, Lady Farwell - ordered the old wing out of bounds, to keep them from coming to harm, you see."

"Very sensible. Such a precaution does not characterize an uncaring hostess, or a negligent householder," the inspector remarked, and after a meaningless exchange of courtesies, would have dismissed her.

"May I ask a question?"

"Certainly, Miss."

"I understand there are quite a few Markles hereabouts. I don't suppose you could be related to any named Joan?"

Startled, the man replied: "Some half a dozen, that I know of. It's a common enough name. Why?"

Felicity performed a young lady's version of a shrug: a slight inclination of the left cheek, a slight elevation of the left shoulder. "A Joan Markle, originally from Gray's Harbour, was once in service here - oh, years ago."

Inspector Markle searched his memory. "It's quite probable," he said at length, "that she was a relation. Some of my people come from down-coast. But I'm afraid we have never been a very tightly-knit family."

"I only wondered," she said lightly, with - she hoped - no discernible trace of the disappointment she felt.

The policeman having no transport of his own, and Cousin Roderick expressing no readiness to return him to Twillingsford, it was decided that he should spend the night and be driven home in the carriage, along with Mr. Forkes and Rosalyn, who planned to take the morning train to London. That Roderick said nary a word about driving his own family was remarked, but not wondered at; husband and wife had barely exchanged a word since the most recent altercation. The scene he had created over her near-accident was evidently motivated by something other than tender feeling. The question of what did motivate him remained open.

Of much closer concern, to at least one member of the family, was Mrs. Sommelroux's insistence upon all of her daughters accompanying her. That she would take Lucy and Lisa, no one either doubted or regretted; Maybelle had already packed their cases, much hindered by the owners' eager assistance. That she would take Bettina, against that young woman's own fervently reiterated wishes, caused much unhappiness. To Roland, obviously - he made no effort to hide it. To Felicity, also - she was certain that with Bettina gone, Esmee would renew the campaign to drive herself and Roland to an understanding, perhaps even to an official engagement. And so, with one thing and another, there was little sleep at Twillingmarche that night. Early in the morning, having partaken of a perfunctory breakfast, all were assembled in the entry hall; even Roderick put in an appearance, however surly. But the children were brighter-eyed than ever and had they been possessed of tails, these would surely be bristling with excitement at the prospect of travel, and at the additional wonder of finding a detective in their midst.

"Are you a Pinkerton?" demanded Lisa. "Are you gonna bust somebody's head?"

Lucy asked: "Have you got a big trunch? Can we see it?"

"Mama was almost killed!" Lisa volunteered happily.

"The Lady threw a big pot at her," added Lucy.

"Which lady would this be?" enquired Inspector Markle.

"The lady on the roof," explained Lisa.

Lucy said: "She's gone now."

The inspector went down on one knee to be at eye-level with the children. In a voice so deep and solemn as to cause all present to fall silent, he asked Lucy: "You saw a lady on the roof, did you? When?"

The little girl nodded, matched his solemnity of mein and trumped him with a sepulchral whisper. "Yesterday."

"Before lunch," added Lisa, her bell-like tone spoiling her sister's effect. "Except we didn't get no lunch, for *ages*!"

Looking into Lisa's eyes, Inspector Markle asked: "Did you see the lady throw the urn?"

Both children shook their heads. Then Lucy, again finding her pace, said: "But she was there!" Lisa reinforced: "An then she went away."

Inspector Markle stood, brushed at his knees and turned to Mr. Forkes, who, smilingly conducted him out onto the terrace. The figure of British Empire was no longer in evidence; she had been laid upon her temporary bed behind the parapet. "The statue which normally stands just in the centre," the solicitor explained, "is affectionately known as 'the lady.'"

"I see," the policeman nodded. "Yes, I see. It would appear, then, that everything is well in hand."

The house was suddenly, strangely quiet. Roderick and Mr. Goldsmith withdrew to the library, no doubt further

134

to plot the ruination of Twillingmarche. Esmee betook herself to her own sitting room with Roberts, where she ordered a luncheon tray brought, indicating an intent to remain sequestered for some time. Roland went out riding, alone with his sad thoughts. Felicity was free to do as she wished. She did not wish to visit Aunt Lettie, with whom she was yet to be reconciled. In the courtyard, Mr. Finch was reprimanding Gus, the boots and knives boy, for some misconduct; as she had no desire to make things worse for the lad by witnessing his humiliation, she hurried on. Men unloading ice from a wagon did not hold her interest very long. At the stables, there was no sign of Will, and she was not about to ask either of the older grooms for a lesson in riding. Desultorily, she wandered through the kitchen garden, where MacRory was busy directing his apprentices in the pruning and training of espaliered fruit trees. Janus was on a ladder with a hammer; Albert was handing up nails and strips of rag.

She might have stayed to watch and learn - today, she was too restless. What, she wondered, lay beyond the greenhouses? The secret garden under the tower? The same to which she had once found the postern gate locked? Was there another way in? It seemed to Felicity that one of the garden's sides was formed by this same greenhouse.

She entered, unnoticed by the gardeners. There was not much here to be seen - vegetable seedlings growing in tidy boxes, dwarf fruit trees in their wooden tubs. Was it not an extravagance, keeping this huge space heated all winter through, when the family would be away in London? Did the servants not disperse to their own homes during the Season? Perhaps not all, and those who stayed would better feed themselves - and Aunt Lettie, of course, who never left - with their own than with imported produce.

Here was a glass door, at the back of the building - for once, a door not locked. Cautiously, she opened it, cautiously looked about. Indeed, this was the little walled garden - and just as charming as it had looked from the tower. There were late roses climbing on the north wall, not yet in sunlight so early in the day, but brilliant with small white blooms. The whole space was divided into neat square beds, stocked with a multitude of she knew not what manner of plant-life. Not vegetables to eat, nor decorative flowers; most of them were leafy things with insignificant, if any blooms on; dark green, moss green and lime green, dusty grey and purplish, nondescript; they looked like weeds.

Somebody was coming through the archway leading to the old abbey. Two somebodies, in fact, deep in conversation. It was their voices alerted the girl, before they might have seen her. Felicity retreated quickly to the greenhouse. Crouching behind a potted shrub, she had a partial view of Edward and Lady Letitia as they emerged from the gloom. Aunt Lettie, outside? Well, after all, why not? Had she not the same need of fresh air as other people? Stairs being difficult for her to negotiate - she had told Felicity as much, but a few days ago - she would require Edward's arm to lean on. Only, she was not leaning now; she was walking briskly ahead of the young man, talking all the while. Felicity could not make out what was said, but the conversation had every appearance of friendly animation. Aunt Lettie indicated one of the beds, which Edward immediately set to harvesting with a small secateurs. The woman, hair tied back, showing a glint of silver here and there when the sun picked it out, carried a basket on her arm. She, too, pulled sprigs from this plant and from that. Dressed in a trim skirt and practical blouse - none of her dark red draperies - she bent agilely to the task. A strange thing, all around. Why should anyone pick greenery without blooms - and unhandsome greenery, at that? More perplexingly, why should anyone pretend to be less able than they were?

Nothing further seemed about to happen; the russet head and the dark one bobbed up and down over their work, occasionally exchanging a comment or a smile. Felicity would have given much to be included in their company, but knew that she must not reveal herself. Aunt Lettie would be angry. Possibly Edward, also. They had become her two most cherished people in the world -

alienating them was the last thing that she wanted to risk. This was another secret. She must wait to be invited to share it. She must somehow earn that privilege.

A tactical withdrawal was in order. To this end, she lightly touched the foliage of a tree, inspected a box of tomato seedlings, pulled a weed from among the lettuces, each gesture a few steps closer to the kitchen garden. When MacRory at last became aware of her, she was idling over a newly-filled cold frame, just outside the greenhouse.

She remarked: "This looks ready."

"Aye," said the gardener. "Got onion sets."

"May I help?"

The morning passed in happy occupation, as Felicity was shown how far apart, how deep, how well tamped down young onion plants should be. MacRory said she had a flair for planting; Felicity glowed with accomplishment. Whatever Roland might believe to the contrary, this was important work. Nothing could be more real, more absorbing - or more pleasant.

After a while, the old man asked: "What do they think?"

"Who?" The girl looked up from her last seedling, hardly more than a green cat's whisker, standing erect and proud, for all its delicacy. "Think of what?"

"Them," he swung a smoothly shaven grey chin in the direction of the house. "You," he looked down at her soil-covered hands. "This."

"Don't know," she said, grinning. "Haven't told em."

"Best wash up in kitchen, then."

"Oh, aye?"

The boys, who had been loafing nearby all the while their overseer's attention was diverted, burst into unabashed guffaws. They were instantly quelled by a MacRory scowl, yet Felicity had already formed a conviction that they were not really intimidated. Respect there was - but no fear. They're probably his nephews or grandsons or something, she thought.

"And get a bite to eat," the gardener told her, without missing a beat or altering expression. He straightened, brushing his palms on the seat of his overalls. "You lot," he tossed over his shoulder at the apprentices. "Clean tools. Lock shed."

The dirt under her fingernails required the vigorous application of a brush to dislodge. She would have to trim them shorter, and remember to rub cream on her hands... if she meant to keep her outdoor activities a secret from the household. Esmee would not approve, nor would Roberts. But did it truly matter? Did they not need her as much as - if not, indeed, more than - she needed them? Her appetite had suffered nothing from the morning's work; she set to with a will. Mrs. MacRory brought forth a fresh-baked pumpernickel loaf, a tub of yellow butter, cheese, cold mutton, cauliflorettes pickled in mustard. None of the dainty slices, either, to which she had become accustomed: this was hearty food, served generously. Mrs. MacRory gave her husband a questioning look before pouring Felicity a portion of brown ale.

"Yes, please," said the girl. "I am permitted wine." Though she had rarely tasted beer before, she found this one admirably suited to the meal.

"Own brew," MacRory gave a satisfied nod, seeing her enjoyment of the beverage. "Best, here'bouts."

As they were only three at table, and at ease with one another, Felicity grew confident enough to ask a question. "Did you always work here?"

"Aye," the gardener answered, "'ceptin my journeyman time at Glendown, south a ways. Herself studied at Pine Ridge, Carter's Arms an such."

"And the Cartwrights? Will told me he was bred up with our horses."

"Aye, Cartwrights, too. Place be infested with um."

"But the maids have only been with us a little while, and Makepeace, and the footmen - even though there are Gillivrays galore." She thought the little doctor would be pleased to have his joke passed on.

The old couple gazed at her intently. "What is't you want to know?" asked the cook.

"I just wondered.... Why are only the inside people new?"

"Ah, well," the woman smiled, "sometimes happen that way."

"I don't think so. I mean, I can't believe it just happened by accident. It seems to me, after Fennimore died..."

MacRory gave her a sharp look. "What d'ye know of him?"

Felicity began to doubt the wisdom of her decision to be frank. And yet, how, without asking, was she to learn anything? And how, having revealed herself thus far, could she now withdraw her trust? "Not much," she admitted. "Only, Esmee wrote letters - while I was away, you know.... " The sharp look had gone, replaced by an indulgent half-smile. "... about how he died, soon after the earl. Was he very old, Fennimore?"

"Old enough," allowed the gardener. "Then what?"

"Then, Makepeace came, and everybody - everybody except you and Roberts."

"Her come with t'Lady."

"I thought so. But all the others, in less than three years? Edward, George, Kate and Evelyn, Becky and Gus - even Mrs. Golightly. While all the people who work outside have been here forever. It seems odd, don't it?"

"Now you mention it," the cook said, "I suppose. P'raps old staff was loyal to Fennimore, didn't get on with new butler. P'raps they give notice, had to be replaced."

"Don't you know?"

"I never meddle, child. Why I've stayed on."

"None of them can remember me from before. Do you? Was I an awful child, like Lucy and Lisa? Or well-behaved and quiet, as the Lady says?"

"Ah, so that's the bee in your bonnet!" said the cook, while her husband nodded, unsmiling now. "That, I can't say, me not knowing you as a tad. The Felicity of old days never did hang about kitchens - nor yards, for the matter of that."

"But," the girl protested, "I recognised you! At least..." She suddenly became confused: where there had been a certainty before she fully realised what she would say, now, hearing it said, she found only doubt. "At least, I knew about you."

"Well, course you did, child," soothed Mrs. MacRory. "Just like we knew 'bout you. But it's not the same, is it, hearing about an sitting down with?"

If she had any further questions, there was no chance to ask them; now the Cartwright boys trooped in, and then the father, for their midday meal, shortly followed by Gus. Noticing her, he snatched the cap off his light chestnut curls, which looked as if they had never known comb. There was something familiar about the boot-boy's freckled, bright face; she had noted it in passing once already, but could not guess to which of the adults he was related. Sometime, when he had overcome his awe of her, Felicity would ask him. Now, she remained only long enough to exchange a courteous word with the horsemen, lest they feel snubbed. "Ah well, that's me a-gone," she announced to general appreciative laughter.

She really must be careful not to fall into the habits of speech that Roberts had worked so zealously to correct. Only, it was so much more comfortable!

There was no comfort at supper. Roland sat like a great lump of immobile misery, picking at his plate and saying nothing. Cousin Roderick was impatient with Mr. Goldsmith, who also had glum lines framing his mouth. Cousin Roderick was impatient with everything: he refilled his own wine glass when Makepeace was a fraction slow to do so; found fault with the roast, which was excellent, as usual; pushed aside the tiny carrots sauteed in butter and dill; wanted more potatoes, and then complained they had too much gravy on them. Esmee, at a loss what to do with such dismal company, turned her attention to Felicity. The girl, though privately reflecting that she would enjoy very much more the same food in a different setting, was in good spirits and did her best to cheer her stepmother. Her diction slipped once only; Esmee frowned warningly, but the men were too preoccupied, each with his own displeasure, to take note.

140

Afterward, Esmee all but commanded, overriding with gentle persistence her son's unwillingness, the young people to dance while she looked on. The older men, much to Felicity's relief, played an apparently unsatisfying game of cards, and then repaired to their respective rooms. In Roland's arms - his mind too far away to require any of her attention; indeed, seemingly unaware of her at all - she closed her eyes and drifted off into a fantasy of sun-drenched gardens. If only these two - grateful as she was to Esmee, fond as she had lately grown of Roland - would go up to London! They would be happier there, she was certain. The woman needed diversion, pretty clothes, society; the boy would come alive again, reunited with his idiotic Bettina. Felicity herself desired nothing more than to be left alone on the estate. It was a vain desire, she knew - for the moment. Eventually, having done her mandatory Season - she had begun to think of that as a sort of penance to be paid, survived, and then forgotten - she would arrange her own life. As mistress of the house, would she be expected to provide entertainment for the neighbouring gentry? Would she be required to attend tea-parties, bridge games and silly masquerades? Perhaps not: there had been no social obligation thrust upon her so far since her return to Twillingmarche. While this suited her temperament, it also seemed odd.

"Why," she approached the problem obliquely, while resting on the chaise longue next to Esmee, "do we never invite people here? Why are we never invited out? My Papa has been dead three years now, surely a decent period of mourning.... Do you not long for company?"

A wistful look passed over Esmee's features, quickly gone and replaced by a tender smile. "Are you lonely, Felicity? Are you very bored?"

"Not at all!" came out a shade too vehemently, but was fortunately interpreted as covering what might have appeared churlish ingratitude. "I only wondered... especially now that Rosalyn and Bettina have gone. Are there no people of our own kind, hereabouts?"

"Of our own kind," repeated Esmee softly, "no. I'm afraid there are none." She shook herself, as one would fluff a pillow, and regained her admirable poise. "Never mind, my dear. We shall soon hear something of this abominable Roderick. Then we may proceed with our own plans."

Felicity allowed the subject to drop. Much has changed in these last few weeks, she thought. We each have different plans.

14

The speedy return of Mr. Forkes brought less relief than might have been expected, and no joy. He had received, at long last, a response from his legal counterparts in America.

"I fear," he said at the impromptu family council that evening, convened as soon as they were able to free themselves of the two remaining visitors, "there is no doubt. The man is proven a legitimate son to the Honourable Raymond, younger brother of the eleventh earl. Far from meeting an untimely end, as had been supposed, during an Indian uprising - Pawnee, I believe, though it may have been some other tribe -"

"Does it really matter," Esmee cut in impatiently, "who *didn't* kill the wretched man?"

"Quite so. At all events, he was merely wounded. He recovered from his injuries and went on to prosper. A certain confusion had been engendered by his use of an abbreviated version of the family name. He was known for a time as Ray Sommer. During their Civil War, he migrated to California and turned his hand to business... as I understand it, with considerable success. Thereafter, he settled in a town named Sacramento - which, as you may not know, has a fine capitol in the Palladian style … "

"Elijah!"

"It is a thriving city," Mr. Forkes continued, unperturbed, "and a busy crossroads of commerce. There, Mr. Sommer founded what the Americans call a livery stable - a changing station for travellers. In due course, he resumed his full surname, married, and begat the present Roderick – in the correct order. I am assured by a source of impeccable repute that the identity and history of both father and son are fully documented." Mr. Forkes, having got all this off his chest, sighed, leaned back, and sipped at his malt whisky.

"Then there is no hope but the courts?"

"That, in a nutshell, is the position."

They both gazed speculatively upon Felicity. The stepmother gave her an encouraging nod. The solicitor, however, frowned. "There is yet worse to come," he said. "As I have been enquiring after the American Sommelroux, so has Mr. Goldsmith been busy, investigating our own branch of the family. He is but lately in possession of a letter from Eastmills House."

A noise, not unlike a muted hiss, escaped the lady's lips. Brief, furtive glances were exchanged. The room became unnaturally hushed. Then Esmee, striving for, and just missing, a casual note, remarked: "Wouldn't the two of you enjoy a game of billiards?"

"Not really," answered Roland.

"Please, Darling, do as I ask." Her tone was silken, but the blue of her eyes was the colour of steel.

Felicity, reflecting that, though she had done all that was asked of her, they did not yet trust her entirely. Nor, in fairness, had she been altogether candid with Esmee. She took comfort in the intelligence that Roland was excluded as well. She saw that Roland, too, would wish it otherwise: as they exited the drawing room, he lingered, waiting for conversation to resume inside. It did so, shortly, but at a volume so reduced as to make its content indistinguishable.

"What d'you know about Eastmills?" Roland demanded, once they were in the games room. He was racking up balls by touch alone, his eyes never leaving Felicity.

"I have been there," she replied thoughtfully. "There were nuns, and a school of sorts, a chapel - that was lovely, the chapel - and an orphans' home."

Roland left off his work at the table. "Really? Are you sure? I always thought they'd made it up."

"Who did?"

144

"Mater and Forkes, who else? After you d-" He broke off in confusion. "I mean," he stammered, "after she...you... disappeared. Is that where you really were? At a convent?"

"Certainly. But that was long ago - my recollections of it are but sketchy, unreliable. I spent only a short time there."

"You were lucky, then. I remember every minute of Bloody Bloorsley - sorry, but that's what all the boys called it. My school. Three endless years!"

The pain was raw, still recent, she could see. "If it was so awful, why did they make you stay? Esmee surely wouldn't let you suffer if she could help it,"

"Well, she couldn't help it, could she?" He met her steady gaze and, finding sympathy there, softened his voice. "Mater wanted me sent to the Governor's old school - Eton, you know? Only, one's got to be signed up at birth, or something... Anyway, he got me into Bloorsley - I daresay he meant it for the best, and I didn't complain - it would only've made her unhappy - and him, well.... I didn't want him calling me ungrateful... So, I had to stay, while he lived. If they'd only got another boy... "

"Did you wish my little brother had lived?"

"Oh, Lord, did I! Sorry, Felicity - Mater would give me proper aitch for the way I'm talking to you."

"It's perfectly acceptable; I have heard of The Lord. I don't see why Reverend Gillivray should be allowed to talk about Him in front of everybody, and yet we, in private, should not."

Roland smiled, took her hand. She did not object, for unlike so many others, his was a light hold, warm but unpossessive. "You're all right, really."

"Well, go on. Didn't you like being the only son?"

"No, I did not. For one thing, I wasn't, if you know what I mean. Not a true Sommelroux. The Governor did pretty much anything Mater wanted, once the old man was gone - he did love her, I guess.... But he drew the line at adopting me. I didn't mind about that - he was no more a father to me than I was a son to him."

"Was he not a kind man, my Papa?"

"Kind?" Roland shrugged. "He never hit me, nor ever whipped a servant or a horse, for that matter - didn't even raise his voice much. I suppose he was kind enough. But cold, you know? Except to ...um... you - but that was different."

"Papa was especially fond of me."

Roland gave a sharp bark of a laugh. "You can say that again! When the two of you were together, nobody else might as well have existed."

"I wish I could remember," the girl sighed.

"I wish you could, too."

While Lady Farwell and her faithful solicitor were of one mind in all things, this appeared not to be the case with Cousin Roderick and his own lawyer. A disagreement of some kind had taken place, a sour note been struck. Whereas, before, they had shared confidential discussions at least three times in any given day, now they met only over meals, and that, in virtual silence. There was a perpetual gloom about Mr. Goldsmith; his responses to his employer were dutiful merely, without alacrity. When Roderick held forth, unmindful of who heard, or how those hearers might be affected, about his plans for Twillingmarche, Mr. Goldsmith would no longer make helpful suggestions, nor embellish the proposal with details. From time to time, he would attempt to broach the subject of the Sommelroux marriage. Roderick would then snort, wave his hand in the air, pour a snifter, and resume discourse upon a topic of his own interest. However, by dint of sheer dogged persistence, the lawyer was at length able to prevail.

"All right," Roderick said wearily, "I'll go. Won't do much good, but I'll see her. If she won't come back, she won't, and that'd better be the end of it. Then, I want you to knuckle down, or I'll find someone else. Got it?"

"I understand," the lawyer said.

"While you are in the London area, sir," Mr. Forkes suggested mildly, "you might like to visit Brentwood."

"Why?" demanded Roderick. "Don't know anybody in Bentwood."

"Brentwood," corrected the solicitor gently. "We have a little place near there..."

"Who's we?"

"Actually," Mr. Goldsmith said, "Mr. Forkes refers to the estate. I have informed you about these holdings -"

"Yes, yes, you mumbled something. House belonged to somebody's ex-wife - that right?"

Mr. Goldsmith had the grace, though his dark complexion did not lend itself to a Roland-style blush, to colour slightly, glancing up under dark eyelashes at Esmee, but going on, if quietly. "It was part of. Lady Beatrice Partridge's legacy. On the maternal side. Two hundred acres. Park. Twelve-acre lake, suitable for sailing. Eighteen bedrooms. Gatehouse. Outbuildings."

"Okay, I remember. So, why would I go out of my way to see it now? It's pulling in a pretty fair rent, for the time being. Better than this place, anyway."

Mr. Forkes said: "Indeed. However, as the lease comes up for renewal in the New Year, and as the property is admirably situated, perhaps you would care to consider it for development."

"As what?"

"Well, we thought," Mr. Goldsmith began, faltered, steeled himself and, in spite of his employer's scowl, continued, "possibly. For a private clinic. It's close to the city. Very convenient. Better climate. Nice countryside."

"And," Mr. Forkes added, "should you feel that the present building is inadequate, investment funds for expansion might be made available, so I am given to understand, at an eminently favourable rate of interest."

Cousin Roderick nodded his head up and down several times. "I get it," he said. "Sure, I'll have a gander, if there's time."

The cast having been removed but a few days before, Roderick's leg was still some way short of full recovery. As he would not entrust himself to Mr. Goldsmith's driving skills, his only option was the train. There was as yet no strike date announced; the journey was in little danger of being upset. This did not, however, prevent Roderick from holding forth upon the dire, if purely theoretical, judgment that would be visited upon the trade unions if they should inconvenience him, if this were the United States, and if he were in charge....

George returned from the trip to Twillingsford with an expression of serenity long absent from his features. Everything was, at least for a short while, normal again. Maybelle was sent back to her parents and siblings; Jane, liking the work, remained as kitchen maid, while Becky was promoted to vegetable cook.

Felicity, being at long last in possession of a reasonably full and becoming wardrobe, was able to have her first riding lesson under the guidance of Will Cartwright. She would not go so far as to call herself a natural horsewoman - the task proved rather more difficult than gardening - but she did not fall off, or otherwise disgrace herself. Just as Will had promised, Petunia was a docile animal, tolerant of her rider's indecision. And, while it was somewhat early to comment, the new rider herself had a premonition that this could be a pleasant activity. After one or two more attempts, she would invite Roland to join her. Some day, she would get him to show her all the infamous sites: where Roderick had the stone roll out from under him, where Grandfather had gone over the cliff, perhaps where she herself had disappeared… Someday. All in all, the rocks round about Twillingmarche were a treacherous lot; perhaps, until she became somewhat more secure in a saddle, she ought to stay well clear of those places....

She was able, however, to pay a visit to her aunt again. Lettie was in high spirits this time, their last unhappy meeting long forgotten. Felicity was not so foolish as to make reference to her most recent bit of spying, nor to the secret garden. But she could speak freely enough of the large one, and of her part in populating it.

"My vegetables are the best!" she enthused. "MacRory let me keep the first cold frame. It's only small, but I have planted lettuce, radishes and green onions in it. I water them every day, open the cloche in the morning and close it at night.... Some days, you can just about measure how much they've grown. Don't you ever miss your plants, Aunt Lettie?"

Lady Letitia started slightly, though the girl's motives were wholly benign. Then she said: "Oh, you mean, the little solarium? No, I can't say I think of it much. After all, they're only plants - you can't make pets of them."

"Why not? They're pretty, and they need loving care."

"All right then," the older woman said, "what do you intend to do with these pretty lettuces of yours?"

"Why, eat them, of course. When they're old enough."

"Precisely. Therefore, it seems to me, you ought not to get over-fond of them."

"Oh, it isn't like that," Felicity groped for an explanation. "It's not as if I'd given them names.... Anyway, I'm starting to like horses now and I know the difference." It dawned upon her then, just how idiotic this must sound, and wondered whether that had been her aunt's intent. "You're pulling my leg, aren't you?"

Letitia smiled. "What a quaint expression."

"It's American, I think. Roland uses all kinds of American expressions lately. He misses Bettina dreadfully, poor thing. I sometimes wonder if he can ever be happy at Twillingmarche."

"Though you seem to have made quite an attachment, young... Roland's state of bliss, or otherwise, does not concern me very closely. Are *you* happy here, Felicity?"

"Oh, yes, Auntie!" She flushed with pleasure at the revelation that her own feelings were of concern to Lettie. "I don't think I could be happy anywhere else. May I tell you a secret? I believe that I was always meant to live here."

"Perhaps so," the other allowed. "Now, tell me about this Roderick. He has gone?"

"Only for a few days. His lawyer convinced him to try to affect a reconciliation with his wife. Either he will return - or they all will!"

"That's bad," said Aunt Lettie. "He is disruptive."

"You can say that again! Sorry, it's another Americanism. Do you know what he wants to do to the house?"

"Yes. And it is out of the question."

"Maybe he'll like Brentwood. Mr. Forkes and Mr. Goldsmith seem to agree that it's more suitable." She added ruefully: "I'd never even heard of it before."

"Well, you can't expect to know much, at your age."

"It is a nuisance," the girl admitted, "ignorance. I am trying to find out more of what I ought to remember. Other people tell me what they think is important, but nobody can tell me the - the..."

"Personal experience?" Lettie helped her out. "No, they can't. You must discover that for yourself."

"Last Sunday, after church, I went to see the graves. Everyone seemed to think it a daft thing to do."

"And?" Letitia looked interested, not condescending.

"Well, I went anyway, because it seems to me I ought to visit the dead relatives. To pay respect, you understand, not just for curiosity. I've seen them once before - a long time ago - anyway, old Lord Farwell's - your dear Papa's, I mean. His monument is very impressive. Did you ever notice the angel on its top?"

"Noticed it? I was present when they set it up."

"Isn't it... don't you think it looks - " She checked herself before the cherished name slipped out; that observation was not yet ripe to share, even with Aunt Lettie. " - very beautiful?" She quickly changed tack: "Of course, my papa's monument is elegant, too. But it was also sad - all those tiny graves.... Not just little Raymond; there must have been a dozen - from long before."

Aunt Lettie nodded. "Yes, it was sad. Those were to be my brothers and sisters. Only three of us lived, all girls. Our mother was not strong enough to keep having more. My dear Papa could never accept it - a son was of paramount importance to him."

The girl said: "Finally, he got one. But at what price! He must have suffered terribly from guilt, when she died. Oh! I'm sorry - I shouldn't have brought it up. Only, thinking

150

of it - having babies, you know - frightens me a little....
Perhaps you were wise not to marry."

Lady Letitia refrained from comment.

Soon, they went on to more agreeable topics.
Felicity quite immodestly detailed her recent feats of
horsewomanship and her aunt demonstrated the correct
way to wind yarn onto a shuttle.

In her absence, Roland had also been out, doing
something he refused to discuss, but which appeared to
give him a private satisfaction like the proverbial cat's
encounter with the canary. Having completed a more than
usually pleasant family tea, Felicity brought forth the hefty
volume of photographs that she had found in the library.
She had removed it surreptitiously to her own room and
had already puzzled out many of the events there
recorded, had already put names to most of the persons
there immortalised. Perhaps she had never been meant to
see it. But, if so, why was it left ready to hand? If, however,
there was no secret attached to the album, why had
Roberts not given it to her long ago? Now she felt sufficient
confidence in her status to ask.

"I wish that we had thought of it," said Esmee.
"Why, I haven't seen this myself in years!"

The two women settled, shoulder to shoulder on
the chaise longue; the one to learn, the other, to reminisce.
Roland, quickly bored, went in search of more active
amusement; Mr. Forkes had excused himself some while
before.

"This is the old Lord Farwell," Esmee indicated a
sepia daguerreotype in the first pages, "as a young man,
with his first wife."

"Aunt Lettie looks more like her father."

"All the Sommelroux children do," said Esmee.
"There he is again."

"And the other?"

"Why, that must be the Honourable Raymond. I
never met him, of course, but the resemblance is striking.
He must have left for the colonies soon after this
photograph was taken."

"This would be Lady Hortense. How young she was! And here," Felicity pointed out a babe in heavily embroidered christening robes, surrounded by a doting family, "is Papa! You can tell by the proud grin on Grandfather's face. Those must be Dorothea and Penelope, with Letitia in the middle."

There were many representations of the only son: as a tiny boy in a sailor suit, with hoop and stick, in bathing costume; as a solemn eight-year-old in school cap, in cricket uniform; as an adolescent, astride a mettlesome horse; with his sisters at a garden party; in Oxford cap and gown. In contrast, the girls were recorded at their christenings and confirmations - otherwise, they were seen only on the fringes of events featuring Randolph.

"Grandfather didn't much care for his daughters, did he?"

"I don't suppose," said Esmee, "he considered females very important. And in the end," she added under her breath, "they all let him down."

"Perhaps that's why they did," the girl speculated. "But wasn't Papa handsome!"

"Oh yes," the widow sighed. "This was many years before I met him, naturally." Esmee flipped the gold-edged wedding photograph. Felicity made no attempt to interfere; she had studied the first Lady Randolph often and long. The bride appeared no older than Felicity was now, large-eyed and fragile. On the opposite page was her only other portrait, done in tender pastels. She was seated in a garden chair, holding a small white dog upon her lap. Felicity had been able to feel no bond of kinship with this ethereal whisper of a girl.

"And there I am!" But for the revealing tint or tone, depending on the age of the pictures, any of the Sommelroux babies might have stood in for any other, so alike were they in the heirloom christening gown.

There was a procession of people wearing black, led by the stout patriarch, with a pale and solemn Randolph at his elbow. A christening, quickly followed by another funeral. This was a sad page, to be hurried past. Then, more pictures of Lord Farwell and of his vigorous,

152

good-looking heir: riding, leading the hunt, their coats painted as pink as their cheeks; in plus-fours and tall boots, each with a shotgun slung over his shoulder. Nothing of a little girl in pinafore and ringlets, until the next wedding. Felicity was charming as a flower-girl; Esmee, as bride, was quite spectacular. Over this photograph, she lingered fondly.

"The old man was *not* pleased," she recalled. "But Randy got his way - he usually did."

"Where is Roland?"

"With his grandmother." The tone of Esmee's voice was so final as to leave no room for pursuit of the subject.

The next event, fully recorded, even to a fine portrait of the white marble monument and its angel, Felicity surmised, was not so tragic for Esmee as it must have been for the newly-ascended Lord Farwell. While nothing could be made of her expression behind the black veiling, he looked ready to weep. And justly so: had he not, within five years, lost a wife, an infant son, and now, a doting father? Was it any wonder, then, that he would soon begin to find solace in the company of his surviving child? It was surely so, for now there appeared one photograph, then another, and then many more, of small Felicity - with Esmee, with Papa, frequently by herself.

"Randy had got a camera," her stepmother explained. "He was forever playing with the thing or hiding in his dark-room. He did so enjoy new gadgets! And look: this was one of Felicity's presents on her tenth birthday."

"A camera?"

"A Kodak Brownie, all the way from America. It was the latest thing."

There now came many - rather inexpert, poorly-centred, some with major body parts missing altogether - small brownish photographs of the twelfth earl. And many more, of considerably better quality, interspersed with the likenesses of Esmee and the house, representing the young girl. The Felicity who saw them now would have spurned the outfits she wore, which tended strongly toward Bettina-like flounces and lace, but she had to admit that Will's assessment was not far off the mark: she did look like a princess. She looked increasingly, too, like her father. There was one especially moving studio portrait of the two, arm in arm, as if stepping out on the promenade, the girl's frilled parasol making a halo for heads expertly tinted to approximate their identical vivid colouring. How happy they seemed, and how affectionate!

Then, suddenly, with yet one more funeral procession, the album ended; only blank pages followed. Esmee sighed. "I suppose that was why I put it away - I didn't like to think of this."

"You must both have missed him dreadfully," said the girl.

While none of the family had expected life at Twillingmarche to continue so peaceably for long, Cousin Roderick's return was an even worse shock than they had prepared for. The reconciliation with Rosalyn having come to naught, he was in a foul temper all the time now; more than ever overbearing and rude. And he was more than ever impatient to proceed with such of his plans as were possible without legal sanction.

"I want an estimate," he told Esmee, "that's all. You can't stop me. That Bentwood place is hopeless. Anyway, it'll keep a few more years, the way it is.... Probably subdivide the land, later on, make a couple of dollars - sterlings - whatever. House will fetch a pretty good price. But it's nowhere near big enough for what I want."

Therefore, it became necessary for the sake of domestic harmony, to accede. After some further argument, wherein Mr. Goldsmith expressed reluctance to undertake the mission and Cousin Roderick maintained that such an errand was beneath his own dignity, the lawyer - a glum, taciturn shadow of his former self - was despatched to Twillingsford to contact the firm of Landry and Cartwright, Masons. "Make sure," his employer instructed, "to get the top man, whichever it is. Both, maybe. I don't want to deal with underlings."

Mr. Goldsmith chugged off in the automobile. He was expected to return with the master builder - for whom accommodation must be found - before nightfall. At supper time, there was no sign of them. Nor at breakfast, although Felicity amused herself by imagining the two - or three - men, locked inside Saint Hilda's, shouting vainly for release.

At last, word arrived at mid-morning by no less a messenger than Constable Golightly. He dismounted his bicycle, puffing, dark red of countenance, sheepish of mien, and requested audience with the lady and Mr. Sommelroux.

"He's not injured," the policeman hastened to reassure them. "Not to say *really* hinjured - a few cuts and bruises, bump on the head.... Doctor Douglas is ready to release him, if you be kind enough to lend transport, M'Lady."

"Yes, all right, I shall send a carriage," Esmee said, not in her most enthusiastic tone. "Can you tell us what happened, exactly?"

Golightly fished out his notebook and read off the salient details. No great mystery was thereby revealed: the vehicle had run off the road on the last steep descent to the shore and hit a tree. Fortunately, this had occurred within a mile of the town, so that help arrived speedily, and the lawyer was rushed by ambulance to the Twillingsford hospital. Upon arrival, he had been conscious and able to recount his escapade to those present, who then sent for a representative of the local police. The constable before them now was, in fact, retailing third-hand information. "But the Twillingsford chaps are on the job," he added. "Questioning witnesses and so forth. It's got to be looked into, seeing as there might be suspicious circumstances. The victim al-leges," he carefully read, "that the brakes on the vehicle in question were kept in perfect working order at all times, and that said brakes, on this occasion, failed suddenly. Therefore, the vehicle has been imp-pounded, taken under the hauspices of duly cons-ti-tuted local authorities, to the premises of Markle and Sons, Automobile Repair. There, said vehicle is to be inspected by a qualified mechanic - to wit, John Markle Senior - in the presence of a hofficer of the law. Said vehicle shall be released to the owner, immediately said inspection is completed, barring the discovery of foul play, in which event it is to be 'eld in hevidence." Having completed this remarkable recitation, the constable heaved a massive sigh, interred the notebook in the depths of his tunic and asked Makepeace for a glass of water.

All eyes came to rest upon the astonishingly quiescent Roderick. "He never could drive worth a damn," was that man's verdict.

15

More astonishingly still, Mr. Goldsmith, when the carriage driven by George and occupied by Cousin Roderick, arrived at Twillingsford Hospital, declined to be transported. He would not under any circumstances return to Twillingmarche. Rather he would, as soon as he felt sufficiently recovered, go to London - thence to take ship for his native continent.

"Bastard's changed sides," Roderick was heard to fulminate, "that's what it is. Wouldn't put it past him to take on Rosalyn's case... thick as thieves.... "

Nothing deterred by these events, however ("Who needs him, anyway?"), Roderick pressed on. While in town, he arranged a meeting with the builders; Mr. Landry was expected within the week to inspect the house and to give an estimate of the time and cost of remodelling it. Finding a new solicitor would seem to be a more difficult proposition, but Roderick had the situation well in hand; he had already approached the redoubtable firm of Gormley, Gormley, Palmerston and Gormley.

Missives arrived and were dispatched by almost every post. Needless to say, easily half this volume of correspondence belonged to Roland - more of the outgoing than of the incoming, yet Bettina, too, was keeping up her end. George, whose regular duties included fetching the mail from Amber, seemed rather to enjoy than to resent the increased demand upon his services.

"And, what d'you think?" he regaled the servants' hall at mid-morning tea with the latest news. "Today, he's got one from Vesey Brothers, Confidential Enquiry Agents."

"What's he want from them?" Mrs. Golightly wished to know.

"Well, I didn't open it, did I?" replied the indignant footman. "T'were a skinny thing, though - one sheet of good paper, I'd say."

"P'raps he's put them onto his wife," Mrs. MacRory guessed.

"And that Goldsmith character," added the housekeeper. "He's gone to the city. I wouldn't be surprised but there was something between those two."

"Wouldn't blame her much," the cook said, "married to that - that - Boer."

"No wonder he needs different lawyers, then. Still, no matter Gormley's be a respectable enough English firm, it's the Goldsmith knows all about his business."

"It'll be tricky, that divorce - cost him dear."

"Serve him right," was Mrs. Golightly's opinion. "He should have never treated her so rough."

Felicity knew all of this, not an hour later, from the faithful Kate, who, having been silently attentive in the presence of her betters, was able to retail conversations with admirable accuracy of detail. By now, Aunt Lettie, too, would have been apprised of new developments; the information network below stairs was a remarkably efficient operation. The girl did not overlook or take for granted her own immense good fortune in being included, nor underestimate Esmee and Roland's loss. Did they realize that all of their movements were carefully observed, their whereabouts, always precisely known, their activities, extensively discussed? Certainly not. Roland would flush the colour of a ripe tomato, were he to overhear some of the servants' remarks. The footmen seemed to find vast amusement, for instance, in his clandestine visits to the old woodshed on his way to or from the stables. Everyone in the household was aware of his fascination with the automobile, his yearning to own such a thing himself. Felicity was more sympathetic; she wished they would not poke fun at so natural an interest. Especially if, as she suspected, at least one of them secretly wished that he could drive it into Amber for the post.

She was aware that her own movements were noted by the staff. Nor had she ever, since that one, first time, tried to conceal anything from them. This might help to explain why she enjoyed such an exclusive privilege. Or, possibly, the servants recognised, without fully understanding the reason behind it, her own identification with their side. For, sides there were, separated by a great, solid wall of tradition. Perhaps she had inadvertently found a champion in Aunt Lettie, who had always been in their confidence. And how or why that unheard-of exception should have come about had yet to be discovered. Tactfully, of course - she would not jeopardize her cherished position atop that wall, not though she was burning to know so much more. It would all come clear in its own good time.

So, Cousin Roderick had hired new lawyers and a confidential inquiry agent! Felicity hoped Rosalyn and Mr. Goldsmith between them would give him no advantage, but a terrible time in the courts. And what of Roderick's proceedings against herself? That case would now be in the hands of solicitors more formidable than the self-effacing Mr. Goldsmith. There occurred to her, too, another possible purpose of a private investigation.... She would talk to Esmee and Mr. Forkes. They must finally confide in her. They must be made to understand that she was not a mere pawn but an active participant; that her interests were inextricably bound to theirs. And how effectively were they to serve those interests, if one party was kept in the dark?

There had been a letter from Eastmills. Its contents cannot have posed a threat to her own ends, else Roderick would certainly have commented; it was not in his nature to forego an opportunity to crow. In point of fact, he had done quite the opposite: of latter days, more especially since the departure of his legal advisor, he had made an effort to be charming. He had, on several occasions, engaged Felicity in - for him - pleasant, inconsequential chat. While these sporadic approaches were less than welcome to the girl, she interpreted them as a sign of weakness on his part. If

Roderick were not so secure in his position as he had initially appeared, that was all to the good.

"I have been at Eastmills," she told Esmee, without preamble. They were at last alone in the other woman's chambers after a tedious luncheon with Roderick and his plans, Roland and his melancholy abstraction. Roberts, tiptoeing around the dressing room, fussing with freshly-ironed apparel, did not matter; Roberts had all along been privy to Esmee's schemes.

The stepmother's surprise was swiftly overcome; it was not beyond imagining that she had half expected something of the sort. "Oh, yes, I know. Only for a matter of weeks, though, and the nuns had no clue as to your real identity."

"Have I also been at Alpenweiss?"

Esmee smiled. "Not as a Sommelroux, naturally."

"Naturally. Only, how did all your sweet letters find their way to me?" Esmee smiled again, enigmatically. It was not necessary for her to respond; at this moment, Felicity herself supplied the answer. "Of course! The salutation is always something like 'My Dearest Daughter'. The letters could have been addressed to any name. What was it? And where are the envelopes?"

"A nurse removed them. In your condition - unable to remember your own name - a different one on your correspondence would have been confusing. Madeleine Shelley Talbot. Do you like it?"

"Not very much. There was a Madeleine in one of the novels Roberts gave me. Does she exist?"

"Is it important? Yes, she does. I happen to be on friendly terms with the Talbots. They would prefer not to have their child's affliction broadcast to the world; the clinic was chosen, in fact, for its discretion, more than any other single factor."

"You mean, they won't reveal the history of patients?"

"Nor anything else. Dr. Weiss is a man of unshakable integrity. However, Mr. Goldsmith has been permitted to ferret out some information at this end - certain payments made by Mr. Forkes every quarter...."

160

"Ah!" Felicity laughed out loud in quite unladylike manner. "The Talbots kept their secret by sending money through a go-between, but it looks as if you were paying the fees. And now that I'm back?"

"The arrangement was altered somewhat."

"Has Madeleine been spirited away to some other clinic? Yes, of course. If Mr. Goldsmith inquires, she's gone. Oh, wait. You said, unshakable integrity.... Dr. Weiss doesn't know. And the nurse...?"

"Still has the envelopes, all duly stamped and post-marked. She *might* give them up, for a... financial consideration."

The girl clapped her hands. "Oh, but that's brilliant!"

Esmee sighed, her gaze lingering on Felicity. "We were given to understand that you're not particularly - ah... quick. We were grievously misinformed. You are really a very clever girl, aren't you? Ah, well, I suppose it's for the best. Perhaps it makes you a greater asset than one had expected."

Should she, in gratitude for Esmee's candour, reveal the most recent assault upon their common cause? No, for that would implicate other allies. In any case, Mr. Forkes must surely be abreast of developments. "What was Goldsmith looking for, at Saint Hilda's, d'you know?"

"Parish records, I should imagine - births, deaths and marriages. They're all in perfect order. By the way, do be careful of your speech - I have been noticing the odd slip."

"Yes, Esmee."

"Good girl. Also, you must be more gracious to your cousin. I know it's a chore! But, think; under the flattering attentions of a pretty girl - yes, you are, and he does have a roving eye, that man - isn't he likely to reveal more than he might intend? Had we not better be forewarned of what he knows and what he plans?"

"Yes, I do see your point." It was Felicity's turn to sigh. "Chore is hardly the word for it - but I shall do my best."

She was able to put this resolve into action directly after church on Sunday. Roderick had only the previous day received his automobile, fully refurbished, from Mssers. Markle and Cartwright. It had been but lightly damaged by its encounter with a roadside tree. The grille and headlight were now replaced, as well as the brake-fluid line. In the mechanic's opinion, officially recorded by the Twillingsford constabulary, the thin metal pipe had sustained a fracture, causing a slow leakage of fluid. The crack might have been caused by a sharp blow, such as might occur when driving at speed over rough terrain, the tyres throwing up stones underneath the chassis. This was no more than speculation on his part, the mechanic admitted, but reasonable speculation, given that county roads were of less than ideal quality for use by automobiles. He and the police were satisfied that Mr. Goldsmith's accident was no more than that. The vehicle was now whole and perfectly safe. Roderick proposed to put it to the test, inviting Felicity along.

"Keep me company, Pretty Cousin. It's awful lonely round here, these days."

Well, she *had* promised Esmee.... But she did have a certain trepidation, both of the machine and of being with this uncouth relative, far from the house - and unchaperoned. "Yes, all right," she said brightly. "Let us bring Roland, too!"

Far from leaping at the opportunity, however, that young man seemed strangely reluctant. Felicity's attempts at persuasion fell on deaf ears. In the end, Esmee had to issue what amounted to a command before he would agree. He, who had always been so keen on motorised transport! Perhaps, she thought, it is that some other man is to be in control of the machine puts him off. No matter; silent and glum in the rear seat, while the girl had perforce to sit next the driver and make such enthusiastic comments as she could muster, he was nevertheless present. She did not so much enjoy the trip as endure it: the roads were, indeed, less than ideal; the bumps and jolts, frequent; the noise, deafening; the velocity, daunting. Unskilled as she still was in the art of riding, Felicity decided that she much preferred horses.

The journey itself gave little scope to conversation; the truly difficult portion of the outing came when they stopped. Roderick had had the foresight to order a basket lunch, complete with wine, of which they were to partake under some pleasant shade by the roadside. Evidently, he had not anticipated Roland as a member of the party; there were but two each of plates, glasses and cutlery. The interloper, pleading lack of appetite, set himself some little way apart, gnawing a drumstick moodily. Felicity concealed as best she could her deep displeasure with him; she intended to give it voice later, in private. Meantime, what could she do, but act graciously?

"It's an interesting way to travel," she said.

"Interesting, ha!" rejoined Roderick. "It's the *only* way. I'm telling you right now, the horse and buggy's dead. Even the railroad. That's a mess, anyway, in this country. Back home, we know how to deal with troublemakers. You people let the trade unions walk all over you. But who needs 'em, eh? Think of it - with a car, you can go anywhere! No timetables, no rules, no crowds. Free as a bird."

"But one does need petrol. You have to take a great deal of it along, don't you? Or else, go only where there are garages?"

"Oh, don't worry. There'll be plenty of garages, and gas stations, too, all over the map. Won't be long, either."

Felicity didn't think she would like the countryside littered with filling stations. "The roads would have to be improved," she said, "and that would be expensive."

"Sure thing, but they will be. There's some good ones already - even in London, and that burg's still crawling with horses. Slow up the traffic. Messy things, too. You oughta see the streets - full of - you know."

"Manure," she promptly supplied. "It's good for the soil. And it doesn't smell half so foul as the fumes from your machine."

Roderick chuckled indulgently. "I see you're not a big fan of cars. That's all right, they'll come anyway, and you'll get to like 'em. Everybody will. One of the first things I got to do here is turn that big old stable into a garage.

Pave some of that lawn and the drive, probably widen it... get rid of those trees...."

Felicity made no reply; there was none adequate to so ghastly a proposition. The row of oaks along the drive was three hundred years old and, to her mind, one of the most entrancing features of the estate.

"Ever been to London, pretty cousin?"

She took the change of subject in her stride. "I believe so," she answered carefully, "but I recall nothing of it."

"Yes, that was a tough break, losing your memory. How did it happen, anyway?"

"If I could remember that, the problem would not exist," she pointed out. "There was no witness, or I would have been rescued."

"You mean, nobody knows anything about it?"

"There is conjecture, merely. I must have been on the cliff overlooking the Twilling gorge. I'm told the view is quite spectacular, though naturally, I have never returned...."

"Why not?" asked the American, for once, not with intent to offend, but from a spontaneous curiosity. "Seems to me, it's the first thing I'd do - see if anything clicked."

"Then you are braver than I, Cousin Roderick. Perhaps I shall someday ask a trusted companion," she glanced at Roland, who appeared not be listening, and did not meet her eye, "to escort me there."

"I'll take you," Roderick volunteered. "Right now, if somebody shows me the way." He, too, looked toward their silent chaperon, and was disappointed of a response.

"No," said Felicity. "Not yet. Much as I wish to recall my earlier life, I am also afraid."

"What of?"

"Doctor Weiss - my physician at the clinic in Switzerland, an eminent man in his field, of course - suggested that there might be some reason, other than the buffeting I had undergone in the river, for my amnesia. He thinks it is best to proceed with caution, one step at a time. I am not allowed shocks, he said."

"Aha," her cousin grunted, beginning to lose interest. "No shocks. Fine. What about this..." his eyes once more strayed to the still figure of their passenger, now stretched upon the grass, "this business of getting engaged? Seems to me that'd be a shock."

"Not at all," she contradicted. "Roland, for all he is not terribly good company today, is a dear childhood friend. I expect him to be a most stable fiance."

"Stable's for horses," Roderick said, wiping his face, then the back of his neck with one of the white linen napkins. "And that boy's for the birds. Look at him! All the energy of a wet rag. Wouldn't you rather have a real man, Pretty Cousin? Don't you want to be swept off your feet - all that romantic girlish stuff?"

Felicity regarded her interlocutor steadily. "All that girlish stuff, as you so aptly put it, is for fairy tales. Marriage ought to provide one with comfort, security, unity of purpose...."

Roderick's gaze was the first to falter, and drop. At last, she had scored a point off this irritatingly self-confident man. Soon, he began to prepare for departure; to collect dishes, napery and utensils, and toss them helter-skelter into the wicker basket. Felicity made another - oh, very small, but satisfying - victory of taking over the task and doing it properly. Or was it really a victory? Did not his careless incompetence exempt Roderick from a chore? And she was not able to preempt or object to having her arm taken, ostensibly to help her up the slope. His touch was very warm; it lasted longer and became more intimate than was required by courtesy. Although she had largely overcome her distaste for all physical contact, this was so disagreeable that, when she finally extricated herself, she resolved never again to venture within range of those freckled hands.

The ride back was uneventful, the girl apologetically claiming fatigue. Roderick himself looked tired and Roland was as lively as so much baggage. Not until after supper did Felicity find an opportunity to take him to task for his ungallant behaviour.

"What d'you mean, letting me go off alone with that barbarian?"

"You didn't have to go at all," said Roland. "You could've had a headache, or something. Anyway, you weren't alone, after all, were you? And," he took the offensive, "you two seemed to get on like a house afire, barbarian or not."

"Ooh," she fumed, "you *are* thick! Don't you see? We have to be friendly, or we'll never know what he's up to."

"Mater said that, too," he muttered sulkily. "You gals have got it all fixed up between you - what d'you need me for?"

Felicity sadly shook her head. "You feel left out, is that the trouble? Oh, Roland, it's not like that! We all have got to work together. We could lose Twillingmarche, otherwise."

"So what?" There was, not so much in the two syllables, as in the hunched shoulder and lowered head, deep disappointment, profound unhappiness. But this was no time for sympathy: he had to be snapped out of the mood, by fair means or foul.

"Some of us might be facing legal action."

"What!?" now she had his attention.

"Think."

"But I didn't mean any harm!" he cried. "They said it must have been an accident. And it's true, honestly."

Felicity was taken aback. "An accident? What are you talking about?"

"The car," Roland explained. "The brake-fluid line. It was a stone, just as that mechanic thought.... Or, well, maybe more than one stone - the farm roads are pretty bad. But I didn't know anything was broken."

A great, brilliant light flooded her brain. "You drove Roderick's automobile? When?"

"While they were in London. I didn't mean to hurt it - just wanted to try it out one time, that's all. Seemed right enough when I put it back."

"Is that why you were so reluctant to ride in it today?"

166

He nodded miserably. "Didn't like to go near it, after what happened. Made me feel rotten, the whole afternoon, knowing...."

"Did you tell anyone else?"

"Of course not."

"Did anyone see you?"

"No. I went after dark. That's maybe why I didn't notice those rocks in the road...."

Felicity put a comforting hand on his arm. "Don't start being racked by guilt now. And for pity's sake, don't blurt out any confessions. For all you know, you're innocent, anyway. It could just as well have happened, as everyone thinks, during Mr. Goldsmith's trip to Twillingsford."

Now that she reflected upon the situation, she recognised another possibility. The shed was never locked; in the usual way, only tools and firewood were kept there. Anyone might have entered. Anyone who hated Roderick might have done wilful damage - never expecting the lawyer to fall victim. She herself might have been tempted to do it, had she thought of it earlier, had she known enough about motor-cars.... No; she could not name a suspect other than Roland who met all of these criteria. And she believed Roland: if he could think up such a devious plan, he would also know better than to admit any connection with the car. Besides, the necessary malice was simply not him. It was the wildest of speculation, merely, arising from the odd series of mishaps that had lately befallen the American Sommelroux. Well, some people are accident-prone: her own branch of the family could hardly be considered immune. In any case, to voice this flight of fancy would be a mistake; Roland required soothing, not further upsetting.

"Mr. Goldsmith wasn't badly hurt. Perhaps he needed that last little push to make up his mind. He wanted to leave all along - now, he's happier, isn't he? So, please stop fretting."

Roland appeared somewhat cheered, restored to his customary - which is to say, for the past two weeks, pretty dismal - spirits. Nonetheless, Felicity concluded, taken all in all, Roland was no great asset to the cause. A very feeble conspirator at best, weak in mind and resolve. Oh, he was a nice enough young man, affectionate and loyal.... He would make an acceptable fiance, just as she had insisted to Roderick, but not much of a husband. At least, not for her.

16

"He's ruined everything," Esmee said, not for the first time. "Everything! We've already missed the best part of the season. If there is a railway strike, we'll be stranded..." Her shapely white shoulders slumped in dejection. "And now, this!"

"The doctor says it is only influenza," Mr. Forkes comforted as best he could.

"Only! Suppose we all come down with it? One had hoped, at least, to get there in time for the Christmas balls. One had hoped, at least to celebrate Felicity's birthday in something like the appropriate style."

"And so you must," said the solicitor. "There is nothing to be done for Mr. Sommelroux that the servants and Dr. Gillivray cannot do. In addition, we should be cheered by the knowledge that he can make less mischief while groaning in his sick-bed."

Esmee protested: "But, how would it look? What would people say, if we all went away to enjoy ourselves, leaving an ailing relative alone in the house?"

"Oh," he said, "it need not look as bad as all that. I shall take charge here. We shall let it be known that Mr. Sommelroux is briefly indisposed, but expected to join the family as soon as he is able. You cannot," he forestalled further objections by holding up a finger, "be blamed for removing your young - and still fragile - ward from a risk of infection."

"That's true..."

"It's settled, then. You and the children must depart as quickly as possible. If not tomorrow, then Wednesday morning."

The children, who had been following this exchange closely, had widely differing reactions. Roland's round pink face lit up like an electric lamp. He had been chafing, scarcely able to sit or stand or sleep or eat or make the most rudimentary conversation, for days. Felicity attributed his sudden increase in restlessness to a recent letter from Bettina. Although he had not confided its contents, Cousin Roderick had given her a clue. That man had ranted and raved at the cost - billed to him, naturally - of first-class passage for four on the prestigious new Cunard ocean-liner, 'Lusitania'. Rosalyn must intend, therefore, to remove herself and daughters from England in the very near future. And now, it seemed, Roland would have an opportunity to say his good-byes in person, whatever comfort that held.

As to her own feelings, Felicity was resigned. The birthday had to be acknowledged; a debut of some kind was unavoidable. It might be best to get it over with, sooner rather than later. Although she would infinitely prefer to celebrate Christmas with Aunt Lettie and the household staff, there would be other Christmases - but no more eighteenth birthdays. She would at least have Kate for company - if the girl could be persuaded to spend the holiday apart from her own family. And poor Esmee, having already suffered so many disappointments, should have this little consolation.

"Felicity," the stepmother broke in on her reflections, "has but one barely adequate gown. She will certainly need something better for the Royal Ball.... Roberts, you must telegraph my dressmakers in London to be ready at a moment's notice. Oh, but this is their busiest time of year! Well," in the excitement of practical organizing, all Esmee's usual animation returned, "they'll simply have to drop everything else, never mind the expense. Still, we can't expect too much...."

"I have an idea," the girl chimed in. "The attics. I found some fine dresses, that time. Remember, when the urn fell, and I got locked in? First thing in the morning - no, tonight! - I shall go and retrieve them."

"Oh, Felicity," Esmee chided, "don't be silly. Anything stored in the attics must be ancient. And I don't think there is time, even if it doesn't reek of mothballs, for Roberts to make the necessary alterations."

170

"They don't reek. They smell of lavender sachet. Everything was packed with the greatest of care. Anyway, you must look. Let me get Kate and a lantern; we'll fetch them back to.... The salon isn't quite the place, is it? I shall bring the gowns to my room. Meet me there."

"And I," said Mr. Forkes, whose presence had been quite overlooked for a moment, "will ask Master Roland, since we men have evidently become superfluous, to join me in a friendly hand of Cribbage before we retire."

He and Esmee exchanged a meaningful glance, which was not lost on Felicity. Roland was to be subjected to a kindly avuncular lecture. Good, she thought, for the boy's mother had not been able to make a very deep impression upon him. Being crossed in love was painful, to be sure, but Roland had known all along how matters stood. He was pledged to Felicity.... Well, he *was* - though both parties might wish it otherwise. In any case, there had never been the slightest chance of Roderick's allowing his eldest daughter to marry one of his adversaries - and an unpropertied, penniless one, if Roderick had his way. Perhaps now, with the object of his impossible affection soon out of the country, Roland would regain a firmer grip on reality and stop behaving like such a drip.

"What's all this in aid of?" Edward asked, preceding the two girls up the stairs. "What are we after?"

"Clothes," said Felicity.

"Of course, I should have known. Don't the Sommelroux always go clothes-hunting by lamp-light?"

Kate, bringing up the rear, giggled. "Felicity's going to London, to see the king."

"Is that so?" asked the footman.

"Yes. It's an awful nuisance, but I've got to. We're leaving right away - by the eight o'clock from Twillingsford, day after tomorrow. And I've nothing to wear for Society."

The little procession arrived at the top landing; Edward stood aside. "Be my guest. When was all this decided?"

"Half an hour ago," Felicity told him. "Mr. Forkes's idea. He said we shouldn't risk catching influenza."

The footman asked: "But *we* should?"

"Not Kate; she's just agreed to go with me. And you'll be safe enough; you never go within a mile of Roderick."

"That's right," Kate accused, "you always make poor Georgie answer his ring."

"Rank has its privilege," said Edward serenely. "Doesn't Evelyn usually find herself with all the unpleasant chores, like cleaning the grates?"

"No, she gives them to Jane, often as not."

"And Jane, if she can, passes them off on Gus," added Felicity. "He and I are the only people in this house who have to do as we're told. We are the lowest of the low."

"Gus'd like to hear that," Kate laughed. "He's madly in love with you."

"He is *not*!"

"Is, too! He's jealous as anything of Will Cartwright."

"Of Will? For Heaven's sakes!"

"You do be awful sweet to him, and you dote on his old horses. Don't you deny it, noo!"

"Well, he's sweet, too - *and* well spoken...."

"Ladies. Decorum, please." Edward was more than half in earnest, but the admonition, far from bringing the girls to their senses, caused further outbreaks of giggles. Oh, it was such a relief to be undisciplined! She had often watched village girls of her own age joke and jostle and laugh in the company of their peers. She had so often envied them! Now she felt - if only for a few stolen minutes - as free and natural as they were. Felicity had become quite light-headed, she realised.

"Why, he can't be more than fourteen," she said of the boots and knives boy.

"You think people can't fall in love at fourteen?" Kate asked, no longer all in fun.

"I'm sure they can," Felicity conceded. "But they can as easily fall out again. Just watch - both my young swains will be mad about Becky, or somebody else, by next week."

172

"Well, I wouldn't count on it...."

Edward, visibly uncomfortable with the turn their conversation had taken, tried again. "Did we come here to gossip, or to fetch some clothing?"

"You're right," Felicity took the lantern he was still holding, and let her fingers brush his. "Let's get on. Prepare me for the capital. Only," she added softly, "I shall miss you all so much. Will and Gus and... others."

"You've not told your aunt yet?"

"There hasn't been time. I shall go in the morning. I want to ask her advice, too."

"I don't suppose," Edward mused, "they'll let you visit Lady Dorothea."

"I intend to try, all the same. D'you know her?"

The footman smiled. "Let's say I have reason to feel warmly toward her. My father was in service there, years ago."

"Then I shall try doubly hard."

"Good. Now," he gave her back a gentle push, "you'd better get busy hunting down those party dresses."

The maid had gone ahead to the little room where Felicity discovered the wonderful trunk. She had known precisely where to look; this was scarcely to be wondered-at, for she herself might well have packed the things. Certainly, they had not been left to moulder undisturbed for half a century; they must have been taken out to air at intervals, their tissue paper and pomander replaced. What did surprise Felicity: Kate was not groping in the dark. There was an electric lamp in the room. How strange! Only days previously, Mr. Landry, the builder, had been heard telling Cousin Roderick that he could not make an estimate on the cost of electrifying the Palladian wing; that different experts must be consulted for wiring, plumbing and heating. Moreover, such specialty trades not being represented in the backwater of Twillingsford, they would have to be brought from Edinburgh or Newcastle. All Mr. Landry would undertake to inspect were the structural elements. It had been an unsatisfactory meeting all around; the master mason had given as his opinion that the building was sound and that any "mucking about" with dividing walls could only do it harm. His firm was not amenable to such a project. Roderick had then embarked upon correspondence with four different construction companies in both nearby cities, with none of which he had, as yet, made definite arrangements for an inspection tour.

This fortuitous delay in Roderick's plans was one reason that Esmee had agreed so readily to vacate Twillingmarche. Not that she could have done very much to keep out anyone Roderick invited. Yet, there was now, with Roderick's illness, a good chance that no such discussions would take place for several weeks. The onset of inclement winter weather, coupled with unreliable rail service, would make any tradesman think twice before travelling many miles from his home base, unless he were driving his own motor. True, quite a number of prosperous businessmen did so nowadays; Mr. Landry himself had arrived in a gleaming porcelain-white creation of Mssers. Rolls and Royce. Still, few would undertake any big job, requiring the scheduled transport of workmen and materials, this far out in the countryside. On the whole, Felicity agreed with Mr. Forkes - Roderick was unlikely to push on with his scheme through the holiday season.

Electric lights in the Palladian wing.... "Roderick doesn't know about this?" she asked Edward, in some anxiety.

"Not yet," he said grimly.

"I wish I didn't have to go away just now!"

The footman shrugged. "Nothing you could do to help, anyway, is there? Not yet," he repeated, in quite altered tones.

"It'll be different, once I have the birthday." Then she felt foolish, for she could not have said exactly how turning eighteen would change anything, except that she should be free to refuse Roland. To gain control of any money at all would take another three years. Even then, so long as she remained a spinster, any major expenditure would be subject to Mr. Forkes' approval. If she married, her husband would have the authority. There was so much that she wanted to do - and could not, due to the accident of having been born female. Felicity conquered her dejection by invoking a deep reservoir of anger. "It is the most foul injustice!" she stormed. "Instead of going to idiotic balls, I shall spend the season chained to railings, or accosting cabinet ministers, alongside Miss. Pankhurst."

"I'll be right beside you," Kate said.

"And you'll both go to prison," Edward pointed out, "and Roderick Sommelroux will have Felicity judged mentally unstable, and take over Twillingmarche."

Felicity sighed. "I suppose you're right. I must behave like a proper young lady.... Will it ever change, d'you think?"

"Course it will," Kate declared, glaring at Edward. "They shan't grind us under their heel forever."

"I'm inclined to agree," said the footman, unfazed by the hostility directed not really at him, but at his gender. "No society has ever yet prevailed against its own disenfranchised elements - especially not when it's more than half of the population - once people know they're being treated unfairly. Only -"

"What?"

He shrugged. "I don't care for the methods, that's all. I mean, so many women today are educated; some control considerable wealth. They have real power. They have the sympathy of clear-thinking men. Of course they'll get the vote, and probably soon. I just wish they could find a more dignified way to carry their point. These antics of the suffragettes do more harm than good - they're turning a just cause into a circus...." Edward broke off, abashed at his own vehemence. "Sorry. Hobby-horse ran away a bit."

The three young people stood looking at one another, their buoyant mood of minutes before, forgotten. At last, Felicity announced: "All right, then, we *shall* be dignified."

The gowns were a great success, particularly the sea-green tulle with the dashing neckline. Esmee was amazed and delighted that such a treasure trove had been so close at hand; Felicity was nothing loath to take full credit for the discovery. She modelled no less than five party frocks, all in excellent repair, and quite becoming. "A little old-fashioned," Roberts pronounced, "but they'll fit well enough. None for daytime?"

"I'm afraid not," said Felicity. "I did find some that must have belonged to... to my mother. But they're hopelessly snug."

"No help for it, I suppose." said Esmee. "Well, you've two decent suits; we'll have Madam Fournier run up another..."

"And if necessary, we shall buy ready-made."

While Roberts stood aghast, Esmee agreed. "Oh, do stop being such a snob," she told the lady's maid. "We haven't time for it."

"We haven't time to do *anything* properly these days," Roberts sulked.

"Never mind," Esmee laid a light hand on the shoulder of her confidante. "Things will improve. After we announce the engagement, you can have a perfectly lovely time, arranging for Felicity's trousseau."

That seemed to cheer Roberts; it did no such thing for the reluctant bride.

Aunt Lettie was already up to date on events. "Well, well! You are to be a debutante, after all. Congratulations."

"It's not my doing," grumbled Felicity. "I understand everyone has to go through this. Was it awful?"

"For me, you mean?" The older woman laughed. "Why, that was in another century. Pretty ghastly, if you must know. I was introduced, along with a flock of other little geese, done up in white organdie, to Queen Victoria. She was a terrible old grouch. The present monarch is quite jolly, though - or he was, as Prince of Wales - quite the blade...." At this point her laughter, barely kept in check, broke out in peals. "Blade..." At last she got it under control again. "Of course, he's getting on. In any case, there is nothing to be afraid of. You come forward, you curtsey, and then you fade into well-earned oblivion."

"But, what shall I say to His Majesty?"

"Probably nothing - just blush prettily."

"You're not pulling my leg again? I won't be horribly embarrassed?"

"Certainly not. Remember, nobody's ever died yet of being presented. Can you dance?"

"A little. Actually, Roberts says, fairly well."

"Can you stand near a wall and smile like a ninny?"

"I expect so," she simpered her best imitation of Bettina.

"You'll do," her aunt declared. "And then, there will be other things. They'll take you to a lecture or two. Hold out for Mr. Clemens – who insists on being addressed by his nom de plume, Mark Twain. I'm told he is most entertaining. There will be tea and soggy watercress sandwiches in salons that all look the same, with identical horse-faced girls and their fat mothers. If I know our Esmee, she won't let you near a music hall...."

The girl disagreed: "Esmee is quite keen on music; she's told Roland that he must escort me to concerts."

Letitia laughed so hard, her makeshift cowl all but came undone. Felicity wished she would give up that ridiculous masquerade, leave off the velvet draperies and show her natural self. This, however, was no time for a confrontation. "Concerts and music halls have little in common," her aunt explained, putting her habille back in order. "Our Esmee is familiar with the difference, even if you are not."

"What d'you mean?"

"Of course - how should you know? Before she became the second Lady Randolph, she was Esmeralda - exotic dancer and, for a short time, headliner at the West End Follies. They tell me she was very good, too. Must have been, to turn Randy's head all the way around to matrimony."

Felicity became aware that her mouth was open with no sound emerging, not because her brain refused to function - quite the reverse; it was racing so fast, no sentence had a chance to form itself before the next one shouldered it aside. At last she managed: "But that - but then..." She finally gained control of her voice. "I mean, where does she get off looking down on Aunt Dorothea!?"

"Interesting attitude - not hers, yours. I like this child," Aunt Lettie said to the marmalade cat, who wasn't interested, being fully occupied in the grooming of the very tip of his tail. "To begin with, Esmee never had the choice of looking down."

"But Roberts said..."

"I know," nodded Aunt Lettie. "That Roberts is an odd bird. She wouldn't thank you for mentioning her past."

"What past?"

"She used to be Esmeralda's dresser. Still is, of course, but she seems to take this ladyship business altogether too seriously."

"Yes," agreed the girl, "I sometimes think Roberts is living inside a Gothic Romance. Well, in a way, so am I.... But not Esmee?"

"Esmee is practical. She had to make the best of living with my dear Papa, who didn't much approve of her and didn't care who knew it. Thea's fall from grace happened long ago; by the time Esmee came, the rule was well established. What else was she to do? Randy honoured the rule, as applied to his sister, then exempted himself from the same standard when it didn't suit him. It's the way of the world."

"Is it still? In the twentieth century? I mean," the girl almost pleaded, "I would *so* like to meet Dorothea! I think she must be rather heroic."

"Heroic? I don't know. I have always been rather fond of her," Lettie said. "If you should, somehow or other, manage to accept her invitation to tea - and there's bound to be an invitation - give her my regards."

"Along with Edward's," added Felicity under her breath. Was this the proper time to broach the subject most heavily weighing upon her heart? It had better be, for she must soon depart and it definitely could not wait upon her return. "Auntie, you once promised to tell me your story. Could you, now?"

"Now? What has it to do with the matter in hand?"

"I was told," Felicity began carefully, watching for signs of irritation, "that you formed an unacceptable attachment. Roberts called it a misalliance. I think she

178

means, you loved a young man of the wrong class..." Thus far, the topic appeared safe enough; her aunt made none of the gestures that she had learned to associate with displeasure. "...and from all I know about my grandfather, that would fit the case. Is it so?"

"It is so." Letitia let her eyelids droop for a second, but offered no help. "Proceed."

"But Grandfather isn't here anymore. Neither is my Papa."

"That, too, is so. And then?"

"And, well, ah..." Felicity heard herself emitting inarticulate Roland-like noises, which annoyed her. She took a deep breath and started afresh. "Suppose I were to form a 'misalliance'? Who could disinherit and renounce me? Who could have me declared mentally incompetent?"

"A fascinating question. Let me see... Esmee and Elijah are your joint guardians. In view of your recent, well-documented illness, it is not impossible.... Do they have the power? Dare they risk the attempt? My dear, I cannot say."

"It's a terrible chance for me to take. Only...."

"Yes?"

"Oh, Aunt Lettie! I'm not in love with Roland. And he's in love with someone else, anyway, so he'd make a rotten husband, even if he was much use in any other way. But, you see, I can't give up Twillingmarche. I want it more than anything."

The older woman regarded her in the same piercing bird-like manner that she remembered from their first meeting. Indeed, almost as if she were assessing the girl all over again. "More than anything?"

"Almost more. As much as...."

"I see. And who is the unsuitable young man?"

"Edward." Having blurted out the bald truth, Felicity hung her head miserably, unable to meet the other's eyes for a moment. "I believe he, too," she mumbled, "at least I think.... He being a special friend - you told me - I hoped you might know how he feels."

"He fancies you, all right," Aunt Lettie said, "But then, I understand, all the boys do."

"That isn't what I mean!" the girl retorted, shame and uncertainty instantly put behind her. "I need to know whether he loves me, truly and forever, because then...."

"Yes?"

"Because *then* I wouldn't mind about the risk. I could stand up to Esmee and Mr. Forkes and... and anybody. I could tell them all to go to blazes."

Her Aunt smiled. "Aha. So that's how it is. Well, my dear, I'm afraid the answer is beyond my ken. You and Edward must speak directly to one another, and plainly. There is a problem still, more formidable than any that Esmee and Elijah Forkes can produce at the height of their cunning."

"Roderick," said Felicity. "Bloody Roderick. Perhaps he will die of influenza. People do, sometimes!"

"I suppose it is a possibility," Aunt Lettie allowed judiciously, leaned back, folding her long pale hands under her cloak. "We must hope for the best."

17

Twillingsford was too unimportant a station for full rail service; only second-class coaches were available on the abbreviated train. There being few passengers, Roberts and Kate had a separate compartment; Felicity was closed into another with a preoccupied Esmee and miserable Roland. The train stopped briefly at several towns, and at one or two places more difficult to explain, for there appeared no human habitation near the station itself. Roland roused himself long enough to predict with gloomy relish: "All these whistle-stops will soon go the way of the dodo. So will the railroad. And the big estates." Not until Newcastle-on-Tyne did they transfer to an express with first-class accommodation.

Felicity had a vague memory of train travel - coupled somehow with boats, though this latter she could not place - of sitting behind a flawed, smoke-grimed window and watching the distorted countryside jog past. That memory, however, was nothing like the London Express, with its sumptuous red plush seats and dusty gold tassels on the curtain-swags, the windows recently washed and closed to retain the heat. Fascinating in the first ten minutes, it soon palled. The journey seemed unconscionably long. She had her first glimpse of a big city: endless miles of rickety wooden fences, hovels and laden clotheslines. Why people should live in such crowding and squalor, she understood: most of them had no choice in the matter. But why cities should be spoken of with enthusiasm, admiration, even awe sometimes, she could not puzzle out. There were villages, too; groups of charming cottages and tidy - if now, all but bare - gardens, pubs like The Carter's Arms and churches identical to

Saint Hilda's. These rural communities looked so much more wholesome than their metropolitan opposite.

The land itself changed: bleak, wind-swept open heath gave way to more and more thickly-inhabited areas. There were more trees, hedgerows, little fields, sheepless hillsides. Past Leeds, she had her first attack of panic. Suppose she never found her way back again? It was too great a distance - too much strangeness between herself and home. Mercifully, she slept much of the way.

The London terminal was not like a train-station at all, but rather like a city contained inside a building: vast, full of people – either frenetically active or zombie-like idle, nothing in between - utterly confusing. It was named King's Cross, even though the cross wasn't there anymore, and anyway, had belonged a different king. Esmee was unsure of its history and displeased to be questioned. The street into which their carriage emerged was broad and lit by electric lamps, but as Cousin Roderick had said, crammed from edge to edge with bustling traffic, both motorised and horse-powered, with men and boys dodging between, in constant danger of death or injury or at the very least a dousing in muck. The ladies were more circumspect, keeping to the lee of commercial buildings. Felicity glimpsed a store's window here, a monument there, but everything far was shrouded in smoke and everything near was covered in grime. During this final leg of the journey, evening grew quite dark and windows came alive in tall, grey, looming houses, built seemingly one atop the other. London was horrible.

After all this, the house in Etheldred Close was a haven of peace and harmony. The mahogany doors were not so grand as those at Twillingmarche but prettily decorated with iron filigree and coloured glass. It swung open to reveal a marble tiled hall, a curving staircase, portraits upon the walls, blue and white figured wallpaper, dark wainscotting, occasional tables with improbably thin legs... In short, it was all familiar, if on a modest scale. The butler's name was Gubbins. He was short and rotund, with a polished pink forehead and no hair to speak of. Felicity formed an impression of one who laughs often and easily - though not, of course, within earshot of his employers - and liked him on sight.

While Roberts knew her way about, Kate had to be shown where everything was. This task fell to a plump, rosy girl named Kitty; Felicity knew that the two would be giggling over this coincidence as soon as they were well through the baize doors. Kitty served hot chocolate and shortbread biscuits before the tired travellers repaired to bedrooms, already aired and heated, for a much needed bath. It was far too late for any exploring tonight, but on the whole, she thought the house would do.

Esmee was, predictably, very busy in the next few days. Invitations, long before commissioned and delivered, had to be sent, and arrangements made for the one terribly important party she must give. Felicity had her own calling cards already printed - raised blue script on a cream linen finish; very dainty, she thought - which she must leave at various addresses. This, Esmee explained, was to let people know that she had arrived. Her only other errand was with Roberts to the dressmaker - a broad woman with an immense white coiffure, who greeted them, but did none of the handling and measuring herself. That came as a relief, for Madame Fournier was rather daunting. The girl who actually waited on her was a pleasant sort, once Felicity had asked her nicely to refrain from so many M'lady's and compliments. Later, though Roberts went extremely tight-lipped at the suggestion, Esmee accompanied her to the shop of the Misses Robinson, two very similar ladies of advanced years, still beautiful, and terribly genteel, who made a great fuss of finding for her the exact right skirts, blouses, frocks and underthings from among their stock of ready-to-wear clothing. *Almost* ready, that is, for everything required some tiny adjustment - at least, according to the Misses Robinson.

Then, for one entire, blissful day, Felicity was left alone. She and Kate explored the house from attics to cellars, from library to kitchen to stables. A pair of greys and brougham were kept here, tended by a man named Tom Tinker. He had a thick, old-fashioned moustache and hollow cheeks, like the pictures of Sir Robert Baden-Powell, but lacked that hero's outgoing nature; Felicity gave up any notion of befriending the horses. On the other hand, the Gubbinses were just as they appeared - cosy and good-humoured. Mrs. Gubbins did the cooking; their two daughters, amiable Kitty and practical Sophie, made up the under-staff. An older son, they proudly reported, had gone to sea. The servant's hall, actually the Gubbins parlour, was decorated, aside from the usual inspiring prints, coronation portrait and needlepoint samplers, with dozens of picture postcards from all parts of the world. Mrs. Gubbins, too, was bedecked, when out of uniform, in one or another of the garishly coloured shawls which Joe was wont to bring back from his voyages. Felicity was instantly at home in this place - and instantly accepted.

Sadly, her social schedule allowed but infrequent and brief retreats. On Saturday she made no less than seven calls, and received twice as many. She even had to meet some of the people. Her very first glimpse of the very first callers almost precipitated a fit of the giggles. Paula was seventeen years old, horse-faced and improbably vacuous; her mother, Lady Cecily Houston, was corpulent and grim; she appeared at every moment on the verge of reprimanding someone for something. Aunt Lettie evidently knew whereof she spoke. Other callers proved more complaisant; some of the debutantes might even be harbouring a brain, though they were careful not to make a show of this. Interspersed with chat about the weather, and who was at which ball, there was much tut-tutting over the latest Suffragette escapade. Felicity thought she detected, now and then, a hint of admiration in the disapproving tones of a young matron, a secret gleam in the eyes of a girl.

And there were young men. Roland, more often than not, disappeared early in the day, did not show himself till suppertime, and then only to change and go out again. Nevertheless, his friends paid their courtesy calls to the female members of the household. Felicity might have found one or two appealing, had she been of a disposition to care; for the most part, they were rather an

184

unprepossessing lot. Their only function in her present life was as contrast to what she missed with daily greater keenness.

She had hoped that stimulation, new experiences, things to learn - busyness - would fill her time and mind, leaving no room to fret over Twillingmarche. She had been absolutely wrong: her homesickness did not abate, not for a single hour. She wrote long letters, addressed to Aunt Letitia but intended for the household at large, then tore them up and posted only a picture-card. To have such quantities of mail arrive for one who had withdrawn from the outside world would look odd. Not until the third week did she send an actual letter. On the previous day, her invitation to take tea with Dorothea Summer had finally arrived, and that morning, she had steeled herself to stand up against family custom.

"Have I not done everything as you wished?" she asked Esmee.

"Yes, my dear; you have behaved admirably," the other woman agreed. "I am quite pleased with you."

"And have I asked for anything?"

Esmee raised her perfectly-shaped, near-invisible eyebrows. "What could you ask for that you haven't already got?"

Her sails deflated, she manfully rowed on. "I should like to visit my aunt."

"Pardon?" Esmee really didn't seem to know what she was talking about; only one aunt had ever been mentioned and she was hundreds of miles away.

"My Aunt Dorothea. She has invited me to tea, and I wish to accept. Please."

"All right," Esmee said.

All right? No opposition, no expostulation? No confrontation or moral victory. "This afternoon."

Esmee nodded. "I'm afraid I have another engagement today that cannot be put off. Roberts will go with you."

Roberts was silent and stiff the whole way: she would have made a contest of the issue, had she the power. Without power, she could only express disapproval in her physical being - even that, Felicity believed, was more assumed than felt. However disappointing to be given her way, rather than winning it, the visit itself was anything but.

Aunt Dorothea's house was larger than Etheldred Close and more handsome, both of architecture and of setting. It faced an open area of brown grass, bare trees and empty flowerbeds which could not belong to the property, for people were strolling about in it. Still, the house did have its own tiny front garden, and the whole prospect must be rather more pleasing, at least in summertime, than the rest of the city. The bell was answered promptly by a young woman in a flowered dress.

"You must be Felicity," she said. "I'm Maud Barry." She took the girl's pelisse, muff and fur-trimmed hat. Felicity, for a second, wondered if she could somehow contrive upon her departure to forget the article last mentioned, which she loathed. "What a lovely hat! All this velvet ribbon is so smart." Maud Barry hung her things upon an empty coatrack: if there were other guests, they had yet to arrive. "We're by ourselves - it's the servants' day out. Thea didn't want you to get lost in the usual multitude." Maude Barry led the way across an entry hall very like every entry hall Felicity had seen in the past weeks; black and white checkered floor-tile, painted wainscotting - the wall-covering was more aggressively ugly: dark gold foil with a fuzzy black pattern - to a drawing room. "Make yourself at home, I'll just go tell Thea to shake a leg."

She had a moment to orient herself. This room, too, was like all the others, with perhaps more of the marble statuary groups and bronze lamps, an extra-large Chinese vase holding dried pampas grass, one occasional table and armchair too many. The furniture was of dark wood and highly polished, or green plush and sleep-inducingly comfortable. But the pictures were different. No oil-paintings of floral arrangements; no pink little maids with baskets of kittens; not even a coronation portrait. Though there was a likeness of the king, it was only a small photograph in a chased silver frame, taken when his beard had been black.

"You admire His Majesty?" The voice was the voice of Aunt Lettie, multiplied by three.

Felicity put the picture on the mantle guiltily, tried to collect herself while turning to the door. "Yes," she began to say, but the other woman continued. "Of course, he was much younger then, and not quite as... substantial as he is now. So, this is the new countess! Come, my dear, let's sit down. I want to know everything about you."

She looked like Aunt Lettie - that is, the one who worked in her secret garden, dressed in sensible clothes and tied her hair back, rather than half-mad Lady Letitia of the tower room - also multiplied. Taller, wider, more amply endowed, though not plump, and also - the girl was not quite certain what, exactly. More like Esmee, perhaps, endowing the space she occupied with some extra quality. She must be in her sixties, but her hair was redder than Felicity's, more abundant than Roderick's. Her skin was whiter than Letitia's, unfreckled and smooth, and her lips, a brighter pink. She was like all of them, only bolder, nobler: the masterpiece of Sommelroux design.

"Oh, you have the look!" Felicity said without thinking.

"Indeed. As have you."

"I've been longing to meet you, Aunt Dorothea."

"Everyone calls me Thea. And I won't pretend I haven't been curious myself. Tell me first, how is the family?"

"Aunt Lettie sends her love. She's well, I think, even though she doesn't like to appear so...." Should she have said that? She was not yet supposed to know about Lettie's life outside of her stuffy room and her interminable tapestry. "Our senior footman," she rushed on, "Edward, wishes me to convey his regards. His father worked for you, years ago - do you remember Makepeace?"

Aunt Thea smiled broadly. "Of course I do. A good man. That child was a terror - but so pretty and clever, one could forgive him any amount of mischief. Is he a heartbreaker?"

"Oh, I hope not!" said Felicity, more sincerely than she wanted anyone to realize.

Dorothea pretended not to. "Esmeralda and the boy behaving themselves? Never mind, that wasn't a fair question. Here comes our tea."

Maud Barry entered with a laden tray, which she deposited on the low table before them. There were jam tarts and buttered scones, sandwiches and iced cakes; all the rich fare that was served at mid-afternoon in every house Felicity must visit. She had learned to make a single pastry last fifteen minutes; else, in the absence of garden and horses, she would grow into a dirigible. Dorothea had no such constraint; she set to with a will, as did Maud Barry, who joined them and poured everyone's tea. "Maud is my secretary," her aunt revealed. "Anyway, that's her title, and she does write a neat hand. But she does so many invaluable things, I wonder if I hadn't better adopt her before somebody steals her away. Even so, she'll get married one of these days, and leave me."

"No, I won't," said Maud. "I'll bring my husband here to live, and you shall have to find a job for him."

"So long as he can make good conversation," Dorothea replied. "There are so few interesting people anymore," she added.

"How can you say that!?" Maud protested. To Felicity, she explained: "Lily Elsie was here only last week. And not long ago, Mr. Twain, that lovely sardonic American, you know - strutting in his Oxford robes. So funny! The Divine Sarah attended one of our soirees before she set off on her last world tour, and so did the great Puccini."

Dorothea waved her white fingers, momentarily unburdened of cake. "He's all bluster; too full of himself. I did enjoy Caruso, in spite of his immense self-confidence. I suppose it's just age creeping up. All the old cronies who have died or retired to stodgy country life - or been transported to the colonies - seem to have been so much livelier than the new people. Unless I decide to cultivate the Pankhursts."

Maud whispered in a stage aside: "She hasn't yet forgiven Sir Henry Irving for dying."

"Ah, he was a wonder. Well," Aunt Thea leaned back on the sofa, satisfied, "enough name-dropping for the nonce. She's impressed. Or *are* you? Would you prefer gossip about the Duke of Kent?"

Felicity laughed. "Of course I'd appreciate that, too, but it would impress me even more to learn that you know Mr. Kipling."

"My dear girl, I know simply everyone. Everyone who does anything worthwhile. That's not to say they're all pleasant company, though. Never fear, your young hero is quite as entertaining as his books and handsome as his photograph. Would you like to meet him?"

Felicity was overwhelmed. It was some little time before she could say anything that didn't sound like Bettina, but she finally mastered her awe sufficiently to give an account of recent events at Twillingmarche. Early in the recitation, Maud Barry took herself off; the Sommelroux women were alone.

"A clinic?" Aunt Thea repeated. "He wants to turn the place into a clinic? That must not be allowed."

"That's how we all feel. Except perhaps Roland - I don't think he cares very much."

"Roland? Oh, Esmeralda's boy. His name's Robert."

"Robert?"

"Yes, Bobby Wilkins - I saw him once. Chubby little thing with big cornflower eyes and yellow ringlets. Quite sweet."

"His father's name is Wilkins," the girl said doubtfully, "but - Bobby? And ringlets?"

"Oh, that was years and years ago. She had to cut his hair *sometime*; I'm sure he took some razzing, even then - he must have been five or six years old."

"You knew Esmee? Before?"

"Not well," Dorothea admitted, "but we met. She was a good dancer and she had stage-presence. Might have been a sensation, only she never really had her heart in it. She married young - badly, from what I've heard. It's not easy to come back - older, heavier, out of practice. I lacked the courage, even to try. But then, she had a child to support."

"Where did she meet Papa?"

"Certainly not here! Though, God knows, enough meetings, for good or ill, have taken place in these rooms. Randy wasn't allowed to come here, of course. I don't know. Perhaps he just waited at the stage door. Many do."

"Were they very much in love?"

Dorothea made a noise that, were she not a lady, might have been called a snort. "They must have been, to marry while the patriarch was still alive. I don't envy her first few years. I imagine she changed the poor boy's name to appease the old man - not that it would do her no good."

"Grandfather was a hard man?"

"Hard is one word for it..."

"But my Papa wasn't like that, was he?"

"No. Your Papa was a spoiled, self-indulgent and extremely vain little boy who never had to grow up."

"That's cruel!"

"It's also true. Listen, my dear," her aunt laid a compelling hand upon her shoulder and gazed deep into her eyes. "Randy was a likable enough fellow, so long as he had his own way. But every girl he had his own way *with* suffered for it. If you need romantic notions about a dead man you never knew, choose a poet - at least they leave you something of value."

Felicity was shaken, less by the vehemence of her aunt's dislike of her own brother than by the implication of this last injunction. Did she mean that Felicity could not have known her father with the understanding of an adult, or that, because of her amnesia, what she had once known was now irrelevant - or...? To obscure the subject, perhaps even from herself, she harked back to a statement earlier. "You said you lacked courage to return to the stage. Were you married, Aunt Thea?"

"Married? No.... He was." And Felicity had imagined this to be a safer avenue of exploration! "But," she floundered, "your name?"

"Summer, you mean? Well, I couldn't use the family name, but getting all my monograms changed would have been wasteful."

"Just like Roderick's father. He called himself Ray Sommer for a while. That's why Mr. Forkes' colleagues in America took so long tracing him."

Aunt Thea gave her a sharp look and asked: "You're sure there isn't any doubt?"

"I'm afraid not. Mr. Forkes assures us that he was the real Raymond. Besides, Cousin Roderick is a typical example of the family."

"Uncle Raymond," Dorothea mused, "didn't get himself killed by Indians, after all. Papa always said he would; he got quite a lot of satisfaction from the news, though he put on a long face for the world. Well, good for Uncle Raymond! He always was an interesting fellow."

"Do you know why he left?"

"Yes. His brother drove him away."

"I've heard they disagreed, but not that..."

"Oh yes. A terrible fight they had - not the first, either. You see, Uncle Raymond couldn't accept... some things Papa did." Looking at the girl's face, avid for information, she sighed. "Oh, very well. Uncle Raymond used to call Papa a brute for the way he treated our mother. He was right about that. But, too, I now think he was fonder of her than a brother-in-law has a right to be.... After her death, I don't suppose there was any reason for him to stay - and Papa gave him reason to go."

"Uncle Raymond was nicer than Grandfather?"

"By far. It's just too bad his son is such a pest."

Time passed pleasantly until Roberts arrived to escort her home. Felicity saw much in her new-found aunt that was, if not exactly heroic, certainly worthy of respect. There might have been much, too, that was shocking, had Felicity not been resolved to slough off what she thought of as the Roberts part of her training. Yet she missed Letitia no whit less than before. When Esmee later asked how the meeting had gone, Felicity mentioned all the famous names she could remember, described every photograph and ornament, managed to refrain from blurting out the truly important new information. But she could not let it pass altogether without comment. "Aunt Thea told me that my grandfather was a hard man. Did you have a very bad time of it?"

"Bad enough," Esmee said, "but it wasn't so long."

Neither this nor any other subject could be pursued at leisure, for they had that night to attend a ball at the home of Sir Richard Gilbert. The two women were fully dressed by eight o'clock, fretting in the blue salon, and Roland had yet to put in an appearance.

"We shall simply have to go without him," Esmee declared. Her cheeks were a much brighter hue than could be accounted for by cosmetics, and her voice had an unaccustomed edge. "I do understand that he has been apart from his friends; he's missed the gaming and the music halls.... I am prepared to make allowances. I've always overlooked his inability to tell time. I have not burdened him with much responsibility; I have no unreasonable demands. But he knows how important tonight is for you - for all of us. One would think he might make an effort."

18

Roland came to the ball unfashionably late, but not alone.

Bettina looked exactly right among the girls - possibly, Felicity admitted to herself, prettier than most, with her rich dark hair and pink organdie ruffles. This was the most appropriate setting for her. Rosalyn, dressed and groomed as impeccably, disappeared in the colourful shoal of matrons without causing a ripple.

"I don't care," Roland told his mother, "if there is a scandal. And why should there be? I mean, divorce isn't exactly unheard-of. So I fixed it up with Fred Gilbert."

"You might at least have warned me," Esmee hissed.

The three were relatively private for the moment in a quiet backwash of the ebb and flow of the ball. Roland said, "Sorry, Mater. I was afraid you'd oppose it. And I didn't want to fight."

"Hm. And now, I suppose we shall have to invite them to Felicity's party."

"You ought to've done it already. Well, I mean to say - they *are* relations, whether we like it or not. How would it look to shun them?"

Felicity stood a fraction apart, reflecting that she had not at all been consulted on any matter relating to her own birthday party, and was unlikely to be consulted this time. Therefore, she volunteered. "I shall ask them formally tonight... Perhaps they won't come, after all that's happened."

But, of course, they would. Bettina had never been one for grudges - nor, indeed, had she ever been threatened or injured. Rosalyn had forgotten whatever she might have held against the other Sommelroux, in her battle with Roderick. And quite a battle it was shaping up to become, according to Roland, who told Felicity while they waltzed together.

"If he doesn't come through with a decent settlement, Sam can dig up all his financial records, sharp practices and so forth."

"Sam?"

"Mr. Goldsmith - the lawyer, you know."

"I know who. I only wondered at your sudden familiarity."

"Oh, that. He's not a bad sort, really, when you get to know him. See, I've been spending time at the Grand." Felicity had already surmised the reason for his many absences. "D'you know what he said, Sam? I don't think he meant it, actually, but he said it wouldn't surprise him, in light of things he'd done before, if Mr. Sommelroux'd mucked about with the brake line, that time he ran the car off the road. Imagine how that made me feel! Of course, I kept mum."

"What sort of things had he done?"

"Oh, business things.... Well, f'rinstance, there was another chap with a garage, only this other chap was some kind of genius with engines, so that he was beating the pants off Roderick in profits.... Anyway, it seems the other chap's premises burned down one night and he was ruined."

"Roderick did that?"

Roland shrugged. "Maybe. Or had somebody else do it. There wasn't any proof, but Sam thinks the coincidence was a little too pat, if you see what I mean. And," he added, his voice taking on a hard note of censure, as if arson were a trivial crime compared to this, "he beat Rosalyn. I'm pretty sure, from things Bettina let drop."

So much suspicion in this family group, Felicity reflected. And so little substance to any of it; nobody seemed to know the true nature of the persons closest to them. At least some of the important facts ought to be clear. "Listen, Bobby," she said.

The boy's head went up and sideways, not unlike that of a startled horse. "Eh?"

"That is your real name, isn't it?"

"Sure. Don't let Mater hear you, though! She'd have a fit."

"I don't see that it matters anymore. Grandfather has been gone eight years. I don't know why everyone is still so afraid of him. Besides, I only wanted to get your attention."

"You got it, all right. Shoot."

"Esmee is planning to announce our engagement at my birthday party."

"I know."

"If Bettina is there..."

Roland smiled. "It'd be all right - I've told her everything. No, no, not that. Keep dancing, or people will notice." Felicity had temporarily lost the use of her limbs; now she was wilting with relief. "I mean, about us. I told her how the marriage was arranged and that neither of us really wants it. You don't, do you?" he added anxiously.

"No."

"D'you think we could just - you know - refuse?"

The music ended and he must now walk her back to Esmee's side. "I shall think about it. Until our next dance, then?" She smiled and curtsied sweetly and he bowed. "Until next dance." Both were in perfect control once again, for the benefit of onlookers.

What to do? If she refused to marry Roland, would Esmee ever let Mr. Forkes release her money? It had been difficult enough to persuade her that Felicity needed an allowance for such small, ordinary things as hair ribbons, postcards and souvenirs. Matters could go even beyond the money. Might not Esmee, in revenge, even disown her? How could she, without risking everything? If Esmee had done all that she had done for her son's sake, and if that son now turned his back upon it.... But Esmee was no fool. And, anyway, Mr. Forkes would surely not allow her to do anything so foolhardy....

"My dear, are you fatigued?" Her intense cogitation was interrupted by its very subject. Felicity was vaguely aware of having heard the voice, but not of what it had been saying. "We shall be going in to supper in a moment. Perhaps you ought to sit out, afterward."

"No...no, I'm quite all right, thank you," she replied. "I did promise Roland one more dance."

"Well," her stepmother smiled indulgently, "I suppose one won't hurt. You two seem to have made up your differences."

"Oh, we haven't any differences, really," Felicity assured her. "We are quite in accord."

That seemed to make Esmee happy, but it caused the girl a pang of guilt. She had been growing weary of deception; especially, she had come to dislike misleading this woman, who had been so unfailingly kind to her, whatever may have motivated that kindness. Why, without Esmee, she would not be here. Little loss, as far as that went, but neither would she be here in the larger sense - with every expectation of returning to her beloved Twillingmarche. How could she dash Esmee's hopes? On the other hand, Roland might well do so, all by himself. He seemed to have a new source of courage; he might be capable of unexpected actions. And if she and he together did not oppose Esmee, their own fondest hopes would be shattered, perhaps their very lives, ruined. They needed time to sort things out. They simply must, and soon, come clean, as Roland and the Americans would say.

A tiny portion of her mind, and all of her well-disciplined social face, had been making polite conversation with the Hon. Freddy Gilbert, who now said, "Look at them!"

She glanced in the direction indicated by his laden fork. There Bettina and Roland were, sharing lobster bisque, heads like morning and evening, bent close together.

"It's dashed romantic, ain't it?" Freddy said. "Makes you wish you were in love too."

"Ah, but I am," she told him.

"Not with.... Oh, I do beg your pard-"

"Don't be silly. I wish them all the happiness in the world."

The situation was becoming untenable.

When their waltz finally came, she would tell Roland to hang fire. If they could not convince Esmee to put off the announcement, well, then it would be made. After all, if marriages can be dissolved, why not engagements? They could even set a date - a distant one. It was possible to go on for months, if need be, officially engaged, yet without making any practical arrangements. In the meantime.... What was Roderick up to? According to the most recent communication from Mr. Forkes, the cousin was out of bed once more and ready for mischief.

"I missed a chance to meet Mr. Kipling," she wrote to Aunt Lettie, "because I had a more Important Person to meet, on the day. You were right about His Majesty. He does seem rather jolly. And Queen Alexandra is quite lovely and slim, and very young. I mean compared to Him. Do you think they are in love? One cannot tell. I did not have to say anything really, and I did not stumble in the courtsey. I was so afraid that would happen!! I practised and practised, until even Roberts was sick of it, and you know how she is! Two of the girls did. Stumble, I mean, it must have been horrible for them, poor things. The King did not seem to mind. He has a very nice smile, doesn't He? But I did get something very precious. Aunt Thea asked Mr. Kipling to outograph? (I'm sure about the ph but not about the first part. When I come Home, I shall want a tutor, Roberts says my spelling is 'atroshus', and that will not do.) to sign his Jungle Book. We already have one in the library at Home, only not with a massege in it adressed to me!

"I think Aunt Thea is wonderfull, and she is fond of me too, thank Goodness. Only she is not like You at all. I miss You every day! Good news. There is to be no railway strike, after all, so that we shant have any trouble coming back. We may be Home in time for Christmas. I hope!

"I have had my Birthday Party. It was not very exiting really, with a lot of silly Debutants (some are not so ignorent as they pretend. If a person can learn French and German, they arent really stupid, are they? So why do we have to pretend?) and there Mamas, and some quite dull young men. Exept that Freddy Gilbert is nice, a friend of Roland. I have two new friends, here in the Town House. Sophie and Kitty Gubbins. Last week I made teribly smart hats for them. Well, I did not make them really, they were mine, after they were Esmee's, but it is quite amasing what one can do with a little vailing and ribbon! The girls I like best could not be invited to my party. I think that is awfully unfair, dont You? Rosalyn and Bettina Sommelroux were here, Roland wanted to invite them, and I think he was right. They did nothing wrong, even if I am not too keen on them. They are sailing on the Lucitania in two weeks. Its the biggest fastest ship in the world, Roland says, exept the Moritania, will be even faster when it is finished. They are sisters, like Lucy and Lisa, is'nt that funny? Roland is very sad. I think he would like to go too. His already half American. Americans are all the rage in London nowdays, but Bettina says they are not all rich, back home.

"Anyway we did manage to talk Esmee out of anouncing our engaigment! She has promised to wait a little while. At least untill we find out what Rodrick is up to. Mr. Forkes arived last night, and I have not been able to learn much yet. He did tell us there was a man from London at the House, and he was not making an estimet. I wonder? Even Aunt Thea said that he must not be allowed to do what he plans. It is really most anoying to be so far away and not know what is happenning at Home! And not be able to do anything!

"I hope Every-one is keeping well? You know who I mean!!

"All my love, Felicity Sommelroux.

"P.S. The picture of the Royal Guard is for Will. They have the most wonderfull horses!

"P.P.S. I shall bring something just as good for Gus, so he should not be jelous."

Felicity folded the missive, slid it into the envelope and sealed it. What else could she find to do? Soon, it would be necessary, in any case, to leave the sanctuary of her room, for the Farquharson girls were expected to tea. She did not mind: Caroline was rather more than half suffragette underneath her fine manners; Alexandra was a still uncommitted sympathizer. Their mother being an invalid of some mysterious sort, they were usually chaperoned by a youthful aunt. Conversation with them could, and often did, take a surprising turn. It was not the Farquharsons she dreaded.

It was her stepmother.

Esmee had scarcely spoken to her in the past week. To Roland, she had spoken at length and strongly on the night before the party - so that, on the day, she had looked pale and drawn, in spite of all her beautifying arts. But Roland had stood firm. He and Felicity had agreed that it was fitting for him to carry this fight. All Felicity had to do when they confronted Esmee was concur with Roland's arguments. Since they were both determined not to marry one another, there was no rush to announce an engagement which would only be broken later. They could not marry, he explained, because they looked upon each other as brother and sister. This was not the strictest verity, but true enough in the circumstance, and Felicity felt it important to make Esmee understand that she had no desire to sunder family attachments.

Yet, for all their careful rehearsal, for all their efforts to state their case with tact, Esmee concluded that both her son and her ward had betrayed her. She had excused Felicity - shortly and coolly, which, though she ought to have been prepared for it, hurt. Then she had set about trying to persuade Roland. It must have caused her some consternation to find him, who all his life had been pliant and sweet-tempered, adamant on this issue. It must have caused her profound unease to find the usually obedient Felicity, suddenly unyielding. Still, she ought not to hold a grudge! Were they not, all three, allies in a common purpose? Well, perhaps not: Esmee had always wanted Twillingmarche for Roland; Felicity wanted it for herself. Even so, this enmity was harmful to both causes; they need not be at loggerheads! She determined at the earliest possible moment to reconcile. Tea with the Farquharson ladies, therefore, was more of a chore than a diversion; Felicity kept wondering what time it might be; how soon they could decently be sent home.

"Esmee?" The room was bright with gas-light, while outside a miserable, wet snowfall turned dusk into night.

"I have a headache."

"You have no such thing," Felicity walked into the room. "You are annoyed with me."

"What if I am?" Esmee demanded in a voice no longer feigning illness. "You and that ungrateful child of mine are about to spoil everything I've worked for."

She sat down, uninvited, in a dainty armchair upholstered in the same yellow brocade as her stepmother's boudoir furnishings at home. It gave her an instant of comfort mixed with an equal part of longing. "We're not, you know. Neither of us wants to spoil anything. Please try to understand."

Esmee heaved a sigh that would have shaken many a strong man, given that she was wearing a peignoir of most delicate silk, and little else. "Understand? Of course I understand! The wretched boy has fallen in love with that American ninny.... Not that he's terribly clever himself, God knows.... But you!" She fixed Felicity with one of her steeliest blue gazes. "I'd have expected more from you, Felicity."

"Mary," the girl said quietly but firmly.

There was a silence in the room so deep that, had the two women no better focus for their attention, they would have been able to distinguish the susurration of the lamp in its glass shade from that of sleet upon the windowpane. Esmee let out breath softer than either. "So it's come to that."

"I really think it has to. You and I - and Bobby Wilkins, for that matter - we ought not to be fighting. We have a common enemy. Don't you see? We simply cannot continue our separate pretenses, and still hope to win against Roderick!"

200

"He's hired a detective," Esmee remarked, not wholly out of context. "Elijah saw him. Rather, he's convinced that the man who came to see Roderick last week was not there to give an estimate on renovations."

"A Vesey Brother, I expect. Well, of course I knew. I kept an eye on his correspondence. Didn't you, Esmee?"

Lady Farwell gave a short laugh, more of rue than of mirth, but still, any sort of laugh was a good sign. She extended the hand nearest Felicity, which the girl accepted with alacrity, and held in a warm clasp. "Erma," she corrected. "Erma Jean."

19

"Of course, if you ever repeat it, I shall wring your lily white neck for you. And now, we had better ask Elijah to join us. But not Roland, I think."

The solicitor was shown in by Kate. "Has something happened?" he asked anxiously, once the door was tight shut.

"Oh yes," Esmee told him. "What we most feared - that is, what we most feared before we came to know Roderick."

Mr. Forkes' eyes flickered over Felicity and back again to his employer, where they made a brief tour and lit, very properly, upon her face. "Oh yes," she repeated. "Not only does she know - the little witch has practically taken charge."

Felicity began to protest that she meant to do no such thing, but was forestalled by Esmee. "She thinks we ought to pool our resources - and I can't very well disagree. She even knows about the confidential inquiry agent."

"Ah," said Mr. Forkes.

"And," Esmee continued, "she remembers everything."

"Oh," said Mr. Forkes.

Felicity explained, "You see, after I became concerned about my figure, I stopped drinking the cocoa, and then I stopped being so sleepy all the time. It meant nothing to me then, only, in one of the novels Roberts gave me - I forget which one - the heroine was held prisoner and drugged with cocoa."

"Those idiotic novels!" Esmee muttered. "And to think of all the trouble we took over them. We had," she informed the girl, "special copies printed, with names and places that we wanted you to learn. But we could not so easily change the plots!"

Mr. Forkes said, "The man Barlow gave me to understand that she wasn't clever enough to work in his shop..."

"Since I am here now," Felicity tartly reminded him, "you may as well address me directly. Mr. Barlow never meant me to apprentice in the shop - that's only what he told the vicar. They really just wanted a house servant they didn't have to pay. And," she added, "I shall always be grateful to you, Mr. Forkes, for bringing me away."

"So I should think." As the solicitor was still far behind, this statement came from Esmee, once again very much in possession of herself. She turned to him, "These Barlows. Are they likely to make trouble?"

Mr. Forkes was certain on this point, at least. "No, I shouldn't think so. They are a greedy pair. Rather than pay them all at once, I have arranged that a certain sum be forwarded on a monthly basis, so long as we are content. Naturally, I did not divulge our true identity. It is in their own best interests to keep the transaction confidential."

"So far, so good. What about Eastmills?"

The solicitor, after some thought, replied: "She was called simply Mary, without a surname. In the strictest sense, this is accurate - the family had never seen fit to acknowledge the poor child.... Nor, one would surmise, were they eager to have it known that they had washed their hands of her. I gather this was their reason for taking her to an hospice far removed from their home ground."

Felicity broke into an unladylike chortle. "And so it'll be fine justice that I shall never have heard of them." More seriously, she added, "I ought to do more than ignore them, after the way they treated my mother - her own kin!"

Mr. Forkes supplied further comment. "They - the family, that is - are fisher-folk, in and about Gray's Harbour, down-coast. One found them rough in manner, unbending in their mode of thought, and unforthcoming. Why, it required months of painstaking - what can be called nothing short of harassment - and quite a handful of disbursements - to glean any useful information as to the whereabouts of the little girl. They had at first led one to believe that she had died in infancy. This, although somewhat difficult to verify, was finally disproved."

Esmee listened patiently, although she must already have known every detail. Felicity, who had not, formed a new understanding - one, furthermore, which warmed her to the depths of her heart. "D'you mean you really were looking for me?"

Esmee nodded. "For the best part of three years."

"Then, you knew about me all along."

"If not all along, at least for some time."

"And you wanted me back..."

"Yes, we did."

"If I had proved unco-operative, would you have returned me to the Barlows?"

Esmee hesitated, then replied, "Possibly. I imagine, though, since you hated the idea so much, another situation could have been found."

"I'm so glad! That you were satisfied, I mean. I did my best - I really did. And now you have got me."

Esmee sighed. "Yes, we have, God help us!"

Felicity took her stepmother's hand again. "And why shouldn't He?"

The solicitor, who had sunk deep into thought, now revived. "Yes, indeed," he said briskly. "The child has acquitted herself unexpectedly well. She is popular with the household staff - not a consideration lightly overlooked, when one is forced to anticipate possible sources of scandal. She is accepted by Lady Letitia - one can but speculate on the weight that may carry. I understand that she has recently made the acquaintance of - ah - the other aunt. However Lord Farwell may have regarded her, in Society, Dorothea Summer is a force to be reckoned with."

Felicity asked Esmee, "Is that why you let me visit her?"

"That, and because you *would* go, in any case: I thought, rather with my blessing than behind my back."

"More to the point," Mr. Forkes continued undeflected, "she has been presented at Court. One really does not see cause for grave concern.... However," he concluded, "this much having been accomplished, one might judge it prudent to return to the manor without delay."

The pre-departure visit to Aunt Thea was neither sad - for Felicity had every expectation of seeing her again - nor private - for Esmee felt it incumbent upon her, as guardian, to be present. It afforded Felicity a source of secret amusement to watch the two women at close quarters. Though hemmed in by the rules of etiquette, their conduct was not unlike that of two dogs, stiff-legged and wary, taking each other's measure, looking for signs of weakness. The encounter appeared, in the end, positive; they evidently each found something in the other to respect, perhaps even to like. Felicity herself kept a modest demeanour; she chatted with Maud Barry, whom she had come to regard as a friend. At parting, she made the older girl a present of the fur-trimmed hat which Maud had so admired at their first meeting.

Parting from the Gubbinses was not so cool and formal; they were a more demonstrative family than the Sommelroux. There was much embracing all around and promises to write and come again. Felicity knew, of course, that her visits to London would never be frequent or long, for, though there had been some pleasure and much enlightenment in the past six weeks, her heart was still at Twillingmarche, there to remain. Still, if she must return to the capital - and the impending litigation against Cousin Roderick would almost certainly require her presence at some time - it afforded her comfort to know that she would always find a warm welcome in the house at Etheldred Close.

Her luggage had doubled in bulk with new cloaks and dresses, and the presents she had purchased for every member of the household. Even Mr. Finch, who had ever maintained a dignified aloofness - and whom, truth be known, the girl had never been bold enough to approach - would receive a foulard of moss green, gold and rust paisley. It was rather more colourful than anything she had seen on that man; perhaps it would incline him a little toward levity. For Mrs. Golightly, there was a dove-grey shawl of finest wool; for Mrs. MacRory, a framed comical portrait of Mr. Kier Hardie, of whose political exploits the cook was an avid follower.

For MacRory, she had bought a smart grey fedora, and, because she did not know any of their measurements, similar gifts for all the Cartwright men: they could sort out head sizes and colour preferences among themselves. Hats, too, for the young women - not least because Felicity herself enjoyed hats above all other garments. For her young friend, Augustus, there was Mr. Kipling's book, Just So Stories - and if Gus could not read, well then, he must learn, and she would help him. It showed little imagination, but some taste, to purchase elegant silk neckties for Makepeace and George, and after a long, agonised indecision, also Edward. This was only proper, for nothing had been said or done to put their relations in a separate category - not yet.

Cousin Roderick would have a commemorative programme from the Opera, and that, though the barest of gestures demanded by courtesy, was that.

Upon the search for Aunt Lettie's present, she had spent many hours, to the evident but unvoiced displeasure of Roberts, who dutifully trailed her through shop after shop. At last it was discovered: a very fine, albeit perforce rather small, example of the weaver's art, all the way from the Orient - a magic carpet. Well, perhaps neither she nor Aunt Lettie would ever find out the secret word to command it actually to fly, but it was very pretty, nonetheless; she had been forced to beg Mr. Forkes and Esmee for its considerable price.

She did not sleep at all on this journey; she did not want to miss a single mile that brought her closer to Twillingmarche. As a result, it was a weary Felicity who greeted George and boarded the carriage. It was a Felicity nearly unconscious upon her feet who finally approached the House, noting the absence of urns and Lady, and said hello to Makepeace, barely able to disguise her anxious glance beyond him. Here were Evelyn, and Mrs. Golightly, hanging back, as was due to propriety. But where was

Edward? The absence of Cousin Roderick registered but peripherally on her preoccupation.

The early winter dark had already closed in. Felicity's reunion with her friends must wait on the morrow; she and Esmee had time only briefly to freshen up for a late supper. They would be four at table, with Roderick: Roland had elected to remain behind a few more days, ostensibly to attend a championship boxing match, really, to spend as much time as he could with Bettina. Esmee had consented; Mr. Forkes supplied him a train ticket and pocket money. The lawyer had made certain that Roland was not in possession of sufficient funds for ocean travel, should ever he be tempted - Mr. Forkes was nothing if not prudent.

One question, though not the one uppermost in her mind, was answered immediately. Makepeace informed Esmee: "Mr. Sommelroux is conveying to the station a person of the building trades. He is expected to return presently."

Ah, thought Felicity in classic Forkes mode, he has had a response from Newcastle, and will now be receiving one of those accursed estimates. It was typical of Roderick, she further reflected, that, knowing they were to come home today, and having himself an errand at the very same terminal, he should not offer them transport. Of course, three people and their luggage couldn't have fit into one automobile, and they wouldn't have liked to ride with him, but a gentleman would surely have made the gesture. Well, let him be rude. And let him estimate away to his black heart's content; it would keep him harmlessly occupied.

But where was Edward? She had to wait for Kate to help her dress for supper.

"Eddie's detecting," the maid reported, her eyes round and brilliant with excitement. "Seems that Mr. Vesey that's come from London is all over the countryside. Eddie's keeping an eye on 'im. He's questioned everybody downstairs - and silly questions he asked, too, Mrs. MacRory says, all about Lord Randolph and his marriage? Nobody but her was even here then, inside staff, that is -

and Mr. Finch, of course, but you can't call 'im inside staff. What he ever saw of the lady, I'm sure I don't know. He - the Vesey person, I mean - has been at poor old Doc Gillivray and the vicar.... And now, they say he's off at Pine Ridge, way and gone t'other side of the gorge."

"What is Pine Ridge?" asked Felicity.

"Why, that's where Sir Alfred Melrose lives. Don't you know? The first Lady Randolph's - your mother's? - people. Them an the Sommelroux hadn't got a good word for each other, ever since the young lord married our Esmee. Stuck-up lot, them. Next, I s'pose, 'e'll be off to the Grossgrains, an then the Sydney-Smythes.... I can tell you right now, he won't find no joy there, either. All toffs, them, won't give 'im time o' day."

Felicity had been assimilating this information as quickly as her travel-worn brain could be forced to take it in, and come to one tentative conclusion. "Were these families friends of my grandfather's?"

"Aye," the other girl nodded, "fossils, all. The Old Earl - pardon, Felicity, he may've been your granddad, but that didn't make 'im any sweeter - was et up with ire, his only boy marryin' a common showgirl.... Leastways, that's what Auntie Rose says, an she says, he told all 'is cronies to give 'er the snub. Course, the Melroses had their own reason...."

"So that's why we don't entertain! And that's why none of the gentry ever call. Esmee once told me there is nobody of our own kind hereabouts. She was right. I suppose they'll turn up, though, now that I - a true, blue-blooded descendant - have come of age."

"Course they will. Anyroad, it's what Uncle Joe expects, any day now."

"Well, I shan't receive them. I shan't even respond. If my stepmother's not good enough for them, then they're none of them good enough for me."

"Bully!" said Kate.

With one part of her mind trying to decide whether to remind the maid to repress her natural mode of speech, unleashed no doubt by excitement, Felicity became aware of another discrepancy. "I thought nobody below stairs cared for Esmee."

"Ah well," Kate shrugged, "we makes allowances. Her not a bad sort, really, an they do say she'd a pretty lean time of it with the Old Earl. Seems he was keen on the first Lady Randolph - picked 'er out 'himself, an' all. Picked out a new one, too, but Master Randolph wouldn't 'ave no more o' that.... Oh, dear!" she slapped a hand across her mouth. "I best - I mean, I had better be watching my tongue. Be mindful of my new station. Speak like a lady's maid, not a milkmaid, as Auntie Rose never wearies of telling me."

"And I had better be going down. Only, I hope Edward is all right; it's awfully cold out on the moors."

"He'll have bundled up, don't you worry. Shell we put ohn the green velvet to-naht, M'lady?"

Roderick was in high spirits, which did nothing for Felicity's own. He had spent the afternoon showing a Mr. Cuthbert all over the House, and now recounted with unrestrained glee how enthusiastically this man of construction had responded to his ideas. "He thinks it would be no trouble at all, dividing some of the large rooms - we could have forty bedrooms, easy, and that's with a bathroom to every two. We don't need to tear the old wing down - at least, not till we want to expand. But, see, they're kind of picturesque, the abbey and those ruins. Anyway, I just might want to keep them - give the place a little character. So, the old biddy can stay put for a while. Time comes, maybe I'll use this wing, and build a whole new house... say, over on that hill." He waved his wineglass in the direction of the park. "It'd be more private and dignified. Got to clear away a bunch of trees, I guess."

When he stopped to drain his glass and replenish his plate, nobody else spoke. They would none of them have been capable of speech, even had Roderick cared to hear their views. He did not; he resumed the monologue directly his carnal needs were met. "Yes, sir, it's gonna be some job! I can hardly wait to get started. So," he changed topics abruptly, "did you see the king, Pretty Cousin?"

"I was presented, along with other debutantes, yes."

"I bet you were the cutest of the lot! Darned if you haven't grown since the last time I saw you. Quite a young lady, ain't you?" Felicity had no answer to this sally, and needed none, as the American now extended the compliment - for, as such it was obviously intended. "It's a darn shame I'm still a married man, or I'd court you myself. That reminds me - where's the competition, anyway? If that popinjay Roland can be called competition."

Esmee had heard enough. Instead of making any reply at all, she said to Felicity, "Shall we withdraw?" and left the unfortunate Mr. Forkes to cope with port, cigars and Roderick - a dangerous mix.

Not until the next afternoon did Felicity once again have to deal with the troublesome cousin. She was by then equal to the task, for her morning had been most enjoyable. Telling her friends as much of her adventures as would fit into the little time allowed, with promises of much more to come, enough to fill many an agreeable future tiffin, was an occupation very much to her taste. They all seemed highly pleased with their presents, too - even Mr. Finch, who actually blushed. He was not standoffish, after all, she decided; he was merely tongue-tied. She had been able to make an open visit to Aunt Lettie. Esmee thought it appropriate to tag along, but mercifully, did not tarry long.

"You had tea with Thea," was the younger sister's first question, once they were left alone. "How is the old disgrace to the escutcheon?"

"Disgraceful!" she said happily. "Shocking. I *loved* her."

"Is she ever going to visit us?"

"I did ask," said Felicity, "but she would not give a straight answer. Perhaps some day. Esmee came along to see her, you know, just before we left, and I think they got on quite well. Oh! Did you know that Roland isn't Roland?"

"Of course I knew. Poor boy."

"Yes. Poor boy. He's madly in love with Bettina Sommelroux. Only, she's going back to America with her mother - they must have left for Liverpool already. So Roland will be coming back, and I suppose he'll be an awful drip." Felicity sighed deeply. "I know how he feels - I wish I could help."

"Love is sometimes a heavy burden," her aunt allowed.

"You never did tell me your own story," the girl reminded, "And Aunt Thea refused. She said, as it's really none of my business, I ought not to snoop behind a person's back. I expect she's right.... But I would like to know - truly. It is a *little bit* my business, isn't it, since I have the same problem?"

"Ah, then you haven't found another? Not even the eminently eligible Frederick Gilbert could turn your head?"

Felicity giggled at the notion, but the amusement was short-lived. "It's no laughing matter, Aunt Lettie. What am I to do about Edward? I haven't even seen him yet! Kate says he's out trailing a confidential enquiry agent all over the county, and I don't even know where he's been sleeping, or if he eats properly and keeps warm enough - I'm half out of my head with worry."

"Well," said Lady Letitia, "I see it's a bad case you've got. Let me assure you that the boy is neither starving nor freezing. And that he will come home very soon. As for the other problem, perhaps I can put your mind at rest there, as well."

"Can you? You've talked to him about... me?"

Her aunt smiled and nodded. "I have spoken to him. And it does appear to be a shared illness. Oh yes, he is quite besotted, my dear. I cannot pretend to underst- " She was unable to finish the sentence for being smothered in a childish embrace, and having many quite undignified kisses showered upon her cheeks.

20

Felicity having made a thoughtless announcement of her intention to go riding, he instantly volunteered as escort. Eager as she had been to resume her outdoor activities - for a sight of the winter-bound farms and a survey of the countryside, majestic even in slumber - Roderick was not her companion of choice. As she could hardly withdraw her statement, and as Roland was not yet available for chaperon duty, she insisted that Clarence Cartwright - not the slight, youthful Will - come along. "I am not altogether confident of my skill," she explained, "Should the horse bolt," (Small chance, with dear Petunia's temperament, but Roderick knew nothing about this.) "I want a capable man at hand." (And if he took offense at the implied evaluation of his own abilities, all to the good.) Therefore, on their whole tedious ride, they were trailed at a discreet four lengths by an unfailingly watchful senior groom. Unfortunately or otherwise, Roderick's conversation was nothing inhibited by this presence.

At first, they merely rode. From time to time, coming upon a croft, or a flock of sheep huddled in a sheltered hollow where grass was still to be found, he would say, "Of course, we'll have to sell most of this off - I've got no use for farming." Or, "Stupid animals. Why anybody'd want to keep them in this day and age..." and shake his head. Felicity, however provoked, had resolved at the start not to argue with him: it was futile, in any case, and would only give away more of her feelings than she wished to. Rather, she would look as ignorant as possible and wait for Roderick to enlighten her; by this approach was the was the most to be gained. After a long while, he stopped his horse (Ginger, son of Petunia, a special pet of Will's) and turned down-slope, westward.

"See that mess of trees? On the rise past the big house? That's all wasted now. Couldn't you just see a house there? Something really modern?"

"Forgive my asking," said Felicity, "but, wouldn't you be lonely? I mean, with no wife and children..."

The cousin snorted. "The kids'll show up quick enough, don't you worry! Anyway, I sure as - as sure - don't mean to die alone. No, sir. Get free of that woman in no time at all. And then I aim to get married again."

"But isn't it rather complicated, a divorce?"

"Why should it be? I've already made up my mind to give in to all her demands."

"You have?"

"Sure," he shrugged, "why not? I've wired Goldsmith to get himself up here before they sail. Nobody can lay claim to what I haven't got yet.... That reminds me, I better tell the Gormleys to hold off. What I had before, she's welcome to it."

"Your business in Sacramento...?"

"Yep. Don't need it. Tell you the God's truth, Pretty Cousin, I was getting bored. All the fun's in getting started, making a business go, winning out over the other guy. I've done that. Been thinking about Frisco - could've picked up some prime real estate for pennies, after the fire.... Could've gone into building. But I figured, in a couple years I'd just get bored again. This is bigger. Plenty of money to be made, if you know how to handle workers - which I do, make no mistake. None of that Socialist road-apples in *my* operation. I can start something here. Be somebody. Back home, I could've maybe got some backing, run for the senate, and if I won - big if - I'd be owing favours all over the place.... Here, I'll be in the House of Lords, for nothing. All's I need now is a few connections and a high-class wife."

"I see," replied Felicity, all but choking on her anger and frustration, and the concealment of it. Could anyone truly be so insensitive, she wondered, as not to feel the eyes of Cal Cartwright boring holes in his back? "If you win," she could not stop herself adding, "big if."

213

"Oh, that. Don't you worry 'bout that, little girl. There's more'n one way to skin a cat." He nudged his horse a few steps toward the lowering sun; perhaps he was vaguely aware, after all, of a need to put distance between himself and the groom.

Her own mount kept pace without urging. "According to Mr. Forkes," she pointed out, "the litigation can take years. Even then, with all due respect, I believe I have the better claim."

"Maybe so," Roderick smiled. "Unless it turns out you're, uh, mentally impaired."

This was too much for Felicity's iron resolve. "Impaired! How dare you!?"

Roderick was not put out, not in the least. "Oh, I don't know," he drawled very softly - if Cal was nearby, he could still not have heard. "Seems there's insanity in the family... some of the stunts old Roland got up to... that woman in her belfry.... And all the time you spent at the Alpenweiss place - hard to believe it was just for a bump on the head. Might have to subpoena that Dr. Weiss." He glanced sideways at the girl's face, and was evidently satisfied to find it drained of colour, ignorant though he might be of the true reason.

She said, staring straight ahead, "I am perfectly competent, I assure you."

"Wouldn't be a bit surprised," Roderick answered, unruffled. "Spunky, too - I like that. And young, and good-looking - I like that a lot. You and I could maybe work something out...."

She had to respond. But how, to a suggestion - less: an innuendo, which she ought, by all the rules of genteel training, not even fully understand - so outrageous? To pretend incomprehension would only draw out the interview - yet it might bring him more fully into the open. To answer levelly, as an equal in intrigue, would be to give herself away. No; she must take another approach. "I am only eighteen," she said as coolly as the turmoil in her breast allowed. "I have not the authority, as yet, to work anything. Perhaps you should be having this discussion with my guardians."

Roderick was not deterred. "I thought about it," he said. "I even gave some real serious thought to that stepmother of yours. Fine figure of a woman! You should dress more like her - those silky things do something for a man! But," he sternly brought his mind's eye to heel, "she doesn't like me. We got off on the wrong foot. Just as well, though. Can't teach an old dog new tricks - I ought to know; I was married to one. Never gave me a son, either.... Well, it's not too late. Esmee's can't own the place, right? Plus, she's not the real goods, anyhow - plenty of class but no breeding. Still, she's nobody's fool. Once she sees which way the wind's blowing, she'll go along with this deal."

Felicity, having believed herself beyond all shock, was shocked to the core of her being. She was altogether speechless.

"Well," he said smoothly, as if he had been consulting her on nothing more out of the way than the choice of waistcoats to a dinner party, "think about it. You could do a lot worse. You could end up, for instance, with that Roland booby. Didn't see your engagement in the Times, by the way. Or, you could maybe move in with the addled aunt...."

She had not the fortitude to see her cousin any more on that day; pleading a headache, she absented herself from both meals. Esmee would have to be the only woman, this once. Given the reason, Esmee would not blame her. *Should* the reason be given? Ought she to reveal the contents of her afternoon conversation with the horrible relative? One part, certainly, was too offensive to repeat. And the other part? Nothing would ever come of it, but even so, Esmee ought to know about the latest scheme before Roderick himself broached it to her. Felicity therefore recounted the barest essential: that her cousin had all but declared an intent to sue for her hand in marriage. Since he had hinted as much on the previous evening, Esmee was not unduly dismayed - nor did she miss this opportunity to point out how wrong Felicity and Roland had been in their decision not to become engaged.

"It can still be remedied," she said, "and the sooner, the better. Meanwhile, you are quite correct in staying away from that insufferable man."

The lovely room seemed more like a cage tonight than ever it had when she was locked in. Bored, apprehensive, restless, she prowled up and down, looking out a window now and then. A cart laden with crates of vegetables pulled away from the garden gate; Mr. Finch waved at the driver, then turned toward the river path. Young Gus caught up with him; the man put his arm across the boy's shoulders - father and son were heading home for the night. And then the courtyard was deserted; there was nothing more to see. No book to read, either - having lacked the foresight to visit the library earlier, she certainly would not venture downstairs now, and risk a meeting with Roderick. The other Felicity's poems?

Oh, how weary you are growing,
You, who have been so strong!
The light of your eyes, no more glowing
When you gaze at me fondly and long.

Oh, what I would give, if only
I knew how to ease your pain...

What an unhappy child she must have been! There was not a verse, not a line, in celebration of all that she had. Why, Mary Markle, living in a nondescript two-room cottage in Twinsdale, with no running water, and sometimes no firewood for the hearth, found more to be grateful for in any single day than this Felicity Sommelroux had found in all the splendour of Twillingmarche. Of course, in fairness, if one were to look at Mary's thoughts during her mother's final illness, they might not see much difference. And again:

Red is the colour of autumn leaves,

216

Torn from the limb by fall's cold breath,
Red is the colour of my heart's blood,
Staining the earth beneath...

Dismal, gloomy stuff. This was not the way anyone ought to be remembered. She shoved the papers back into their hiding place. Her own poetic effort of some time before, she tore into small pieces and threw on the fire. No future occupant of this room would read it, and think such thoughts of her as she was now thinking of the other girl. The very idea that there should someday be another occupant indicated how morose her mood had become.

Dear Kate it was who came to her rescue. She brought Felicity a supper tray, along with the good news. "Eddie's home," she announced happily. "Only he's dead on his feet, poor lamb, and been sent straight to bed. You can see him tomorrow. He's been gone all of three days," the maid added. "You'd think one of them would'uv noticed - asked after him, or something."

"I noticed," said Felicity.

"Oh, aye. Poor lamb, yourself. Anyroad, the Vesey person got short shrift at Pine Ridge, he says, and din't fare much better with the Sydney-Smythes. The Melroses never even let 'im in the door. But the best part! D'you know what he's been askin' after?"

"I have an idea," Felicity said. Then, realizing that she would only spoil Kate's story, asked, "What?"

"He's been wanting to know, does anyone remember any of the Sommelroux acting funny? Touched in the head, he means. Well, for pity's sake! Some of 'em's been high-handed, all right, and some of 'em's been wild - leastways, it's what the old folks say. But mad - I ask you! It's the daftest thing I ever heard."

"Not so altogether daft," Felicity told her. "My aunt was declared incompetent by her own father."

"But we all know he did that in a snit."

"Nevertheless, it is on record, and most people would think it very odd, the way she lives. I myself am known to have spent three years in a clinic for the chronically ill and well-heeled. I do know what he's after - he all but blackmailed me with it, today."

"He never!"

"Yes," Felicity reinforced, "he did. He's made up a scheme - quite clever in its own horrid way. He wants to marry me, as a way to get hold of Twillingmarche without spending time and money on the courts - where he might lose in the end."

"The devil!" Kate responded. It was perhaps relief enough to have the sympathy, undiluted by self-interest, of one true friend, however powerless to help. Enough it may have been for the heart, but the heart did not rule in matters of inheritance.

"Oh, I wish his father had been... No, I don't; he was nice. I wish Roderick himself had been killed by the Indians!"

"There's more," said Kate. "I heard them at dinner. He's got another of those construction blokes. All the way from London, this one is. I s'pose they'll be a-pokin around the place again. What a bother! One of em's bound to notice something. Oh, and Master Roland be coming home tomorrow, as well."

Roderick was in fine fettle at luncheon next day. He had been host, earlier, to a most secretive visitor. The infamous Vesey, Felicity surmised. The man had not come to the front door, nor given his card to Makepeace. Rather, he had waited in the drive, and Roderick gone down to him, and the two carried on a huddled conversation in the dank, chilly outdoors. Those watching from various windows could make nothing of what was said, nor could they have described the stranger afterward, bundled up as he was in hat, muffler and overcoat.

Roland having duly arrived, and being in the mood she had expected, Felicity felt obliged to attend that cheerless meal, and to bear without comment the winks and smirks her odious relative directed at her throughout. It was not so hard as it might otherwise have been; she had had her own secret meeting that morning.

Edward had been waiting in the butler's pantry. On his face was no sign of fatigue or privation; it was as beautiful as ever. Nay, more beautiful than ever, for at sight of her it broke into a smile that seemed to illumine each corner of the little room. All uncertainty behind her now, Felicity had rushed into his arms, and fitted there as snugly as if it were the hundredth time she'd done this, rather than the first. And it would be so, the hundredth time, and the thousandth, and always. The ease and warmth of this reunion, and above all, the understanding they now shared, gave her armour to withstand a dozen Rodericks, if need be.

Esmee was subdued, watching her son with a mixture of irritation, pity and speculation. To see all these expressions, and especially to see her vain efforts to conceal them beneath an ever-more strained social veneer, might have been a curiosity, had the girl felt less compassion. She had become so fond of them both! Esmee's early treatment of her was long ago forgiven - she counted it a paltry price for what Esmee had thereby opened to her. Roland said almost nothing, merely affirming, when Roderick asked, that Rosalyn and the girls had gone on to Liverpool.

Roderick said, "Fine. Well, that's one thing done right. Tell you another." He relieved the passing butler - still, after weeks of this man's obtrusive presence at table, not quite fast enough - of a bottle of hock. "Get a new one, Peacemaker, don't be cheap - this is kind of a celebration. Yes siree, things are going my way, all right. My man that's been digging around - and he's a darn sight better at it than that turncoat Goldsmith ever was. Well, he's been at the Eastmills place." This was accompanied by a broad wink at Felicity, who lowered her eyes. "That's neither here nor there; those nuns are a pretty tight-lipped bunch. Your fine neighbours are something else again. They can tell stories...! Well, now I've about decided to send him off to Switzerland. What do you think of *that*?" He drained his glass and poured from the freshly uncorked bottle, heedless that the wine had had less than one minute to breathe. "Something ought to come of it, eh, Pretty

Cousin? Course, I might still decide against, if you come around.... Fill 'em up, boy, I haven't got all day. There's a man coming from Pringle and Lyecaster to look at the house. I figure to sound him out on that idea - you know, the one I was telling you about. So, right after we finish this here fine meal, I'm going to scout out a site. Might interest you." The last remark was addressed unmistakably to Felicity, who had been unable to resist looking at him, and was forced to meet his smiling eyes. "I'd be honoured, Felicity," he said, "to have you come along."

She groped for a negative reply sharp enough to serve as discouragement without antagonising him. Upon reflection, however, there was nothing to be gained by courtesy: he knew perfectly well how she felt, and cared not a whit. She said, "Mr. Sommelroux, I would not, under any circumstances, willingly go with you, anywhere, ever."

If she fancied this statement the pinnacle of rudeness, she had underestimated Cousin Roderick. He laughed out loud. "That's all right, I'll pick out the site myself. Surprise you, eh? Peaceable, just time for one more refill. Then I have to get moving. The Leycaster fella's getting here about three."

Mr. Leicester arrived at three fifteen. By that time, Roderick Sommelroux was dead.

21

Mr. Leicester was a large, modest man. He gave up his top-coat reluctantly, explaining how Mr. Sommelroux was meant to be expecting him, and had wanted particularly to show him something out of doors while the light was still good. He waited ten minutes, twenty. He paced the front hall until Makepeace, having sent to look in bedroom and library, drawing, dining and games rooms, finding no Roderick anywhere, grew tired of him. He sat down and stood up, fidgeted and rubbed at his broad greying moustache until Esmee, taking a peek from time to time, began to feel sorry for him. At last, able to stand it no longer, she sent Roland down.

"I don't know where Mr. Sommelroux could have got to," he told the tradesman. "Why don't you come into the games room? It'll be more comfortable."

When they had gone from the hall, Esmee summoned the butler. "Give that person a sherry. No, he doesn't look the part; perhaps a whisky. Well, whatever he wants. Then send one of the footmen to fetch Mr. Sommelroux."

"I have already done so, M'lady. Mr. Sommelroux is not in the house."

"No, of course not. He intended to go to the park, don't you remember? Send for him there."

"Very good, M'lady."

Returning to the drawing room, she told Felicity, "He has never been notable for his manners, Heaven knows, but lately the man's rudeness is astounding."

"I think it's because of losing his wife," the girl suggested. "Rosalyn so wanted to be a lady; I imagine she kept his behaviour in some check."

"Whatever the reason, it's become intolerable." Esmee set her jaw and pronounced: "I shall ask him to leave."

Felicity did not for one moment believe that this would have the slightest effect. Roderick's arrogance knew no bounds: he would simply refuse, and there was nothing short of causing a scandal that Esmee could do about it. She said, "You don't think he has gone?"

"Without a fanfare? And without luggage?"

"No, it would be too much to hope for. Well, then, perhaps he had a secret meeting with that sinister Mr. Vesey, and forgot all about his other appointment."

By four o'clock, dusk had closed in. George returned to the house, unsuccessful. Makepeace came to report that Cousin Roderick's automobile was still in the woodshed, undisturbed, its engine cold; that no horse had been taken from the stables, and that the Palladian wing had been thoroughly searched.

"We shall have tea," Esmee told him, "in here. I suppose Mr. Forkes is still closeted with Finch? Ask my son, and that poor Mr. Leicester to join us. After that, you'd best send out more men. He must be on the grounds somewhere."

She tried to put the builder at his ease with questions about his work, but these appeared only to make him more uncomfortable. "The thing is, you see, Ma'am, Miss, having seen the house now, I don't feel all that keen on changing it."

"Mr. Landry from Twillingsford said the same thing, not very long ago."

"Landry? I know him. Sound man. You say Landry's been consulted, and refused the commission?"

"That's right," Felicity put in. "He said mucking about with the walls would only spoil the building."

"Ta, it's a goodly while since lunch." Mr. Leicester allowed his cup to be refilled and took another sandwich. "But, that being so," he raised hound-like brown eyes to Esmee's, "might I ask why you should want it done?"

"Oh, we don't!" she replied. "Have a cream horn. No. It is a fancy of Mr. Sommelroux's, which the rest of the family most emphatically does not share."

"Ah," said the builder, visibly relaxing. "Mister Sommelroux - not Lord Farwell. Wonderful," he said of the pastry, "I don't know if I've ever tasted as good. But why in the world would Mr. Sommelroux want to change such a fine historical landmark?"

"That, I'm afraid, you must ask him." Esmee said primly, but Roland, at the same moment, volunteered: "He wants to turn the place into a clinic."

"Into a what!?" The builder's hand froze mid-way between plate and mouth. When he noticed, he put it down again, but continued to stare fixedly at the boy. "*This* house?"

"Well, not to say this one, exactly," Roland explained, blithely ignoring his mother's steely glance. "Just the Palladian wing. At first, anyway. He figures to bring in a couple of well-connected Harley Street physicians, and make a lot of money. It's not such a bad scheme. Well," he stared defiantly at Esmee, "it's not! This whole enormous pile's been going to waste for years. Might as well get some use out of it."

"But not," Mr. Leicester protested, "by chopping it all up! That... Why, that'd be like a slap in the face to the architect. Who built it, by the bye? Couldn't have been Inigo Jones himself? No - one of his students, probably. The lines, the proportions, even the placement of the windows - it's perfect. I don't suppose," his eyes dismissed the philistine Roland and beseeched Esmee, "I could have a look at the inside?"

"That, I think, was Mr. Sommelroux's plan. It's unfortunate the light has gone."

Mr. Leicester pulled a huge turnip watch from his waistcoat pocket. It even had a gold chain draped across from a buttonhole, just as Dr. Gillivray kept his timepiece, only on his lean front, it looked more imposing than comical, if rather old-fashioned. "It's gone five. What can be keeping him?"

Felicity had wondered this herself; it was not like Roderick to miss an opportunity to plot the downfall of Twillingmarche. Though this Mr. Leicester, with his passion for the artistic in his trade, would certainly fail to give satisfaction, the cousin had not known it. Where was he?

And yet, as night closed in, there was no sign of him. Esmee was less put out than one would have expected; even after Mr. Forkes joined the family, the best part of her attention remained with the uninvited guest. And why not? He was comely enough in his middle-aged way; tall and well-formed, with more than a hint of the outdoors in his bearing. A very masculine sort of man was Mr. Leicester, prominent of nose and cheekbones, weathered of skin, and yet with those soft brown eyes and hesitant manner of speech, also gentle. Nor was he unmindful of Esmee's charms, however discreet his glances in that direction. Their mutual attraction charged the air with an undercurrent of excitement Felicity could feel. So, she guessed, did Mr. Forkes, who was not pleased by this development. Could he be jealous? She had not been aware of any such relationship between him and Esmee. Of course, when she had first encountered the pair, she had known nothing of such feelings. No, not until she had come to know Edward - not, truly and fully, until yesterday. Had she, in her self-absorption, her preoccupation with material things, overlooked a circumstance so potentially significant? Esmee, at any rate, appeared oblivious to the black looks directed by the solicitor at the builder. Mr. Leicester, however, was not.

"Well," he said, "I doubt there is any point in waiting longer. I shall have to return in the morning. Is there, do you know, Ma'am, a place in the village where I might find lodging?"

Mr. Forkes replied, with near-unseemly alacrity, "Certainly. The Carter's Arms is quite comfortable. One has not had occasion to spend the night, you understand, but one has partaken, once or twice, of a meal there. The cooking, although plain, is perfectly adequate."

Felicity thought: he is not doing himself any good by being so pompous, but he probably can't help it, poor lamb. Felicity had grown more sensitive, of late, to the inner suffering of people crossed in love.

"Why don't you spend the night here, Mr. Leicester?" Esmee offered. "As you can see, we have plenty of room."

"Oh, no, Ma'am. Couldn't possibly impose. I have a motor out front; won't take but a few minutes to run down

224

to the village." And from this resolve he could not be budged. They watched him drive away - Esmee, with a hint of disappointment in her eye.

"M'lady," Makepeace said, after closing the doors, "there is as yet no sign of Mr. Sommelroux. I have taken the liberty of calling on Golightly, and mobilised the outside staff. All available men are searching the park with lanterns. I hope that is satisfactory."

Esmee nodded. "I can think of nothing more to be done. We shall be in the drawing room or the games room, if there is any word."

To the others, she expressed herself more freely. "That wretched man! He has been nothing but trouble from the very first day. He's likely fallen into a well, or tumbled off a rock and hurt himself again.... And here he will be, with a broken something or other, in a foul mood, no doubt, making a nuisance of himself, spoiling the holidays for everyone."

And it was so. Even in absence, Roderick somehow managed to spread a pall over supper. Shortly thereafter, the company being less than jolly, Felicity went up to her room to enjoy her thoughts in solitude. She wished that Edward could join her there, for a long, intimate talk. Although she had a strong suspicion that disappearing couples at the village fetes she recalled had not been engaged in conversation - what would the rustic lads and lasses have found to say, spending all their impoverished lives on the same street? - and although she felt that the odd kiss might not be unwelcome, it was talk she most craved. There was so much that she had yet to learn about him. And he, about her! Soon, she must make an opportunity to tell Edward her secret. Would he find it repugnant? Would he be angry, and think the less of her, once he knew? No; of this Felicity was confident: he loved her for herself, not for her name. Just as she loved him - and had loved him, even before she had a word for it, from the very first moment - for what, not who, he was.

If she could change their stations, either or both, she would - to end this painful separation. Never had they been allowed, by dint of those stations, to linger over a cup of tea, to take a walk, to dance together.... Why, the most strictly-chaperoned of debutantes took those pleasures for granted. Never had he and she been free to idle over a household chore, to meet behind the garden wall, as the meanest of servants did daily. How long must she keep quiet? At the moment, it would be a grave risk to reveal her attachment. And yet, soon, it *must* be brought into the open. Aunt Lettie knew, and Kate, which almost certainly meant that all the women in the house knew, except Esmee and Roberts. Makepeace? Here was a thought to give one pause: what form would the butler's disapproval take?

These were obstacles for another day. Whether she and Edward together could surmount them was no question at all: of course they could. The only question was how to proceed; it was this, more than any other of the million as yet unexplored topics, that she longed to discuss with him.

Kate joined her for a short while, to tell about the search for Roderick. After they had looked in the park, Edward had all the men fan out and walk the length and breadth of the estate. There was no Roderick in the folly, nor in gardens or paddocks. By now, the party had moved on down to the riverbank. Then Bernard Golightly had arrived and taken charge. He fared no better.

"They can't do the gorge," she concluded, "in dark. If he's not found anyplace around the home farms, they'll have to wait till morning."

"I hope he's never found at all," said Felicity.

But, finally, he was. House staff and horsemen, gamekeeper and gardeners, shepherds and field-hands had been out at first light in the rough terrain of Twilling Gorge, and met with no success. Then someone had presented the idea of recruiting dogs. There was not a trained hunting pack closer than Pine Ridge, but a brace of bird dogs and a dozen sheepdogs were rounded up from the home farms. As no man present had expertise in tracking, the animals were simply shown an article of Roderick's clothing and let loose in the grounds, to go where they would and find what they could. Quite soon, three of them - the rest, failing to apprehend the purpose of the exercise, having quarrelled among themselves or bolted after hares or flushed a grouse - converged on the same blackberry thicket.

Close by the knoll that Roderick had pointed out to Felicity as a likely site for his new house was a hollow, shaded in summer by ancient trees. Here, one of the past earls of Farwell had had his ice house built. (Circa 1800, guessed Mr. Leicester, and he was not more than a decade out.) It had been in annual use up until the time of Roland, who had been persuaded of the superior economics of a cedar-insulated sheet metal ice-box close by the kitchens, replenished weekly by a merchant of Twillingsford. Stocking the old ice house had required the labour of ten men through all of January and sometimes beyond, chopping ice on the river into portable blocks, then hauling it two miles up the hill with a sledge and four horses.

The structure itself was little more than a great round well dug in the ground, forty feet down and twenty in diameter, the floor and walls of it lined with fieldstone and topped by a shallow dome. This had been covered over with a thin layer of topsoil on which vegetation was allowed to grow each summer for improved insulation. In the centre of the dome, a four-foot square hole had been fitted with a double plank trap door through which the ice would be lowered. For its retrieval, there was another door, reached by a down-sloping tunnel, in the base of the structure. Ingenious, for its time, certainly, but hardly convenient.

Roderick was directly under the open hatch, his neck broken. The colour of his skin was indistinguishable from that of the stone floor where he lay, stiff and cold as any block of ice. Even in the dim light from above, before MacRory and Edward wrestled open the underground door, they saw that nothing could be done for the man. Edward stopped the gardener from shifting the body. He set MacRory and the gamekeeper on watch, relayed word to the constable, sent the shepherds and dogs away, informed such of the search party as he found within earshot that it was over. Then he went up to the house with the news.

Dr. Gillivray came in his buggy. He was led by Edward and Bernard Golightly to the icehouse. Roland, Mr. Forkes, Makepeace and Mr. Finch all trooped along behind. Esmee and Felicity were commanded, each by the man she was most likely to heed, and in the nicest possible way, to remain indoors. Mr. Leicester, who had returned shortly after breakfast and taken a peripheral and wholly unproductive part in the search, elected to keep the ladies company.

In time, Roderick was brought up, decently draped so as not to shock, but the outline he made was grotesque enough to give nightmares, even so, to all who beheld it. His entourage, shivering in topcoats, fur hats and mufflers, stamped about the front hall. Dr. Gillivray, though with much hand-wringing and without actually finishing a sentence, had taken charge; Constable Golightly seemed content to remain in the background, scribbling notes. Both were agreed that the case was beyond their jurisdiction, and that all further action must wait upon the Twillingsford authorities who had been notified by telegraph, and were, presumably, on their way. Kate, alone of the female population, found occasion to mingle, watch and listen, while distributing welcome cups of cocoa to the chilled men and relieving them of outerwear.

More time passed. At last Inspector Markle, with a sergeant he introduced as Beale and two young constables he did not introduce, arrived just after noon. However like an eternity the interval might have seemed to those waiting, he had made excellent speed in his official car, followed by the heavy police van. After a cursory look under the blanket, he had Roderick loaded onto his vehicle and set one policeman on watch over it. Then he asked to be conducted to the site by Constable Golightly, ("Just the officer, if you please.").

After another long interval, he and the sergeant came back.

"Nasty place, that," was Inspector Markle's comment to the hall at large. "Nasty thing to happen. Now then, let us attempt to make sense of it all."

"Welcome to use my room again," offered Mr. Finch, perhaps knowing that it would be commandeered in any case.

"I'll bring you both some cocoa, shall I?" asked Kate.

Inspector Markle agreed to both suggestions, "And if you could send a hot drink down to the ice house? I've left Golightly and my lad on guard there." He stopped by the blue drawing room only long enough to pay his respects.

22

The police van bore the remains of Roderick Sommelroux off to Twillingsford hospital where they would be subjected to a post-mortem examination. Dr. Gillivray, his fat mare given into the care of a Cartwright, rode along, to review his first findings with the coroner. (And what a lovely time the old dear must be having! thought Felicity.) Mrs. MacRory and her girls quietly prepared a cold buffet to substitute for both luncheon and tea, and set it out in the dining room. Something similar - nay, it seemed to Felicity identical, except for tea and ale, instead of coffee and wine - was laid on in the servant's hall, for the parade of men filing in to give their depositions. Inspector Markle and his trusty sergeant were still in Mr. Finch's office. The manager of farms, who felt it his duty to remain, and Gus, whom no father, nor home and bed, nor wild horses could have dragged away, spent the afternoon in the kitchen. Not altogether unpleasantly, nor amid any great show of sorrow.

As Mrs. Golightly pointed out to her nephew the constable: "It'd be a big lie. He was a dreadful boor, and that's no secret. Why should we start pretending?"

The Sommelroux, having given their statements early on, wandered about their house like lost souls. It was their property now - or, rather, Felicity's. This fact had just begun to dawn upon the heiress: the one who had intended to take it from her was dead. Yet, with the police installed, it did not seem like home.

Mr. Forkes had had the presence of mind to wire Mrs. Sommelroux the sad news; she and her daughters would, no doubt, cancel their berths and come back. They would have to be accommodated. Funeral arrangements must be made, or else arrangements to ship the body to California. Had Roderick wanted that? Would he have wished a full church service? Had he left instructions or a will? These were questions more properly within the scope of Mr. Goldsmith and Rosalyn. No decisions could be made, in any case, before the inquest. Esmee and Mr. Forkes occupied themselves with such matters, practical or imponderable, while Roland sat here or there, paced or stared out windows, with a stunned look upon his pale face, hands clasped between his knees - no earthly good to anyone. Mr. Leicester had told what little he knew and, assured by Esmee that he might return for a tour of the house on a more convenient occasion, departed for the Carters' Arms.

Felicity, whose presence was required by no-one, was free to go anywhere she pleased. Having refilled the coffee urn and eavesdropped a little on conversations that could not hold her attention, she brought empty plates back to the kitchen. Things were livelier here; there was an air of subdued festivity. She gave Jane a hand with the interminable washing-up and nobody reprimanded her, so she stayed to take some refreshment.

The gamekeeper, finished his interview with the police, joined Mrs. Golightly at the big central table. "Well, that's done. Would there be any partridge pie, I wonder?"

"This was the last piece, I'm afraid," said Felicity.

"Cut us a bit of ham, then. And pour a mug of ale, there's a good lass. I'll bring you in a nice bird or two in the morning," he told Mrs. MacRory.

"Carter's need a couple brace," said the cook, and the housekeeper added: "Don't forget that Twillingsford order."

Settled with his plate and mug, Golightly grumbled, "All this business," he stabbed the air over his shoulder with a brown thumb, in the general direction of the manager's office, "keeps a man from his proper work. Everything at sixes and sevens."

"Well?" prompted his wife, "How was it? What did Inspector Markle ask you?"

Golightly shrugged. "Usual things."

"Oh, come on, Charlie, tell. The girl's all right."

The girl sitting across the table from him was, in fact, dying to hear, and more than a little heartened by the housekeeper's confidence. She met the old man's measuring stare with her own most innocent one. "I really am, you know."

He laughed, "S'pose you are, at that. But young ones ought to know their place. Seen and not 'eard, eh? Well, there isn't much to tell, just the same. Did I see the Sommelroux man, muckin aboot in park? Did I warn him o' the ice-house? Was it kept locked? So much foolishness."

"He's got to ask," said Mrs. MacRory.

"Waste of time," the gamekeeper insisted. "If a grown man pokes his nose where it don't belong, it's 'is own look-out."

Mr. Finch interrupted his spirited game of cards with Evelyn, Becky and Gus to remark, "You'd think he'd have learned from the first time, or second..."

"Some people never do," said Mrs. Golightly comfortably.

The cook nodded, "That's true. Look at the Earl - one broken bone after another..."

"Course, he was gettin' on in years,"

"So he was. But then, *this* feller," the gamekeeper said, "was three sheets to the wind, most time."

"Do you have any fives?" asked Mr. Finch, and Becky's answer, "Go fish," was the only speech by any young person.

"And some people," Mrs. MacRory pursued her reflections, "are plain accident-prone."

"Maybe," speculated Mr. Finch, "it runs in families."

Felicity, in the face of a history that would appear to support this theory, fervently hoped that he was wrong. She served MacRory when the gardener was done with his brief statement, but left Terry Cartwright to serve himself. She wandered to the drawing room, brought a stack of empty cups back to the kitchen; went to the dining room to fetch away a platter. At last, the moment she had been seeking on all these contrived errands came: she found herself in the back hall, otherwise unpeopled for the moment, face to face with Edward.

"How are you holding up, Nosey Parker?" His tone was light, but his eyes betrayed anxiety on her behalf. Actually, she had not been very much upset. But perhaps Edward had.

She replied, "I'll do; not to worry. Was it really horrible for you, finding…. him?"

"Bad enough, but it's over - and I can't say I'm sorry."

"I believe getting killed is about the best thing Cousin Roderick ever did."

Edward took her free hand. "We'll talk about that, too. We have a good deal to talk about, don't we?"

Another voice broke into their conversation. "Children," said Makepeace, very softly, "there is a time and place for everything. Please try to observe the proprieties."

"Yes, Dad," Edward said meekly, dropping her hand. It felt cold, suddenly. And to Felicity, "After breakfast. The chapel."

In their comings and goings throughout the afternoon, they were able to exchange glances and smiles, and once a half-accidental touch, but no more private words. I ought not to be so impatient, Felicity admonished herself; we have all the time in the world. Why, there is nothing to come between us anymore. Well, perhaps Esmee... but what, really, can she do? Roland will soon come out of his trance and realize that no disapproving father can any longer stop him marrying the girl he loves. Esmee has lost her power over him, and over me.

Everything's changed.

Lady Letitia was in her room, but not in her chair. She wore an ordinary blouse and skirt; her hair was neatly tied back with a green ribbon - not the style most flattering to her narrow face, the girl thought, but infinitely preferable to the mad-woman disguise. She stood leaning her elbows on the windowsill, oblivious of the cat Grimalkin pacing back and forth, sweeping his tail across her chin at every pass.

"It's growing dark," she said. "Not that there's much to see. No activity in the last hour." She came and sat down, as Felicity pulled up a small table for her tray. "It was quite interesting, for a while."

"Interesting? It was awful!" said Felicity .

"Do you think so?"

"Well," the girl admitted, "I'm not sad about Cousin Roderick. But I *am* sorry for the little girls. I don't think they knew how vile he could be, though perhaps Rosalyn and Bettina did. Still, to have something like this happen here..."

"It's not the first time. You don't find it all just a little bit - thrilling?"

"All right - yes, I do. The detective is still here, you know. He's asking everybody when they last saw Cousin Roderick, and where he'd been, and was he warned? He's asking about the ice-house, and when they started looking for him, and why it took so long.... It wouldn't have mattered, though, if they'd found him right away; the doctor says he broke his neck. Died instantly, he says. So, it must have happened yesterday, quite soon after he went out."

"And what does the inspector say?" Aunt Lettie picked up a triangle of buttered toast, spread a delicate layer of mustard upon it, and, hesitating over the ham, chose a slice of turkey breast instead. She took a dainty bite. "Thoughtful of you to bring this. There's nothing like high drama for giving one an appetite."

"He hasn't said anything yet. He's not come out of Mr. Finch's room all afternoon. But, according to Mr. Forkes, there will be an inquest. That's a sort of hearing, to -"

"I know what it is. I have attended one."

Of course; Letitia's own father had died violently. And, of course, Letitia knew a great deal more than her reclusive habits would suggest; she probably knew more about everything that went on at Twillingmarche than Felicity did herself, however apt the nickname Edward had lately used. Well, then, if I am nosey, she thought, it runs in the family; I come by it honestly.

234

"Has there been any more heard from that investigator, Vesey?" Aunt Lettie asked.

"No, but Roderick meant to see him again. He was teasing me about it. Said he would send the man to Switzerland and bring Dr. Weiss here - Could he do that? - if I didn't agree to... to marry him." The girl shuddered, "I would rather have died!"

"I doubt that," her aunt replied serenely, constructing a sandwich of watercress and ripe cheddar. "But it's better that he did."

"He was so rude and selfish. And so sure of himself! He frightened me."

"You haven't told all this to the police?"

Felicity shook her head, "No. It hadn't anything to do with Roderick's falling into the ice house. And I'm sure Esmee wouldn't have mentioned it, unless to Mr. Forkes."

"Elijah Forkes can hold his tongue, though he doesn't like to. Who else knew?"

"Cal Cartwright was with us the other day, but I don't think he could have heard Roderick threaten me."

"Cal's all right."

"I told Kate."

"Naturally. How, precisely, did Roderick threaten you?"

Understanding that this was a matter of grave concern, the girl tried to reproduce her cousin's exact words. Lady Letitia nodded once, decisively, when she had finished. "Good. He was only hoping to establish mental incompetence. He hadn't learned, as yet, that you've never been at the Alpenweiss."

"I'm sure not. You see, somebody was..."

Aunt Lettie interrupted. "The Talbot girl, yes. She is no longer there and her fees were paid through an intermediary. The problem is, she looks nothing like you."

Felicity felt her mouth drop open, made a mighty effort to regain control of it. "But how did you...?"

"Never mind. There will be time for that."

Felicity recovered quickly, even to being, in some remote part of her mind, amused. Only a few minutes ago, she had been reminding herself of Aunt Lettie's many sources of information, and here she was, once again taken by surprise. "That's what everybody says - about everything," she grumbled.

"Now," said her aunt briskly, treating this last bit of childishness as it deserved: ignoring it completely, "since Roderick was awaiting your answer, he won't have given his agent new orders yet. Good. Beyond an oblique proposal of marriage, which you found flattering..." She held up one thin hand to stop the girl's protest, and firmly repeated, "...which, should it come to the attention of the police, you found flattering and embarrassing, as you did all of his flirtatious banter. You did not take it seriously, of course, he being so much older, and still married. Therefore, neither you, nor anyone in the house, had reason to fear Roderick Sommelroux."

Felicity dared not contradict, but felt compelled to point out, "The whole county must have known about his lawsuit - and his plans for Twillingmarche."

"True. And the whole county disapproved of them. That's neither there nor here. What everybody doesn't know, and must not learn, is that you have no right to inherit."

"I do have a right!" flared Felicity. "I am the daughter of Randolph Sommelroux!"

"Of course you are," said her aunt. "It's Randy's shame, not yours, that he never married your mother. It's the law's shame to dispossess children like you. Nevertheless, it does. Had Roderick found out, he could have cut you off with nothing."

Felicity said softly, "Then it's lucky he died when he did."

"Indeed. Fortuitous. And now, I think you had best put your face in order and go back before you're missed. Don't fret too much, my dear. Just be the best Felicity that you can be."

Meanwhile, the house had settled into quiescence. Farm hands and stablemen, gardener, steward and boot-boy had all gone to their own homes. The maids had finished clearing the dining room; there would be no formal meal served tonight. The footmen were not in evidence, though Makepeace kept to his post in the front hall. The family was listlessly disposed about the drawing room.

"Where have you been?" asked Esmee.

"I took a bite of supper to my aunt. The servants were busy and I thought someone should tell her what has happened."

Mr. Forkes looked up from his game of solitaire at this, but made no comment.

Esmee said, "Very kind of you. I should have thought of it. One tends to forget about the poor old thing. How did she take the news?"

"She's only met the man once, and then didn't like him; she isn't grief-stricken."

"I'm not, myself," Esmee admitted. "Relieved, just between us. It's an ordeal, all the same. You seem to be wearing it quite well."

"I shan't miss him."

"That may be true, and it's quite in order to be candid amongst ourselves, but we must put on a decent show. Whatever else he may have been, he was a relation.... We must do our best for his poor family."

Mr. Forkes, still holding a red knave which he had been about to place on a black king, said, "They'll all be here tomorrow or next day. All of them," he repeated sadly.

Roland, in the corner wing chair with his feet propped against the fender, smiled into the fire and held his peace.

"You can't do that," Felicity pointed out to Mr. Forkes. "It's cheating."

"So it is," he agreed, and placed the card.

"What'll you do with the red queen, when it turns up?"

Mr. Forkes nodded thoughtfully, took the knave back again and shuffled the deck.

At a quarter past eight, Inspector Markle finally emerged.

"Well, now," he announced a few minutes later to those assembled in the hall - which was the entire household staff, it seemed, as well as the family. Word had passed rapidly.

"I have completed my preliminary investigation. I now propose to outline the salient facts. If any here present have relevant facts to add or details to correct, please do so.

"It appears that the deceased, after a heavy meal accompanied by much wine, went to the park to inspect a possible site for a house which he considered building at some future date." The policeman paused in his remarks, glanced about his sumptuous surroundings, shook his head minutely, cleared his throat. "Be that as it may. Mr. Sommelroux had made his intention known to several persons. Mr. Leicester, by prearrangement, arrived at approximately fifteen minutes past three o'clock. At that time, Mr. Sommelroux was not in the house. As he did not appear in the next hour, one George Gillivray, a footman of the household, was despatched outdoors to remind the deceased of his appointment. He was unable to locate Mr. Sommelroux. A search was organised, at first by members of the household staff, later including all able-bodied men in and about the estate. Very efficiently conducted, I might add." Inspector Markle gave a small, approving nod to the Makepeaces standing against the wall, side by side, in attitudes of respectful attention. Edward allowed the impassivity of his features to slip a fraction in acknowledgment of the compliment; the butler's registered nothing at all.

The detective continued. "No trace of deceased being found yesterday evening, the search continued at first light, under the leadership of local constable, Bernard Golightly. At this time, dogs were recruited. The body was discovered at," he glanced at Sergeant Beale, who, without checking his notes, supplied: "At twenty-one minutes to twelve noon, sir."

"Quite. Mr. Sommelroux was discovered at the bottom of a long-disused ice house which had been previously overlooked, because of its obscure location. I am informed that the trap door to this, ah, building had been securely latched. The hasp and hinges, though rusted, were strong. The door itself appeared, upon my inspection of it, to be sound, and of heavy construction. In order to fall in, then, Mr. Sommelroux had to have unlatched and lifted the trap door, which needed considerable force. Mr. Sommelroux, as I understand it, was a vigorous man in his prime; the task was within his capabilities. What remains unclear is why he should have wished to do it alone, when help was readily available. That, and also how he might have lost his balance and fallen, is perhaps explained by the, ah, reported condition of deceased at the time. This is mere conjecture, pending the coroner's report.

"Does anyone have further information? Clarification? Comment?" The policeman looked slowly around at the faces, all alike in their blankness. "Very well. Witnesses required to give evidence will be notified of the time and place of the inquest." His voice changed from the studied neutral tone of officialdom to one of human warmth, "I would like to express my thanks for the cooperation shown by all of you in a circumstance so naturally distressing. And my personal opinion that this accident does not reflect adversely on any person here. Or any other person," he amended, noting the absence of Golightly, in whose purview the ice house was located, "here employed."

Collecting his taciturn sergeant, Inspector Markle bade them farewell and disappeared into the night.

23

She had paid especial attention to her toilette this morning. She had endured breakfast with Esmee, responding to that lady's mundane remarks with ever-increasing abstraction. At last, she was free. The intervening doors no longer kept locked, she didn't need to tell anyone of her destination. The chapel stood open, breathing out ancient sanctity.

"Edward?"

"Here," he answered in low a voice, though there was no real need for secrecy. "Come, sit down."

She joined him in the nethermost pew, pleased at the familiar way in which his arm went round her shoulders; she leaned against him and gave a little sigh of contentment.

"We mustn't relax our guard too much, just yet, "he warned, "It isn't quite over."

"All but the shouting," Felicity replied, "You said so yourself. But what a lot of shouting there will be! Rosalyn and the girls and Mr. Goldsmith are coming. And then the inquest," she shuddered, "I shall hate that."

"No, you won't," contradicted Edward with a laugh. "You'll have a grand time - you and the doctor, both. He will have to give evidence, of course, but you needn't go..."

"Of course I must go -"

"See?"

"- if only to give you moral support."

"We shall all be there, don't worry."

"Even Aunt Lettie?"

"Possibly." His tone changed. "So. Little Mary Markle is to be chatelaine of Twillingmarche."

Felicity looked up sharply. "You must not say that!" she hissed, "not even in fun. If it were to get out..."

Edward nodded soberly, "You're right, I suppose. If Goldsmith or Rosalyn got wind of it, even now, poor old Roderick might have died in vain."

"How long have you known?"

"Some little while," he said easily. "The first time I saw you in Roberts' window -"

"You were surprised then, I could tell."

"Surprised!? I was astounded, Love. We knew that Elijah had brought home a girl, but not how closely she resembled the original. I thought I was seeing a ghost."

"A ghost is it? And there was I, seeing an angel. It seems I'd got the better of the bargain." She snuggled comfortably. "How long d'you think we'll have to wait?"

"For what?"

"To get married."

"I haven't proposed," Edward reminded her.

"Well, then, you'd best get on with it, unless you'd rather I did. It's all right, I'm an emancipated woman."

The arrival of the other Sommelroux was as noisy and disruptive as she had expected – even more perhaps, because after two days, the household was settling into its accustomed ways. The niche lately carved out by Cousin Roderick was shallow; the gap he left was quickly closing up. His bedroom was generally avoided - as it had been for years before ever he came. And now Rosalyn and the girls blew in like the fabled tornadoes of their homeland. Maybelle was called upon once more to supervise the little ones lest anything further befall the luckless family. Bettina cried quite a good deal, though without serious damage to her smooth face, and was duly comforted by Roland. Mr. Goldsmith, in the absence of his ebullient employer, kept a modest demeanour, taking his cue from Mr. Forkes. The widow, decked out with new and quite elegant weeds, had more an air of competence than of grief. The initial shock, however unfeigned, was dissipating fast; she concerned herself with things to be done, rather than occupying her time in fruitless lamentation.

Lucy and Lisa, on the other hand, were preternaturally quiet. They behaved, for a wonder, like two young ladies: spoke when they were spoken to, but otherwise kept much to themselves. They were, Felicity imagined, the only people of whom Roderick had been genuinely fond; they were the only people whom he had given no cause to wish him to the devil. Irritating as Felicity had found them on their earlier visit, she felt an unexpected sympathy now. She knew what it is to lose a parent. That, and their double reflection of herself as a child invoked a sense of kinship. Therefore, she was at pains to invent small acts of kindness, although she understood that only the passage of time would console them.

Dr. Gillivray - the younger, clerical one - came to call. After completing his examination, the pathologist had released the body to the ministrations of Adams and Archibald, funeral directors in Twillingsford. Felicity was not involved in the discussion of burial rites, but learned that Roderick was to be interred in the Sommelroux plot at St. Hilda's. She reflected, irreverently, how much easier this might have been, had one of the past earls seen fit to build a crypt: frozen ground must make heavy work for the gravediggers. Flowers were to be supplied by the estate's own greenhouse, to be picked at the last possible minute by MacRory. In this, at least, Felicity could help, and it struck her as appropriate.

All was done with pomp and ceremony. The entire village of Amber turned out, as well as every denizen of Twillingmarche itself. Both carriages were harnessed, the horses caparisoned in black satin and tassels, each with a brass and feather head ornament. They looked magnificent, and seemed fully conscious of the solemnity of the occasion. The footmen on the driving seats wore black and gold livery. Edward looked exceptionally distinguished, she thought; even young George had an air of mature dignity. Behind them came a long line of buggies and traps and two motorcars. Mr. Goldsmith had elected to drive Roderick's; Mr. Forkes joined him, in order to ease crowding in the carriages. Makepeace rode in a commodious black automobile driven by Mr. Finch, occupied also by a very comely Mrs. Finch, a most grownup-looking Augustus in Sunday best, and two watchful, dark-eyed fledglings. With Esmee, Roland and herself, and to their unvoiced astonishment, sat Lady Letitia. She looked slight and frail, swaddled in a cloak of black velvet, slightly rusted by age; a family heirloom, no doubt. Upon arrival at the church, she was helped down by Edward, when it came time to follow the coffin, supported on her other side by Makepeace. She said not a word throughout the proceedings.

As Roderick's father was buried half a world away, he would be laid next, on the left, to his uncle Roland's second wife. To the right of the eleventh earl was his only son, Randolph, his wife and child beside him. On the baby's white monument, a small cherub played its diminutive stone harp. The whole next row was given over to similar markers - eight of Felicity's aunts and uncles had not survived long enough to be named. What sort of gravestone would Roderick get? Rosalyn had not as yet been able to decide - certainly nothing so imposing as that of the patriarch Roland.

Afterward, chilled to the bone, everyone was happy to return to the Victorian house. Fires had been laid in every room, and all interior doors thrown open. Mrs. MacRory had set out a vast array of funeral meats and pastries; Kate served hot drinks and Makepeace, strong ones. There was scarce need of such quantities of food, for the nine people most immediately touched, but everything was done in the strictest of traditional style. The vicar was, of course, in attendance, and his brother the doctor; Mr. Leicester came, because, encountering him at the church, Esmee invited him. Aunt Lettie, for the first time in living memory, joined the party, if only to ensconce herself by the drawing-room hearth. Here Felicity, Makepeace and Kate came at frequent intervals with a tid-bit or steaming cup. Both Gillivrays stopped by to pay their compliments. Esmee, having expressed surprise only by the merest rise of her brows, made a brief courtesy visit; Rosalyn followed suit, though she had evidently no idea what to say. It ought to have been the widow sitting in state with everyone flocking to condole at her; Rosalyn seemed unaware of this. Nor did anyone else presume to question Lady Letitia's pride of place.

Finally, it was over. The guests went home. Aunt Lettie was escorted to her tower by Edward. The residents repaired, each to his or her room, for a much-needed rest. Except Felicity, who stayed behind to help move victuals down to servants' hall for another wake - an altogether less constrained and happier affair, attended by Cartwrights, Finches, MacRorys, Gillivrays, Makepeaces and Golightlys and their various dependents from around the estate. For this second assembly, it was an unabashed celebration.

Not so, for Roberts. The woman had made herself alien among the servants and, unlike Mr. Forkes, was not at home in the drawing room, either. It was a shame, after all she had done, for Roberts to be so isolated. Felicity decided to repay, in very small part, those many times the lady's maid had brought trays to her room, by taking supper up to her now. It proved a short, unsatisfactory visit. Roberts thanked her politely but declined to engage in casual conversation. Felicity could not understand why the other should persist in observing a formality she knew to be false. Had she not, in large part, herself created this Felicity? Why then, would she insist upon keeping her at arm's length now - the same girl whom, but three months previously, she had been lecturing and reprimanding at every turn? Prisoner of her own snobbery, perhaps of her own private fantasy, Roberts was not, and never would be, open to friendship.

The sound of the bell was unexpected; everyone they knew had but recently gone away. Makepeace was therefore slow to emerge from the back of the house, and Felicity hesitated on the landing, not certain she ought to arrive at the door first, or whether she should answer it. It was George who responded, hastily pulling on his splendid formal jacket.

The visitor stood irresolute upon the threshold. "I wonder," he began. George stepped well back into the hall, forcing the man to follow, so that he might sooner curtail the invasion of December air. "I wonder, now, who it is I should be asking for?"

"If Sir would entrust one with his name and the nature of his errand, one could perhaps be of assistance," said George.

The stranger searched his inside coat pocket and eventually came up with a card, which he thrust at the footman. "My name's Vesey," he explained. "I had some business with ... er.. the late Mr. Sommelroux. I've only just this morning heard, you see,"

"Quite," George replied smoothly. "Then Sir would no doubt like an interview with Mr. Sommelroux's solicitor."

"Yes, that'd be fine," replied Mr. Vesey in evident relief. "He's here?"

"If Sir will step into the library, I shall enquire." He deftly removed the unprotesting investigator's hat and coat, and ushered him through. Normally, Felicity thought, persons with the appearance, not to mention the occupation, of Mr. Vesey, would be left standing in the hallway; possibly the nature of his business, or the present sad circumstance, imbued him in the footman's eyes, with an unaccustomed importance.

Mr. Goldsmith was roused. Mr. Goldsmith hurried down, past a Felicity occupied for that moment in the study of an ancestor she had never before considered particularly engrossing. The library door closed.

"What d'you suppose will happen now?" she asked, running lightly down the last flight to George. "He wouldn't report to anybody besides Cousin Roderick, would he? A confidential inquiry agent?" The young man pantomimed: who can tell? She said, "You did that very well. 'If Sir would entrust one with his name...' I enjoyed that."

George grinned, "Watch Uncle Joe long enough, you learn how to be snotty as h- "

"Ahem." Makepeace had, in his eerily silent manner, materialised upon the scene; they both sprang to attention, like children caught making sport of their elders. "I hope I don't have to remind you - either of you - yet again of the necessity of observing proper decorum. What would an onlooker make of this: the Countess of Farwell and one of her footmen, whispering and laughing together?"

"I'm not sure I care," retorted the countess.

"Please make an attempt," the butler drily told her. "We're not all the way out of the woods yet, M'lady."

Felicity sighed, her small flame of rebellion thoroughly quenched. She had no wish to get on the wrong side of this formidable man, especially as he was to be her father-in-law.

"Pst," George warned, "here comes Goldsmith. Alone."

The girl made her way without unseemly haste, and George more sedately followed, to the butler's pantry. This narrow space adjoined both the dining room and library; if the occupants of either room spoke in normal tones, most of their conversation could be heard by ears pressed to a wall. At the moment, there was but the sound of one man pacing back and forth between windows and fireplace. Soon, however, the listeners' patience was rewarded; not only did the lawyer return, but he had Rosalyn in tow.

"Well, what is it you want?" she demanded without preamble.

"Mrs. Sommelroux? Let me introduce myself..."

"That won't be necessary. I know that my husband hired you. If you have been spying on me ..."   Mr. Vesey here interjected three or four rapid No's.

"...you'd be well advised to drop any such investigation. Well then, what were you meant to snoop out?"

Given a moment to collect himself, Mr. Vesey outlined his assignment. It did not take long to tell.

"I see," said Rosalyn, no longer hostile. "He was clutching at straws. The girl is no more crazy than I am - maybe less crazy than poor Roderick was."

"Then, you do not wish me to continue?"

"Certainly not."

"Mr. Sommelroux had mentioned the possibility of my travelling to Switzerland..."

"You can forget that," said Rosalyn.

Mr. Goldsmith ventured, "If it's a question of your fee..?"

"No, no," the investigator hastened to reassure them. "On the contrary, I find myself with cash in hand. The retainer, you understand, is not refundable, but your late husband advanced me a generous sum for expenses."

"Keep it," Rosalyn told him. "As compensation for the inconvenience."

"And my report?"

"Keep that, too. No," she amended, "Mr. Goldsmith will dispose of it. I wish you a pleasant journey home, Mr. Vesey. Good bye."

Makepeace, ever at hand, showed the visitor out. Employer and advisor were left alone.

Mr. Goldsmith asked, "Why let him keep the money?"

"It can't be much, and the man was obviously disappointed. He wanted that trip."

"Even so..."

"And I want him to go away, with no more possible claim on us. Get rid of those - there's still a good fire."

"Roz, are you sure?" persisted Mr. Goldsmith. "You won't read this?"

"Quite sure."

"But, suppose he did find. Something useful. Suppose Rod had a case, after all? Don't you want to? Follow it up. For the children?"

"No," said Rosalyn decisively. After a moment's pause, she continued in a gentler tone. "Look, Sam, we don't *need* this. I admit he turned my head for a minute. The idea of being aristocracy all of a sudden was - well, pretty exciting. I did enjoy the parties and balls; I know Bettina loved every second, and I'm glad she had the chance. But we don't belong here. Or in London, for that matter. We might be welcome, even popular... sure, it's fun... for a little while. But we couldn't afford to keep up very long, the way these people spend money. And we'd never have been accepted as British nobility - we'd always be the upstarts. No, the girls and I have everything we need in Sacramento. We're respected there, and no pretending. We have friends, a pretty good business that's being neglected..."

"Henry Harrison has it under control. You know he does. I showed you the statements."

"And I miss my own home. I've never liked this house; never trusted it. Poor, big-headed Rod became obsessed with it, and look! I told him it wouldn't end well. We should have stayed at home. The divorce would have been final by now.... He could be chasing women, having a good time, taking a comfortable twenty years to eat and drink himself to death. Instead, he's got nothing but a flashy Sommelroux tombstone. I will do that for him - a really big one."

"So. We go home."

"As soon as you can book passage. It doesn't have to be the Lusitania - any ship with half decent quarters will do. This weather, we'll be stuck inside the whole trip. Wait much longer, we'd run into icebergs."

"But, the inquest? What if the coroner. Rules foul play?"

"Why should he? It's obvious what happened: Rod had too much to drink, as usual, went where he shouldn't, as usual; didn't think… as per. Just the same, I guess we ought to show up. When is it?"

"Monday afternoon."

"All right. When it's over, we'll drive straight to Liverpool. And don't think they'll be seeing us off with tears in their eyes."

Mr. Goldsmith said something so quietly that Felicity and George were not able to catch it. Rosalyn's answer was as soft; perhaps a sigh, but she immediately resumed her healthy volume. "Yes. We'll have to talk to his mother, if he hasn't already. I don't know what Rod had against the boy - he's sweet. And," she added, "not so air-headed as I used to think."

That was that, as far as Mr. Vesey was concerned. By now, he would be half way to Amber. By tomorrow, he would be a faint memory. George gave Felicity a nudge; she smiled back. They left the pantry by the doors at either end; he, toward the kitchen end of the house, to give his report; she, through the dining room and thence next door. The confidential agent's notes were smouldering satisfactorily; Felicity checked and stirred the grate before drifting over to the shelf where she kept her set of white leather-bound poetry books. Or, rather, the other's poetry books; she herself had little patience for such things, as a rule. Only, it was that sort of day. She pulled a volume at random and let it fall open where it would.

I'll not leave thee, thou lone one,
To pine on the stem;
Since the lovely are sleeping,
Go, sleep thou with them.

Thus kindly I scatter
Thy leaves o'er the bed
Where thy mates of the garden
Lie scentless and dead.

Thomas Moore had been addressing the last rose of summer; he could not have known how aptly these verses of his would fit into a winter's afternoon, a hundred years later. Nor that he was sending a coded message down that century. The present Felicity suddenly realised that there was a service she still owed to her predecessor.

The secret panel sprang open with a well-practiced click. Some day, perhaps, she would find a more fitting use for the secret compartment, though she hoped not. How wonderful to anticipate a life free of concealment and prevarication! Of her only remaining secret, no written record must exist, anywhere. She brought out the sheaf of dog-eared pages and leafed through them, stopping at the last page.

Without you, the sun grows dark,
The stars have lost their shine:
This life is dust
And still I must
Continue to repine.

Without you, the bloom of youth
Is a hollow mockery.
How could you, my love,
Ascend above,
And leave me in misery?

Without you, this earthly coil
Is heavy, cold and slow.
I should give my all
If only you call,
If with you I may go.

Well, the child never would have become a poet,
even had she lived to a ripe old age; these really were not
very good. Still, she had put down her true innermost
feelings, and it was wrong to make sport of them. It was
discourteous, indeed, to read them at all. No-one else
should be given that opportunity: the girl, however foolish,
was entitled to her privacy, wherever she might be. Felicity
gathered up the pages and placed them, one by one,
gently upon the grate, where they flared up in imitation of
the Vesey report.

24

The youthful Albert Gillivray, magistrate of Twilling County, did not disappoint Rosalyn: the inquest was a short one. Detective Inspector Markle's extensive notes were scarcely consulted; he recounted his investigation simply and succinctly, leaving little for the jury to ask. Dr. Gillivray and the district pathologist, a reticent, soft-spoken gentleman named Ferrier, described the body as they, respectively, had found it. Constables Golightly and Ribble related the results of their experiments with the trap door. It had very likely been Roderick's undoing - somewhat under the influence of spirituous liquor, struggling with the rusted hinges and the heavy planks, he had lost his balance and tumbled forty feet onto the stone floor below. So concluded the coroner, and thus was the verdict of six good burghers, and true: "death by misadventure".

Rosalyn had ordered the grave stone, a great polished black slab with scroll and wreath, but no angel; she thought that far too elaborate. As it would not be ready before the spring, Mr. Forkes promised to send photographs of the emplacement, and the reverend Gillivray would, naturally, officiate, "God grant," he added piously.

There was nothing further to keep the Americans at Twillingmarche, except the deep reluctance of Bettina and Roland to part. They had already declared their intention to marry; nothing Esmee said - nay, though she spent a goodly portion of the night saying all that she could think of and then repeating it more loudly - would deflect her son from this resolve. She had, at last, acceded. To her greater chagrin, Roland was also bent upon emigrating. Rosalyn and Mr. Goldsmith together made a convincing argument: there was a place for Roland in the family business. He would learn all there was to know about motorcars, than which nothing could make him happier. The wedding had to be put off at least six months, and even that might be considered an insufficient period of mourning. Of course, Rosalyn had no intention of staying so long; arrangements would be made when the time came, for a second journey. Whether Esmee and Felicity should travel to California or the other Sommelroux return to England was yet to be decided.

It had been a crushing few days for Esmee. Felicity, now in unchallenged - if still, for some time, superintended - possession of the house and lands, was making her own plans. She would continue to run Twillingmarche just as it had been run for years, under the guidance of Mr. Finch. Only, the new chatelaine wanted to know every detail of every transaction, and be always in residence. She had no desire to spend months at a time in the city; she had no need for any society outside her estates. The fate of Etheldred Close was uncertain; Felicity would, very soon, confer with Mr. Forkes about the current state of finances. Could she afford a town house? Was there sufficient capital for improvements in farming equipment? Would there be money enough, then, to refurbish the Palladian wing? She had given up the idea of hiring a tutor, nor had she any desire for expensive dresses or entertainments, yet these were economies of small significance. The Brentwood property was producing an income; so long as it continued profitable, no change in its status was required. MacRory's clandestine trade in hothouse produce and Golightly's in game-birds brought in something; these operations ought to be encouraged and expanded. There must be a hundred other such ways, with proper management, to enhance revenues.

Her intention to marry the footman and someday to install her friends in the big house, she kept secret from Esmee. It could wait; that lady had more than enough to trouble her mind.

With Aunt Lettie, she had no such constraint.

"I know I'm still ignorant," she explained, "but I can learn. I don't want to sit in the drawing room, embroidering useless flowers…" She broke off, blushing at her tactless slip, but as her listener didn't appear offended, soon

252

regained her stride. "I mean to work along with everyone else. If we all pull our weight, I don't see why the estate shouldn't support itself. And I don't see the point of this enormous building sitting empty while the people who take care of it live in pokey little rooms under the roof. Besides, Kate and George are getting married - did you know? Of course you did. We thought, a double wedding, one big party, next summer. They'll need a private apartment." Letitia smiled indulgently and let her continue. "I know the Finches have a house of their own - it's quite nice, and they're happy. So are Aunt Rose and Uncle Rob.... You don't mind my calling them aunt and uncle? The Golightly's have rooms downstairs - I'll have to see whether they're good enough. Where does Makepeace live, do you know?"

"Certainly I know," said her aunt with a sly little smile. "He won't need a new apartment; he's quite well situated."

"But where?"

"Here," said Aunt Lettie, her smile broadening to a veritable grin. She had discarded her velvet draperies for good. In contemporary blouse and skirt, she now looked the healthy, capable woman that she was. "Well, not here, precisely; this is meant to be my sewing room, but everything that doesn't have a place seems to end up in here. We live upstairs. That's our solarium you discovered."

"Our...? Here...?"

"I'm half surprised you haven't ferreted it out by now, Nosey Parker."

"You and...?" Felicity was not yet able to assimilate the information, much less to articulate a question.

There was no need, for having sprung the news, Letitia was prepared to give details. "It's entirely proper - we're married. Oh yes, have been for years."

"How many years?" the girl at last managed a whole phrase on a subject, suddenly, of vital importance to herself.

"Eleven, next March."

"Then you are Edward's stepmother? No wonder you called him a special friend!"

Aunt Lettie shook her head and gave vent to one of her witch-like cackles of old. "More special than you know. He is my natural son."

"But that means..."

"He is a bastard, like yourself. The Sommelroux have a long history of consorting with domestic help."

"But then," the girl made another attempt to voice her real concern. "We are cousins! And he never said."

"Don't blame Edward. He wanted to tell you everything. It was I who would not permit it - not until we were sure of you. Oh, do stop fussing; half the married couples in the shire are related by blood. Besides, Randy and I had different mothers."

"That's true," Felicity was starting to recover. "Who else knows? Makepeace, obviously..."

"All the youngsters call him Uncle Joe."

"Yes, I know, only it's hard to change - and he's so..."

"Forbidding? Butlerish? All a facade - though, I must admit, he is awfully good at it. Perhaps those years at Thea's turned him into a bit of a ham. Never mind, you'll soon get to know the real man." Aunt Lettie smiled in a private, tender way the girl had never seen before. Why, she thought, these two are still as much in love as Kate and George, or as Edward and I. "Are you ready to hear my story now?"

"Ready!? I've been begging you for months!"

"Very well, then, pour us a glass of sherry. It happened twenty-two years ago. We came together, much as you and Edward did. Joe was a footman here, and I... I was somewhat younger than my sisters. Penny had gone off to Africa with her planter; Thea was enjoying her disgrace in London. Hortense - Randy's mother - hadn't much use for me - and Papa never had. Like you, I was happiest in the servants' hall. But for a governess who disliked me almost as much as I disliked her, I had no-one. I was raised, more or less, by Rose and Robert MacRory. Incidentally, you had quite a champion in Rob - he said from the first day that you were like me as a girl: good, hardy stock, if a little too inquisitive."

"He is a dear man," said Felicity, "and a fine judge of character. Go on."

"Well, living in the same house, being thrown together every day..." She hesitated, sighed. "It happens. When Papa found out, he created a dreadful scene. Of course, he wouldn't hear of letting us marry. He sacked Joe without references. Threatened to shoot him on sight. Make no mistake, he would have... *and* gotten clean away with it - the magistrate at the time was his old hunting chum. Me, he shipped off to a posh and very discreet nursing home. All the best families of England had sent a daughter there, at one time or other. When Edward was born, Papa meant for him to be adopted out on the quiet..."

"But Aunt Thea took him instead!" Felicity picked up the story, thoroughly enjoying it. "And hired Uncle Joe, so they could be together."

"Yes, it was the safest place: the only house in London in which Papa would never set foot - nor Randy, either, once he grew up. I was brought home, locked in, declared a lunatic... That was hard."

"Couldn't you have run away together? To the colonies? You had a sister in Africa, an uncle in America..."

Aunt Lettie sighed again and shook her head. "As far as we knew, my uncle Raymond had been killed. Whatever the long-term result, I'm glad that he survived.... Yet, perhaps, in spite of all Papa's precautions, I might have contrived an escape. I dreamed about it, made up elaborate schemes in my head, but never really tried. I was too afraid of him, of what he could do if he foiled an attempt. He killed my mother, you know."

This was said in such a matter-of-fact tone that it took the girl a second to apprehend it. Then, she could only gape. Aunt Lettie hesitated, looked hard into Felicity's eyes at her own reflection, and decided.

"Oh yes. I can't remember, if I ever knew, what his rage was about - he seemed always to be angry in those days. Mama was in the family way - she usually was – and crying all the time. Being six years old, I listened at doors,

255

convinced that if only I understood the trouble she was in, I could help her somehow. That night, late, they were coming upstairs after one of his dinner parties. I'd been put to bed hours before and slipped out again, hid under one of the marble hall-tables. Papa was scolding in that awful acidic whisper he had - so that the servants couldn't hear... too arrogant to realize that servants know everything.

"Mama, for once, answered back. She didn't, as a rule - I don't know what possessed her that time. Perhaps she just didn't care anymore.... He picked her up by the arms and shook her. Then he let go, and she tumbled backward down the stairs.... I heard every thud of her fall, every moan and whimper. I still do, sometimes...." She shuddered and was still for a moment, then took a deep, slow breath. "My mother lost the baby that same night, and her life, two days later. She was never fully conscious, thank God. Papa made a big show of being upset by the accident. Uncle Raymond took him to task – I think he suspected the truth, though I never said a word to anyone. And Uncle Raymond was cut off. He had no money of his own. Papa offered him the price of passage to any of the colonies, and nothing more. I hated the man," Letitia continued in the same level tone, as if commenting on the weather. "I feared him even more. But I had another reason," her voice now took on some animation; the bad story was finished, now the good one resumed, "for not running away. I loved - I still love - Twillingmarche. "When at last Papa had his fatal accident - he was a tough old bird! - Joe came to live in Amber, took a job at the Carter's Arms. We were married at St. Hilda's by George Gillivray, of course - a good friend he has been. Once Randy was gone, too -"

The girl interrupted, "What did my father die of?"

"He died, that's all. Oh, very well," sighed Aunt Lettie. "If you must know, he'd got a vile disease that sometimes catches up with libertines."

"I still don't understand," Felicity complained.

"That can't be helped. Do you want to hear this story or not?"

"Yes, please."

"Well, Joe worked his way up to brew-master at Carter's, an estimable profession. For years, we shuttled secretly back and forth between here and Amber. It was better than nothing, and fairly good when *they* went up to London, but we never had a proper home life. Once Randy passed away, he gave it up to work here."

"How did you manage that?"

"Very simply. When I tell Elijah Forkes to hire someone, he does. Of course, Joe still supplies the beer for Carter's - and for half the independent pubs in the county. We grow the finest hops. If you want to get on his good side, ask to see the brew-house. It's downstairs, in the abbey cellar - very handy." She nodded a final punctuation. "And that's *my* story. Now, tell me yours."

Felicity began: "My mother was Joan Markle, maid to the first Lady Randolph.... Oh, Aunt Lettie, I'm quite sure you know this!"

"Nevertheless," said the older woman, "I should like to hear it from you, just once. None of this must ever be repeated."

"All right," the girl agreed, and inwardly commanded herself to do as Letitia had done; to recite without emotion or commentary. "Mama was fond of her mistress, but she could not resist Lord Randolph - I don't think anyone could, and she was just a young girl. D'you know, she told me almost nothing about the old Earl - I wonder why?"

"I expect she was terrified, too. Papa became more unpredictable as he aged. By that time, I was safely shut up in my tower."

"She did speak," Mary continued, "quite a lot about... my father. She was still in love with him, even then, years later. She might have married, but she never did. My mother had a romantic nature; she was not very practical." Realizing that she had already twice broken the rule she had set only moments ago, Mary took a deep breath and mastered her voice. "Lady Randolph was... in the family way, and her husband missed the - ah - wifely, um... Oh, fiddlesticks!" the girl burst out. "His wife was pregnant with Felicity, and he was used to getting his own way. And why not with a pretty maid? I'm sure it wasn't the only time - Esmee all but said so. Roland, too. When the maid got pregnant, she was sacked in disgrace. Mama had nowhere else to go but back to Gray's Harbour to her family. And they were horrid. Later, Lord Randolph sent her some money, so that we were able to run away. We moved to Twinsdale, where Mama set up a little hat shop. It was a modest living, but respectable - especially as she changed her name and called herself a widow."

"And that," Aunt Lettie softly interrupted, "was how we lost track of you both. We could not have helped very much while Papa was alive, but afterward we did look for Joan."

"I remember!" Mary exclaimed. "I remember the churchyard. It was Saint Hilda's, just as I thought. Mama brought me on a train to see the old - that is, my grandfather's - grave. She still believed, till then. She thought, with his wife and father both gone, Lord Randolph would bring us back to Twillingmarche. She used to tell me such wonderful stories...."

"Only, of course, Randy had married Esmee and forgotten all about poor Joan."

"That must have been when Mama discovered the truth. Because she hardly talked about him anymore, after that. And she stopped teaching me how to be a young lady, and began to train me in the milliner's craft." Mary sighed. "Her dream shattered for good and all. It must have been heart-breaking. Poor Mama!"

"And for you?" asked Letitia gently.

"I couldn't miss something I'd never known. To me, it was only a story. I was quite happy, really, until Mama got sick. That was a bad time. She was desperately ill for weeks.... Mistress Carey, the vicar's wife, used to come and help with the nursing. They were good people. She told Mr. Carey our real name at the end, and asked him to send word to our kinfolk. When Mama died, all our money was gone.... Then a repulsive man came, who smelled of fish, and hated me, even though he didn't know me at all. I was glad he took me to Eastmills House, not to Gray's Harbour. He made me swear never to use their name - as if I wanted any part of it! The nuns were kind, most of the time, even though I was a Protestant."

"You were not yet fourteen?"

"Almost fourteen. That's why I had to leave the orphanage."

"And so?"

"And so, I was sent out to earn my living. The vicar at Wyn Fell was a dear man, but quite doddery - not so energetic, nor, I think, as intelligent - as Mr. Carey. He thought I might do for a shop assistant, being as I could read and do sums. He placed me with Mr. Barlow, the draper. Sure that he had done all that he should, the vicar never came again. He died not long after. The Barlows had me help in the shop, as well as do the work of both nanny and maid, all for the cost of my food..."

"You were there three years...." Aunt Lettie took the girl's hand in both of hers, stroking it as if it had been a small animal in need of comfort.

"It's all right," Mary said. "It's all behind me now. I shall always be grateful to Esmee and Mr. Forkes for cooking up their little plot. And to Lord Randolph, because he has given me the right look. I wonder," she added, "how many more there are? Sommelroux bastards..."

"We could never keep track of his movements in London," said Aunt Lettie, "In the district, we have three."

"Really? Where?"

"One, here at the house - Augustus Finch. Yes," she nodded, "Julius loved the girl; why should he not accept her baby? And a fine lad he's turning out, too. We'll make an engineer of him some day. Dottie Ribble married a Gillivray and named her girl Victoria. Maureen MacBride vowed never to marry, which is a pretty tired joke by now.... She operates the post office in Amber with her daughter, Gwendolyn. You'll meet them, in due course. And now," Letitia concluded, "we've got our ancient troubles off our chests. From this time on, you must always be Felicity. A shame it makes you four months older..."

"I don't mind about the age," said Felicity. "Only, it's too bad she was such a drip. The stupid girl killed herself, didn't she?"

"Yes," sighed her aunt, "but perhaps you should not be so quick to judge."

"Why not? She worshipped Lord Randolph. I don't blame her for *that* - he must have been, in spite of his loose morals, rather splendid. Even Esmee, practical as she is.... And I'm sure Papa treated his Felicity better than he did other women - he certainly wasn't gallant to his wives and sisters. I understand if the child was devastated when he died, and droopy for a while. I suppose she missed him dreadfully. Of course I understand - have I not been an orphan? But I didn't go jumping over a cliff! *She* still had a family. I can't imagine Esmee being very unkind to her. As for Roland - well, she could have done worse for a step-brother - or even for a husband. She had so much to live for - she had Twillingmarche. There is no excuse for what she did."

The older woman raised one eyebrow slightly more than the other, gazing intently at the girl's face. "Are you jealous?"

Mary shrugged, casting down her eyes. "Perhaps. Yes, a little. At least she had a father - and a doting one - for fourteen years. I never had him for a single minute."

"Perhaps that was your greatest good fortune. You might have ended like Felicity, given her circumstances. On second thoughts, you'd have been safe from Randy, if anyone was."

"What d'you mean?"

"He didn't like his women too clever, or self-confident. You have turned out both. Possibly a bit too much of the second..."

"Papa wouldn't have liked me?"

"Well," said Aunt Lettie, considering, "you may be lucky to be spared the knowing, either way. Felicity had an overly affectionate father, and it killed her. I had a hateful one, and it killed *him*." She forestalled the question forming on Mary's lips. "Another time, my dear. It's quite close to supper; you must go now, and be a young lady."

260

25

Next, Felicity broached the subject of living quarters to Kate. They were twining holly round the newel posts in the Victorian hall, decorating for Christmas. "I think we ought to put the tree in the ball-room next door, don't you?"

"What, in the old wing?"

"Yes. I'm sure we could scare up some chairs and things, from the attic. There must be a hundred people on the estate - none of these rooms are large enough."

The maid, catching her drift, burst out laughing. "You're not serious! I'd like to be there when you tell Esmy you mean to entertain the servants for Christmas - *and* outside help!"

"All right. You can come along - now, if you like. The sooner I tell her, the better."

"She'll have kitten-fits!"

"That's what everyone thinks of Esmee. It's not fair, you know. She's a good deal more sensible than people give her credit for - and she's not forgotten where she comes from. Now that the Americans are well away, I think it's time we - all the family - understood one another. There has been altogether too much secrecy. It is certainly *not* the way I mean to go on."

Kate shook her head, still unable to speak for the giggles that choked her.

Felicity resumed, "I have done quite a lot of thinking in the past few days. Mr. Finch says we have enough money to keep up the London house. But if we rent it for income, and furthermore, the price of wool is rising, I'm sure we can afford to install plumbing in the Palladian wing.... I know just the contractor. Mr. Leicester has such respect for the building, he can manage it without spoiling anything."

"I should like that," her friend said. "It was an awful nuisance, trekking over here when I wanted a proper bath."

"We shall also need central heat..." Then Felicity realised the implication of the other's statement. "What d'you mean, it was a nuisance? Your room is just upstairs."

"Now, it is," Kate agreed, "but only 'cose you all stayed and stayed."

"And before?"

"I've only been here since fall of last year, when Esmy and Roland and that snooty Roberts were gone up to town. I had the Caroline room. Evelyn was to have the Albert next door, only she never got the chance."

"The Prince Albert room..." Palladian wing, second floor, south-west end, decorated in royal blue and gold. Felicity tried to conjure up the diagram in her pamphlet. The Princess Caroline, in grey and lilac. "But that... But then...?" Understanding flooded her mind. Of course! Why had she not guessed the truth? "That *is* quite a trek. I suppose George will have the Albert, once you're married. We can easily cut another door on the dressing room.... Where, then, shall we put Evelyn?"

The maid, ever unsympathetic to her younger sister, said, "We'll find something. P'raps she can sleep over the stables."

"Kate!"

"Be close to Terry, anyroad."

"You're just a little cat. Your dad would never hear of such a thing. Why, she's barely sixteen! Now, be serious - I'm trying to make plans."

"Oh, aye?"

The skeptical tone woke Felicity to the presumption - not to say absurdity - of her approach. Who was she to make plans, when there was so much that she still had to learn, that everyone in the household had known for ages. "All right, Smarty-pants, score for you. Well, one thing at a time, then. What about putting the Christmas tree in the ballroom?"

"Always used to be there, far's I know."

"Then, it's settled. Shall I tell Esmee, or will you?"

"Oh, you must do it, M'lady; tis your devising." Kate brushed off her skirt and ran down the staircase. "But I think I shan't be wanted there. I'd best alert the *other* ladyship."

"And," Felicity concluded her monologue, "those rooms have been in use all along, ever since Lord Farwell's death. Electricity was laid on two years ago. George is studying to be an electrician, isn't that interesting? When you and Roland came for a few weeks in summer, they would move to the servants' quarters upstairs, and store the valuables in the attic. Quite a lot of bother, considering you never took an interest anyhow."

Esmee had been listening patiently, showing little surprise throughout these revelations. Now, she murmured, "Yes, I see. I see."

"Is that all? Don't you mind?"

Esmee, her face set in unbecoming hard lines that made her look both less genteel and older, replied, "Oh yes. Not," she added, "so much that the mice will play - I always thought something was going on. But I mind very much that Elijah should have been part of it."

"Perhaps he wasn't," the girl tried to equivocate. "He mayn't have known."

Esmee nodded soberly, staring straight ahead. "He arranged for the sale of paintings, furniture, ornaments... all of them stashed away in the attic, you say. Indeed, Elijah must have been an arch-conspirator."

There was little that Felicity could say to make her feel better about this: she had trusted the solicitor as she had trusted no-one else, even her only son. To be hoodwinked by him, howbeit for her own protection as much as that of Letitia and her people, must be deeply wounding. Esmee did not deserve such disappointment. Why had she not been invited to join the community of Twillingmarche?

After a lengthy silence, Esmee said, "I was a proper fool. I tried so hard to be the silly bit of fluff Randy loved... to be the lady that old monster, Lord Farwell wanted. Hopeless, of course. I ought to have realised; nobody ever pleased him, except perhaps your mo - Beatrice - poor thing. And Randy lived his own life. He hadn't much time for anyone but..." Esmee's eyes flickered to the girl's face and as quickly away again. Then she sighed. "Ah, well," folding her hands in her lap, "I have had a pleasant few years. Roland seems to have found his own way.... What's to be done with me, Lady Felicity?"

"Oh, don't mock me, Esmee. After all, you rescued me. You practically invented me! I shall be forever in your debt. It is not my place to decide anything for you. Esmee?"

"Yes, Felicity."

"Do you hate me now?"

Esmee looked fully into her eyes at last. "Of course I don't hate you."

"D'you think you could go on being my stepmother?"

Esmee smiled. "Well, I suppose we have no choice in the matter. Though one might be tempted to give the show away, if only to see that pompous, lying old buzzard in leg irons.... No, I really would rather not go to prison."

"Will you and Roberts help to plan my wedding?" Esmee, for a second, looked confused; she had to explain. "I'm to marry Edward. In May, we thought - is that too soon?"

"Edward? The gorgeous footman, Edward?" Felicity affirmed this. Esmee shook her head; a sound rose in her throat, and then another. "You little minx!" she gasped, as it kept bubbling up like a spring from the ground, try as she might to repress it. "Your grandfather must be tossing and turning in his grave. Serves him bloody well right!" In another moment, she was helpless with mirth. Felicity was soon infected, too.

It was thus, hugging each other, laughing till the tears ran down their cheeks, that they were discovered by Roland and Mr. Forkes, coming in for their tea. The men froze in their tracks. The women, at last noticing their presence, subsided. Felicity resumed her chair, groping for the handkerchief in her sleeve; Esmee sat up, then slowly rose, confronting the solicitor.

"Elijah Forkes, I want to speak with you."

His eyes sought Roland's, then, immediately dismissing him as a source of reassurance, Felicity's. She looked away; he had no option but to face his erstwhile mistress. They stood so for a long minute, silent. The man could clearly see that he was in trouble, was clearly searching in his mind for clues as to what order, and of what magnitude, that trouble might be. He waited. Esmee, her icy displeasure suddenly breaking, exploded in a fresh wave of laughter. "It's all," she struggled to articulate, to catch her breath, so that Felicity became concerned for her. "It's all so... so ridiculously apt! I'll be... I'll deal... with you... another time."

Later, after tea and sandwiches and fairy cakes, after some time to collect themselves, Esmee and Felicity were summoned by a solemn butler to the library.

A council of sorts had been assembled there. Lady Letitia was already seated in her great armchair by the hearth; Mrs. Golightly, as head of her clan, was placed on her left. Elder Cartwright was present, and Mrs. MacRory; the chief gardener sent his regrets: he wasn't much for palaver. Mr. Finch was there to represent the agricultural interests; he explained, "I speak for the lads - always have." (If this were so, Felicity thought, the lads must be a right quiet lot: she had scarcely before heard Mr. Finch put seven words together.) Makepeace courteously seated Esmee, before taking up a position next to his wife. Mr. Forkes had been invited, naturally, but Roland was gently excused. So would Felicity and Edward have been, along with all the other young people, but for their very special role as figureheads.

Aunt Lettie began by pointing this out and explaining, "We'd all but given up on finding the right girl. The two we had are too old and too young. The situation was so desperate, we were almost ready to bring forward little Augustus.... A grave risk, for the death of that baby was too widely known. It was only Elijah's perseverance that saved us. Now we have a legitimate heiress - soon to be married," she glanced at Edward, who smirked like the proverbial cat, "to a young man of impeccable bloodline, for whom a suitable history is in production - and so, we anticipate no legal problems."

She turned to Esmee, "Felicity says that we've treated you shabbily - and I'm forced to admit the child is right. We have become too insular, too suspicious of outsiders.... For what it's worth, I apologise on behalf of us all." Noticing Esmee's eyes turn to where the solicitor had removed himself, on the farthest side of the room, she added, "Don't blame Elijah - he has been in a difficult position. He did want to include you. We kept voting him down."

"Is that what this is," asked Esmee, "a... a Parliament?"

"Yes, of a sort," Letitia answered. "Though I rather think it's more effective - and more equitable - than the other one. Well, now you are in the conspiracy, like it or not. Elijah says you liked it well enough, that you were quick enough to see its merits, when he presented our little scheme. I must congratulate you on carrying it off like a trouper. Will you join us?"

Esmee thought this over. She shook her head slightly. "I should still be an outsider, the butt of jokes. And what about Roberts? She is my best friend in the world, the only one who has been loyal to me - and truthful!" her eyes flicked briefly over to Mr. Forkes. " - always. This would destroy her."

Mrs. Golightly muttered under her breath, "She's a silly woman!"

Felicity offered in Roberts' defense: "She's a romantic. I think she's half dreaming, half play-acting, even to herself. If she wants to live in a fairy tale, where's the harm?"

"Very well," Lady Letitia turned to Esmee. "You have sufficient income, as Randy's widow, to live in modest comfort anywhere you like. Elijah controls the funds, but I'm sure he's amenable to whatever arrangement you prefer. If you choose London - and I understand you have many friends there, including my sister - Etheldred Close is at your disposal."

266

"That would be best," Esmee agreed. "You must already know that my son is planning to leave the country. His future is assured; it's what he really wants. Without Bobby.... Well! I shall make the best of things as they stand."

"May we," Felicity shyly asked her aunt, "give Roland – Robert - a motorcar for a wedding present? A Roll-Royce? They haven't anything so fine in America, he says."

Lady Letitia gave a magisterial nod. "Your proposal will be considered. Is there any other current business?"

Mrs. MacRory stood. "Angus asks that Felicity be apprenticed to the gardens, if her's willing."

"Well, child, what do you say?"

"I should like nothing better, Aunt Lettie."

"So long as you don't neglect your lessons. An heiress must have education, as well as a useful occupation. Anything else?"

The company clamoured for attention. Most of their suggestions and queries, however, concerned the Christmas festivities: as far as the elders were concerned, the subjects of Felicity, Esmee and Roland were happily settled. The chairwoman made several decisions, arbited one or two disputes over jurisdiction, consulted Mr. Finch about the supplies of fresh meat, approved Mrs. MacRory's schedule for extra kitchen staff. At last, people began to drift away. Mr. Forkes made his way to Esmee and the two departed, deep in animated, intensely private conversation. At least they are speaking to each other, Felicity thought. It would be a terrible shame if their friendship - or whatever connection - were utterly sundered. She noticed Makepeace - Uncle Joe - taking his leave. Edward, with a friendly wave to her, followed.

"Where have they gone in such a hurry?" she asked Aunt Lettie.

"The cellar, I imagine. There was some disagreement over the quality of the last brew.... I swear that boy is getting too big for his britches. Thinks he knows everything about beer - and everything about herbal remedies."

"That's what you do?"

"That's what I do. Perhaps I shall teach you some day."

"Lessons! Always more lessons. I imagined the life of a countess to be more glamorous."

"It's not too late to join Esmee in London."

"Oh, no! I mean, I should like to visit Aunt Thea and Esmee sometimes, but I never want to live anywhere else. I shall study gardening and herbs and grammar and history and anything you tell me to - even French, if I must."

"You forgot Latin, but you've grasped the gist."

"I have some questions now."

Lady Letitia raised her eyebrows - both; Uncle Joe alone had the knack of raising just one - but did not object.

"Whose clothes have I been wearing?"

"Kate's, mainly."

"I thought so! That's why she looks daggers whenever I put on something nice."

Lettie smiled. "I suspect it's more because they look better on you."

"Who locked me in the attic, when the urn fell?"

"Edward did."

"Why?"

"To keep you safely out of the way."

"And who pushed the urn?"

"I did," Aunt Lettie calmly replied. "I meant to frighten Roderick, not Rosalyn, but he was too quick."

"The twins caught a glimpse of you, I think. They tried to tell Inspector Markle, but Mr. Forkes explained it away."

"Tom Markle would have found some way to dismiss it, I suppose. Still, I was a bit careless that time...."

"Who let the dogs out?"

"What dogs? There haven't been dogs on the estate since my dear Papa died." She looked at the girl steadily, green eyes locked with green eyes, her expression as still and unforthcoming as any that Uncle Joe could assume.

Felicity thought better of her next question. There were some things she need not know. Instead, she asked, "Shall we live happily ever after?"

Lady Letitia answered, "I see no reason why we should not."

- The End -

Vera Mont is the author of three other novels:

A Tidy Killing,

The Ozimord Project

Chronicles of After and Before

And a children's book:
The Trouble with Whatchamacallits

and co-author of a fantasy novella:
A Dark and Stormy Knight

and a short story collection:
Meandering

Ordering Information

You can order a copy of this book at the following venues:

www.montland.ca

or by sending email to the author to the following address:

vera@montland.ca

I will respond to queries within 24 hours.